A TOUCH OF GINGER

Little India Trilogy - Part 3

SP Venkata

SP Publications

ISBN 979-8-9921756-1-5

Cover design by: Ray Chisesi

Made in the United States of America

To the late, great Molly Ramanujan
Of The Clothesline School of Writing
- She made me possible

CONTENTS

GRATITUDE

Editorial and Copy Services were generously provided by:

Tierney Noll Throws you into Chicago's Little India...

Margo Berlin It was my honor to beta read your novel.

This book could not have been written without the
gracious indulgence of some mighty fine people
including: Mike Oppenheim, Justin Tate, Robin, Fran,
Gail, Rachel Feeck, Ien Nivens, George, Sander,
Tina Olive, Chelsea, Olivia, Susan, Ralph, Papa G.,
and too many others to mention.

APRIL, 2005

April is the cruellest month, breeding
Lilacs out of the dead land, mixing
Memory and desire, stirring
Dull roots with spring rain.

T. S. Eliot

The Burial of the Dead; The Waste Land - 1922

Nobody's Fool

I am nobody's fool but my own. I often think that the world is pretty straightforward, same as me. I know people.

The farewell at the airport had been a grim affair, and I wanted to check up on my friend Lalu Ganesh. Stress had built up in him over the previous weeks due to his brother Phani's departure to India. Lalu could use a friend, and I could use a free meal. So, I headed over to the *Blue Mountain Indian Restaurant.*

It was well past the lunch hour when I entered the restaurant, and once the front door was closed and locked, it was just us Indians. Lalu was toting up the numbers from the lunch crowd's business while the rest of us gathered around a large round table that Shetty and Ghose helped set up. We owed Lalu support, I thought, after the debacle of his brother's visit to America. If Lalu was pleased that we rallied for him, he didn't show it. Yeah, that's how grim the airport send-off was. Lalu was forlorn.

"After everything I have did for that *bewakhoof kutha,*" Lalu kept muttering. His style of English didn't bother me, I knew it was broken. The other Indians didn't even known that it was was broken. They only knew that Lalu's heart was broken.

Each one of us gave a slight variation of that Indian nod of agreement, which ranged from a tiny tilt from me, to a vigorous 'don't you know it' kind from Shetty. Even the young and handsome Warangal, already steeped in American mannerisms, couldn't resist the Indian nod.

I felt Lalu's pain alright, but there wasn't much I could do to ease his sense of frustration. My friend was not only the proverbial model immigrant, who worked hard to support his parents back home, he also helped others to come to America. Now his older brother ran away, as he poetically said, like a dog with its tail tucked. I let Lalu fume.

Shetty brought out a large round platter laden with samosas, bajjis, mirchi and *bonda*, and dips and chutneys. He set it down in the middle of the round table. We partook of it in the communal eating style more typical of Arabs and Chinese but seldom practiced by Indians.

Lalu cast a quick glance at Warangal, and said, “Like this all his life. Marriage, becoming a father made no change. Phani only get worse.” The finality of a vigorous shake of head. He ran his palms down each opposite arm, alternately scratched elbows and grabbed his shoulders. The pale ghostly light of fluorescent fixtures in the false ceiling didn’t help the look of his skin any. Between sips and rants, he kept running his hands over his head and across face, using a napkin to wipe moisture off his person.

Turning to me, he said, “Like this, Kumar, all his life, even when we were just boys. I think that he change, I prayed that he change. Just a little bit. I think that if I bring him from India and join with his daughter, they live good. I think wrong.” Lalu spread his hands wide, “Big mistake.”

I nodded slowly, and prepared myself for the outpouring that was still to follow. Lalu started pacing the dining room floor, while the rest of us munched on a favorite snack. Noises continued in the kitchen suggesting that the Mexican crew was at it with the pots and pans.

“America is not for everybody, I suppose,” said Warangal. He sat tall in his chair like the policeman he was. The comment drew a sharp turn of Lalu’s head.

"Easy for you. You can say that, yes. You young and lucky. No history of a miserable life," Lalu's lament was not off the mark. I knew a little something about how Lalu's whole family struggled back home. We also knew a little something about how complex Lalu's brother Phani was. I let it go.

It was Lalu who settled the matter eventually, "My brother crazy, but you all help him adjust to America. I think may be he work hard like us and succeed." Again he spread his palms wide, "Total mistake." He stopped pacing, looked at each one of us in turn, and declared, like it just dawned on him, "My brother too crazy." He strode into the kitchen. I was sure that wasn't the end of it. So, I malingered while the rest of the group disbanded gently.

****

Lalu returned from the kitchen bearing a plate of freshly cooked chicken and pushed it towards me with expectant eyes.

"Try it," he said.

"Delicious looking," I took a bite of it absently.

"Chicken taste good? It taste different today?" he asked.

"I love it. You make the best authentic tandoori chicken, Lalu," I said.

"I put crushed star-anise in the marinade, you like it?" he asked.

"I didn't notice," I confessed.

"I also smeared some on the chicken before putting it in the tandoor. No difference at all?" Lalu scratched his elbows, with hope in his voice.

“Now that you mention it, I do sense a difference in taste. Couldn’t quite place the flavor at first,” I said. “Just assumed you left it in the tandoor too long. You know, the strange almost sweet flavor.”

Lalu looked pleased. “Yes, yes. That’s because of star anise.”

I nodded again, still absent minded.

“I was thinking how much Francis would have loved this Sunday. If that bewakhoof would have stayed in America longer.”

Ah, Francis. The name adopted by his brother Phani following his conversion. My gluttony had me totally side-tracked, and I forgot all about Phani, aka Francis, Easter and other such stuff. Still --

“What would you have done different, assuming he stayed?” I asked.

“That’s what I am saying. I used spices and flavors used by many Christians on Easter Sunday. Tried them on the chicken.”

“Not bad at all, Lalu. Quite tasty. It actually enhances the bouquet created by the hot clay,” I said.

“I knew Easter was coming. I planned a whole special menu for Francis to enjoy. Make him feel Christian is okay,” said Lalu.

“You are a saint man, still thinking of your brother and his new faith, even-though he was so unpleasant towards you all.” I said.

"He never give any chance.. no chance," replied Lalu. "My brother never chance to himself, make money, get better."

"I say again, you're a saint. Saint Ganesh."

"*Chee Chee*," Lalu burst in mock derision. "Don't put Christian words along with names of Hindu gods." He was in a full laughter mode now.

"You are an odd Hindu, Lalu," I said. "On the one hand you are quite ready to cook an Easter meal even though you aren't Christian yourself. But then you turn around and worry about a nice title like Saint attached to a god's name like Ganesh." I joined in the laughter.

"I was very angry last week, when Francis quit America, like a loser. Now I try to laugh, I have to," Lalu said.

"To each his own, we'll let him be. Like Warangal said, I suppose America is not for everybody. Though, god knows a million illegals will dispute it," I said.

"Truth is," said Lalu, "my brother Phani is a complete *bewakhoof*, *gadha*, *houla*, a total *Tuglak*. But, he is family."

Lalu wasn't laughing any longer, but I was. The epithets he hurled at his brother were so redolent of Hyderabad-style Urdu language - fool, jackass, simpleton - it had me in stitches. Everyone of those words was apt. But that last one, referring to the Moghul ruler, Tuglak, was most caustic. In any Indian language, in any Indian town or village, being called Tuglak was the ultimate insult. Even school children know of the last of the moguls as Madman Tuglak. History books branded him as an insufferable lout. Who'd suffer that moniker?

When I finally stopped laughing, I said, "You should have talked to Gita about your plan for an Easter feast. She might have convinced her father to stay longer?"

"Maybe. I never told her about it. Menu idea was still just cooking in my mind."

"It's his loss, Lalu. I can imagine the great feast. Americans make some fun dishes. Put pineapple on ham, cloves and carrots in cakes, glaze foods with caramel. And, your chicken with anise. You think Phani would have liked it?" I asked.

"We will never know," Lalu shrugged.

"You know what, I'll call Gita and tell her about this. The next time she calls India, she will tease her father about what he missed," I said.

Lalu was quiet while we sipped the remainder of our chai. I didn't know what his thoughts were, but mine were suddenly all about Sundays, anise, lamb cake, and chocolate bunnies. My mind wasn't on Indian food, but on the Indian mindset. I marveled at how effortlessly Indians in America, Hindus specially, eased in and out of the 'culturally other' ways. Put up Christmas trees, cobwebs for Halloween, say Shalom Shalom or *Id Mubarak.* Or, make Easter chicken. Was such an easy habit rooted in a sense of human bondage, an eclectic world-view? Or, was it some crazy compulsion? In the case of Lalu, it had to be family love. That idea began to lull me into an unseemly warmth all of a sudden.

Bitter Tendrils

The start of the month of April, 2005 promised no fanfare or tomfoolery. Like instances of Aprils past, it was full of good auguries: birds sang in the elms, ice crunched underfoot, and helicopter leaves twirled down to the ground with a regular irregularity. The sidewalk in front of my three story graystone building, which I called the Headquarters of Everything, had so many that I had to call called my assistant Virginia. “It’s a regular Mogadishu out here, Ginny. Helicopters crashing to earth like in the movie, Blackhawk Down.” Yup, I said that. That’s the kind of an edgy wit I used to be back then.

Virginia replied, “Kumar, you need to get a life beyond movies. Glad you called though. I am going home early today.” Click. She hung up without so much as a sniffle. And, she was supposed to be *my* assistant at *Wings of Ether*, Internet Cafe, Proprietor, Anand Kumar.

But what made that April in 2005 different was what happened later that day. I didn’t see it coming. It was an April that fooled me…

I went to the fridge to forage, and found some leftover slices of pizza. Walking back to the lazy-boy, I noticed that the weather scenes of TV news showed lots of blues and yellows. Clear skies and sunshine all across Chicagoland. The graphic of rising temps for the week, from high thirties to mid forties, looked like a staircase climbing, going somewhere.

“An epidemic of shirtsleeves broke out,” said the mid morning anchorperson, and turned to the weather reporter. She was all excited about the new front coming in. My philosophy about TV News had been that if the the weather girl looked happy, all must be well with the world. The more so if her dimples danced. A good weather show put me in my happy place.

But, it all changed with one phone call that afternoon. How could I have known that the call would be about Gita Ganesh? After all, the caller-ID said it was my friend Lalu Ganesh, Gita's uncle calling. What could be wrong with that? I answered the trill since it would always be nice to talk to Lalu. He just might be trying out a new recipe?

I was wrong right off the bat. The voice of my friend was a rattle. Raspy, broken, and laden with some heavy breathing. Gasps and some choking up.

"Kumar.., you must ... come ....immediately."

" Hey Lalu, what is going on?"

"Please come soon, quickly."

"You said that already Ganesh. Immediate, soon, quickly, they all mean the same thing."

My wit was not received at the other end of the phone line. Instead, there was a sibilance that was his sigh. I instantly regretted my humor. Something was amiss.
"Alright, alright, coming over."

****

I got on my way over to Devon Avenue, (not day-won, but De-Vaughn, is how we pronounced it). A mile long stretch of De-Vaughn Avenue was taken over by hundreds of Indians, and came to be fondly known as Little India. It was a slice of the subcontinent on the far north side of Chicago, er.. ShiK-Awe-go, that's how our venerable mayor pronounced it. De-Vaughn Avenue in Chic-Awe-go.

Thoughts about the odd request from Lalu distracted me from choosing my wardrobe. It wasn't the writer's sports coat with leather elbow patches, which I also wore to art galleries. It wasn't the dweeb-y red plaid shirt I had taken to wearing lately either. No. I just threw on a fleece jacket over an old rumpled tee shirt and left the condo.

City bus Number 11-Lincoln arrived at the bus stop at the same time as I did. That coincidence turned out to be the only happy thing to happen, on what would become a lousy, no-fooling, miserable April day. I should have remembered poet TS Eliot's line about how April was the cruellest month, "mixing memory with desire."

I sat at the back of the bus and tried not to notice life on the street. It was an attempt to put myself in a neutral zone of the mind - a sort of a bus yoga. I was preparing myself to better receive whatever news my favorite cook of Indian food was going to dish out. But, I was tensing, bus ride yoga wasn't working.

The desultory bus ride got easier once I began to doze. I sensed then, that Ms. Agnes, the tabby I left back in the apartment, seemed to ride alongside me. Her presence could be felt in the fleece and fabric of my clothing. Quite reassuringly, in fact. I didn't have to scratch or stroke my beard, or strike any pose in my mind. Ms. Agnes did that sometimes, she grounded me in the moment better than any form of yoga.

****

Lalu had the usual hospitality already setup. A pair of samosas and spicy tea, with a diet coke to boot, were on a table. And on his face, a wan smile and dull eyes. A severe stoop rounded his shoulders. He greeted me with the usual invitation to 'eat something first'. He pushed the steel plate toward me, past a plastic vase with a plastic flower. I reached for a samosa.

In my book, when Indian people say eat something first, it's the same as someone asking over the phone, are you sitting down. It was a poor preface to a conversation: not much good came after that. Eat something first, set you up with a belly full of curry, while the meat of the matter lurked in the wings.

But, I eat when so commanded. I eat knowing full well that that gesture of courtesy might couch a serious anxiety, even despair. That's the Indian way.

Evidently, Lalu did not actually intend for me to eat or imbibe. He plunged right into a wail as soon as I took one bite off a samosa.

"Why these things happen, Kumar," he too sat down now, palms rubbing his face. "Tell me Kumar, are we all not good beings, pious as we can manage. But horrible events happen. Why god punish like this?"

I nibbled gently, listened, and waited. For form's sake, I told myself. One must feed, while one is being fed an obviously serious matter, I told myself.

"I try to do good, Kumar. To everybody in my clan, and to all the customers, and to my investors. I cook food good, I make people money. Then, why gods punish me like this. You know these things better..."

Lalu's voice trailed off into the familiar elbow scratching and forehead wiping. He stared into the corners of the room. But, the corners of the room had no answer. I followed suit, looked around with slight tilts of my head in empathy, and just awaited the story.

"Why things happen, Kumar, tell me, why?" He looked straight at me now. Steady, composed, his visage overwhelmed by a darkness greater than the dark pigment of his face. Light had gone out of his large marble sized eyes. His round face became featureless: broad, black, flat. The staff became invisible even as they did their chores. They went totally quiet. I realized that the place emptied of diners, the front door was locked, and the 'Closed' sign put up.

Lalu's palms were cupping and rubbing each other, suggestive of an ancient submissive gesture. He was a mute worshipful supplicant in a temple with an equally mute stone idol. I became nervous on the inside, but managed to look straight back at him. I was keen to be supportive of whatever troubled him, and wished for him to go on.

He wailed again, "Kumar, tell me why things like this happen..." and then burst out, "Gita is dead. They are saying Gita is dead."

Chokes and gasps in the air. His chokes and my gasps. Long before I could recover fully, and while I was still shivering and swallowing air, I heard Lalu go on..

"....Some place, some small town they are saying. Police saying Gita was found dead near a highway. What highway, where? Accident? I don't know. They not telling me what happened. Why so far away, Kumar. Tell me why?" Lalu paused after raising that floodgate, but I got the impression there was more. More questions and much more agony waited. He was breathing really hard. So was I.

It felt like my being had punched the pause button hard. Was my heart beating, could I move my tongue? Was I breathing? I wasn't sure. Was my mouth dry, frozen? Yes! My mind raced and got way ahead of my breath and body. I felt warm and chilled at the same time.

The samosa crumbled in my hand but I didn't know it then. If it weren't for Lalu's continued staring and his eyes engaging mine, I probably would have ended up with fragments of peas and potato in my mouth. What was I supposed to do?

I shuffled my feet to get my blood pumping again, and made a serious effort to breathe in and out deliberately. I tried to make fists, and opened my palms, a few times. Forced myself to un-pause. Of one thing I was sure, Lalu did not intend to shock me. He was too agitated to be intentional. I knew too that he didn't intend for me to react verbally. Good thing too, I was totally at a loss for words.

Shetty, one of Lalu's assistants arrived quietly at the table and filled our cups with fresh chai. He took my plate away too, and replaced it with a small plastic saucer bearing a dessert. After you eat spicy stuff, you also eat something sweet. It is the Indian way of snacking. One must always eat something sweet. Even if the heart were breaking.

The back of my brain was furiously active, but none of the thoughts made it to my tongue. I forced myself to take a bite of the sweet *kalakand* milk cake. It exuded a delicate aroma quite familiar to my palate. But the name of thing that caused that exquisite bouquet escaped me. I saw in my mind's eye, threads of a spice bitter to taste but fragrant. Short slender filaments of burnt-brick color. What's the name? I racked my brain in a fury, as if just the word for that condiment would somehow save my sanity. As if recalling that word right then, would restore me to a reality that threatened to slip away. But those threads of tender fragrance refused to form a life-line to my sanity.

At that moment, that piece of kalakand wasn't tasty to me. I knew, however, that whatever gave kalakand that bouquet, that word would come to me, sooner or later. Words returned to memories and lives, The dead never did. So we suffered. All of us at Blue Mountain suffered. In that universal way humans loved those taken away too soon. That special suffering with which people loved their dead.

Lalu recounted the phone call he got from Detective Sergeant Mike Mullins of the Chicago Police Department. He was an old acquaintance of ours.

Mullins was ever so polite, remembered Gita from his previous visits with Lalu Ganesh, inquired after her. He asked Lalu when it was that uncle and niece got together last. And finally, after some more drawn out chit chat, Mullins let it out that Gita was possibly a victim of foul play. Someone should ID the victim, of course. But the physical description Mullins had was close enough to get Lalu going. Details of the personal effects only added to the misery.

I sat quietly, digesting the information which poured out of my friend, piecing together a story from snatches of Lalu's bursts. Mullins was careful not to be cruel or conclusive, but he also wanted to be informative, subject to protocols and procedures. In the lingo of the game of American football Mullins was 'threading the needle.' An expression I learned to love in the new country.

Growing up in village India, I had known strangers who arrived on a bus, or even a passing lorry driver who pulled over, to deliver news of a death. It wasn't that unusual that persons not known to a family at all would stop by the house, to give news that some relative, in some distant village had died. Not so in the American way. News of death couldn't be so casually conveyed. In my new life, news of death had to be communicated in ways proper and official.

Our friend, the detective, wanted to be informative informally. He also had to be officially proper. That was the rub. In his desire to do the right thing, tell his Indian friends what happened, he had to be proper in ways he couldn't be. A tender uncertainty crept into our comprehension of that certain moment of finality, death.

The earth did not care where a person was born. It is the vain humans who fussed about birthplace. Death was different. In death, the earth claimed a person totally. And the place where a person died, was where the person truly belonged. Battlefield, cancer ward, high seas: earth absorbed that final breath. Gita's would be an American death. She became American in death. Yet, those of us who lived in America knew so little about the circumstances of it.

Some three hours after my arrival at Blue Mountain, an unsmiling Lalu was back to giving orders to kitchen staff. They had been trying to give him some distance, now they ceased hovering about in silence and went to work in a flurry. They put out fresh linen tablecloths, glass flower vases with real flowers, silver cutlery, cloth napkins etc.

I reassured Lalu that I would go visit our detective friend, and 'do everything I could' to find out the facts. Of course, I would accompany Lalu if he so wished. He nodded, turned to his staff and mumbled a final slew of instructions.

"People will come and want to eat, you know," he said to me. "It's dinner time."

Yes, Gita or no Gita it's Dinner Hour in America, and as the expression went, the show must go on. It's the American way. I got up to leave, but a piece of my heart was left behind. Crumbled like that samosa. As my hand reached to turn the door handle, it hit me. I said to no one in particular, "Saffron, it is saffron." Bitter tasting saffron tendrils gave kalakand an exquisite bouquet. Recalling the name saffron helped to shed a little bit of my dark mood, but it didn't make my heart whole.

Call to Mullins

My call to Detective Sergeant Mike Mullins was, I would like to think, not quite as frantic as the phone call I received from Lalu. But, I didn't feel any less pressure from within. The detective seemed to have anticipated my call.

"Kumar, good to hear from you, how you been?"

"As good as can be, Detective Mullins. Thanks for taking my call."

"Of course! You're welcome to call me anytime, you know that."

"That's great, Mike. Hope you're well too. Made Lieutenant yet?"

"Working on it, Rama.."

"Keep at it, detective. You'll be one soon, no doubt." I genuinely believed that.

It was reassuring to me how easily he dropped Rama into our conversation. It was my ancient and discontinued first name. He extracted it out of me over beers some years earlier, and he hasn't forgotten.

Rama Ananda Venkata Easwara Kumar-Swamy was the name which appeared on my high school record. It got compounded in college, to just three words (Ramananda Venkateswara Kumaraswamy). My parents' piety earned me a lot of ribbing, as to why I hogged the names of all the gods. Or, as to why I left some out!

The name was further shortened to Anand V. Kumar when I

got off that proverbial boat and set foot in America. I joked that the USA could use fewer gods and one less swamy. Mike loved that tale and used Rama, my original first name, to cue in a personal chit-chat mode.

"So, my Hindu friend, how's Lalu saab taking it all?"

"Mike, I don't know what exactly you told him, but he is totally shook up. Stunned, actually."

"He give you the gist of it, right?"

"Well, yes. He's carrying on with the restaurant business, but I can see that he is on auto-pilot, sort of. Fact is, if you ask me, he is quite perturbed."

What, perturbed? Oh well, sometimes words just come out like that. Sort of an old habit of mine, words tumbling out like that. The hazard of knowing too many words, I suppose. So, yea, Lalu perturbed was right.

"Can't blame him Kumar," Mike was back to my popular public name. "I did hit him hard, I probably should have asked you to be there, but I could not. Not at first. You know the protocol. Immediate family, next of kin, etc. It was really his news to tell other people...."

"Can I ask what is known so far, Mike?"

"Not much more than what was told to me," a short pause and then, "I conveyed to Lalu saab what I could. Our friends downstate said that a farmer stumbled upon a dead body. The local sheriff secured the area, the coroner estimated that the body had lain there about two days if not longer. But not very long, is how they put it."

"How much have local cops uncovered? I mean, as far as you can tell me." I was holding my breath.

"The coroner confirmed that the young woman lived in the Chicago area. The state investigator went through some databases and found that she was not reported missing, or a wanted felon, or a convict. Her prints came back negative for terrorism watch list etc. He didn't know what to make of it, referred back to the bosses in Springfield. Well, they contacted my boss's boss's boss. It only came down to me because of my earlier work with people from India."

"You know Mike, that's a lucky break for Lalu Ganesh and those who loved Gita." My interjection was neatly side-stepped by Mullins who continued in an even tone.

"The reports or the material in NCIS, didn't specify ethnicity or national origin or place of birth. So I didn't recognize the name Gita right away. But the name Ganesh triggered my memory, I casually touched base with Lalu saab. I knew he would call you, and he did."

"So, are you are investigating the case?" I asked.

"It's not a Chicago case, yet."

"Whose case then?"

"I don't know, Chicago Police were contacted for courtesy and confirmation. The state cops knew from her personal effects that we would be involved somehow in the case. How much and who ... er the whole thing is above my pay grade. It's up to my boss's boss's....."

"Boss, eh..." I cut in.

Mullins remained silent. I suppose my silence was less bearable, so it was he who resumed. He echoed my mind.

"So what's your plan, Kumar. I know that you like to meddle and explore."

"Meddle, explore? Oh, no. Not me, sir. This time I will just follow the developments from a distance." I said.

Mullins's broad smile was easy to sense over the phone line. "Still modest, huh." A short pause, and then, "Kumar, all smart people are restless. They solve puzzles and seek explanations. Admit it, you trying to do something?

"Oh no, Mike. It is all so... distant, so incredible. I wouldn't know how to begin... er the meddling. Unless, of course, a detective friend helps me along."

Chuckles very clear over the phone line. Followed by the sound of paper shuffling on Mike's end. I held my breath again and the detective finally spoke up.

"Don't you go sticking your neck in police matters, Rama. This is no time for amateur hour."

"Oh Mike, you don't really mean *that*. I can't just sit idly by while my people are dying from curiosity. Oops, sorry, Mike. A poor choice of words by me. The 'community is desperate for answers' is what I wanted to say."

A clear chuckle from Mike Mullins, and "I hear you." Followed by a more serious tone: "Kumar, I know you. You get involved in stuff because you care about people. That's admirable. You are a good communicator, and that's good too. But, in terms of police procedure, don't poke your nose or stick your finger in..." he trailed off.

"Hmm, nose, fingers, neck. Any other body parts I should be minding, Mike?" I asked with a small laughter in my own voice.

That cost him all the sternness in his speech as he laughed heartily. I let our laughter settle down naturally. I told Mike how grateful the Indian community was for his friendship. He remained quiet for a while, but eventually: "Kumar, I am serious. Stick to writing blogs, okay? Don't go short-circuiting the state police. You can do stuff I don't have time for. Like sleuthing about on the Internet. By the way, how is your Internet Cafe doing?"

"It's actually good, Mike. Thanks for asking. This Cafe thing seems to be the real deal. Lots of people come in to connect to the net. I put in a couple of printers, copiers and a fax machine. People come to use them too."

"You figured it all out, huh," said Mike.

"Not quite all by myself. I took some classes so I could help folks with their basic computer tasks, the older folk, specially. You remember the lady from New Delhi, Sarada Sashanki, from a couple years ago?"

"Oh yeah, Sasha, I remember her. How is she doing?"

"Quite well. She emails me often, sends recipes to try out, and inquires about things Chicago. Even gives me tips on how to run my business. Of course, if I run into a technical problem there is always a 'cousin' to help."

"Glad to know you and Mrs. Sasha kept in touch. Tell her I wish her nothing but success, will you?"

"For sure, Mike, for sure."

"You going to visit her. I hope," said Mike.

"I have a standing invitation to New Delhi, so to speak."

"Well, then..."

"Yeah, but, you know, visiting India is no casual matter. For me, it's akin to an expedition, like exploring a continent all over again."

"Naw, Just like riding a bicycle. It will all come back to you. I say, go and say hello to the lady in person," Mike let out a murmur of light chuckles.

I changed the topic. "It's been a while since you visited Wings of Ether, Mr. Mike."

"Yeah, we'll have to rectify that." Easy to imagine another smile.

"Look detective, I'd love to meet you to talk further about Gita. I really must come see you. Lalu needs my help. I need your help." I didn't need to lay it really thick on him, the detective would help, I was sure. All the same, I offered to ride downtown to Precinct One.

My old detective friend was a good sport. He offered to come up north himself. To Little India, stretched out along Devon Avenue on the North Side of Chicago. "I miss the samosa," he said.

Detective-uncle

Unlike the previous time Mike and I dined together, the *Blue Mountain* was super busy this time. Lalu obliged by improvising with a small round table brought in from a back room. He set it in the only spot available, a corner by the kitchen. Mike didn't seem to mind it and I was silently thankful for that. The air was thick with curry and I worried that it might hurt Mike's eyes. Or, cling to his clothing and go home to annoy his wife.

I was about to say something, when Mike rubbed his palms together and said, "Ooh, I just love this. Let's eat samosa." He said it as though it was his word for Indian food. But then again, sometimes a samosa is just a samosa. One never knows with detective Mike. On the other hand, Chef Lalu Ganesh took samosa to *mean* Indian food, lots of it.

Minutes after being seated and given water, silverware etc., Lalu was at our table but there were no samosas. Instead, it was a huge plate loaded with aromatic delicacies. Lalu knew Mullins's tastes well enough by now, having hosted him a dozen times in recent years. He set down an extra large *thali* for the detective. It was a giant round steel plate with a number of smaller steel bowls lined up in a half-moon arc. Each bowl was filled with a dish more flavorful than the next. In the remaining space on the round thali, Lalu piled rice, chicken, flat bread, and a skewer of kabob. Mike smiled broadly, "Thank you sir, for your kindness," and dug in. I followed suit, making a messy mix of rice and curry on my smaller thali tray.

I had to deal with the constant swing of the kitchen door near my back, offering some amusement to us both. I was just happy we were seated. I was happy that Mike came to break bread, er break samosa, so to speak.

Lalu did not wish to sit with us. "I can't bear to hear horrible details, Kumar," he had said when he learned about the detective's visit. "You find out first, the details. Then tell them to me the way you know I can handle it." Well, it *was* Lalu's special personal misery, and he dealt with it anyway he could. I felt sorry for the poor bugger, and did as he wished. Let him stay immersed in his daily toil, while I took on the detective with endless inquiries. *But eat something first.*

It was pleasing to see an American police officer eat Indian food with familiarity, even gusto. He smoothly reached into each of the half-a-dozen *kathori* placed around the dinner plate. And, grabbing a piece of nanbread wrapped it around curry comfortably. Or, slurped liquid sambar right out of a small bowl. He didn't rotate the big thali plate like it were a lazy-susan, as some Americans did. His natural Indian style of using the thali & kathori system was a delight, and made it easy for me to get to the point.

"So, do you think Lalu will get some detailed info soon… You think your fellow officers will share more?"

"Yes and no. There are issues, you understand, of jurisdiction and authority. We will get information, but I just don't know how much, or how quickly."

Mike put the skewer down on his thali, wiped his lips with a moist napkin. A finger bowl also appeared magically at his side, courtesy of the head server. The detective gave me a steady look. "You know, Rama, I have to ask a few questions too. Mind you, it's just for me. I am not taking notes or any such thing. All investigation belongs to Illinois State Police right now. But, I do need to know some things."

I was already done eating. I opened my arms in invitation, "Ask away Mike, anything."

"How well do you know Gita Ganesh?"

"A little over five years. She came on some sort of a domestic worker or ethnic service worker type of visa. That sort of thing became quite popular during the late Nineties. Her uncle Ganesh put up the sponsorship papers for her."

"Interesting. I didn't know such things existed. I know lots of your cousins come here on computer visas."

"H1-B visas," I chuckled. "Hi-Tech workers. They get paid well. They are the new middle class in India."

"Um…okay. So you knew Gita all along?"

"Never met her alone, if that's what you mean. I knew her socially." And without pausing, "Mike if you are wanting to connect me to Gita, just ask. She is Lalu's blood niece. That makes her almost my daughter," I said.

There was a quickening of my voice when I said those lines and I regretted it at once. Getting upset with Mike, or cross-questioning him served no purpose. He was trying to help us. I took a sip of ice-water from the glass tumbler. Again, things appeared on our table courtesy of the ever hospitable Shetty.

Mike steepled his hands on the table and asked a totally different question. "Tell me Kumar, who do you think might have a reason to kill Gita? If she was in fact killed on purpose. For all we know, she might have just died accidentally."

"Oh, come on Mike. You tell us she was found far away from a road. in the middle of a farm, in the middle of nowhere. And then you say she could have died accidentally. What are you getting at?"

"I am trying to get at facts on this end, our end, Kumar. This is not my case and I don't know what to think. Help me put together a picture of Gita. What was she doing so far from Chicago?"

A long sigh, "I just don't know Mike."

"Do your best. Guess."

"How can I? The girl probably doesn't even know what it looks like beyond Chicagoland," I said.

"So, nobody here knows anybody anywhere else in the state. Is that what you are telling me?"

"Of course not, Mike. I know lots of people, all over the place. You actually know that for a fact. You even met some of my doctor friends." I had to pause again, drink more ice water to douse the fires of spice and anger.

After gathering some cool, I said, "Oh man, you are really cross-examining me now, aren't you? You do know I know people. Are you trying to connect me to Gita's death? That's just not fair."

"I am not linking you to anything," Mullins soothed. "I must be on solid ground as far as facts are concerned. I must know all about Gita before I can ask reasonable questions of detectives downstate. I need rock solid facts."

The level of noise in the dining area was dying down, the place was emptying out. As Lalu was flying by, I asked him to join us. He gave a gesture of wait and disappeared into the kitchen.

Mike popped another one of those police questions: "Did Gita know many people in Southern Illinois or downstate, any Americans?"

I hadn't thought along those lines. Actually, it didn't occur to me that she might know people on her own. She was a kid, Lalu being her only family here in America. Every person she knew would be a person she knew only through Lalu, right? Right.

Mike was watching my face. He shrugged and said, "I was wondering, I have to. You know Kumar, if I ever called the sheriffs down there, they would ask me. Do we know what Gita was doing traveling over there?" That gave me pause again. But, something clicked in my mind and I set my chai down.

I spoke slowly, haltingly, "Aren't we assuming Mike that Gita traveled willingly, under her own power, so to speak?" I trembled as I asked it. There was silence for some time.

Eventually, I finally broke the tension, wishing to explain how Indian people connect with everybody around them by making up a familial relationship. It was time to let Mike in on some Indian-ness.

"Look Mike, Gita and I were not family but she always referred to me as uncle. Nothing odd about it. That's how all Indians relate to others. Every person an Indian meets socially is an instant relative. Really..."

"You mean.. are you saying all you Indians are related to each other?" The detective was hiding a chuckle.

"Mike, it works. It's a disarming way of relating to people. A bonding type of thing."

A smile still lurked behind Mike's facade, though he now appeared to be curious.

"Mike, the point is, Gita regarded me as family from the very first day we met. I was her Kumar-uncle. An odd way to phrase it, but that's the Indian way too. Place a person's name first and put the word for relationship after it. Kumar-uncle, Radha-auntie, Shetty-brother, etc. Really. That's the way Indians speak, Kumar uncle."

Mike looked quizzical, "That would make me Mike-detective?"

My turn to chuckle. "You'd think so. But, no. Job titles like doctor, captain, president etc., still come before the name. Saying the name of a person before a title of respect is done only in family or close relationships. To Gita, you would still be Sergeant Mike. Unless, of course, she regarded you as family, then you are Mike-uncle. She might have even called you Detective-uncle."

I thought he would chuckle. Instead, his face turned grave. "Imagine that," he said, "Detective uncle, he has a dead niece."

Gita - Wisywig

"Why don't you get a car, bro?" asked the bus driver. "You sure spend a lot of time riding my slow beast."

"Well, Larry, I'd probably spend just as much time in traffic, stop and go driving. This way I get to think, while you do all the work," I grinned.

"For sure, for sure," a big grin of his own. "You own a store around here?"

"Naw, I just get hungry a lot," still grinning, "for Indian food."

The black bus driver mirrored my humor.

"Long way to go to be with your culture, bro." Larry said, nodding, with that knowing look. "I get like that sometimes. Which one you like the best, you people like ribs and stuff?"

Some persons might get upset by the phrase 'you people,' but not me. I disliked identity sensitivity just as much as I disliked parochialism for its own sake. People are same all over, but also different. Very different, sometimes. I celebrate the differences. Plus, I wasn't above making stereotypes out of people including myself.

I smirked, and said "*My people*, Larry, don't eat pork or ribs. A few eat steaks and such. Many will even eat turkey on Thanksgiving Day, just to be good Americans. As for me, I just eat whatever is cheap."

"My man, my man. *Aw-eight,*" Larry said,

"Back to your question, the best chicken and rice dishes can be found where my buddy Lalu cooks, the Blue Mountain restaurant, near Devon and Western," I said.

"Blue Mountain, huh."

"Yup. It's named for a place in India, with lots of mountain peaks that look bluish and cloudy. Just like the Smokies in America."

"Right on, right on," said Larry, focused on the traffic. The bus inched along a stretch busy with shoppers on McCormick Boulevard. Larry spoke again. "You like this smoking or blue something mountain restaurant, huh. Good chicken you say?"

"Blue Mountain, yes. Great food all around. You can sample it all at a buffet table. Some 25 or more items. The owner and cook is a buddy of mine."

The 'Lincoln bus' stopped at a big multi-road intersection. Larry turned totally in his seat to face me and said with the big grin, "So, I go into the mountain place and tell them you sent me, what do I get then?"

"All you can eat," I laughed. Horns sounding behind us made him turn back to face the traffic, but the grin just wouldn't fade off his face.

I was tempted to tell Larry all about Gita, but a certain reservedness came over me. It was hard enough talking about Gita with people who knew her. Talking about her with someone who didn't know her at all, it was not something I could do at the moment. What I didn't know was how much all of that would change in just a few short weeks hence.

****

It's not like Gita was known to me that intimately either. She was my friend's niece and that was all that mattered. Kumar uncle didn't have to sit down and compare notes with Gita, or 'hang out'. Our bond was implicit, the Indian way.

In Little India, we were all nosey, and we knew each other in that gossipy way all ethnic enclaves functioned. We knew who was related to who; who just got married, or had a business shut down by authorities. We all knew who sponsored who for a visa. And if I may whisper, we also knew who quite didn't have 'the papers.'

There was a word we Indians in America use to describe ourselves. *Desi.* It meant countryman, a compatriot. Russians have their tovarish; Italians say paisano; Indians say desi. To an Indian, every other fellow sub-continental person is *desi.* I know, I know. Our American friends can't resist asking, "Everyone of you is Desi? You mean, all you guys have a wife named Lucy Ricardo?" Oy vey.

It is the Indian way of the immigrant street, to live within the comfort zone of made up relatedness. If a real relationship didn't exist, we invented one. Every Indian we came across was, somehow, an instant relative. We didn't have any mysteries, and we wore our truths on our sleeve. The world of computers coined a word that said it all. WYSIWYG, what you see is what you get. Ours was a wysiwyg reality in Little India. No mysteries. Every person we met was a relative: uncle, aunt or grandpa.

Our happy sense of certainty and familiarity was shattered that April. Suddenly, we didn't know what to believe, or who was who. We weren't even sure of what we knew. All due to Gita's death so far from our *bustee.*

The incoming

The 'incoming' was ferocious, and we had to take it. I expected news of Gita's death to be received with shock and dismay, mixed with sadness and sympathy. I expected a thousand different questions. But, not the sort of reaction we actually got. Sure, there were sorrowful emails, letters, and sympathy calls. But the incoming from India had a lot of invective, a barrage of criticism. The hurtful phone calls came at random intervals. Lalu played back for me the ones that went to his voice mail.

“So irresponsible, you are, Lalu. You took father and daughter to the America country. Now both failed, you failed both.” That was from the drawing teacher at Lalu's old high school, who was also a distant uncle (many times removed on the maternal side).

“I am shocked, I am sad. Just when I thought my children were doing well in life,” Lalu's father. There were other phone calls his father made which Lalu picked up directly. But in this one, there was the sound of others sniffling, wailing, in the background.

And then there was this: “Hoy-yo-hoy, Lalu. I heard a lot about crime in America. You better leave America.” Lalu said the speaker was a bicycle repair man who was once happy to see Lalu go overseas.

I sipped my tea, trying to think of something not banal to say. Lalu was shaking his head between button presses on the answering machine, and tried to control his breathing. The invective, on top of the tragedy, was just too much. How to minimize the venom, without minimizing its effect? “People say stuff when they're excited. Don't pay no mind to them.”

Lalu retorted, “They blaming me, I don’t know why? It’s upsetting.”

“Of course, it’s upsetting. Those callers,” my finger pointing at the phone,”are just as shocked and upset as us. I don’t know if they are cruel. Foolish, maybe. They have no idea what life in America is like.”

“I am upset. You saying, Kumar, I should not be upset?” He shook his head. Before I could give a soothing answer, the phone came alive, and I nearly spilled my chai. Lalu jumped up quickly and jabbed his fingers on the machine with surprising speed. The caller’s message came through the speaker phone:

“*Ayyo,* Lalu, What bad thing this is. I knew you will be sorry for going to America. Ask anybody here, I always said, go to America and get ruined. Now see what you did. Father failed, daughter dead...” The rant would have gone on, but Lalu smacked the phone to disconnect. “Listen to it. Will you listen to it. That mad fool...” He said, stabbing at the phone with a finger. “I know this fellow, Rajmani, carries bricks on his head at building sites. Can’t even make a wall with them. He preaching to me?”

“There is a lot of grief back home, Lalu. Your family is well liked,” I said.

He paced slowly, trying to calm down and breathe. “International phones should not be this cheap. Every riffraff is using it these days.” It was hard for me to watch my friend feeling abused. It was as if the whole of south India relocated into his ear, giving him grief non-stop. I decided to hang out with him for the rest of the day. Lalu appreciated that, and asked me to answer the phone for him. I didn’t really wish to, but braved it for him.

My turn at dealing with the inquiries wasn't any easier. It was like being in school and taking a test, every caller had lists and lists of questions. What were the police doing, what have they told so far, is Lalu demanding answers everyday, has a TV station been contacted, are the wealthy Indian doctors helping, and on and on.

The variety of questions fired across the oceans was matched by the number of insults directed at Lalu personally. He became too Americanized; he thinks everybody should act like him. He wants to be a big shot in America. He is sponsoring all sorts of people to come live in Chicago. What's Lalu trying to prove? That he is some sort of 'Godfather of Indians.' Who does he think he is, a Hindu Columbus, setting up his own colony there? When it rains, it pours. Soon, it was a monsoon of blame.

I was at a loss myself, and turned to a friend from New Delhi for help with my sanity, Sarada Sashanki, whom I got to know as Sasha, for short. She and I first met a couple of years ago during her visit to America for a trade show. She had inadvertently gotten into some trouble, and I aided her through it. She met Lalu, Gita and a number of Indians in Chicago. She was a kind and dignified lady who kept in touch with me. She was also a good listener, and I could use one.

Dear Sasha, I hope this missive finds you in good health, and your business in good stride. Thanks for the news clippings you shared last month. Wonderful profiles of you and your business smarts. People in Chicago still ask about you. They are pleased when I tell them that you are doing nicely.

Now, there is some sad news to share with you. Gita Ganesh, hope you remember her as Lalu's niece, died suddenly a few days ago. There is a lot of mystery as to how and why it happened. It's a police matter now. Her uncle, Lalu, is hiding his feelings. But I can tell he is stewing in sorrow. I feel confused as well, as to what I could or should do.

Gita was independent minded and lived by herself. An unattached Indian young woman of marriageable age, living and working in America with only an uncle for family. What might she have been going through? Even though I was her Kumar uncle, I feel incapable of answers to such questions.

My friend, I have known you to carry on through tragedies with grace. Surely, you can offer me some insight? I need to find out what happened to Gita. And, I must help Lalu Ganesh. Write me your thoughts soon, won't you? And keep me posted on your latest mustard creations. You know that I rejoice in your triumphs!

Your friend Kumar
Chicago, April 8.

Sign, seal and stamp, I found it easier to fall asleep then. But it turned out to be a lot harder to stay asleep. Every little noise sounded like a telephone trill to my sleepy head. At one point, the purring of Ms. Agnes confused the cells of my lizard-brain enough to conjure up a cartoon phone rattle. I woke bolt upright, much to the cat's dismay. My eyes smarted, my mouth was dry, and I needed a cold drink to restore myself a bit.

The things people said in some of those phone calls were not all that weird. They were seeds to questions that sprouted in my mind. The vitriol was what made it too much. I began to feel within myself some of the angst Lalu must have suffered since Gita's death. He sure was taking some heavy verbal uppercuts.

I fired up the computer and began to browse police websites for information on death investigations. What did forensic people look for? How was cause of death established, and how did it differ from the manner of death? What did the manuals in different jurisdictions have to say about murder. Chemistry, physics, biology - it was like going to school again.

The inter-webs revealed a new-fangled something called Internet Sleuthing. Amateurs and armchair Sherlocks who poured over publicly available data. They speculated away in an attempt to solve a whodunit. Should I join such a group? Could it work in Gita's case? Or, might it disrupt the good relationship I had with Mullins? There were tons of items to ponder and organize in my mind. Before long, I was back in bed sliding into a happy drowsiness.

The next few days kept me busy at Wings of Ether, the Internet cafe I owned and operated with the help of my assistant Virginia. I replaced some desktops, rearranged tables, rerouted cables, upgraded cable connectors, and so on. I also took care of Ms. Agnes's quarters, situated next to a small bookshelf. After all, it was quite often 'take your kitty to wok day,' at the Wings. The tabby loved her home away from home as much as I did.

When I eventually made it to Devon Avenue, Lalu greeted me with the usual 'eat something first.' It wasn't until he returned from the kitchen with a platter of samosas and soda, that I noticed the changes.

A new grimness took over his dark face. There were raccoon rings, and a puffiness which threatened to make slits out of his eyelids. His shoulders became rounded, and the orders he barked lacked the usual bite.

"You need to sleep, my friend," I said.

"Maybe I should just lie down in the kitchen," he said, "You know, I used to do that in the early days. Slept on an army cot right here. So many things to fix here in those days. No time for home."

He settled in a chair across the table from me, sipped his diet coke and watched me bite into my samosa. After that ritual of hospitality, he placed an envelope on the table. It was from his village, his father's return address. Having faced two weeks of the incoming, Lalu was somewhat gun shy.

"Open it, can't be that bad," I said.

"How many people you think are inside?" he asked, feeling out the thickness of the envelope between his thumb and index finger. He was referring to a habit common among Indians who wrote to the USA. One family wrote the main letter, and people in the village added their own notes to the envelope. Saving postage by letter-pooling.

"Go ahead, let's at least see who all joined in. Maybe Phani had some questions he couldn't ask over the phone," I prodded. Lalu complied after finishing his soda.

I used to fancy myself as shrewd, insightful, wise, and all that other stuff. I thought I knew the world, and the ways of its people. Going through that pool of letters proved me clearly wrong. All sorts of people put their little notes in that envelope. But, not Gita's father.

Admittedly, I was never that good at remembering time zones, seasonal time shifts, and have been often late to social events. But, even I could tell day from night, and Monday from Tuesday. Phani would have been back home days before their village learned about Gita. Why didn't he put a note? A callous vagabond he might have been, but even he would know of his daughter's passing. Yet, nothing from him in the envelope. Not a wail or a peep. Not even a second-hand diatribe.

The man with multiple interests, the man who was wildly curious about many gods and many religions, was oddly incurious about the death of his daughter. Blood did not bind, it thinned his curiosity. It was a weird sort of a mind

I should have been alarmed perhaps, but wasn't. In my bid to help Lalu, I too fell into an odd sort of a zone myself. I was flailing, like a free falling skydiver who loses his fix on the horizon, panics, and doesn't remember to pull the chute. Instability leading to missed judgment.

On the other hand, the letter from *their* father, the elder Ganesh, was riveting. Written by hand, in a chain-linked cursive script, mixing words from four languages - Urdu, Hindi, Telugu and English - the letter ran over three pages long. The letter from the elder Mr. Ganesh's reeked of gentle sorrow, the fountain pen bled on paper. As Lalu read it aloud, I noticed how warm and tender the written words were, compared to comments during his first phone call. He wrote feelingly about grief, purpose in life and rebirth. Towards the end, he wrote that Gita's father became mournful and gaunt. "He is not touching his food."

"Hogwash, Kumar, total hogwash," said Lalu. "They exaggerate. I know my brother. He saying nothing at all." He swung his index finger like a windshield wiper, "He is not suffering, not shedding one tear."

"Suffering quietly, probably," I said.

Lalu turned his index finger to point at me. "Now you

exaggerating. My brother is rat. Always running away. No news good, no news bad. Just rat." He spat out the words.

"Oh come now, lost his daughter, after all."

Lalu let out a cackle. "They lie. I am sure Phani is not at home. He got on some slow moving train without buying ticket and took off. I am sure of it." He sat again across from me and rested his head between crossed arms. I couldn't see his eyes.

"Um…still, his…um..own daughter…" was my final attempt.

Lalu's head jerked up, "Nonsense, Kumar, Phani has no feelings for anybody, or anything." He took a deep breath, "You know, sometimes I think he hate everything, even god."

I was appalled, but saw no point in pressing. Why compound his emotions? Can't soothe him? Leave him alone. Eventually, I said, "Write to him, explain the situation. He's bound to read your letter sooner or later."

"If they even know where he is," Lalu's teeth gritted, fully convinced of his brother's foolish simplicity, an ignoramus. I had a notion too. That when a man runs away from America, the ultimate prize, he could walk away from a whole life. And, a person *that* sure of himself wouldn't allow anybody to be sure about him at all.

Whatever. There was good news, Lalu's brother wasn't my problem. The bad news? Lalu's dead niece was.

News Reports

"What will you be doing, Kumar? What's the next step?" asked Lalu.

"I'll go over every news item that's out there. Compile a full dossier. All the known knowns," I air-quoted the last part, a phrase made popular in the US news media by the great, grinning Rumsfeld.

"Clipping newspapers, huh," Lalu snorted. He might have thought it to be too banal or useless, I wasn't miffed. Just carried on with my explanation. "Once I record every thing known, I will be ready to ask the right questions. I will know who can tell us what."

"So you will make news clips first, okay. But, you are not going *there?*" His voice dropped on the last word.

"Of course, I'll go." And then, more slowly, with conviction in my voice, "I must go visit the place." Lalu should have no doubt about my going to the place where Gita's body was found. Of course, I would go. It was about two hundred miles away. The distance added to the mystery of what Gita was doing there in the first place. And, the mystery only added to the misery.

"I better get back to my computers so I can get started straight away," I rose to leave. Lalu's face remained impassive, though it was obvious it was killing him on the inside. After all, he was no Buddha. He was only shaped like one.

On the way home I felt that I must have, somehow, lessened Lalu's misery. However, a subtle new question arose. Was there something we didn't know about our Gita? That doubt was the worst devil of all.

***

Agri-Dispatch Online, an Internet-based news service with a focus on issues around Logan County, Illinois, covered Gita's death early and often. It posted a number of brief reports, starting with one about a body found in the fields, where the interstate ran alongside the old Route 66. Subsequent reports were in the form of updates, each one a different day, a different hour. The website made no effort to organize them in any way, its own internal links didn't always work. One such link to an update only returned the original piece. The Dispatch was just one of about eight sources of information I started out with. I saved a search of the radio reports for later.

Google search results were jumbled even worse. It took a lot of time to tag each download with a time stamp of the original report. Next, I loaded each report into a separate tab of Firefox and played with the order of tabs. It gave me a semblance of a time line. And, made for a meaningful starting point.

The earliest item I found was a Dispatch post that began with a sheriff's spokesperson confirming that a local farmer did indeed report finding a body in a field somewhere off Route 66, north of the capital city Springfield.

In a video that accompanied the report, there was a brief tight close up of the reporter pushing her hair back while holding a mike toward a sheriff's deputy who read from a statement. This was followed by a long shot of the farmland, from an aerial sequence, and then switched to a medium shot of a farmer extending his hand out somewhere toward the left of the screen.

The next *Dispatch* post in the time line, as I had it sorted it out, came some six hours later. It showed fluttering ribbons of yellow crime scene tape, a pair of official vehicles, technicians flitting about, and a sheriff's deputy standing near the tailgate of a truck, pushing his hat back with a finger. More people, civilians likely, could be seen milling around. The same reporter appeared, now in a fleece vest, with a notebook in one hand and mike in the other. She was saying:

"What is certain, is that the body found in this spot, to my left, last evening, is that of a woman possibly in her thirties. Sheriff's office wouldn't give any details about how death occurred, pending medical examination. However, I can report exclusively this morning that the deceased is not believed to be a local resident."

More shots of technicians and a quick cut to Sheriff Bob Crawford saying: "She's definitely not local, as we know of. I will have more after the coroner's report. Please, let my crew do their job, appreciate it."

The Dispatch Online also published a longish text report about five hours after that video report. The 800 word piece detailed the story of how this old man working in the field heard the sheep dog barking. The dog, named Buddy, barked where there were no sheep or cattle. The farm hand went over to where the blue heeler dog was. "The hound's ears were swiveling, tail flapping and stretched its neck out, it was barking," the farmhand was quoted. The man got off his tractor, followed the dog, and seen him looking under a small tree and bark once. There it was, what looked like a small human body. "Them dogs, they know things, you know," the man said into the camera, his hat held against his chest.

The report went on to say that the owner of the farmland called the sheriff, and the two discussed who the victim might be. Deputies came to the scene right away, and taped the area off. Mr. Will Bennett, the farmer, was quoted as saying that the sheriff's office responded real quick, and it was a good thing too that crop hasn't been planted yet, else the body would have lain hidden, who knows for how long.

An overview map of the county was printed, with a skinny arrow pointing to a vague spot off the Interstate. There was a picture of man and dog together, and a side piece about Australian Blue Heeler dogs.

The Dispatch followed this up, some two hours later, with a related story centered on the Sheriff's office. It summarized what it has discovered, any evidence gathered, results of medical examinations, and what clues as to the identity of the woman. The report was actually just a repetition of what was already known, except that it added speculation from an unidentified source, that death resulted from loss of blood due to multiple stab wounds. It was now a definite case of homicide. It quoted the Sheriff again as saying the dead woman was not a local resident, without any details.

That last Dispatch post garnered a single reader comment. The anonymous reader speculated that the deceased woman might be a migrant farm worker since television images suggested a dark skinned person. Also, planting season was about to commence. *Follow this story*, said a link appended to the post, but the link was dead. Some sort of a breakdown, 404 something.

***

There was a rushed edition of the local college's student newspaper. The *Daily Scholar* asked in a front page article if readers knew of persons that went missing inexplicably, or under odd situations. It also asked readers to be cautious in thinking about 'missing' students. After all, it was a break time in the school calendar and many students traveled out of town. The article urged officials to release the ID of the victim soon. A student editor wrote a human interest story, in an absorbing style, about dying in a field. Probably a worker who planted crops the year before, and now lay dead in the same field. "What did the migrant worker think, as she lay looking at the sky one last time, did it look same as the sky back home?" was the last line from the future-Pulitzer hopeful. The Scholar promised a diligent follow up report.

There was a single news story printed by the Logan County Gazette & Courier, which was one of the larger surviving newspapers. Its Local News section carried a three inch column about the grisly discovery. The report appeared two days after the actual discovery, and it basically quoted the sheriff as saying the investigation is ongoing, and that he contacted the State Bureau of Investigation for help.

Three days after the sheep dog barked its alert, news reports began to diminish. Hard news pieces faded away. The Dispatch too moved on, after the initial flurry of a dozen or so posts.

I continued to scan all other local news sources, but there was little other original reporting. A reporter went down from St. Louis, in the Show Me state, and reported on the body's discovery for a paper based on the other side of the river. The highlight of her report was that the deceased was not a migrant farm worker, for sure. There was no elaboration.

I had known since the early days of my Internet Cafe, that You Tube and other video platforms could be a haven for news clips. I scoured the stream sites for coverage of the story. There was no network news coverage of Gita. I probably shouldn't have expected any. Only local television stations carried the news. Of the seven different stations beaming to that part of Illinois, only four had any stories about 'a female found in the fields'. But their coverage and visuals were no different from those of the Dispatch. I logged them anyway.

News stations that beamed to the far southern Illinois towns like Carbondale and Cairo didn't bother to mention the news at all. I didn't expect them to either, since I thought of that part of the state as Kentucky, (not that Paducah cared one way or the other).

I took a break from staring at the screen, and made myself a fresh pot of coffee. I took the cat off the desk and laid her down in her bed, where she yawned once and rolled on her back to sleep, in a body contortion that yoga people would envy. Light, early-spring rain began to caress the window panes. Streaks formed on the glass that became smudgy, opaque, and eventually boring to look at. I returned to the computer.

Search results of news coverage took a nosedive. On the morning of the sixth day after the first report, there was a recap post published by the Dispatch. It had a joint byline, of the female reporter and one male reporter who wrote the long text piece three days earlier.

It was a well written report, a detailed narrative, and not too sentimental or lyrical about death. The story began with a dog bark, unfolded through different deputy sheriffs and farm workers, finally ending with a woman who died. It recapitulated some of the facts already laid out in earlier reports, the farmer calling the sheriff, the coroner conducting the post-mortem, the office of the State Bureau of Investigations withholding any comment. Etcetera, etcetera.

The recap pointed out that questions remained as to why the woman was killed, or by whom. Pointedly, it said that answers to those questions may lie elsewhere. The victim was not a local citizen but a resident of the Chicago area. Death most likely occurred elsewhere, and not under that little tree. It was too early to tell if this was an isolated killing, or part of a series.

The rain outside faded and the wind quieted into an eerie silence. So too did my brain. What did I have to show for a night of surfing? Not much, it seemed.

I yawned. It's true that I filled many blank spaces with information, but my knowledge didn't advance to any great extent. Should I have been surprised? No. After all, the internet doesn't know why Gita was there, or how she got there. Somebody somewhere knows, but who?

Killers everywhere

By the time I was ready to head out to Little India, there was a sizable stack of news reports printed out. I also had a clear idea of how to present it to Lalu. But, something odd happened once I reached Devon Avenue. The street felt different, like I entered another world than the one I knew. Or, quite possibly, it was *a different me* that entered the same old Avenue.

Years of reading detective novels in four different languages, and watching thousands of TV crime shows set on three continents, set me up with the fabled police cliche, 'everyone is a suspect'. The catchphrase that worked for so many fiction writers and fictional cops, now laid siege to my mind. It became a literal answer to every one of my questions about Gita's death. An answer the internet didn't provide me the night before. I couldn't go ten paces on Devon Avenue without seeing someone that looked like a killer.

"What is wrong, Kumar sir, you look like you were dealing with ghosts?" Shetty asked.

"Gita *beti* is on my mind," is all I said. Shetty nodded. But, I don't think he quite understood my neurosis. Yes, it *was* a neurosis of sorts. Seeing suspects when I should be seeking clues.

I tried to explain to Shetty and Warangal, but couldn't, why some people set me off on the street. A person hurrying across the street with a bag of rice, an uncouth fellow spitting red betel juice into the corner of a closed doorway, or a youthful, greasy-haired miscreant who giggled or snarled - suspects all.

Shetty wasn't concerned, "You should relax with a cup of chai, Kumar sir, and eat something first". Well, eat something first, at least the anthem of cordiality hasn't changed. And a platter of snacks did sound like a welcome treat.

Settling down to the tray of tiffin, I hoped my inner Walter Mitty would take the rest of the day off. With some delicious-looking samosas seeking my attention, I wanted Walter to give me a break, and let me get comfortable again with familiar places and faces.

"Killers everywhere huh, Kumar?" said Lalu when he emerged from the kitchen to sit with me. His voice was without irony, but there was a twist to his lips that bordered on a smile. It was a welcome sight to see some humor from him. I granted Lalu this line of ribbing since he was close to my age. All the same, I met his zinger head on, "Let's go on the street, I'll show you more suspects." We all laughed out loud, but it had been no laughing matter for me.

"Don't be doing all the detectiving by yourself, Mr. Kumar," joked Warangal. "What will the police be having to do then?"

Lalu surprised me with a further dose of humor, "Careful, Warangal. Kumar is trying to steal your job, hehehe."

My smile didn't change the fact that there were no clues whatsoever as to how Gita died. Nothing could be gleaned from news reports. Police gave no new information about the case. Mullins gave no hints as to how things were proceeding. The so-called news cycle touched Gita briefly and rolled on nonchalantly.

"So, nothing in the newspapers of the computers, huh, Mr. Kumar sir," Shetty said, shaking his own head.

"No new things from the police either, Shetty," I said. And, to no one in particular, "The weather is getting warm while the case is getting cold." I let that pearl hang for a minute, not knowing what response to expect. *Forget about forty-eight hours, we were now well up to four hundred...*

“You should tell your bosses to get the case moving, Officer Krishna,” said Lalu. We all looked at Warangal. He remained silent and played the fingers of his right hand over pursed lips.

Shetty ventured, “I think our brother Krishna opheessir has many questions. I am right?” The lanky man resumed shaking his head, “Policemen are always having many questions.”

“Where do you see all those killers, Kumar saab,” asked Warangal quietly. No mockery there, nor a real inquiry. His face was turned away.

“No, no,” interjected Shetty. “I meant police questions. Opheessir, please ask police questions. I mean, ask other people, not Kumar sir.”

“Krishna cannot ask questions. Other people are in charge of the case,” said Lalu. “Any question Warangal asks is totally unofficial, right, Kumar?”

I nodded, but the silly diversion to our talk didn’t minimize the mood that came over me overnight. Obsession with suspects. I let the group in on some moments that startled me, if only momentarily.

“I smelled some *attar* on this fellow coming around the corner, suddenly I felt a revulsion like I seen a killer. And then there was this guy with a scowl on his face and stroking his beard, standing alone at a street corner. He looked dubious. Just before coming in here, I saw a man in a turban that was so nondescript I couldn’t tell if he was a Muslim, Sikh, or even an Indian at all.” I paused for a breath. “They all stirred me up. Every one of them looked very suspicious.”

“Oh, I know what’s going on," said Lalu. "Unusual people look like suspects to you. People different from ..er you, ..er different from us; doing quite different things,” said Dr. Lalu, the Psychologist. Except, he didn’t say it like he was proposing the idea, he made a proclamation of it. And just like that, he up and headed into the kitchen. Hmm, it really was not that simple, was it?

There was no reaction from anybody for awhile. Not from Shetty, with one of his laconic queries, nor fromWarangal with his silent quizzical looks. A buzzer or chimes went off in the kitchen. The entire staff swung into action setting up the buffet, like it were a military drill. Lunch seekers were already clustered on the sidewalk.

Warangal and I left the Blue Mountain and went for a walk down the Avenue. It was his idea for me to talk things over with the police side of him, though I knew that Mullins would not let him near a case that involved Lalu’s niece. No harm in bouncing ideas off a younger mind.

We went to a *dhaba* on a side street off Devon, and ordered two large cups of chai. The place was run by a Sindhi man. It was known for its *dal makhani*, chai and *chole*, and it served Indian tea in giant foam tumblers (and charged pretty high too). It proved to be a fine idea, carry our oversize cups, walk around Little India, and chat while people watching. I couldn’t help the thought of it being an Indian version of white people strolling with lattes.

“So, what do you really think, Kumar?” asked Warangal. “I mean about who might have done it?”

“It’s got to be a young scoundrel of some sort. Can’t be an old man, or a woman. The way the cops described the body, it sounded like some disturbed, wrathful fellow," I replied.

"You think robbery gone bad?"

"Could be. Me personally? I think it could also be love," I said.

Warangal looked at me over the top of his foam cup and said, "You really think it was an angry, jilted lover?"

"Well, it doesn't have to be an angry or jilted situation. Or, even a lover. It could have been a one-sided love. Quite possible some guy had a crush, or a severe obsession with her."

The young man didn't seem convinced, so I added, "Yes, such things do happen, officer. You know, even a homely Indian girl like Gita. She could be attractive to some men. Some unstable character might have found her hot enough."

"I don't know how somebody can kill a person they like," said Warangal. "It's got to be a stranger, like a theft gone out of hand."

"Look around, Warangal. Take a look at the faces. Who here would Gita have trusted enough to get in a car with. And gone on a drive?"

Warangal turned the question back to me. "Kumar, I am not on the case, it's not even a Chicago case. *You* are on the case, for our good buddy Lalu. *You* tell me who around here looks likely to have done it." I took the bait.

I pointed to a middle-aged lady carrying a small bag of groceries, and said, "Look at that mean looking auntie over there, Krishna, she could have done it." Warangal laughed, saying, "All aunties are mean looking, in my opinion."

"You're supposed to like the aunties, officer. All Indian men like aunties," I laughed.

" Kumar, you see the oddity?" Warangal said. "Your suspects include young men and middle aged women. You don't seem to get the same vibe from men your age."

It gave me pause. Did I unconsciously give older fellows a break? I didn't consider Lalu or his brother as suspects, nor any number of older fellows around. I might have briefly worried about Shetty, but disregarded it quickly. Did Warangal have a point?

From where we stood, under a leafy tree on a side street off Devon Avenue, I had a good view of the intersection a few yards away. The area was busy with cars waiting to turn, people crossing against traffic lights, and entire families darting diagonally across the intersection while adults signaled for drivers to hold.

Warangal nudged me and said, "There goes a group of killers, Mr. Kumar," tilting his head to the left of where we stood. A group of four young men in good shape, and wearing stylish jeans and tees, were gathered near an SUV they had just exited.

Oh yeah, that was a group alright. What the CNN types called military age men, repeating it like a mantra. No additional description needed. "Oh, yeah," I said, "tough young military muscles, killers alright."

Warangal laughed heartily, and said, "You know, Kumar sir, none of those fellows would ever volunteer to be in the army. And, if they are drafted, their rich fathers will find a way for them to go back home and find nice Indian wives."

"Perhaps, Krishna. But, I do like that short-hand-speak,

military age men. It suggests killers. I bet one of them could have …."

Warangal punched my shoulder, "Stop it Kumar. I was kidding."

"We have our work cut out for us, Krishna. Lots of people knew Gita. We'll have to go through a long list of customers, suppliers, people who work around here…"

"Whoa whoa," Warangal interrupted me. "*You* have *your* work cut out. The department won't like it if I go around asking questions. Specially your detective friend, Mullins."

We headed back to Blue Mountain, walking slowly, observing people, and silent with our own thoughts.

I didn't realize that we had been gone so long, that Blue Mountain had almost cleared up from the the lunch rush. Lalu sat at his usual corner round table perch. His head down and dozing, and unconsciously scratching his elbows. A handful of diners were scattered about, all Indians. They looked like workers on a lunch break from other shops on the strip, judging from their business-like assault on the buffet line-up.

Warangal and I joined Lalu. He didn't open his eyes. Ghose came and placed silverware and cloth napkins. And when Shetty too came and sat, Ghose brought out a 'Lalu Special' tray. "Where did you fellows go?" asked Lalu, his eyes open now, looking from Warangal to me and back to the young Indian cop. Shetty was already loading up his own buffet plate.

The last of the diners left. A young Mexican r went and locked the front door. It was now just us, Gita's people, and time for Gita talk. Or, rather, Gita speculation.

“Kumar and I walked around and made lists of suspects ,” said Warangal.

“You were gone for some time, must have been very difficult, making up the list,” said Lalu, closed his eyes again.

“No, it was easy. Big list, little time. Everybody is a suspect,” Warangal laughed at his own wit. Lalu opened his eyes again and fixed us both, looked from one to the other, shook his head and leaned back.

A quietness descended and lasted a while, with only the clatter of the cutlery keeping up with the sounds of 'Bollywood muzak' in the ceiling. All humor aside, there were a lot of possibilities when it came to what happened to Gita. And an equally bewildering number of ways I could go about investigating them. Lucky, I thought, that poet Robert Frost had only two roads diverge. I was faced with a multitude of forks, and equally unable to choose my path.

Shetty, who missed some of Warangal's verbal shenanigans, looked up from his thali and asked, “Mr. Kumar sir, before you and Krishna opheessir went out, you said cybething will help Gita. You will do it?”

Warangal jumped in. “What cybething, what are you talking about?”.

I smiled, “No Warangal, not cybething, Shetty here just mixed up the words.” Turned to Shetty and said, “It's called cyber-sleuthing.” I separated the words for him, “Cyber Sleuthing.” People act like they are detectives and solve crimes. Everything happens on computers, on the internet.”

Shetty repeated the words a few times and asked, “Is it

expensive to buy this game?"

I laughed, "No, Shetty, not a game, and nothing to buy. People use the computers they already own. Somebody will write about a specific crime, other people will suggest answers. More facts are published, and then more solutions are suggested. Someone will put it all together and point out who did the crime."

Lalu spoke up. "Sounds to me like trying to get something for nothing. Crimes should solved by police who are paid to do it. Not lazy people sitting at home with computers."

Warangal raised an eyebrow. "We don't get paid enough, you know." Lalu closed his eyes again. Ghose walked up and asked Shetty in a low voice, pointing at Warangal and me. "What game they are playing?"

"No game right now, Ghose. It's computers," said Shetty. He turned to Warangal, "You explain."

"It's like a big game of Hide and Seek, Ghose," said Warangal. "Somebody is hiding behind a tree and others have to go find out where." He smiled.

Ghose snorted and threw up his hands, "Grown up men, children's games." He huffed back into the kitchen. Lalu kept his eyes closed but laughed heartily.

"Kumar sir, everything you showed us this morning, is that the only news about Gita?" Shetty asked.

"For now, yes. But, I will keep tracking them for updates. I will also cast a wider net, see if I missed any small entries ."

Warangal had a question, "Kumar, can I come and use your

computers to search for news, separately on my own?"

"Sure, you're welcome at the internet cafe anytime."

"You'll show me to login and so on?"

"Sure, sure. Anytime you like."

Lalu was fully awake now, "You two don't like your real jobs? Kumar sees killers, Krishna don't look for clues. Maybe you two stop doing each other's work, huh." The words he said were silly, of course, but the absence of a smile in his eyes said different.

I said, "You know something, fellows? It feels to me sometimes that Gita left this world, and got herself a green card to live in my mind permanent." It was only a feeble attempt at commiseration, but it turned out to be the wrong thing to say.

Lalu burst into tears, and wouldn't be consoled for a long time. Krishna Warangal paled and shriveled, no longer tall like a policeman. Shetty wilted, and turned to sit side saddle in his chair, looking the other way from me. Only Ghose, who didn't follow English too well, flitted about with a confused look.

I didn't see that coming. One simple throwaway line triggering them like that. But, there it was. As the silence extended, I too began to feel something. My body trembled. *Gita belonged to us all, right? Why then do I feel this monopoly over grief?*

During the bus ride back home, I went over the complexity of the problem and my own inadequacy to tackle it. I needed to scout the Avenue for sources of information and clues. I would have to look under every bag of basmati rice, turn over every Japanese-made sari bolt, and every crate of mangoes. Though

I lived and worked on the North Side of Chicago, far from the world of Devon Avenue, I could never be quite disconnected from it. Little India, that old stomping grounds of my college days, will have me acting like a true Indian all over again. I was sure going to address a lot of women as auntie, and lots of fellows as *bhai*..

****

Back at the internet cafe, I asked my occasional, part-time helper (and incessant nail file user), Virginia, to set up some web logs. I wrote out the protocols, queries and categories, and a blank database she could use to fill in, and sort sources and ideas. I also created three different profiles of 'inquiring minds' which I planned to use to seed discussion boards and get a buzz going. It might help to see what folks smarter than me would say about murder mysteries.

Naturally, Virginia did her usual best to dissemble and ignored the topic altogether. Instead, she started about women in my life, or the lack thereof. I tried to steer her away from that direction, and reiterated the protocols and forms she was supposed to work on actually. Virginia's matronly smile morphed into a tease.

"Oh come on, Kumar, you can tell me. What's the latest on your mustard girlfriend in New Delhi?"

"Nothing to say Ms. Ginnie, nothing. No - new - news. Okay? Nothing new about Mrs. Sashanki."

"Oh, now she's *Mrs.* Sashanki huh. Isn't she a single gal? I promise, I won't breathe a word. Tell me, she write to you this month, yet?"

"Miss Virginia, this is not time for gossip, please. Time for work on some cyber-sleuthing ideas," I paused, and for emphasis added, "for Gita's sake." I thought that was fairly stern. Virginia continued to smile with mischief in her eyes. For added drama, she poised her hands above the computer keyboard, fingers floating an inch above it. As if she were saying waiting for an answer.

I laughed and said, "Yes, Ginnie, Sarada and I exchanged letters recently. It was not personal, just some business matters."

Virginia beamed, and tapped out a rapid storm of keystrokes - real ones, not fake, it turned out. She sighed deeply and said, "Kumar, you protest too much," and kept typing away, god knows what.

"Focus, Miss Assistant Manager, focus. The check-list, please." I said.

"Oh, I am the assistant manager now, huh. Does the title come with a raise?"

I maintained a broad smile on my face, and gave her a big shake of head.

"Ah okay, I get it," she came back in her theatrical style: "Virginia is neither assistant, nor manager, discuss."

"Touche," I laughed at her witty redux of the famous Saturday Night Live TV shtick.

I brought her a tray bearing a mug of hot water, a bag of her favorite herbal tea, and honey. She received it with a broad smile. She dug through her purse and fished out a pair of vials, and tipped some potions into the tea. While it steeped, I told Virgina about how I spent the entire previous night surfing the net, and about how the fellows at Blue Mountain reacted to the things I said. It was an awkward, but comforting, confessional.

"You gotta stop obsessing like that, Kumar," said Ginnie, "You'll drive yourself crazy." A short pause was followed by an expansive smile, "But, it is kinda cute that you are so moved by what happened to your friend's little girl."

I was pleased by that remark, but still miffed at her for taking too many shifts off work. I was about to say something when Virginia raised her cup, "You're a true mensch, Kumar. Thanks for the tea. Happy sleuthing."

What can I say? I am a sucker for moments of tea and sympathy.

When windmills invite

When the windmills invite me to tilt at them, I oblige. Lack of a lance and armor notwithstanding, I mount an imaginary steed and go off...

Hence, this fool's errand. Writer, blogger, and Don Quixote. Lalu wished to know everything I could dig up about Gita's death. He didn't want to hear official jargon, or news piecemeal from the police at random intervals.

"The way police answer everything, Kumar. They use nice calm words, but those words don't mean anything," said Lalu, scratching his elbows.

"Yes, saying without saying anything," I replied. "Quite a habit of politicians too. Cops do it when they are forced to say something but don't want to. Equivocation, it can be frustrating."

"Why they do that?" Lalu asked, and without waiting for an answer, "I don't care. Just find out what happened, Kumar, please." He stopped scratching his elbow and gently cracked his neck. "Please, no police snake talk. Two tongues talking nonsense when they can't tell truth with just one." I suppressed my impulse to chuckle at Lalu's native metaphor. Forked tongue critters are believed capable of ambiguous speech, talk from both sides of the mouth: what Americans describe elegantly as double talk.

I nodded agreement with Lalu's sentiments. He was one of the more straightforward persons I knew. Instead of stiff replies, and useless answers to even simple questions, Lalu wanted truths. The raw details of the reality of how his sweet beloved niece ended up in a raw farmland so many miles away.

"Then come tell me what happened, Kumar. You know how to ask questions," he said.

I translated that to mean that unlike cops, Kumar knew how to handle Lalu's feelings. My punches land soft. I don't tease or gossip. I won't embellish. Ironically, those were the very traits that contrasted with how Lalu touts me to people, "My friend Mr. Kumar. He is great writer. Lots of imagination."

That's me then, Kumar, the trusted pal. Full of imagination when inking words, but rock solid and country-simple when it came to telling truths to my abiding brother-in-curry.

In a way, it was exciting to realize that Lalu's confidence added to my own enthusiasm. But I saw the irony too. That Lalu should have more confidence in me than I did in myself. "You know how to do these things." He seemed to trust me to handle the puzzle, the police, and his feelings. A tall order. Was I truly equipped to ferret out the truth *and* handle it too? I would need all the medieval bravado that I could muster, wouldn't I? What I didn't know at the time was that the windmills I tilted against were no match to the *windmills of my mind,* like the song said in that great Steve McQueen's heist movie.

Captain Jones

I wasn't fooled by the shabby exterior of the building - its once-pretty cream color, now faded to a distasteful Chicago grime. It was home to some of the toughest cops around. And, its once-dazzling facade, emphasized by glittering modern art created out of glass beads and airframe wire, now elicited a yawn. The building which housed the First District of Chicago Police Department still intimidated the good citizens who entered it. I was no exception.

A stop at the proverbial front desk, show drivers license, explain reason, get patted down, etcetera, etcetera. And, I was on my way through a labyrinth, unsure if each turn led to a window or to a hasty dry wall partition, erected after the building was carefully planned. Mike was waiting for me on the seventh floor. He hung up an internal wall phone, and led me down a long row of filing cabinets, then a less forbidding maze of desks and homey smells of office workers, to his own seat of power.

"Good news, Kumar," he said. "The Captain agreed to give us about five minutes," Detective Sergeant Mike Mullins had a broad grin. He ushered me into his office, not a corner office, but one wedged between a room marked SUPPLIES and a wider door marked simply MEN, no explanation needed.

"What do you think of my little pond?" Mullins gestured, and pulled a chair out for me.

"Pretty as the Irish Sea," I said.

"Liar, you've never seen it," Mike laughed.

"True that, but I used my imagination," I smiled.

"That you do quite well, blogger man," said Mike. Just then a buzzer rang on his desk.

He picked a folder off the table and led me down the hall. We paused at what appeared to be, for sure, a corner office. Chief of Detectives, the stencil on the mottled glass of the door said. A newer, carefully applied stencil beneath it read, Deputy Commissioner. I shivered. Mike's big pond was nondescript, and I didn't quite feel like a fish. Now, I was about to enter an ocean. It had unknown currents that made me feel like a minnow.

***

"Mr. Kumar, I gotta admit that's a lot of information you've compiled. I am impressed," said the Captain. He tapped the folder on the desk.

For my part, I was more than impressed. I was rattled. The air about Chief Jones's office - capacious, spartan, symbols of authority such as flags and seals, plus the vast blank desk surface - made it forbidding enough. Caught between gratitude and anxiety, I tried to still myself, and not shuffle on my feet. I merely nodded. Nodding never hurt nobody, right? Right.

"Kumar is taking this very personally, Chief. The deceased, er the young lady, Gita, thought of Kumar here as an uncle. He adored her," Mullins said.

"That's the way families should be..." said the Captain.

My mind was on my arms. Crossing them in front of me would have been a gesture of attentiveness in India, but it could be seen as a gesture of resistance by Americans. I couldn't bring myself to place my arms behind my back, like a prisoner about to be cuffed. I tried to look dignified while resisting the urge to stick them in my pockets, I didn't really care to sit. So, I lurked to a side of Mullins, facing the huge mahogany desk. *Five minutes will pass soon enough, I am lucky to be here at all..*

"I will put in a word to the Sheriff, Mr. Kumar. That should get you at least a meeting or two with local officials," said Captain Jones, the Chief of Detectives.

He took a quick look at the buff folder that Mullins laid sideways in front of him, "Far as we're concerned, you are part of her family, Gita..." Mullins looked on and nodded.

After that, Jones found his finger nails fascinating, and after staring at them awhile, ran his hands through his swept back silvery mane. He looked from Mullins to me and back.

"You are a good friend of the department Mr. Kumar," he said. "The kind of a good citizen we like to see more of. You earned a good turn with the help you gave Mullins on the trade show case last year. But don't go half cocked during your look-see trips."

"I don't think he will, Chief," a quick intercession by Mullins.

"I don't think he will either," Captain Jones said with a piercing gaze in my direction. "Mr. Kumar is level headed. Quite different from the other gent..." Jones left the other gent's name unsaid.

Mullins and I both knew that the 'other gent' the Captain referred to was Chidanand, an agitator of Devon Avenue, known informally to the CPD as 'the angry Indian'. I stayed clear of Chidanand, and Chidanand stayed clear of Blue Mountain.

John Paul Jones's service rank was Captain, but he also held the appointive rank of Deputy Commissioner (one of six). At one time, he was Chief of Detectives, and many in the department simply called him Chief.

The top cop stood up. The meeting was over. His physique was imposing, every bit the boss man. Mullins grabbed his folder and I followed him out.

Mike and I parted at the elevator. “I still think you should let events unfold, Kumar,” said the detective. “Keep doing your searches using computers, and leave real work to real cops. Don’t go over there. Don’t rock the boat.” He shook my hand. There was a seriousness to his grip as well as his voice. The elevator doors opened, I turned and waved at Mullins. I didn’t say anything to him. Not because I didn’t want to, but because I feared my own response.

Sheriff Bob

Sheriff Bob Crawford sounded affable right off the bat. “Well, mister, it’s darn awful good to talk to you too,” when my call was put through by the receptionist. His voice boomed through the telephone speaker. I was mumbling my thanks, when he continued talking over me, “You sure took the trouble to call us all the way from Chicago.” It all sounded pleasant, as if the chief lawman of Logan County, Illinois, was actually glad to be contacted. I felt encouraged, even as a part of me worried that his good cheer might be an act and not last long. All the same, I shed some of my trepidation in broaching the matter of Gita’s death.

“Once again, I appreciate your taking my call, Mr. Bob…” He cut me off abruptly, but with no curtness in the voice.

“Sheriff Bob, that’s what folks call me. Sheriff Bob. Unless somebody gone and done, broked the law. Then, I’m just *Sheriff* to them. You go right ahead and call me Sheriff Bob. Now, what can I do you for, mister?”

It was getting to be dinner time already, and I was glad to be talking to him, finally. I needed to make the best of the chance. There was a saucepan laden with soup, warming up over a low flame on my stove, and me parked on a stool in front of it. Hey, even canned soup labeled ready to eat, won’t heat itself, right? I had a wooden spoon in one hand and the telephone in the other.

Into the phone, I said, “Sheriff, it’s about the case of the young woman whose body was found off Route 66.”

Silence at the other end.

"I am sorry, mister, didn't quite catch your name there," now the Sheriff sounded like he was really trying not to bark. "Bessie here done write it down for me. Wait...um..." (shuffling of papers), "it's Kuuner, isn't it?" He rhymed it with crooner. And before I could respond, "Bessie's hand has gone bad lately, forgive me if I got your name wrong." His voice sounded like it was struggling to stay low and level.

I pulled my best aw-shucks tone, which had been well-honed from decades of interaction with diverse Americans. I also lowered the pitch of my voice, and slowed down my speech some. "No worries, Sheriff Bob. Folks get my name different *all* the time. My name is Kumar, k u m a r." I spelled it out for him like military alphabet. "That's Kilo, Urgent, Mama, Alpha, Romeo." And without a pausing, I added, "By the way, Sheriff, the name is of Indian origin. East Indian, not Native Indian. You probably guessed as much." For added good measure, I pronounced the word 'probly' instead of probably. We just being folks.

A slow growl came from the other end of the telephone line. "Yeah, Indian, from India. That's what one of my deputies, young Shane, wrote down here in his notes. Seems you talked to him already about things." More sound of shuffling of papers.

Sheriff Bob was back in talking form. "Deputy Shane. See, his kids go to school in Champaign-Urbana? Says his boys know many students same background as you, India. A big country ain't it. What is it that you want, Mr. *Kuummer*?"

"Well, Sheriff Bob, there sure is a lot you can do for me, sir." back to my usual foreigner self. Standing at the stove, stirring minestrone, keeping the non-stick saucepan just hot enough to simmer - still missing the aromas of Indian *sambar*.

“You see, Sheriff Bob,” I said, “We could go over the circumstances under which the young lady’s body was found. What the coroner found, cause of death, and maybe some details about the location etc.”

I counted the items off with the fingers of my left hand, and played the wooden spoon softly in the saucepan. With the cordless phone wedged in the crook of my shoulder, and boxes checked in my imaginary list, I hoped to come across as a methodical person. “Also, Sheriff....”

“Hold on, mister,” said the man, cutting me off. This time there was no mistaking the voice, it was a full throated bark...

“Hold on mister,” he repeated, “just hold your shopping list right there. Tell me why I am even talking to you. You know, I could be heading home right now to a nice steak dinner the missus is making, as we speak.”

More sounds of paper shuffling at the other end of the line. I wished him to keep talking, and hoped he’d offer a spot, somewhere in his rant, for me to continue the dialog. He did.

“You a private investigator, Mr. Kumar?” He asked.

Finally, he got the name and pronunciation right. That was a good sign, but I still worried that that correctness of my name could just be a prelude to a polite dismissal. On the other hand, the sheriff asked a legitimate question about my interest in the matter. And, there was no telling how he’d react to my answer. I got on with my spiel.

“No, Sheriff Bob, I am not a private investigator. And, I am not connected to law enforcement either. All I am, sir, is a close friend of the family. Sad but true, the dead girl’s own father is not in this country. He only recently returned home after visiting his daughter. Her closest relative in America is an uncle, and he is my best buddy. I just wanna help him, being that I have a lot more American friends and contacts. You can see how I would take interest in the matter?"

"That's something else again, Mr. Kumar. Being loyal and all. Doing what her own family should be doing. Tell me, why isn't that uncle of hers making these inquiries?"

There was a hint of softening in the sheriff's tone. But, the question opened a new can of worms. I braced myself to more inquisition along that line. I wanted the sheriff to talk about Gita, but he asked about everything else but Gita.

I stopped stirring the soup now, set the wooden spoon aside, covered the saucepan, and turned the heat lower. And, settled in a chair by the window. A light pleasant breeze threatened to diffuse the aroma wafting off my soup. I let it.

It was partly a relief that the sheriff didn't push questions about Gita's father. In fact, I dreaded any questions about Gita's father, from anybody. Who could ever explain that person? The odd phenomenon of a man named Phani/Fakhri/Francis, and his tale of many religions. Gita's father was a lunatic, beyond the grasp of anybody, let alone a rural American lawman.

My internal dithering helped. After some moments, Sheriff Bob launched again. "Tell me Mr. Kumar, do you have any background at all in these matters. Crime investigation, police work, etc."

Well, I saw no value in making stuff up, or concoct a phony story about college courses taken. Of course, I could lie about stuff convincingly. But, it was a shrewd old owl of a country cop I was dealing with. Truth seemed to be working so far, so I decided to pulled Mr. Aw-shucks back out again.

“Sheriff Bob, all Americans consider themselves expert in criminal investigations, don’t they? God knows, there is altogether too many crime shows on TV. They even show murder trials live on television. Everybody who watches TV is an expert, sir. And this thing called the internet, people are looking up everything.” I let him have all of that, but didn’t want to come across as snotty, or downplaying the value of real cops. So instead of leaving him hanging, I just said, “But I gotta admit, Sheriff Bob, that I am no super expert like you.”

“Well, Mister, what’s the bottom-line, what do you want?”

“I’d love to come down and visit the site where the little girl was found, and maybe talk to y'all some.”

The sheriff grunted. I hoped that meant an assent, though there was no telling how he took all this, while his mind was on lamb chops or whatever.

MOTHER ROUTE 66

Go West, Young man...

Go West, was the old dictum which most *roads* in Chicago had no choice but to comply. Many a road that didn't go westward from State Street came to a dead end at Lake Michigan. Worse yet, the road could fade into the nowhere land of Indiana. My well-traveled roads on the north-side of Chicago, such as venerable state highways, numbered 20, 64, 49 - and their poor cousins - all wended their way West.

Other great paths out of Chicago went southward, in the manner conveyed by an Arlo Guthrie song. Snaky ribbons of asphalt rolled past factories, junk yards, and small towns. Looking at the map of the trip I planned, I couldn't help but hum-start a country song of my own lyrics, 'Oh, go to the south, if you really want the truth'.

It was in a little dark blue rental sedan that I set out on one such famous road, number sixty-six. Leaving the urban scape behind, I drove across the drab flatlands of Illinois. I imagined myself as a post-war, middle class American road tripper, traversing the remnants of the legendary Route 66.

I drove past towns with names that were familiar to me from watching Chicago newscasts three times a day: Joliet, Dwight, Pontiac, Normal. After some hours, I entered Logan county, turned the car westward, and headed toward the spot I was directed to in the email.

With the car windows down, and the grime of the cities a distant memory of the lungs, I inhaled goodness. It was the mother of all historic roads. Route 66, elegantly nicknamed Mother Road. She seemed to smile in the sunshine, smile at me.

The prairie grass dividing - its special odor breathing,
I demand of it the spiritual corresponding...

The lines came to mind, and I too smiled. Once censored and banned, but now celebrated, Walt Whitman was special to me, ever since I discovered him all on my own. His poems were not in a class book or assigned by a teacher. Nor was Whitman an author preached about by a nice American, or a friendly, true-believer Peace Corps Volunteer. I stumbled upon Whitman in a library perchance, and the poetry became a lighthouse beacon instantly. His phrases sang out even more urgently than the Romantic poets of England who first infected me with Anglophilia.

Lines from Whitman flooded my brain as I breathed in the country air. He was so right to say that *air* was at the center of the word *prairie*. Though most of the American prairie has been gone, so much abided. For just a wee bit of time, old Walt replaced Gita. My little rental and I hummed along as winter cover crops rolled by outside. The land still brown, just starting to sprout greenery, awakening from death, awaiting new birth. I was strangely excited, like I myself was awaiting to be reborn.

The America Fever which I suffered in college gave rise to some odd longings. One fantasy involved two words that could never be joined together in the India of my youth: Road and Trip. That could happen only in America. And now, driving to some godforsaken place in a rented car, with the sense of prairie grass in my happy nostrils and the sound of Whitman's lyricism in my ears, I felt alive.

Off the rural road some miles later, I turned left. Passed an enormously long drag line of spidery frames and tubes, a watering system on wheels, now idle. I continued to scan the roadside for a tool shed with a cement bench in front of it.

With a sigh I ended my mental journey to face the sight facing me.

Jimmy Redds was waiting for me on the bench in front of a pre-fabricated synthetic tool shed. In the glare of the noon light, the little structure looked more aged than it should. He rose slowly while I got out of the rental, "Howdy, you the young feller from Chicagaw. Right? Yea, call me *Jimmee.*"

A big beefy shovel of a palm came slowly forward and engulfed my hand. He loomed over me and the car. With arms akimbo he eyed the sticker of the car rental company, and the gleam of the car which had by then acquired a fine pale brown coat of dust. Tilted his head, which I took to be approval or acceptance.

"Thanks Mr. Redds. Nice of you to take time from your chores to meet me." The halting delivery of my sentiments sounded stilted, even as I spoke. But, I had to deliver them.

"Don't bother me none, young mister, I am jess a worker. The big man's over there," jerked his thumb over his left shoulder. His hand shook some. "The boss said no harm in taking you around." I reached into the rental and pulled out a baseball cap (of Chicago Cubs, if truth be told), and we set out on foot.

"I comes out here daily, you know, to check up on stuff. The conditions, the weathering, browning. Check on the cattle, make sure the goats didn't stray." Jimmy stretched tall, looked around, scratched his ears and drummed fingers on his belly. He then eased into a slight stoop and resumed walking, "Them goats is as good as lawnmowers, you know. Keep the vegetation down. Muck up the soil, and all." I nodded.

"I gets to all corners of the field, that's my job, you know what I mean?" He said. I nodded again.

"That how you discovered the body, Jimmy?"

"Yes, sir."

We walked along an earthen bank, shifting between the two sides of it, dodging hard packs of earth, and stumps that threatened to twist my ankle. Jimmy, of a heavy foot, just trudged on. We reached a larger structure with a wider door. "You wait, mister," said Redds and went in. The noises from inside sounded like machinery or pumps, so I let him be.

Jimmy Redds drove out in a front loader, the shovel filled with some bags. We weren't going to go riding in that thing? I worried, but just then I heard and saw a handsome giant yellow tractor coming around the corner. It came to a stop on the crumbly gray asphalt apron in front of the barn door.

A wiry lean man with jet black hair, blue eyes, dressed in casual-Friday office type clothes jumped out, rubbed his hands together, and stood erect, looking at me.

"So *Jimmee* been showing you around, huh. I am Will Bennett. What exactly is it you do Mr. Kumar?"

"Yes. Will Bennett, the owner," I gestured to the land, sweeping my arm around to cover the fields, "You own all this. Very kind of you to let me come visit."

"You're welcome sir. I was told you are not with the police or any such thing."

"That's correct sir. I am a close friend of the family. The deceased young woman is a niece of my buddy. He is just too distraught, and asked me to help out. You know, make inquiries on his behalf."

"That's mighty decent of you, mister, to put yourself out so. Sheriff Bob, you know he is the big man around here, the sheriff said you're okay. Seems you checkout okay with Chicago Police."

I nodded. "Mr. Bennett, I realize this here is a tricky situation. You know, with issues of jurisdiction, chain of authority etc. I am just a friend of the family, trying to give aid and comfort to folks I call community. Naturally, I am bound to stay within lines set for me by law enforcement."

"I can go along with that, Mr. Kumar. Seems you are a writer of some sort, and friendly with some cops back in Chicago, er excuse me."

Bennett turned to the tractor and gestured with his hand. That's when I saw the handsome dog perched on the seat of the harvester. It sat erect, poised, and close-mouthed. But its full beauty could be appreciated only when it jumped off the vehicle on some invisible command from its master. It went over to stand by him, but kept looking at me intently. The farmer caressed it behind the ears and tapped on the neck.

The dog wagged its tail gently but remained standing alert, still looking at me. Its coat shone brilliantly under Illinois sun, a blue sheen on top of dark gray, and milky pale bluish eyes. "This here is Buddy," said Will Bennett. "He is a real pal, goes with me all over the farm. He is good company too. Good Boy." The dog acted like some body else was being talked about, and even the mention of the word buddy had no reaction. He just continued to look at me, though not so intently anymore.

"He is beautiful. Can I pet him?"

"Just let him come to you and sniff out a bit. He is not scary but he is mighty protective of me. You are my friend, so you are his friend. Right Buddy?" Mr. Bennett tapped its neck again. I extended my hand out and the beast came forward, took a whiff, looked me up and down, sniffed some more around my legs and thighs and stood next to me. I petted its head and ran my palm down the back. Buddy's tail wagged a couple of times.

"Seems he likes you, Mr. Kumar," Bennett said. "Not bad for a city man," he chuckled. "Let's go see where we found the poor thing."

Bennett retook the driver's seat on the tractor, "squeeze in here, Kumar."

I rode shotgun while Jimmy Redds hung out on a small steel plate that stuck out the rear. He, held on to a roll bar, and swayed with the vehicle in a fluid manner. Buddy bounced along next to us.

When we got out into the open, a ways away from the barn, Mr. Bennett pointed to a small stand of trees. "That's where my house is." Sure enough, what I hadn't noticed before, was a longish, low, gray-roofed house, barely discernible through a copse of trees. About half-a-mile away.

"There is a proper road over there, but you would have needed to approach it from yonder, near where you see that old abandoned factory thing," said Bennett. I took it all in as the tractor lurched on.

Mr. Bennett said, "I could've gave you proper road turns, or sent you one of those GPS directions, Mr. Kumar. But you would have had to drive some forty miles out of the way. Crazy, huh? That's how it is around these here farms. Very few municipal roads. Jimmy here thought it best to save you the hassle and bring you this way."

Buddy stopped occasionally to bark a couple of times, and then resume his loping alongside. I looked in the direction he barked, some cattle and goats - the animals grouped tighter whenever the dog barked. Evidently, just Buddy's bark was quite effective. I was glad to not have to test his bite.

"Yup," said Mr. Will Bennett the farmer, "Buddy is a good animal minder. Keeps livestock proper, from straying too far."

"His coat is fabulous, blue and shiny."

"Yes sir, he is what they call Australian Blue Heeler. Not the doctor kind of healer. You know, the heels, he'll nip at the heels of the cattle lightly if needed. But just barking works mostly."

"Yes, I've heard of sheep dogs and such, but never seen one in action. Remarkable." I couldn't help but smile.

"Yup, Buddy is also family. Sleeps in the same room as us. The wife gets annoyed sometimes though, like when he sheds too much. He is good hound."

The tractor finally reached a small tree. The farm men hopped off the machine and looked on as I uncoiled myself to get onto the land. "For a city feller you ain't in bad shape, Kumar," the farmhand Jimmy Redds said. Even as I suppressed a groan. Mr. Bennett gestured with an extended arm.

So, this was it, the silent witness to Gita's last moments on earth?

It wasn't as I imagined

My mind expected a large tree with a canopy that offered a sheltering shade. Something benevolent. Instead, what I actually saw was a tallish above-average plant, in a spread of land caught between seasons of death and rebirth.

What had you been up to Gita? I am here. Talk to me.

I approached the small tree step in step, almost reluctantly, certainly reverentially. Midday sun made for a dappled ground. Nothing stirred in the slightly damp air except for some leaves. And the shifting patches of light stirred me.

..this little tree here saw it all?

Its gray stem, thick as my upper arm. The ground around it tinted as pale a brown as Gita was. Some debris at the base. Not entirely certain about what I should be looking for... A small shiver ran through my spine, at the thought of how lonely it must have been under that tree at *that* moment. Was she alive then, or had breath left her already? I felt an intense chill. Would I even tell Lalu about this?

("Not much to see there, Lalu, just one single bush..")

I could make out pieces of tattered yellow tape, a stout pillar of a half-burnt votive candle in a glass jar - painted with purple clouds and a pink Jesus - and deflated balloons. A cross fashioned out of picket fence slats lay to a side.

I circled the little tree once more, without being aware of actually doing it. Days later, I'd think back to the moment, and marvel at my instinctual behavior of circumambulation in a temple. I'd also wonder, if the spirits of Gita's ancestors, peering down at that corner of the earth - might they have noticed the solitary Indian circling the death spot like it were a shrine? Would the spirits be pleased?

But back at that hour, when I was stumbling around the tree looking at the ground and not knowing what I was looking for, I did see a cluster of stones. It couldn't have been more than a couple dozen pieces stacked in a pile, come to think of it, like a pyramid. I didn't makes sense of it right at that moment. The word for it would come to me later. Cairn. Some unknown person created a rock cairn for Gita. Another odd thing too. I knew that word in some deep corner of my mind. But, the tears didn't start until word cairn surfaced in my mind.

There was something else that shimmered and drew my eye. I stooped down to sweep my hand about. It was an old-fashioned crucifix. People of faith, people who cared about victims. While some raged about the rights of the perp, there were others who prayed. I pocketed it.

Being close to that collection of memorials, under that tree, felt like I was at the side of a dying person. I had stood near real deathbeds earlier in my life: aunts, uncles, college buds, and one roadside stranger too. They all exuded a smell. At that hour in rural Illinois, beneath that silent witness of a mere shrub, the air still smelled of death long after the body was taken away. There was the stench of death in my nostrils, the prairie grass no longer dividing.

I stepped back, and turned away from the two men. And, tried hard to not sob or choke up. My chest tightened, my torso quivered. As I let out a long slow exhalation at last, Buddy, the shepherd dog, came near me and touched his head to my legs. It was impossible not to reach down and caress. The dog looked at me for a few seconds, tapped its tail twice, and sat on the ground at my feet. The farmers stared into the distance.

***

It would be some hours later that day, during late evening hours, that Jimmy Redds would show me damage to the ground made by trespassers. From a nearby dirt path to that shrub, a span of a couple hundred feet. Large vehicles, pickup trucks probably, or SUVs, traversed the stretch flattening out dry brush and earth.

Vehicles turned off a frontage road to an old battered road that went nowhere, and then the dirt path. They drove through a gap in the fence, and came to where the body was found. All done with no fuss or fanfare, the mourners came.

Regular folks from rural Illinois had come bearing balloons, teddy bears, and candles. It was a show of heart-felt caring, the sort that bloomed into instant memorials and roadside shrines at accident sites. So typical of the soft heart of the heartland, and an unexpected sight to come upon during any modern American road trip.

It became evident to me, that when news broke about the grisly discovery of an unknown dead woman, nameless faceless mourners came. And when they could see the shrub shown on TV, but didn't know how to get near it, they just dared to trespass. The mourners didn't have GPS directions either, or a *Jimmee* Redds to escort them. I stared in astonishment at the path created out of that intense human impulse to memorialize.

Jimmy Redds said that his boss told him not to mind all that trampling, oh just let folks be. "You know, Mr. Kumar, I'd come down here to tidy up some, but they kept bringin' them things. Stuff just popped up under this here little tree," Redds shook his head.

****

When Buddy eventually left my feet, and we humans all moved out, I debated whether to return to Chicago right away, or look for a motel. Get a good night's sleep before heading home. Let Lalu wait.

What would I do in the middle of nowhere? Go visit the Sheriff, perhaps. Go see some reporters? Maybe. Or, visit a nearby truck stop to gather scuttlebutt?

The decision was made for me by Jimmy Redds being in a talkative mood. Hopping once again onto the worn steel plate back of the vehicle, he kept up a chat about the chores he planned to do. Partly for my benefit, but mostly just telling the boss. Apparently, it was all a-okay, since Bennett said nothing. Jimmy Redds was clearly turned over to me for the day.

In his light banter, I saw something deeply human, an essential decency, and a willingness to connect. Of course, it could all have been my imagination. Whatever. After Mr. Bennett dropped us off back near the original tool shed where my rental car lay, I too took a chance to connect.

"How's about a beer, Mr. Jimmy?"

The big beefy man gave a crack of a smile, "You could use one after that visit, couldn't you? I could do with one, myself."

We piled into my vehicle. To my amazement, his large frame squeezed itself into the little rental car with ease, knees in his face and elbows straight out. He navigated us to a tavern some two miles away.

****

Tilly's said the peeling brown paint. Graying clapboard siding and a rust-colored front door. And noticeably, no neon beer signs in the windows. Redds and I made it inside, and bellied up to the counter. "Howdie Diane," said Jimmy. And Diane, looked at me kind of curious and asked, "Hey, *Jimmee,* who'd you bring?"

Jimmy laid a heavy hand on my shoulder. "This here is Kumar. He is Indian, from India." Jimmy Redds's voice dropped. "He is an uncle to that Hindu lady, you know, found on Mr. Bennett's property." Diane's smile faded as his voice dropped even lower. 'I am so sorry,' she mouthed, and we all looked at each other in silence. I blinked and nodded.

Diane retreated to the tap station and returned with three hefty steins, and set them down in front of us, including one for herself. We raised the glasses high, didn't clink before partaking, and imbibed in silence. I drank deeply, thinking about a girl who probably never so much as touched a liquor bottle. Diane whispered low, questions about the dead woman, her family, was she married, etc. The big farmhand answered in equally hushed tones. His voice had a softness remarkable in so large a frame. Between sips, he bent his head to wipe his lips on his shirt's sleeve. I devoted myself to draining my stein fast.

I was tense from Gita. But, was already wrestling in my mind with the matter of a presentation to Lalu. What exactly would I tell Lalu; how would I word it; could I meaningfully convey my impressions of the site, etcetera, etcetera.

("A very quiet place, Lalu... Not much to see there, Lalu... Kind people, Lalu..")

I could, of course, keep it all simple and flat. Say that there was a tree and not much evidence left, the cops probably have it all. But will that cut it? Probably not. I had a chance for a catharsis of sorts. But, what of Lalu? Then again, I wasn't above crying in public. Lalu, on the other hand grieved privately, out of my sight even. The only tears he shed were over chopped onions and sputtering spices. His true habit was only to smile in public, like some sort of a Buddha.

When Diane got called away by a customer, Jimmy Redds turned to me and whispered a question. "What you intend to do next, little mister?"

I shared my thoughts about the evening, possibly visiting the truck stop, etc., but Jimmy wanted to share something else.

"I think whoever did this to your niece is long gone," he said. "That little lady we found in the field affected a lot of people. I wanna show you something, you up for it?"

That's how we ended up at that spot off Frontage Road, a spot with no direct access to the farm and would have forced *me* to drive an additional fifty miles to get to the Bennett home. A spot on Frontage Road that led to a dirt road and a breach in the property line. That spot would be a clue in the case, and I would be blind to that fact for umpteen days.

****

We finished another round of beers and left. Jimmy Redds wouldn't let me pay, saying in that good-natured way, "Your money is no good here." Friendliness or pity, it didn't matter, did it?

After all, he had taken me to the trampled path in the field; shown me the way of the collective responsive of middle America toward the death of a woman they didn't know. Jimmy Redds was sensitive to it all.

I was reeling from the intensity of the whole afternoon. I sorely needed settle in a motel and calm down. I needed rest.

“Thanks for everything, Mr. Redds, hope you’ll have a restful evening,” I said when we returned to the tool shed.

“Oh, I will get on alright,” he brought out an aging mud-splattered three-wheeler out of the little building with the cement bench in front of it, and got on it. I raised my hand to wave. Jimmy Redds waved back, and turned its starter on, saying, “Vaya Con Dios, my Hindu friend,” and took off.

His parting salute used a language that would have irritated me at any other time. But on that day, at that spot, and right at that moment, I was ready to receive comfort in any tongue. I exhaled long, as his huge frame swayed on the three-wheeled vehicle.

Setting sun gleamed off his red plaid shirt in vivid hues of ruddiness, that lived up to his last name. Watching that shifting, receding farmhand’s shiimering redness of a figure, it occurred to me that the color of blood was never so disarming.

The tattoo virgin

It was the farmhand's idea that I join them for the unofficial interview. "Let's go listen to what the tattoo virgin says, Kumar," he said over the phone. "My old friend, the sheriff, wouldn't mind." I was intrigued. Informal interview? Tattoo virgin? Oh well, it was 'their' source, their witness, and their nickname. I went along, curious about tattoos and virgins, and watched amused, as the sheriff and the farmhand talked up the 'coolness' of having tattoos.

"Tattoos aren't just for sailors and bikers anymore, you know," said Sheriff Bob leaning back in the booth. He had the same air as an expert on TV, with an added twinkle in his eye. "Lots of people are getting them these days," and looked around the booth, like inviting responses. The farmhand and I exchanged looks. I looked at the 'seed guy' seated next to me in the booth, over the rim of my beer glass, and waited. This *was* going somewhere. Jimmy Redds already said, ya ya, while the sheriff spoke. He picked up the relay-race baton. He took the toothpick out of his mouth and said, "This generation seems to love tattoos, even in the cities. Ain't it so, Kumar?"

"True that, Mr. Jimmy," I said. Turning to Sharky, the seed guy, I said, "Bike messengers, cabbies, nail girls, college girls, even lawyer chicks. Everybody got tattoos in Chicago." For added measure, I pointed my beer toward the sheriff, "Like the man said, tattoos aren't so much about sub-cultures these days, they are more about personality statements."

Sharky, the seed guy, kept shaking his head, and now he stood up. He parted his hands, twice quickly with palms down, like a baseball umpire calling safe. "Naw, naw. That's not reason for *me* to get a tattoo. I am okay if everybody gets one, though." His jelly-belly nudged the table's edge, and he looked at me. I showed my agreement with vigorous nodding. Well, the seed salesman thought he was a cool guy by his own estimate. Who was I to argue the point? I smiled and looked at Sheriff Bob and Jimmy Redds. *They* could argue it up a notch, get Sharky talking more. I was along merely to hear something first hand.

Sharky sat back down and took a sip of his lager. "Okay, okay. People get tattoos. I get that. Don't mean that I gotta get one, though." He looked from the farmhand to the sheriff and back at the farmhand, who were seated across the booth.

The sheriff raised his beer for a long pull of the amber liquid and leaned his large mass farther back in the booth. His left arm rested easily atop the back of the booth, over the farmhand's shoulders. Jimmy was smiling now. Sheriff Bob leaned a bit into the farmhand, but tilted his head toward Sharky, "What we got here, *Jimmee,* is a tattoo virgin. A cherry. A regular tattoo virgin."

Jimmy Redds nodded slowly with a steady look at the seed salesman. Sharky's face didn't look bothered by the cherry reference, didn't turn red, or offer any sign of boiling. On the contrary, he seized 'tattoo virgin' as a badge and doubled down. With a chuckle and a shake of the head, he rolled up his long sleeves, "See here, unblemished skin. I am not damaged goods, gentlemen." With that he pulled his sleeves back down over plump white arms and re-buttoned the cuffs. But, it wasn't over with.

The sheriff's hand waved in the air like he was painting, dismissing the value of pristine skin. "Having a tattoo these days is almost the default situation, isn't default the proper word, Kumar?"

Without waiting for my response, the sheriff turned his whole torso the other way and bellowed, "Hey, college girl, git over here, hon." And, as she neared our booth, "You got any ink on you, girl?"

Diane 'the college girl' ambled over, a round bar tray tucked under her left arm. She rolled up her blouse's right sleeve as she approached our booth. "Sure, Bob. Remember last summer, I got this at the county hot-dog eating event?"

I got the impression that the sheriff either didn't remember or care. He put his glasses on to inspect the college girl's tattoo as she showed her upper arm around the table. A nice horse head with a generous mane in vivid rainbow colors. "That's the spirit," mumbled the farmhand as the rest of us oohed and aahed.

"Nice," said the seed kid as Diane adjusted her sleeve. We looked at Sharky, and he repeated, "No, that's really a nice picture," as if trying to convince somebody of something. Diane gave Sharky a piercing once over before turning around.

Sharkey shifted in the booth, rolled his shoulders, looked annoyed even though nobody said anything to him directly. He sighed and said, "Folks can do as they please but my skin is gonna stay pristine. God made it nice for me, and I am gonna keep it nice for him."

The farmhand spoke up, "But, young man, that pickup truck guy offered you a free tattoo, a one hour job. Be worth over a hundred dollars, if you had to pay for it." Surprise and disappointment came through in Jimmy's head shake and lip curl. The sheriff waited. I waited.

From the talk I had earlier with the sheriff, *something* was expected to come out of this bar room banter. I now started to doubt if anything would spill out of this young man, the tattoo virgin.

His refusal of a free tattoo wasn't the issue, curious as it was. Neither was his preoccupation with a clean skin, nice as that was. The sheriff said Sharky was an honest young man who would make a good witness if it ever came to that. But the kid needed to relax first. There was time. After all, this was just a first go at him for Sheriff Bob.

"You people don't get it do you?" The seed guy threw his hands up in the manner of all those who fail to win an argument. Sheriff Bob nodded and looked on quietly, and Jimmy picked his teeth with the end of a paper umbrella in his new drink. He took a gulp, belched, and said, "So you toldim that you wouldn't lose your tattoo cherry….hehehe. 'Least, your mama be proud you stayed clean cut. Good thing for a salesman, I guess," he belched again.

"Ain't nobody getting me inked," The young man snorted, with a shake of head.

Sharky opened and closed his mouth a couple of times, as if he wanted to talk but changed his mind. Beer taste and dry mouth, combined to cause him to cluck his tongue. And when he closed his mouth up tight, the upward curve of the slit of a smile showed why everyone called him Sharky. I let the silence in the booth hang, and let my eyes wander around. My first visit to Tilly's with Jimmy Redds was emotional, and I had been too busy to get a good lay of the land.

Diane waddled by - I never did learn why they called her the college girl - carrying sodas and wedges of pizza to a trio of youngsters at the far end. There, stood an aged and wobbly old fashioned pinball machine with reluctant lights and feeble dings. I didn't see a big screen television or a video juke box in the place. Less than a dozen tables of assorted sizes and shapes were strewn about, looking less like a pub and more like a rebellious cafe owned by an unrepentant beatnik. Customers sat around speaking quietly or dozing. A pair of family dogs stretched out on the creaky floorboards next to their owners, with snouts poised on front paws. Tilly's was having its midday rush, what with the sheriff himself just come down with some men, four more drinkers than usual.

"Tell me more about the pickup truck the inker was drivin', " the lawman asked.

"See, sir, he had his stuff laid out between us on the seat and all, I was wedged away, close to the passenger windah," Sharky's hand indicated a spread of space next to him. I shifted to make room.

Sharky continued, "The inker kept going on about new types of needles, self-calibrating injectors, tints and such. Like how my skin had a real special glow and could take some cool new designs, chicks would dig me, and the like." He was breathless. It seemed to me that the youngster was pleased not to be arguing, to be on solid ground. Telling Sheriff Bob interesting things, facts he alone knew, and the sheriff himself buying beers.

He pushed his spectacles back up the slope of his nose, looked around the place, the ceiling, the wood-dust floor, and the kitchen door swinging lazily. "I am sure it was a crew cab, Bob. Sort of a dark color, maybe muddy like." After a momentary pause, "It was definitely an open bed, regular length, no doubt."

He looked straight into the wizened face of the lawman, but the sheriff showed no reaction. Sharky continued, "Come to think of it, there was a slight wobble on the front end, on my side, the passenger side like, maybe, the tie rod going bad or something. Could be just a bad rim though. I remember saying to him to get it fixed before it gave out."

He stood up looking toward the washroom, but sat back down, and spoke slowly, "It was for sure a Silverado, on account of I saw the tailgate as she pulled away after I got dropped off. The Chevy bow-tie flashed. Yeah, a Silverado regular bed for sure." The last part was slow and drawn out, like he was certain about it.

Finally, there it was. A vehicle description. The Sheriff still didn't say anything. He must know it was just a start. An older squeaky Chevy truck with an open bed and no other markings. One of many such trucks, and just one of many possible clues.

The tattoo virgin wasn't done. He made his trip to the men's room and returned to settle down next to the sheriff - buddies with him now - and to a new round of drinks. His memory refreshed too. He had more things to tell about that night. After all, the Sheriff did ask him challengingly why he refused a free tattoo from the pickup truck driver. Tattoo worth a hundred dollars or more. He spoke now with less nasal railing, more beer-moistened tongue.

***

Sharky, the seed man, wouldn't have been at Tilly's at all, were it not for a chance eavesdropping at the truck stop. People there talking about how Sheriff Bob Crawford would love to talk to anyone who had hitch-hiked the previous week anywhere along the frontage road that led out from the old refrigerator plant. What on earth for? Sharky didn't care about that. His car had broken down just around that area, and he walked a couple of miles before being given a ride by a tattoo guy from Missouri. If the sheriff is going around asking questions, Sharky would be mentioned, and Turk's Auto Shop will be visited by deputies anyways. So, why not be a good citizen and tell the law what he knew. A good turn by a citizen never hurt nobody. Even if it meant, as it turned out, arguing about tattoos with the farmhand, Turk the engine genius, and the sheriff.

***

"So, I didn't want no ink, Bob, I just wanted a ride outta that miserable back stretch onto the state route. All I wanted was a short lift to the nearest phone booth. But, the weirdo rode me in all the way into town. Don't say I don't appreciate it. But having needles in my skin, getting punctured, no way, Bob." Sharky shivered as his arms sprouted goose pimples.

I noticed two things. The excited kid kept calling the sheriff by just his first name, and secondly, the sheriff acted like he didn't notice that. Catch more flies with honey, or something like that. The sheriff did have more questions, however.

"What else you saw in the pickup truck, besides inks and needles?"

"Nothing."

"Something on the dash? Maps, magazines?

"Naw, nothing of the sort."

"Anything on the back seat?"

"Don't think so."

"On the floor, behind the front seats."

"Nothing,"

"You turned your head and looked behind the seats?"

"Well, no. I didn't do that, but I don't think he did either, Sheriff. I mean if you think I thought was he hiding something or what."

Patience, patience, said the look on the sheriff's face.

"And you saw nothing in the bed of the truck either? No trunks, tool boxes, ladders etc."

"No sir, he was weird, but in a nice way, giving rides to people like he did."

What was that, rides or ride?

"Hmm," was all the sheriff said to keep the kid going.

"Oh nothing sir, he didn't seem to mind giving rides."

Rides!

I saw Bob Crawford tense up, hold his breath.

"Sheriff, just after I got off the truck, the guy waved goodbye, I was thanking him real good, he shrugs and mutters, "Guess this is my night to give rides." I figured he gave someone else a ride too."

Sharky drained his beer and set it down with a plop on the tacked-down plastic laminate. A long slow sibilance out of the lawman; a short strong snort out of the farmhand; and a return of even, easy breathing by the seed man. I tried to contain my heart which was 'a-pumping'. *Rides* - something of note, or no there there?

A tattoo shop owner from Missouri, driving through Illinois near Interstate 55, on a less used stretch of the Mother Road - Route 66 - in a Chevy Silverado pickup truck with a bad front end. That guy gave rides to two people during the night which just *might* be the night in question. It wasn't quite settled for sure, but it fit the time frame of Gita's death.

One of the people who got a ride was Sharky. Who was the other one? Gita? Did the guy try to take liberties with her? Did she resist, and that's how it went down? Whoa, whoa. Wait, wait. Wait one darn second there. Why would Gita be there at all, in the middle of nowhere? Why would she be hitchhiking?

The tale made crystal sense one second, and utter nonsense the next. When I came back down to earth, I saw Sharky chewing his nails. He had more than one finger in his mouth at a time. Like an infant oblivious to its surroundings.

I exchanged several glances with Sheriff Bob, even as Jimmy Redds looked on, nodded slowly, and not said anything either.

There was nothing to say. Except answer college girl Diane's questioning looks as she approached the booth, 'go another round, guys?' The answer would have to be, yes.

Sideways

"What you found out, Kumar?" asked Lalu, over the phone, his voice flat and without a question mark.

I was a bit unsure how to strike the right note, but eventually said, "No solid evidence, Lalu, that spot doesn't have clues." That much was true enough. I wanted to save the full details of my mission for a face to face talk.

"But, Kumar, you said a personal trip by you will tell us many things," again his tone didn't convey anything. No, it wasn't an effect of the motel telephone. It wasn't an electronic signal flattening. I knew Lalu, and what I heard was definitely his brave-face voice. Guarded and plain, it was a cultivated non-eagerness, intended to stave off any lurking disappointment.

I gave him a quick overview of the huge farm, the unplowed land, the single small tree, and the farm hand and his sheep dog who found the body of Gita. Much of my tale conveyed to him what the news reports had already told me. I did leave out the broken fence and the many heavy vehicles that beat a path to the tree. I also saved for a personal time, later on, my description of the memorial stuff.

Finally, a long sigh, "Kumar, you were supposed to find out how she died, who killed her."

That's my buddy, Lalu. Infinite trust in his friend Kumar's ability to do wonders, solve a crime in just a day, well ahead of the cops. He really couldn't have believed that. Or, maybe he did?

"Really, Lalu, there is too much detail that I can't say over the phone. We will talk about it tomorrow. Police are on the case. They are working hard." After a pause, I hastened to add,

"There is a lot of local kindness for Gita here. People are moved by what happened."

"People's kindness won't find the killer, Kumar." After that abrupt reaction, I expected Lalu to hang up, but I could still hear him breathing.

"I will see you tomorrow, lots and lots of interesting details." I hung up.

After showering, I sat on the motel bed and flipped through some digital photos I took. A long shot of the lonely tree. The shrine underneath, picket fence cross, the alert dog. I looked closely at the file of photos before deleting obvious duplicates, and resolved to purchase one of those thumbnail size things that slid into the side of the camera and stored hundreds of photos, even short videos. I put the photos in a certain order, hoping to tell a story, like a movie. Hoped that my images of the scene would somehow soften Lalu. The impromptu memorial moved me. Surely it will touch Lalu too?

I lay down on the bed for a while, and turned the crucifix over and over in my hand. Why did I pick it up? Out of all that stuff under the tree, why that one? The cross was most likely left by a nameless mourner? Maybe it was draped on the wooden cross itself. It would be too fantastic to think of the crucifix as a clue. After all, it wasn't like it was pried free from the fist of a victim, as they show in movies. On the other hand, I was quite wound up under that tree, feeling primal, groping in more ways than one, and highly keyed up when I picked it up. Probably just a natural act in a moment of unnatural desperation.

I held the crucifix up to light coming from the window and studied it. Made of metal, it had a heft to it, and filled the area of my palm. Something made me go to the wash basin in the bathroom and clean the crucifix with soap. Was I thinking there must be a secret writing on it? Of course, not. It was simply that the impulse of idol worshiping ran so deeply in my veins, that I couldn't bear the idea of desecration implied in a dirtied crucifix. Some things in this world were ever holy, weren't they? After washing, I noticed that it showed wear. On the top side were the letters INRI across the post. I had seen hundreds of them in my life time. Even though I couldn't recall exactly what the letters stood for, I knew it was Latin.

When I was all packed and came down from my room, a somewhat somber and downcast Abhilash Patel printed my invoice. While he collected the bill and checked me out of Prairie Shores Motel, his wife vacuumed the lobby, and his son played with a toy car behind the registration desk.

"Anything you found out, Sir?" he asked softly.

I shook my head.

"So sorry," he said, "maybe you will come back in a few weeks and try again."

"Perhaps, Abhilash," I said. "Thanks for your sentiments."

He gave a shy nod and put the paperwork in an envelope for me.

"Maybe, next time you will come, you speak to different people that time. Get answers you looking for," said the young man.

Abhilash belonged to what some Indian wag once described as the Motel-Patel tribe, who took over the American roadside in recent decades. Sleepy, low cost Indian-owned lodges lurked all along the Interstate Highway system. As a Chicago cop-friend of mine once said, every person named Patel or Gandhi must be a cousin of Kumar, cousin being a cop's synonym for a compatriot. Abhilash, my cousin. There was a time when I used to wrinkle my nose at the phrase Motel-Patel, but have since grown to enjoy its humor. Motels owned and run by Indians always had a room available, and I often enjoyed a Cousin Discount.

Abhilash's farewell was sincerely sad, I could see that.

"Our Gita sister is fortunate to have an uncle working so hard for the truth," he waved goodbye.

I kept thinking about that, how easily Indian people found a way to relate themselves to strangers, even dead ones. Indians referring to someone they don't even know as a brother or an aunt; a grandma or a little sister. In the middle of nowhere, my Motel Patel found a sister to refer to. Other cultures probably did that too, but Indians seemed to do it so easily and naturally.

Abhilash Patel made my anguish diminish momentarily. But, even as the interior of the rental car warmed up, and Farmland, USA flew by, a sense of cold anger began to form. What was so lucky about a dead girl having a living uncle? And, what was so lucky about a futile quixotic effort like mine? What truths had I really discovered about her murder during this trip? Nothing, nada, zilch, zip. A big fat original Indian zero. *Had Gita been truly lucky, I wouldn't even be here.*

The remainder of my drive back to Chicago was filled with no ordinary anguish. An older, more ancient sort of grief seized me. The morning phone call to Lalu didn't help at all. I only called him because I said I would.

The hours I spent driving back became a looped replay of the time I spent near Gita's tree. I couldn't help recall how that little tree just began to cast off winter's grayness by putting out a few hopeful tender green shoots. It had stood sentinel over Gita's lifeless body for many cold hours. And now, random pieces of roadside vegetation began to remind me of Gita's little tree and stirred me to tears.

Any sudden sight of a length of mangled guardrail would take me instantly back to the broken-through fence near 'Gita's tree.' As the miles rolled by, even the sight of rusted out farm equipment with weeds growing about them, took my mind back to the farm I was fleeing.

I desperately wished to get past it all, wished for my memory to develop lesions, and set me free. Free from images that bred depression. A darkness was beginning to seize me, urging me on homeward fast.

My front door opened easily enough when pushed, making me think that there wasn't a worthy stack of mail behind it. I would be wrong about that. Nothing in this junk mail pile will lift me up, I thought. I would be wrong about that too. But, the very first thing to hit me was the stuffiness. My windows had been sealed against drafts with plastic sheets, Chicago style.

I propped the front door open, and turned on a table fan I kept for just such a situation. While it oscillated, I went about stripping the windows of the double-sided tape that held the plastic sheets. Trying not to peel off too much paint from the wooden frames. I raised the sash and let fresh air in.

The duffel bag fell on the couch. I settled down to a bottle of Guinness picked up at the corner convenience store, also owned by a cousin (but no cousin discount for booze). I took a swig of the dark liquid, and looked around for the cat to come out and rub herself against the couch. I was wrong about that too. There was no yawning, stretching cat to welcome me home. Looked like it was going to be just me and Mr. Guinness for a while.

What I needed was something nice, something bright. Something tangible to hang a hope upon. I picked up the stack of mail. Looked like all bills, but I was wrong again. Sure, there weren't any bulky stuff like packets, books, or newspapers. But, nestled in there was a long narrow manila envelope, slightly larger than the standard number ten business envelope. *This one had a flap on the short-side.*

The sight of it warmed me instantly. Long manila envelopes that opened on the short side. Only Indians used those envelopes, and only one Indian would write to me. The return address confirmed: Sarada Sashanki, New Delhi. The bottle of Guinness earned an extra pull.

I leaned back on the couch and shook out the contents of the envelope: a fullscap sized, hand-written, letter wrapped around four postcard sized color photos.

My Dear Mr. Kumar, Today's India Times newspaper in New Delhi had an article about the need for a symbol for the Rupee. Imagine that! Money used by a billion people has no graphic, like they have the American dollar sign. Why did they select the letter S, by the way? Another article said all Americans pay taxes by the 15th of April. I hope you didn't forget. Don't be a scofflaw! Now, as for...

There was no mention of Gita, or my letter, or the request I made of Sasha. I double checked the dates and realized that our letters have crossed paths. All the same, it was an informative letter in a different way- the photos it included.

I turned to the photos and looked at each one, not in any hurry. Palpitations and gasps were okay in my book, as far as those things go. It's never easy to deal with memories of a deceased daughter. Being in the midst of grief over Gita, I was receptive to seeing photos of Sarada's own deceased daughter Durga. The four photos in my hand were all of Durga, at various stages of pregnancy. All happy photos. But, that happiness now passed. It made me realize that the patience and forbearance of people like Sarada and Lalu were not of this world. It takes mythical, biblical, levels of dignity and sufferance. The lady from Delhi could teach me some of that...

***

The tabby, Ms. Agnes, did at last emerge from the bedroom, all mewls and twitching whiskers. She approached the couch real close, abruptly raised her tail and scurried out of sight. Hmm, something in my briefcase? Something about the six-pack of beer? Not likely. Must be something else. I couldn't think of anything reasonable that might have irritated her. Dust, dung, dairy, dander. I found myself, unwittingly, on a roll with words starting with the letter 'd'.

I tired of the exercise and decided to turn in. I put fresh food and water out, waited, and watched the cat munch happily. As for me, it was time to sleep, and seek a better morning. It was not until I laid in bed that it occurred to me, that an entirely different d-word explained the cat's behavior. She sensed that I brought home the stench of death.

Letter to Sashanki-1

Dear Sashanki,

I am moved by the photos of Durga. Particularly the one in which she is dressed in loose maternity clothing during her fateful stay in New Delhi's Sarojini Women's Hospital. I could see in your late daughter's eyes - just like yours, a deep brown mustard color - a joyful tender love for life growing in her belly. That photo must have been taken when she was near full term. There was also a closeup of her face in which I detected a lip in mid-quiver, as if she were lonely, missing you, wanting you by her side so much. But, you were stuck here in Chicago...

And the one showing her knitting a scarf for the baby that was to be your grandkid, had the gods been kindly disposed. Forgive me, I don't intend to rake up sad memories, but only to convey that I feel as though I knew your daughter Durga all along.

On quiet nights at Wings of Ether, I am reminded of those long conversations we had during our train rides in Chicago. Laying on my couch, I'd ponder your cryptic words: *"A fine mind like yours needs a fine heart to accompany it, Kumar."* I'd Often prefer to think that you meant to say that *we* - my mind and your heart - make a good combination...

The recipe you sent for a spicy drink with mustard powder and ginger turned out to be a big hit with computer
users in my Cafe. Looking forward to more missives from my Mustard friend.

Kumar

Letter From Sashanki

My Dear Mr. Kumar,

Thank you for your most recent.

It was kind of you to 'remember' Durga and speak so well of your impressions. You're kind.

Chicago will remain an unforgettable chapter of my life, in no less part than due to your kind presence there. Throughout my ordeal in that city, you were a great source of comfort and assistance. My friend, you are remembered fondly. As I told you before leaving Chicago, there will be at least one place for you to stay, if you ever decide to visit your own homeland in the future, mine.

In other news, as they say on TV, my company is marketing a Durga branded mustard paste specially targeted to Bengali cuisine. I am also making an entry into South Indian markets, but that's proving tough. You have any tips for me, as to how 'Madrasis' love their mustard, (just kidding).?

Yours
Sashanki

Letter to Sashanki

My dear Sashanki, Greetings from America.

I apologize for not responding sooner.

That was a nice idea to create a Durga branded, bottled mustard paste specifically for recipes used in the Bengal region of India's northeast! The concept is brilliant. The Bengalis deserve it. I hope it brings you lots of new business. Of course, your new brand's name references your late daughter, Durga. It's nice that it also invokes goddess Durga, held in reverence by the people of Bengal. Kudos.

The links to news stories from the local press which you emailed me, back during the Holidays, were quite interesting. Of course, I mean holidays in the American sense, Christmas time, not the summer vacation time, as Indians use the word.

Your business seems to have grown strong in the time since the Chicago Spice Show. You must feel really good about it. Everything I read online shows how well the ideas you mentioned succeeded in practice. It's a tribute to your fortitude and resilience. I am proud of you, friend!

Yours,
Anand Kumar
- a Madrasi, yes.

Death of News

Death came to the news-cycle of Gita's passing, as suddenly as her own demise. Like last rites performed in a compressed time frame, instead of the long stretched out ceremonies of a Hindu funeral, news ended suddenly. Death of News was palpable by Monday, it was cremated by mid-week. Come Thursday, there were only ashes of a story.

Little India News & Gazette, our beloved local rag, existed mainly to sell advertisements. In fact, the same two owners did ad sales, and cut-pasted wire service news stories. They too pushed Gita off their 'newspaper' pages, when Lalu stopped paying for "Reward for Information".

Online stories promised earlier: sign up here to get updates. Signing up didn't result in any updates - there was nothing to update. Instead, there was plenty of push marketing, sale coupons, and invitations to press more clicks. One week after the first full report, Gita ceased to exist, virtually. That second death was no less painful.

In my agitated mind the words death and dearth melded visually and phonetically. A dearth of news on Gita, the death of news. I shouted at the internet, who killed Gita? And, the internet shouted back, Gita who? The chance I took with the form to 'enter you mail for follow up stories' was a bad mistake. I learned not to do stuff like that ever again. Like liquor store owners I realized that it's okay to push your product on others, just don't consume too much of it yourself. So, I changed tack and emailed directly the reporters, the editors, and bureau chiefs.

I posted comments on week old posts hoping to trigger talk. I did everything except hire a blimp to circle Gita's little tree.

A great and wise wag once proclaimed, "There are known unknowns, and there are unknown unknowns..." Virginia, my office assistant, and I came up with an inventory of the former, questions to suggest to our cyber-sleuths: how Gita got there; how the killer got away; was she actually killed where she was found, or killed elsewhere and taken to the farm.

As to the unknown unknowns, there probably was much that I didn't even know that I didn't know. My brain hit a dead end there. Online sleuths spent their energy on that one by asking all the predictable questions - was she married, where was her husband, did she have a boyfriend and if so where was he; did she go out with her boss and if so where was he; who lived next door to her; was she promiscuous; did she go clubbing a lot. The cyber sleuths offered a plethora of motives. It all amounted to a big pile of unknown unknowns.

Warangal in distress

It was a long grand table laden with trays of Indian food, starting with chutneys at one end, through breads, veggies and meats, and ending with sweet things. I walked the gauntlet of curries, dodging the dishes that called out to me to sample them, and yielding to the ones I could never stop loving. Pick and chose from among an abundance of appetizers. At the same time, decisions of a different sort were taking shape in my mind.

When I entered the place, the first thing I noticed was how different the young cop looked. Of all the people, Warangal had changed most since Gita's passing. He looked forlorn and too distracted for a policeman, and distressed beyond the pale. It became my mission of the day, to somehow lighten his burden.

The other thing I noticed was that, in a rare occurrence, Lalu invited Shetty to sit with us for the late lunch. The right hand man wasn't used to that. "I still have kitchen work..." he started to say. "Ghose will clear up later," Lalu insisted, referring to a kitchen assistant. And, that was that.

"Don't be a stranger, Krishna," I said beckoning the young policeman, "Come, join us." He complied in mirthless silence.

Shetty approached me and said, "Mr. Kumar sir, welcome again, sir. Lalu is talking all day. You will tell us," he lowered his voice, "about Gita. Some new news?"

"I don't know how much of it qualifies as news, Shetty. But we do have things to talk about," I replied.

"Is okay, Kumar sir, we talk about Gita sister, it will be good." He picked up a plate and proceeded to the line of curries. Of course, I didn't assume that Shetty meant there were 'good' things to talk about. He only meant to say he hoped there was news, and that was a good thing. Sadly, there really wasn't. At least, not in the forensic sense.

"Officer Warangal, how is the precinct"? I asked.

"It's going fine, Mr. Kumar," Warangal took his hands out of pockets, rubbed his ear with the left. The right fumbled with the buttons of his shirt. The two hands met at his waist where they tugged his pants up. Warangal losing weight?

"You see Detective Mullins recently?" I asked.

"Yeah, a few days ago. He said to say hello to you."

"Anything he wanted you to convey to me?" I inquired.

"Naw, nothing about the case."

I handed him a plate and nudged him again. He took it and began to serve himself. Dal palak, garlic *nan,* and cucumber-in-yogurt dressing.

Good, he is eating. Because he cut a sorry figure otherwise. A gauntness was developing in his face, he struggled with poise, and lost something off his policeman's bearing.

Shetty was at the end of the buffet spread, already near the dessert section. He piled everything on one large oval china plate, like an American new to Indian food.

Lalu didn't have to do any such thing. As soon as he returned from cleaning himself up in the washroom, Ghose had a plate ready for him. Two pieces of Chicken Tandoori, a single unspiced papadam, and a small bowl of *semia payasam*. That was it.

I felt like a piggy. It was a loaded and well appointed plate of servings which I carried back to the table. As I dug into my heaps of okra and eggplant curries, I kept an eye on Warangal, none too furtively. He nibbled on his food, looked stressed, and lacked gusto. He didn't exactly 'play with his food,' he ate in fact. But not enough, which explained his changing body.

We made for an odd mix of physical changes to our bodies after losing Gita.

Lalu grew rotund, became stoic and slow.

Shetty stayed lanky, but became nervous and talkative.

Warangal seems to have suffered most, becoming sullen and slovenly.

As for me, it seemed that when I began to tilt against the windmills, my taste buds had eloped with Sanity. And, when I spent time under Gita's tree, I lost a lifelong lust for spicy food. But, I had every confidence that I would recover before others.

What worried me most was Warangal's looks. He put on weight in all the wrong places. It was a short time in which it happened. He was a policeman who should show off his fit and trim look. But, he sat there quietly, stooped, pretended to be hungry. Amd, acted like he was eating, and then ate like a girl. Light, leafy stuff...

I gave them a general idea of the news coverage, local, regional and national sources, what the television and radio stations said. Finally, I gave a gist of my searches online. "Same in every medium, hot story one week, and not a single mention the next." Blank stares all around.

I showed photos. Of the bare tree under which they found Gita, the sheep dog, the farmhand who discovered Gita, and of the shrine that grew there. Sighs and moans from the group. Ghose stopped by to look at some of the photos. When I showed him the digital photo of the little tree, Ghose joined his palms and bowed his head, and gave himself a Siva-slap of contrition. The shots of the memorial elicited a moist response, even from Lalu.

"The computers you researched, Mr. Kumar, sir?" Shetty asked. They have nothing?" His face had that curious, childlike wonderment and innocence.

"No, Shetty, nothing in the computers. But, I do have an idea though." At least two pairs of ears perked up. I turned to Lalu and explained cyber-sleuthing. That I joined a forum and solicited ideas. That I presented Gita's case as an example, to see what shook loose. Lalu, Shetty and Ghose listened attentively.

"The police department allows such things?" Lalu asked.

"It's a free country. Plus, it puts a subtle pressure on them to speed up the investigation."

"Private detectives on computers, why?" asked Shetty.

"Many minds make thinking light work," I said.

Out of the corner of my eye, I saw Warangal roll his eyes a couple of times. His face eventually settled into a thin black line of tight lips. He shifted in his chair a bit, now really played with his food.

"So, it is like a race? Police find out first, or the computer people find out first?" Lalu asked.

"Why, Ganesh? I think possible, Kumar sir, will solve the case first?" Shetty said.

"He will," Lalu's confidence in me on full display. Warangal snorted.

Lalu got up, he was done. Ghose came in and started clearing up the place, the rest of us lending a hand.

I invited Warangal to my apartment for a beer and maybe watch an old Hindi movie. "I should like to know what you think, professionally," I suggested.

****

With beers in hand, and Amitabh Bachan hamming it up on the screen, I asked, "Alright, Krishna, what's going on?" Nothing. Silence.

"I can see that you are genuinely upset since Gita is er... was a dear friend to us all."

"Kumar, you don't know that I am upset, or why."

"Hey, easy. We are just buds having beers. Okay to unload."

"Mr. Kumar, I have nothing to unload, upload, or download. It's just a sad thing what happened."

"And yet, you are losing sleep and getting out of shape. But, er. never mind, forget about that part. Just put your policeman's hat on and tell me what you think. You must have learned a thing or two from Mullins?"

"Kumar, only psychopaths kill strangers for no reason. Most people are killed by people they know."

Sure, we all watch TV and know that stuff.

"Nobody kills nobody they don't know." He explained like to a child.

A few years in the USA, and Warangal had begun to sound like a regular Chicagoan, double negatives, and all. If times were different, he might have passed for a member of the local political machine, or a ward heeler. And, if times were different, I might have chuckled at his accent, and the way the words slithered out of the corner of his mouth. Nobody came out as *noo-bawdy.* But, times were *not* different. All of us were seized by the same grim reality, and that's what weighed on him.

"She didn't deserve it, Mr. Kumar," Warangal wailed, suddenly. Grief contorted his body and limbs.

"Nobody ever deserves such fate, Krishna," I tried to sound soothing.

His breath caught in his throat, and after he recovered, "I owe her many tears, Mr. Kumar." That was a rather poetic way of saying, and I was touched by it.

"We all owe Gita tears, officer," I said. He looked at me with a slight shake of the head, like he disagreed, or I didn't state it well. All the same, we raised our glasses, tilted toward each other, and took sips in silence. Tears and toasts for Gita.

"So, who is the most likely suspect, you think?" I asked when we lowered our beers.

“It’s got to be someone she knew,” he said flatly.

“What are you saying? One of us killed Gita?” I asked

“Could be, Mr. Kumar, could be. One of us could have killed Gita.”

“Warangal, that’s crazy talk, man.”

“You wanted to know! I am just saying that’s how cops think. I don’t know one way or another. That’s just the breaks though.” *That’s the breaks,* is that what the young Indian just said? When did he become so expressive in American English?

“She had a father and an uncle.” I said. “And, a person like me, who regarded her as my own daughter,” I said.

“Cops think everybody is guilty unless shown otherwise,” he said.

“You are taking this way too personally, Warangal.”

“And you are not?” he retorted. “Look at you, Kumar. I notice that you have lost weight, don’t eat much, and run around looking for clues as if you are a detective.”

“Maybe. Er… maybe I lost a bit of my taste for spicy foods after visiting the farm, but I am still strong in mind and spirit.”

“But Shetty says you don’t eat much any more.”

“What, he told you that? When?”

“He realized it a couple days ago. Said not to say anything to Ganesh saab.”

I stared at him. Since when does everyone know everything that I do or don't do? "So, you think I am running around like a detective, huh?" I said.

"Oh, you don't know? Maybe I should buy you a round magnifying glasses and a trench coat, so people know you are Sherlock Holmes." Warangal let his thin dark lips curl in a quick wry smile of triumph. Triumph over what? "And, here you are, Mr. Kumar, telling *me* not to worry," he tapped his own chest before continuing, "so funny you are Kumar saab."

Warangal was on a roll and relishing it. I snorted. 'So funny' he said, but I didn't think he actually meant that he found my activities humorous. If he did, he would have chuckled or something. The grim look on his face, and the steady but silent stare he gave me, were unsettling. Why was he so stung when I said he was taking Gita's death too personally? Why wasn't he troubled, when I resisted his idea that I was the one taking the whole matter too personally? It was almost like he disliked my involvement, but didn't want to admit it. Just attacking me pleased him.

Like the dog that didn't bark, which *was* the clue in some Sherlock Holmes story, the fact that Warangal didn't chuckle at my excessive protestations, made me uneasy. I couldn't put a finger on the reason why, other than that he might be hiding something.

But the one thing he didn't hide was his contempt for my efforts. "You keep doing your sleuthing, Mr. Kumar. We both know that you are not a real detective. I do work with some real ones, you know."

The movie ended, though neither of us followed it. Warangal looked like he was doing okay. It was I who felt the stress.

Sayam Sandhya

I was bewildered.

How come, my attempt to ease Warangal's distress ended with me stressed, while he seemed so blase. After he left, I sat in the window, and watched the light in the sky stumble through changes. The birds roosted already, the early stars came out, and my mind stewed a medley of thoughts about the past and future, all at the same time. I hung on to watch the colors in the sky, hoping to cling to the moment, and stay in the present. I failed. It was an hour tailor-made for bittersweet nostalgia.

Hindus wrote poetry about memories suffered during that hour. *Sayam Sandhya*, when light and color changed the sky inexorably. Like children who *walk* to school but *run* home, the sun sauntered upward slowly, but rushed to sink and drop into the sea precipitously. Time passed during the day somehow. But, as the day ended, each man needed to take charge of time. Sayam Sandhya, a Happy Hour for Hindu poets who created moving *raga* scales to reflect the uncertain hour. The approach of night was something more serious than simply end of daylight. It bode a daily, recurring, end to the Self. Honoring that moment of decline clarified life itself. Like watching 'cattle dust' rise as the cows came home from the fields, the setting sun turning dust into gold, and then, nothing.

I didn't live in *that* world anymore. Heck, that world probably didn't even exist anymore. Gita's death didn't change the order of the world. Nor did Gita vanish from my world. She was very much with me at that hour, and in that window. The sun did not take my grief with him into the ocean.

***

Hunger. I felt it, but I couldn't pick up a utensil, or open a can of soup. My mind buzzed with memories, and memory of memories. Like my wish for a light that never changed, the memories kept wanting to pause time, or enliven an earlier time. Maybe, go back just one hour, just one *ghadia* - regain the moment when the moment was golden. My friend Sarada Sashanki, was once stuck in a legal limbo in Chicago. She read voraciously, during the many hours of her, non-imprisonment detention, by Detective Mullins. She told me about the Welsh word *hiraeth.* With no equivalents in the English language, that bittersweet word about nostalgia - hiraeth - led me to a single question, *Gita, what happened to you?* Hiraeth, a word of lament over something unrecoverable, as futile as the lament of someone displaced, someone who couldn't go home.

As I prepared to turn in for the night, the thought uppermost on my mind was, nobody has yet mentioned the final disposition of Gita's body. Where will the last rites be held, who will light the pyre. Will anyone feed the crows at the cremation grounds? If not, how will her soul ever migrate to another life? Even more paramount, who was the vulture that flew off with Gita's recent life?

Night at Wings of Ether

Instead of sleeping, I decided to 'go to work' and spend the night at Wings of Ether and try to make a list of suspects. April's weather in Chicago often became a tug of war, between icy blasts reminding of winter on some days, and the promise of spring with bouts of warm breezes on others. It was at such an uncertain moment that I arrived at my internet cafe that night.

It was somewhat chilly inside. I set up a cocoon of comfort and prepared to do some serious thinking. My supplies were all set: a heavy fleece blanket, thermos filled with *cafe-Au-lait,* biscuits, and a moleskin flip notebook. A low-grade hum emanated from the computer equipment, and a weak glow permeated the space giving it the proverbial ethereal vibe. The first thing to do was to make a list of lists.

- people who Lalu or I felt were untrustworthy.
- people who might have a grudge against Gita.
- people who coveted Gita, known to lust after her.
- people Gita trusted enough to keep their company.
- people who appeared in more than one list.

Yay, quite a systematic way to go about it. I was pleased. Yes, make a big composite list, exclude some. Refine the list, eliminate more. Rinse, repeat. Good plan, I thought.

Wait, there might be another way! Should I first make the elimination list itself, a list of people Gita *non-suspected*? People she totally trusted, or would have trusted, I suppose? Maybe, I could start at one end of Devon Avenue and go through all the businesses, see who should *not* be on the suspect list.

I poured myself a mug of hot coffee while the wheels spun.

After a couple of sips, it was decided. Just start with the obvious, people Gita trusted implicitly. People 'eliminated from suspicion' will be the first list.

Besides her father and Lalu, Gita loved and trusted me. I was her Kumar-uncle. It's true that I didn't kill her, but for the sake of academic reasoning, shouldn't I be a suspect? Would Sherlock Holmes put himself on any list? He would, just so the lack of proof against himself would perforce show that someone else must be the culprit. So, I put myself on the list just to rule others in. Nice logic I thought, but for some reason I couldn't see right then the torturous absurdity of that logic. Anyway, father and uncle - a duo eliminated as suspects, with me Kumar uncle, almost. It got harder from then on.

People that Gita would have known well included workers at Blue Mountain, kitchens of nearby Indian restaurants, people in the banquet hall and catering business. In fact, a very large number of Indian workers on Devon Avenue would make the list. But who particularly should I worry about?

Note to self, ask smelly Patel at the *P & P Mall*. Patel and Patwardhan Mall, a giant food store, employed many Indians, Pakistanis, Mexicans and Caribbeans. My old buddy, Keshubhai Patel (no relative of the namesake owner) knew them all. The mall was a world apart, a little third world unto itself. My garlicky pal not only was steeped in that world, he also had a grandfatherly affection for Gita. He would know if someone at P & P Mall held a grudge against Lalu and Gita.

Another place to inquire at would be *Khana Khazana*, a behemoth of a grocers-cum-restaurant. Located at the far end of the strip, Khana Khazana *was* a wild place, with a diverse clientèle, long hours of operation, and regular customers who ranged from the raucous to the devoutly solemn. The place was worth visiting more than once. Its owners, two Muslim brothers, were not only upright fellows, they were friends with Lalu Ganesh. But, it is possible that someone who frequented there had an eye on Gita.

Kamini Sundaresan came to mind out of nowhere. I was surprised by it myself, since Kamini never truly belonged to the tribes of Devon Avenue. She held herself above us all, but as had been happening lately, the stronger my wish to forget beautiful Kamini, the more unexpectedly she popped in my head. Sundaresan knew Gita and had employed Gita at one time. Everybody in our circle knew that. But we also knew, Kamini, aka *Mustard Princess of Chicago*, had been in jail for a year now. No means or motive to kill. I shivered from the memories of Kamini, and my adventures with mustard jars. I sat up, shook my head loose of random thoughts, and poured myself more hot coffee to restore myself.

There was a salesman at a jewelry store on Devon Avenue who often invited Gita into the store, unlocked the always chained and locked door, even when she didn't have an appointment. He'd show Gita bangles and necklaces, "New items just came in," he would say. Single out items which Gita's aunt might buy her as wedding gifts, saying "Oh, who will be the lucky man." And smiling, "Try this new-style bangle," gently tug on Gita's hand, a sly caress, and push a pair of bangles on to her slender wrist. What bangle salesmen habitually did. But, he would know that Gita didn't have an aunt, or no wedding plans. Might the salesman have filled her head with visions of wedding music, fragrances, shimmering jewelry and gold embroidered silk sari? The smug salesman Nandubhai, his mouth reddened with betel leaf, lime and rose paste. Slowly letting Gita's hand go, slide away, and seeing her out the store. A smile laden with a leer. Could Gita have lowered her guard in some such dreamy mood?

I knew a little bit of Nandubhai. A grease ball for sure, but not craven. Was he even in-country? Worth checking out. Imperative that I talk to his boss, the portly Mr. Ranajee. Lakshmi Jewelers went on my list.

The list-making exercise was getting unwieldy. It lead to more questions rather than candidates. Who could Gita have known well and trusted - trusted enough to travel out of town with? Lack of clear cut answers was tiring and depressing. I turned my mind to people on the Avenue I knew really well.

Shetty, the lanky reserved waiter. A nice guy, but I knew him to never take his eyes off Gita whenever she visited Blue Mountain. Was it simply a brotherly love for the boss's niece, or was it lust?

Imtiaz, the man who owned a big video store on Devon Avenue, used to ask about her whenever I went in to rent a movie. "Your girl Gita got married? No, not yet? Oh why, oh why," in that baleful tone. His sing-song Hindi language with a South Indian accent, sounded like a wounded street dog running away from pelted stones. Did Imtiaz have lewd notions about Gita?

Well, it had to be asked, given her age: was there a secret lover? And if so, who might that be? Where could they have met? I went over various social and cultural events where it might have occurred. I couldn't recall a specific person Gita hung out with. The scenario of a jilted lover didn't seem tenable. Even if she weren't a strictly conservative Hindu, such a thing would have been quite far fetched anyway. Few Indian girls dared to believe in what our people called 'love marriage.' For almost all the girls from the sub-continent, arranged marriage was the rule. Pretty much.

The later the night got, the darker my thoughts got. Was she hounded by a client or a supplier? If she were, a coworker would have known about it and informed Lalu right-away. So, that was out. As the cops often say, murder was most personal, nothing casual about it. All the same, it was worth looking into her catering assistants, kitchen helpers, and competitors for possible stalker-suspects.

I imagined an American, quite possibly a white man, shy and wealthy, who had a love for 'Eastern Culture' and was smitten by Gita. With natural warmth and sensitivity, "oh, what a culture," he might have drawn Gita's eye, and coaxed her into a day trip or picnic. And then what, things don't go…well?

The lists that could be made, with all the possible side branches of motives and circumstance, got out of hand. My body oscillated wildly, alternating between feelings of doubt, anger and numbness. There were random palpitations and an occasional wave of chill. I drew the blanket tight around me.

How exactly did Gita die? Her body held the clues. Facts will emerge in coming days. Captain Jones, the Chief of Detectives, told Mullins that local authorities will handle the case, not State level investigators in Springfield. Gita's body was still in Logan County downstate. Might they keep it there and only send results to Chicago Police? What if they don't do even that? I lay on the sofa brooding, the blanket all the way up and over my head. Would Mullins be of no help to me?

Outside, the midnight air shook with thunder. Wind picked up and rain began to splatter the glass. The storm that raged outside somehow calmed and eased the storm within me. As the barometer fell, so did the speed with which my neurons fired. First came drowsiness and then an abrupt slumber.

***

I woke up in cold sweats and ague at about five o'clock in the morning. Having slipped off the couch at some point during my sleep, I found myself on the wooden boards. It was the chilly floor which caused me to shake and shiver. Or so I thought, at first.

While I putzed around trying to regroup, with a blanket pulled tight and a mug of hot instant coffee, a new realization came to me that was far chillier than the floor. An utter darkness had taken over me during sleep. I had the most disturbing dreams in a very long time -

Apocalyptic images. The end of things I knew and accepted unquestioningly. My personal world dissolving before my eyes, projected onto my mind. Bits of movies and photos in galleries I visited. Myths and tales I had imbibed over a lifetime. Disturbing bits of early morning dreams which used to wake me up in the past. Pieces of old nightmares that were never forgotten. Unrelated things juxtaposed and melded into one prolonged dream stream. Dark clouds, vapor, scowling gods, and multiple twisting, morphing, figures that whirled and danced to a frightful rhythm. It was the twirling image of many arms which had me in cold sweats. The Dance of Shiva, remembered from movies, dances and dramas. Dance of death.

I shivered again under the fleece blanket, took deep breaths and attempted to steady my heart with breath control. Sleep came over me afresh. But not before the thought that the so-called Dance of Shiva represented the universal truth of life and creation, the cosmic dance of the Endless Being.

BOOK OF PHANI

Lalu's Brother
Phani, aka Fakhri, aka Francis

(Flashback: February - March, 2005)

Phani Arrives

When the day finally came to meet Lalu's older brother Phani, it turned out to be the Second of February, Groundhog Day. I didn't see that one coming, and I didn't like it at all. It ended my decade-long routine for the day: stay home, order a pizza, and wage war against winter with the aid of all the drinks mentioned in the movie named after the day.

Year after year, the same movie, the same two creatures named Phil, the same one and only alluring Andie McDowell, the same non-holiday holiday. Rinse, repeat. I thoroughly enjoyed Groundhog Day every year since it come out. But not this year? I was not a happy camper.

It started with a phone call from Lalu while I was checking out local pizza menus.

"Kumar, Phani is coming today. Me and Gita are going to receive him. Come here, we'll go to the airport."

"You realize what today is, Lalu? It's Groundhog Day."

"Yes, but it's not a holiday. You will have no parties to go to."

"Exactly. That's why I make my own party every year. You should join me, it's a great American movie. Bring some tandoori chicken. You *will* like the movie. Guaranteed."

"You are not listening Kumar, Phani is coming. We are all going to the airport to receive him. Bring the DVD, we can watch it at my house after Phani comes."

"Ah, come on Lalu, your brother isn't going to care. He will be too jet lagged to even know that he arrived in Chicago. He'll be sleepy for a few days. Remember, we all did that?" I knew even as I spoke, that there was no getting out of this one.

“Really Kumar, you saw the movie already, why watch it again? I don’t understand people watching the same movie again and again. Only kids do that.”

“Listen, Lalu. It’s not just the movie. It’s the whole experience. Pizza, pretzels, Tom Collins, Vermouth on ice, members of my movie fan circle on speaker phone. The whole package.”

Lalu was not buying it. He just spoke slowly, halting after each word, “Kumar, you remember, right?. You promised to go with us.”

I kicked myself for losing track of it. Lately, Wings of Ether, my internet cafe has been taking a lot out of my mind. What with the demands of the computer customers, the need to keep them happy, warm and connected. I forgot all about Lalu’s brother.

Darn it! I did make that offer to Lalu and Gita quite a while back. Back on a day, when I might have even thought that I would enjoy meeting Phani. Not so sure now. I was ticked off and ready to dislike a man I had not even met. The plane was due to arrive in a couple of hours. To be precise, it was 145 minutes before landing time.

Like thousands of other Indians, I knew the schedule of flights between Chicago and India by memory. An enduring fantasy of all Indian immigrants is that a visit to the homeland could be just around the corner. While waiting for that mythical future day, just keeping up with the airline schedule was good. Just thinking about a plane taking off at the hour it did, felt like being on it. Indians flocked to international airports at the drop of a samosa. Go to the terminal, feel like a traveler.

I took my time in the shower, letting the water rinse away thoughts about furry rodents, and replace them with thoughts about the Ganesh brothers. The talk since before the Holidays had all been about how the latest, and the oldest, member of the Ganesh family, would impress everybody with his hard work. He'd start a business, become a wealthy American. Redeem the whole village back home. Great Expectations, Indian style. I should have kept Phani on my mind.

If I didn't present myself at the airport, Lalu might forgive me, but not Gita. She regarded me as uncle-like, and would want me there to welcome her father. She was the main reason he was coming to America. That was all everyone at Blue Mountain talked about. Gita was dying to reunite with her father and would love for her uncles to be there too.

Lalu Ganesh pulled me aside as I was about enter his car. "By the way, Kumar, whatever you do, don't address my brother as Phani."

"What, Phani is not Phani? I don't understand."

"Just call him Francis, okay? He might get angry if you don't. Maybe not at first. Best if you don't use the name Phani at all."

"But, he is Phani, right? All this time, you never said Francis...?"

"Yes and No." Lalu was pleading now. "We'll talk later. I will explain everything."

"I see. But, he is still called Ganesh?"

"Yes, yes, yes. Please, here is Gita coming. Remember to use the name Francis, okay?" I nodded, somewhat reluctantly.

It was too much. The man I didn't know had a name I shouldn't use. The man I was about to meet had a name that didn't make any sense. I was already annoyed by the disruption of my festive evening. Now the intrigue about a name change. And, pleas that I act natural and not look mystified. Groundhog Day was turning into a hogwash day.

In the car, I tried to guess what Gita was thinking. She must know more than what I knew. Does she think I know more than what I do, which was actually nothing. She sat in the back, all smiles. Running a nail file along her fingertips, holding them up to inspect in passing road light.

"So, what's your brother really like, Lalu?" I asked.

"You will see," said Lalu. "But one thing, we are not like each other. You will see that right away." His belly shook.

"That's true, Kumar uncle. They are not," chimed in Gita. "Actually, daddy is more like you than he is like Lalu uncle." I was not sure if that was a compliment, and Lalu's extended belly shake only gave me pause for concern.

I turned and asked, "Gita, how is your father more like me?"

"Oh, I don't know. Daddy is very different. He is different from all others. Just as you are quite different from all others I know. Yea, that's what I think I mean," said Gita. Held her fingers up to light for a final check, and put the nail file away in her purse.

Lalu's belly settled down, and we reached O'Hare in silence. He managed to find us a parking spot and I quickly got out, and held the door open for Gita. After all, this was her special hour. We crossed the walkway that led to the terminal building, Gita checking herself in the glass panes.

I caught glimpses of a sparkle, and turned to look at her. Silvery, bell shaped earrings that dangled on thin links, wide expanse of her eyes, a sequined clutch, full moist lips, and a dainty diamond shaped mirror glued to her forehead in place of a bindi. Gita glowed. She was a very happy girl, full of anticipation. I was pleased, glad that I went along to the airport.

The three of us headed toward a sea of Indian-ness in the arrival area. Sari and chudidar clad women, men in *kurtas* and children running around or just wailing. Mumblings in a multitude of tongues and phone conversations that used two or even three languages in one sentence. I tried to locate a monitor showing flight status. After confirming that the plane landed, we settled behind a throng of people near one of several video screens that showed travelers exiting the customs area. A long vestibule that reached the greeting zone.

Lalu tapped my shoulder, "There he is," and I felt Gita grow tall on her heels in front of us.

The luggage cart he was pushing in front of him obscured a part of his body, but I could make out a sinewy man whose facial features jarred. The nose pointed one way, the jaw the other. Eyes were set close and deep, but steady. Dark thick lips pulled back, with an indecisive tongue stuck in between. A full head of hair, greasy and slicked back without a part. And, what might be either a slight limp, or just the gait of someone cooped up in a plane seat for almost a whole day. His head swiveled atop short collar bones till he spotted Lalu, and then Gita. The eyebrows knitted and his lips pulled farther back now, as white teeth flashed. His gaze more upon his brother than upon his daughter.

Lalu took the cart from him. I took the cart from Lalu. And, pulled it aside to let the Ganeshs reconnect.

Gita rushed to her father. A brief hug, and then she fell to her knees to touch his feet. "Daddy, daddy, you are here at last." A few moments of obeisance, after which he urged her up and they hugged briefly again. Lalu patted them both. Gita pulled away to let the brothers hug, and reached into her purse for a tissue.

"Welcome to America, big brother," said Lalu, with a big smile on his big round face. Gita rejoined the huddle and the three hugged, for a far longer time. When they finally separated, I was introduced.

It was hard not to notice that the tears that drenched his shirt and sleeve, came from Gita and Lalu. The latest member of the Ganesh clan to arrive in Chicago remained dry-eyed. I extended my hand in an automatic greeting, "Nice to meet you." Phani/Francis shook it. His hand was callused, dry and leathery. And his eyes, steady and steely, bored into mine with a terrifying probity.

"You must be very tired," I said to him, as I steered us, and the luggage cart, out of there.

"No, not tired," came the reply from Phani, er Francis. It was a chilly, sleety voice that grated, like wind whipping across a frozen Lake Michigan.

"And you," he said to me, "you come to receive me, why?" Again, the voice pelted icy shards, and the head swiveled probing each of my eyes in turn. His own eyes glowed. They were quiet while he was quiet. But when he talked, they shone.

I smiled, looked at Lalu and Gita in turn, and said "Francis, I am a friend of your brother and daughter."

"Yes," he said, "but, you want something. I am going to find out."

We fell silent while waiting for an elevator. A slight burning sensation began to form along my spine. I didn't know if it was some sort of a premonition. Whatever caused my spine to tingle, it was assuredly not the serpent of my kundalini. I wondered if it might be due to the rodent in front of me. After all, it was Groundhog Day.

Gita's Father

After welcoming Francis - as Phani must now be called - to America, I insisted on taking the subway back to my apartment. Lalu objected, "Nonsense, Kumar. I drive you home. Not a problem."

"That's *waay* out of your route, Lalu. Moreover, the three of you should spend time together first," I said. "They built a billion dollar train system, you know. I might as well use it." I helped load Lalu's car with his brother's luggage, and took off for the subway.

I slept happy that night. An odd thing to admit, but just being at the airport often lifted my spirits. Watching planes and people coming and going, fulfilled a tiny part of my longing to go places, even homeland, maybe. Pangs of nostalgia suffered by the immigrant can only be eased piecemeal.

Two days later, I went to the Blue Mountain hoping to chat with Lalu's brother, to catch up on happenings in the old sod, so to speak. And, talk of cabbages and kings, or rather, rhubarbs and rajahs. But, I found Lalu alone, seated at a large round table in the middle of the floor. His head bowed down, but no deity in front. A small smile broke on his tired face, and faded away just as quickly.

"Where is Phani?" I asked.

"Staying at Gita's apartment."

"Hmm, I thought he would be staying at your house," I said.

"Better this way. Nice they meet after long time. Thanks for going with us to the airport."

“I wouldn’t have missed it,” I said. A flip quip perhaps, but my sentiment was true.

Lalu nodded, examined his fingernails, and looked up at me. Clear eyes, but a face with no joy in it. “Kumar, I say this only to you, never to others,” he began. “My brother is, um, thanks by the way, for addressing him as Francis at the airport, and not as Phani."

“No problem. I figured you will explain it all when the time is right. Phani, Francis, same diff,” I said.

“Good,” said Lalu. “Okay, I don’t tell this to anyone, this.. um um my brother is a bit...” he moved his index finger in circles in front of his temple. The universal gesture that spelled ‘screw loose.'

“He did look a bit frazzled at the airport, long flight after all,” I said.

“Come on, we have all taken that long flight. Ten or fifteen years ago they used to be even longer. Which one of us became cranky?”

“True that,” I said, still not willing to say what needed to be said.

“You remember it Kumar, right? Every Indian who flew from Bombay to Chicago for the first time - it was like magic for us. It was the first plane trip for most of us. We loved it from the moment we got on the aeroplane. We floated in air. We felt like floating for months afterwards.”

“But, remember, the jet lag hit us as soon as we landed, and we slept for hours and hours the next day,” I had to point out.

"Yes, yes, yes," he said, obviously with a No on his mind. "We had America in our dreams for weeks before we got on that plane. Nobody, nobody landed in the States feeling crazy and cranky. We were in heaven."

Lalu left the unsaid, unsaid. His brother was different.

"Well, I must admit, your brother's behavior was odd. But, it's a long way to go from there to calling him crazy."

"He was like that always. Different, unpredictable…"

"But, he is here now, with his daughter." I said that with some real hope.

"Kumar, I know what you are thinking. My name is Ganesh, our family Hindu. Francis comes from where, right..?" I braced myself for the explanation I had been waiting for.

Lalu took a long breath and said, "Short and quick answer. He got under the influence of some 'fathers,' you know those fellows."

Oh, I knew them alright. Bible carrying street preachers. They pushed, badgered and enticed distraught folk at the vegetable market, butcher stalls, and cigarette kiosks. They dressed in different styles, but all used the same tactics overall. The words were pretty much the same always…

"Stop worshiping stones and clay figurines. Don't spend your life in hopelessness. Brothers and sisters, place yourselves in the hands of the real son of god. Here, take away a free tincture-bottle and a gauze-cloth roll." Etcetera, etcetera..

Yes, I had seen them all. Fathers or Fatherys as some were called. Indians badgering other Indians over how to worship.

Sometimes it worked, mostly it didn't. A sideshow at a busy town center, was what it mostly amounted to.

"Your family is devout, aren't they?" I asked.

"Not too much, but yes, quite traditional. We had all the festivals, idols, and ceremonies. My mother, more than my father, I will say." It confirmed what I suspected. *Lalu's brother was a seeker.*

"Phani gave up the name Fakhri, which some imam had given him a year earlier. He became Francis Ganesh. His new Christian 'brothers' were pleased. It was Phani, or Fakhri as they knew him, who approached them on his own. Even asked for 'the Book' to read. "That Arabic book is too difficult to follow," Phani said to his new brothers. They beamed, "You're a natural man of faith, Francis," they said.

The conversion was celebrated with a feast of bread, curry, and pudding. An elderly Father came down from the town of Tandoor and gave the blessings. Francis also got a handsomely bound copy of the New Testament printed in America.

"It all sounds so...formal, so ceremonial," I said.

"Oh, yes. Christian events always lot of ceremony. When Phani became a Muslim it was quite simple and quick. Very serious people," said Lalu.

There was more involved in Fakhri becoming Francis. A lady came down from Zahirabad, a Mother Miriam. "You are an inspiration, my son," she told Fakhri. She gifted him a brand new string of prayer beads made of Himalayan quartz, with beads shaped oval, like *shivling* almost. The older Ganesh brother remembered to cross himself before tentatively rolling the beads, with much tenderness. Their pure translucent glow caught the sun's rays and bounced it on his face which glowed. Mother Miriam chose the name Francis personally. Saint Francis, the kindest man in all universe, second in compassion only to the Lord himself. He was kind to all animals. Just as Phani or Fakhri grew up being respectful of all life. Francis knelt, faced the Holy, and crossed himself with the ease of someone who had done it all his life.

Whew, that was an amazing story of serial religion. Which American hippie could compare to this native version?

"Didn't your parents kick him out of the house after the second conversion?" I aske in Indiad Lalu.

"No," he replied. "Nobody wanted a divided family, Kumar. My parents wanted that Phani stay and we all live in the same house."

"And Phani agreed?" I asked.

"Yes." Cryptic.

There had to be more. I prompted "And happily ever after?"

"Sort of..."

I put together a narrative from the bits and pieces of stories Lalu related about the days following Phani's latest 'seeking.'

Phani's problems started right after Gita's birth. Her mother died due to afflictions she contracted after delivery. For a year or two, Phani kept it together, but with the child growing up fast, he couldn't handle it. I guess his search for meaning of life led him to all sorts of wanderings. At first he just went to different places, then he went to different faiths, eventually settling in the Church.

The elder Mr. Ganesh, their father, let Phani continue to live in the same house with the rest of the family. Phani could eat and sleep with the rest, as long as he didn't become a nuisance to others. Mother Ganesh learned to cook foods she herself wouldn't eat. She made chicken and egg dishes, mutton, and custards to feed her son according to his newly acquired tastes. She then took a full cleansing bath and cooked pure vegetarian food for herself, her husband, and Gita. She used a separate set of pots to prepare Phani's new foods, but the love she gave him never diminshed.

"Your mother is a saint, Lalu." I said, and didn't even realize the word I just used.

Phani was even given a portion of a wall for his new gods. Put up a picture of Jesus, Mary, Mother Theresa, whoever he worshiped. Decorate it with flowers, mango leaves, anything. His mother continued the family practice of making rice and milk pudding, and gave a small cup of it to Francis to make an offering to his new gods before meals - the timeless Hindu practice of *prasadam.* After all, humans shouldn't eat before gods do.

"Let's just stay together as one family," their mother wheezed.

The new Christian laughed at the idea of floral garlands. Instead, he found a length of tinsel to drape around a color photo of Jesus. He found incense sticks scented with rose, not sandalwood.

"Did he worship at the wall regularly?" I had to know.

"Actually he did. He lit a candle daily and prayed."

I had questions, but let it drop at that. It was a revealing narrative. But one question I couldn't pass up.

"And what about Gita?" I asked. "She didn't convert? Follow her father and change her name, or stop wearing sari?"

"Come on, Kumar, what conversion? Phani was just a boy when this religious crazy stuff started. Be was not even thirty years old. Yes married, yes daughter, but no real responsibility. Phani do nothing about real life." The look on Lalu's face wasn't so much a sneer as sadness.

He went on, "You see, our parents handle everything, and all Phani and I had to do was study and be good boys. Phani never have stability. He always struggle. No money, no job, no business. I was lucky to escape all that."

Once again, I chose to not press for details. Sure, I wanted to know how my buddy 'escaped' all that. But it was his brother's adventures I wanted to hear about. The story of Phani, or Fakhruddin, or Francis, was more absorbing. And somehow more urgent.

"Is that why you sponsored Gita for the visa?" I asked. " To save her from conversion?"

Lalu rubbed his face vigorously. "God gave me a blessing, good help. Now I help others. My parents very happy I got Gita out of there."

"Francis didn't object? He let go of his young daughter?"

"My brother only concern with himself, not others. I was going to sponsor her anyway." Lalu sounded tired by now. "I don't know what he thought. Lucky for Gita, our parents were strong about it. They took charge and they handle my brother's moods."

"And look at her now," I said.

Lalu grinned. "Yes, I am very happy she's here. She learn everything I know about kitchens and cooking."

"And now her father sees what a success she made of herself," I said, basking in the reflected glory of my friend's accomplishments.

"Kumar," Lalu with a certain finality in his voice, "all I want is for Francis, yes, I think he finally is Francis. I want Francis to get a job or start business. My parents will be happy."

I looked at my friend long and hard. He deserved better than platitudes. He needed doses of reality.

"Lalu, do you really think America will change your brother? Will he adapt to this new chance like we did?"

Lalu paused a long while, then shook his head. More vigorously than needed to just say No. Like he was shaking something loose out of that big gourd of a head. He looked calm, but I knew better. Watching him waddle into the kitchen, I didn't envy him. Gita's father was, as the cliche went, a many layered individual. His mind had silted over several long years.

Francis, the Christian, covered over Fakhruddin the Muslim. And, Fakhri the Muslim, layered over Phani, the angry Hindu. And now, an American Francis who arrived at O'Hare Airport overlay them all. I wondered what really lay buried inside that *matrushka* doll? I couldn't have known, at that time, the twisted darkness my curiosity would lead me to.

Kitchen Album

“I loved her like she was my own, Kumar. You know that,” began Lalu, when he emerged from the kitchen. “I used to hold her for hours when she was a child. Crying and asking for her father. Phani was never home,” his voice rasped.

I nodded. "Where was Phani?”

“Who knows? He was a vagabond. Once he was gone for over a month, to live near a temple in Kerala. You know the one, *Ayyappa* temple.”

I knew that tradition. Adult Hindu men went on a *deeksha*, or observance, for periods of up to forty days. They wore black, abstained from intoxicants and spicy foods, and married men took a vow of temporary celibacy. Many prayed or read scripture. Some went on pilgrimage to the state of Kerala, to live in the shadow of the temple of *Ayyappa*.

“That’s a laudable thing, isn’t it, Lalu? Nothing wrong with that sort of piety?” I added, “My uncles used to do it. I know that some companies offered space for quiet meditation.”

“You don’t understand, Kumar,” Lalu was quick to respond. “My brother didn’t do any of it. He only *claimed* that he did. He wore the ritual black shirt and loose pants, alright. But, there were people who saw him smoking and drinking coffee. He might have done deeksha for a few days here and there. Just like all his other ideas, it was just talk.”

“Better than nothing, right?” I said.

Lalu snorted. “And there was the time my brother was gone for three months, ‘to help people’ he said. Earthquake happened somewhere in Central India. Phani stuffed a bag with some clothes and took off. Where he lived and how he survived, nobody knows. But, he sure told stories when he came back. Kumar, even a writer like you couldn't make up tales like that. I always thought he was actually in some jail during that time."

"Jail, why do you think that?" I asked.

"Strange people were coming to our door claiming they were owed money by him. They spoke different dialects, from distant provinces. Not family types, more like criminals," Lalu snorted again.

"An oddball alright," I said. Lalu smiled as if he liked the word oddball.

"Please, Kumar. I say all this and we keep it private. As long as Francis is in America, I say you don't bring up his past. For Gita's sake."

"I have no problem with that. But, he seemed just a bit cold - not nice - at the airport. I will be real glad to help him adjust to America."

Lalu's face beamed. Around us the kitchen staff began to wake up from their siesta and slip back into their roles, setting up the restaurant for the dinner hour.

"I will show you something," Lalu went in the back. I played with my samosa which was somewhat oily and over-crisp at the corners. I tried to wash out the taste of it with a sip of chai, but it had gone tepid. Lalu must have a sixth sense, he returned with an enameled jug of fresh hot chai in one hand.

It was what he carried in the other hand that caught my eye. A large green tome which turned out to be a photo album. It was a remarkably aged and decrepit thing. Definitely not bought in America. He set it down between us. However, when he opened it and leafed through, I noticed that some photos looked recent.

"This thing looks so old, bring it with you on the boat?" I asked with a chuckle.

He grinned. "Been in the family for years. Bought by my father when I was a baby." He flipped through the thick dark green pages, about the size of an old LP record's sleeve. Many of the photos were held snug by corners, a few slid about loosely. He opened it to a place where a spread of some nine photos stretched across two facing pages. I turned the album toward me and Lalu drew his chair next to mine.

Photos of old folks posing with grim tight faces, children with toothy frozen smiles, idols festooned with garlands, cattle adorned with sacred pastes and powders, and people seated in a line and feasting at some special occasion.

Lalu launched into a recitation.

"That's Phani and me playing in the courtyard of our house; that's us decorating the house on the day Gita was brought home from the maternity hospital; this one, her First Letters ceremony, our father holding her hand and tracing the five sacred letters in rice." Lalu wiped his face discretely, and resumed, "We always knew she would be a fast learner."

I turned the page over and there it was, just hanging on by one photo corner, an image that caught my breath. Lalu seemed to have anticipated my reaction. He stabbed at it with an index finger and said, "Yes, that's Phani, in his Fakhri avatar."

"When was this?"

"A few years after my niece was born. He became a Muslim overnight. He wore a brand new fez hat, walked around the village wearing a *sherwani* coat, and smelled of attar."

"Amazing, did he read the Quran too?" I asked.

A dry laugh before the reply. "He tried. An imam tried to teach him. Phani memorized a few poems or something like that."

"I think they are called *Sura.* Similar to our Hindu sloka."

"Yes yes. That's what he said they were. He learned a few by heart. Here is the thing. He changed his name also. The mullah gave him the name Fakhruddin, or Fakhri as a short form."

"What did the name mean, did he say?" I asked.

"Something to do with faith, I don't remember exactly. None of us would ever forget that fez cap with its black tassel, or that smell of attar. He dabbed a drop or two on a piece of cotton and stuck it behind his ear."

It was getting curiouser by the minute. Lalu's older brother had more sides to him than I could have guessed.

"None of the villagers laughed or mocked?" I asked.

"Nobody had the courage. Phani would have shredded them alive. He had a temper." That, I believed.

A few more pages of the album, and some riveting pictures of Lalu's elders, some in closeup, some in group actions. All faces deeply etched with life, staring intently into the camera with varying degrees of vitality. Unlike Fakhruddin's dreamy face with a distant look in his eyes, the other faces were full of reality and awkwardness.

It was obvious from just a cursory glance, how much that album got thumbed through over the years. The thick individual sheets that held the photos were not just curled, they were cracked, chipped or entirely rounded. Even without trying, I detected grease and curry odors on it.

Lalu noticed my reaction to the album's aroma and gave a big, healthy grin.

"Yes, I know, it stinks," he said. "It used to sit on top of the spice shelf. Like that for a few years. Now, I wrap it in plastic. Put it inside a box."

"Why do you have the family album here?" I asked.

"Keep memories close," he said..

"But why keep it here at all, why not at home?"

"Some days it gets to be too much, Kumar. I give it a quick glance. Or, maybe look through some photos. Reminds me why I am in business, why I am in this country," said Lalu.

He grabbed a napkin, moistened it and wiped his face. Tired, and looking at nothing in particular, he spoke slowly.

"Things happen here that wear me out. Chopping vegetables or checking stock gets tiresome. The mixture of spices goes wrong sometimes, and I have to slow down and work out exactly how to salvage the curry paste without throwing it all away. Sometimes just the stress." Lalu shrugged.

He drew the album toward him, tapped its cover a couple of times and said, "This helps me slow down on those days.

Reminds me of what I am doing."

"A source of inspiration for you," I said. "That album is your touchstone."

Lalu took a deep breath and arced his hand around him, "I do all this for the people in the book. Even the dead ones. The faces I left behind to come to America." He took a sip of his diet drink and said without any affect. "New photos are nice, but I need the old ones sometimes. I need to see their faces, see them the way they were when I left India."

I stared at him in silent admiration for the calmness with which he stated it all. And also moved by the lack of heaviness in his voice. He simply sat there with his palm laid on top of the album. Like it were a holy book, like he was taking an oath of office.

The unbearable solemnity of that image unsettled me. What would I take an oath for, where was my holy book?

Francis is taken on a trip

Francis walked around the vehicle, eyeing it like a kite circling overhead, curious and keen. But, this car wasn't like a carcass. It was a metallic beast that could come alive any moment. He was stunned by the very looks of it. The large gray car, SUV they called it, took up the entire width and nearly a third of the length of the driveway of his younger brother's house.

Its large tires, the shiny chrome metal strips that ran its length, an enormous front bumper that rivaled the cow catcher on a locomotive, big side mirrors that spread out like a rat's ears - the SUV loomed over Francis. And then, there were those shiny bulges of yellow and red plastic covers over light bulbs, they looked to Francis like beady eyes of some alien creature.

He became aware that his own eyes got big and beady, and his mouth hung open. He felt he wouldn't be able to close his eyes if he tried. The voice of Kumar, as usual, interrupted everything. The fellow behaved like a boss and Francis didn't care for that. As soon as Francis got into the passenger seat, Kumar issued an order, "Clip your seatbelt." Annoyed though he was, Francis complied. He saw Kumar go about using different controls of the car quite familiarly. Radio, the air flow vents, window glass and so on. Francis felt only a slight grudging admiration, but a whole lot of disdain toward the talkative man.

Gita, Lalu, and Warangal, all got in one after another. Shetty, the fair-skinned right hand man of Lalu Ganesh was the last one in. Shetty joined Warangal on the third row seat, stretched out and settled sideways, a cushion at his back and a backpack on the floor by his feet.

Francis smiled at the lanky head waiter who was making himself comfortable, and said, "Shetty, I have never seen three rows of seats in a car before."

"America is full of wonders," came the reply. Francis couldn't tell if the waiter-fellow was being sarcastic or dismissive, but decided that Shetty's comment would be disregarded.

Gentle warmth spread throughout the interior of the vehicle, and Francis found himself in a cocoon of a bucket-seat comfort. This wasn't so bad. This tourist drive they were taking might actually be enjoyable. It might even reveal to him some things he never was sure about. About America, Indians in America, his brother, his daughter. Did they love driving SUV cars, or hate their own families? Why are so many Indians eager to run away from homeland.

Now seated comfortably in the warm belly of the beast, Francis looked at those seated behind him and asked, "All ready to go?" Since this road trip was arranged for his pleasure, he would take charge of it.

Kumar backed the vehicle out of Lalu's driveway, *long like a runway at an airport*, and started them on a route toward the expressway. After going only a mile, instead of entering the highway, the vehicle slowed down and pulled up at a 7-11 store. "Let's get coffees," said Kumar, as if *he* were in charge.

Francis's irritation with Kumar only increased when they got back into the SUV. Kumar became a non-stop tour guide. He felt Kumar's taps on his shoulder every few minutes and was forced to turn his head in the direction Kumar pointed. And listen to some stuff Kumar had to say. The number of taps, and things to say, increased along with the speed of the car on the expressway.

Just to change the conversation, Francis himself tapped Kumar on the shoulder and said, "You look quite skilled driving this, a very long time you driving this?"

Kumar said, "No, not really. Got it only this morning. Just fifty dollars a day to rent it. Comfortable ride too."

That surprised Francis. Both because it was so cheap to rent, and because Kumar acted so nonchalant about it. Yes, the ride is comfortable thought Francis. It would be even more so if someone else drove it, and not the annoying Kumar.

Gita was seated directly behind Francis, and carried on excitedly with Lalu and Shetty. About banquets, buffets, menus, and stuff like that. She was all smiles and shiny eyes. At one point, when Kumar had nothing to point to, Gita leaned forward and said, "You will enjoy this trip so much, daddy. I like going to see places with you." She put a hand on his shoulder, "Remember all those places our whole family used to go and picnic together, when I was in grade school?"

Francis snorted. Now she started calling him daddy. What was wrong with *ayya*. He had been called ayya by her all along. Sitting in the big car, driven by the Kumar fellow in the USA, Gita has a daddy now? He blurted out his annoyance. "If you liked all those picnic things, why did you leave home and come here?" He felt Gita pull her hand back, but not before she gave him a gentle squeeze. "Oh, my father," she said, " I was talking about when I was a child. It's different today. I am a grown woman now." She shrank bank into her seat, shifting a bit away from Lalu uncle, who had said nothing at all.

Even as he maintained a gritted-teeth silence, Francis felt her gaze upon him. He avoided looking at her initially. But eventually, turned around and mumbled, "You don't have an answer, do you? Why you abandoned home, abandoned your father, abandoned your village." She didn't answer. Still turned around, and showing neither sadness nor anger, Francis stared, and sought out her face.

It was a calm oval face, hair pulled into a tight braid, baby fuzz that still clung to her cheek bones. There was a flame-shaped yellow-painted bindi on her forehead, the dark lines of *kajal* on her eyelids, Francis saw it all. It was as if he were seeing his daughter for the first time. Her dark deep-set eyes were steady, unblinking, and bored into his own.

Francis saw an attempted rueful smile on her lips. The short upper lip and strong wide lower jaw parted. Her mouth opened briefly but clammed up at once. He was not surprised. *That's right, you have no answer as to why you abandoned your birthplace.*

The SUV was going past an enormous overhead highway sign that shimmered in mid-morning sunlight. The bckseat became bathed in bright light momentarily. In that fleeting flood of brilliance, Francis noticed something quite peculiar, something he should have noticed the moment he got off the plane from India but had not. In the light bouncing off the highway sign, during that moment when Gita started to but didn't answer her father's question, her teeth sparkled!

While growing up, Gita's teeth always had a slight mottling. Her front teeth were quite even, but somewhat brown due to bad minerals in their district's water. Her cousins had mottled teeth too. But the older generation which had grown-up farther away didn't have such affected teeth. What happened to the brown tint? Where did the mottling go, and when did it happen? Did Gita get her teeth painted or covered?

Francis felt pained. She became such an utter faker. Fake teeth, fake eyelids, face paint. America did this. It made his daughter vain and smug. That briefest attempt at a smile exposed more than her teeth. *Good thing I agreed to this trip.*

Right here in this SUV, in the midst of a group of people who were all younger than himself, he got no answer from his daughter. Not only that, she dared to stare back, stare him right in the face. What kind of disrespect was this, and who taught her to be so bold?

He felt anger rising. He slowed his breathing down and began to pray in silence using the special lines he used for such agitated moods. If Gita had really thought about him so much why didn't *she* come to visit him? Instead of making her father come all the way to the USA. Francis tried to tamp such thoughts down. But, out of nowhere, a refrain echoed in his ears. The refrain of his family, of his village, nagging him day after day: "Go visit your daughter."

He turned forward and stared ahead. Gave no response to Kumar's taps, talks, and exclamations. He decided not to care if mister know-it-all had no audience anymore. *Kumar can talk to himself all day long.*

Francis was jolted out of a reverie by a prod from a smiling Kumar. "You look bored, Francis."

He said nothing. Kumar continued looking at him intently. In turn, Francis stared back. He wiped his face on his sleeve and turned to see who in the back might make a snide comment about him dozing off. But nobody seemed to pay attention to people in front. Francis said mildly, "No, no, not bored. Continue, continue."

"I thought you wanted to sit in the front seat because you were eager to listen to me." Francis felt the poke by Kumar again.

He knew that to be true. He did insist on sitting in the front passenger seat. He had told the group before getting into the SUV, "Kumar explains everything. I don't want to miss even one word." Francis looked at each person in turn, and bared his teeth to show them that he could smile broadly, be friendly. The group beamed at him as they had all piled in.

But now, after being called out, he didn't blush or cringe. He even got over the anger he felt toward Gita a while ago. Stifling a yawn and an urge to stretch out, Francis forced himself to smile at Kumar, "Yes, yes Mr. Kumar, good commentary. Please, continue. I like sightseeing."

****

Francis had made it his habit after arriving from India: whenever he was taken along in a car, he insisted on sitting in the front. It might be a party, a festival, or just shopping, he declared right before the start. "I sit in front. So I can see everything nicely." Anybody who raised an eyebrow, received an earnest explanation: "Just sitting in this seat, I feel like I am driver." People shrugged.

Some food workers started calling him shotgun Francis. They grinned at him and made gestures with their hands. Francis didn't know what that was all about, and didn't care. But, one afternoon, Warangal explained it all to him over lunch at the Blue Mountain. American farmers often 'rode shotgun' on their tractors and pickup trucks. American kids often called out their desire to sit in the front seat next to the driver. The food workers were play-acting, mimicking loading, cocking and aiming long guns.

"You are just like a little boy, Francis," Shetty had said. Francis nodded with neither a smile nor a scowl, and said, "Yes, yes, I am shotgun." Silence took over the table and the topic of his seat preference was dropped.

Francis observed the people who gave him rides keenly. He didn't care what *they* thought, he was imagining himself as *the* driver. American cars were pretty easy to drive, everything automatic, everything powered electrically. People didn't seem to mind being watched by him and forgot all about Shotgun Francis.

The Kumar fellow, however, seems to have kept the topic in his head. On one occasion, a particularly turbulent and windy day, it was just the two of them that went for a drive on State Route 49, Lake Shore Drive. "It's the Windy City, let's go watch." Kumar drove up and down the highway a couple of times. Enormous waves rose up and doused the roadway. The earth, sky and water fused into one gray mass to the east. The only sparkle came from a dozen police vehicles who kept vigil with flashing blue lights. "Nature's fury my friend," Kumar kept saying. On the way back, Kumar brought up the topic. "You know Francis, according to car crash data, the front passenger seat is the most dangerous. People in front are injured often. I don't mind if you sit in the back."

"In the backseat, I don't feel like American," replied Francis. "In front, I am shotgun." He mimicked using a rifle, as he had learned the gestures from food workers. Kumar dropped the subject.

****

Their SUV left the suburbs and entered a rural stretch of the highway, and picked up speed. Kumar's lecture was now becoming somewhat fragmented and meandering. There were big expanses of farmland on either side with no great edifices to point to. Except the big, green overhead signs with lots of names and numbers.

Francis felt boredom again. Everything about driving in

America vexed him. The oddity of cars being driven on the 'wrong side' of the road didn't bother him, but everything else did. The speed, the colors and sizes of the cars, the roads, the traffic - Francis was bothered by it all. It occurred to Francis that it wasn't the people. It was the damn cars, they were too big and went too fast at the slightest press of a foot. The hardest part of America to comprehend was the bloody road system. The roads were too wide, too smooth and went too far. They seemed to go on for ever. Don't any of these roads ever end?

Kumar was carrying on with his tour guide act. Less excited now, he chuckled at times. Francis couldn't tell what was so amusing, and felt his mind drift again, until the vehicle slowed down considerably. "We're getting close to our capital city," he declared with another chuckle. 'Land of Lincoln,' Kumar said, and craned his neck to the back, "You all ready to visit Abe Lincoln?"

Francis heard Kumar reading numbers off the sign poles on the roadside, repeating to nobody in particular, what routes they needed to take and in what order. It bothered Francis even more. Since first landing in America, he saw numbers everywhere. Big roads, little roads, tiny streets. Americans numbered roads like there was a shortage of names or something. There were numbers on every sign. And, by god, those numbers passed by in a blink. It was all so silly, the number of numbers!

Now off the Interstate, their vehicle moved at a much lower speed. There were a lot more things to observe now: bridges, intersections, shops, motels, gas stations etc. Kumar looked for what he called local route numbers. Francis, in spite of his irritation, tried to follow Kumar's lead, and he too now swept the roadside for indications.

They came to an intersection at the outskirts of a tiny village, and Francis burst into laughter. It was the metal post as stout as a streetlight pole but not quite as tall. It had seven different number signs with one stacked on top of another. He counted them again to be sure. Yes, seven signs. Seven metal plates. Each had a thick black number on a silver background, and an arrow pointing a certain way. Even more funny, the numbers weren't in any order. Seven metal plates, some of which were shaped like shields, and one which said INTERSTATE.

He pointed to that pole and said, "So many numbers on this just one road. It's very funny." He resumed his hearty laugh, but soon regretted saying anything at all to Kumar. Because, as soon as that simple observation tumbled out of Francis's mouth, Kumar launched into an instant lecture.

"Oh, that. It's pretty simple, Francis. Those signs don't refer to the road we are on..."

Francis tried to nip the lecture in the bud, saying, "They don't? Okay then."

But, Professor Know-it-All had an answer for that too.

"See, the state route and the county road run together for a mile here, so the plates are together even though they have different numbers. Also, part of the stretch ahead is also called a US Route, but it is not an Interstate Highway. The US Route sign is a shield also, white in color, not blue, with its own separate number. Further along, all these numbers will go separate ways but right here they are all the same road. Oh, by the way, there is a junction up ahead, hence those two signs, see the arrows in different directions? North bound and South bound...."

Francis tore himself away from Kumar's lecture and didn't

even pretend like he was listening. He didn't care if Kumar thought it was rude behavior. Instead, he occupied himself with a look at his hands and fingers. Suddenly, Francis realized how soft his hands became in just a few weeks. No longer callused or leathery, his fingers and palms felt nice. No dirt under fingernails. His hands weren't like that when he left India. His daughter's good cooking and America's creams and lotions softened his hands nicely. Away from all that digging and hauling of dirt when he worked at the brickyard near his village.

He kept feeling his hands while Kumar droned on about roads and numbers. And long after Kumar ceased, Francis continued to run his hands over each other. He kept on rubbing the tips of his fingers, almost like rolling prayer beads. While his hands might have become clean in America, *there was dirt lurking elsewhere.* He has seen enough of America

At the Khana Khazana

Francis Ganesh was overloaded. Yet, he moved nimbly, even gracefully. He walked step-in-step, swaying, his hips and waist pushed this way and that, and not too slowly either, despite the precarious load. Stainless steel plates stacked in threes and fours perched precariously on his outstretched left arm. Smaller round plates close toward rippling biceps, larger squarish ones rested on spread out fingers, and odd sized ones in between. His right hand carried a pail, actually an old paint bucket with handle, now filled with small items: forks, spoons, teacups, bowls, and food scraps.

Near the double doors to the kitchen, employees and diners made way or held the door open for him. At the sink in the back of the kitchen, a young Mexican boy with a fuzzy face and a missing front tooth, methodically took the loads off and dropped them into a large sink. Like a villager with a life-long habit of carrying multiple bags of rice perched atop his head, or a railway porter who carried the luggage cluster of an entire family, Francis calmly carried loads of dirty dishes to the kitchen. In the big city of Chicago.

Again and again, Francis, aka Phani Ganesh, aka Fakhruddin, returned promptly to the dining area for more dirty dishes. Circus Francis, the others in the kitchen often said. They couldn't know if Francis heard that comment, or minded it. Francis quietly continued shambling with loads of dirty dishes without comment or complaint.

"How you liking your job, circus man?" somebody asked him once. Francis didn't sit down to chat or reply. What is it to them, he wondered. Don't they know that he, Francis, didn't talk lottery numbers or TV shows or baseball scores? When pressed, he merely said, "Why complain about what everybody knows? It's a rotten life but we must all live it somehow."

Francis did just that, only without resting. The smoky heat of the kitchen, the din of the dining area, or the crazy hours he was asked to work, none of it bothered him. The noise made by steel plates and cutlery was just so much the sound of dollars jingling.

Who could have imagined such a place existed in America? For the one thousand and one time, Francis marveled at the sheer size of the dining space, let alone the entire Khazana. The enormous dining hall required constant watch as people came and went, and all he had to do was just clean tables constantly.

It's called busing tables, explained the head cook Khan, a fellow of an uncertain nationality, due to the odd combination of a middle-eastern cut of beard and a very Indian-looking fez cap. Khan had shown Francis how to use a large deep pail, the busing tray, to carry dirty plates. In fact, Khan repeated the suggestion the next three days, but eventually gave up.

Francis ignored all advice given to him and continued with his acrobatic style of clearing tables. *Busing, what a silly name for a job!* It was nothing like driving a bus or lorry. Just a donkey hauling things. *That's what you are now Francis, a donkey*. Deep in thought, Francis kept a vigilant eye on the floor. A group of diners just got up and left.

Go on, make your haul of dirty dishes. Be a good donkey of a daddy and clear dirty dishes, while your daughter Gita preened with glee, after cooking to feed a hundred in banquet halls.

****

"Looks like busy out there, huh," said Castillo the Filipino - a junior cook - without pausing the chopping of vegetables.

"Yes, very busy dining room," Francis replied, unable to take eyes off the knife in Castillo's hands. The Filipino had the fingertips of one hand rest on the vegetables while the sharp knife in the other hand came down repeatedly to slice. The rapid chopping action was mesmerizing and terrifying to Francis at the same time. How did the man ever slice the cucumber and not his own finger?

"Try and use the busing tray, it helps," said the junior cook, still with no pause in the action of the knife. Francis tore himself off, nodded, and returned to the floor, but with bare hands.

It's fantastic, isn't it, he asked himself. That mindless slog could yield such money. That drops of sweat turned into dollars, dollars then turned into rivers of rupees. No brain needed at all. *My little brother Lalu knows a thing or two about this country.*

Francis felt his jaw tighten and his stomach go sour. He sensed his angular face darken and his long thin nose, that sat askew, twitch. Little brother taking care of the older one. And now, everybody in the world telling him how to do things.

Gita admires and emulates her uncle. Gita, his Gita, his own flesh and blood, so enamored of this god-forsaken country. How could she live so far away from parents and grandparents? How easily she seems to be coping with being so far from childhood friends!

But Francis also knew that the same gods who gave Gita that kind of thinking, they also gave him, her father, a special strength. Francis knew it all his life, that there was a special force within him. What that force was supposed to do, nobody foretold. He just knew that it was there and would be revealed sooner or later. A sign will appear. His life will become meaningful.

***

"The immediate goal for us is to get you some money," his brother Lalu had said a month earlier. "We should get a job for you, at once." Lalu sounded like a controller of the universe, able to summon up events to take place, thought Francis.

"You will do work, right? Not hesitating some hard work, huh Phani, sorry, Francis?" Lalu had asked. No, Lalu was not asking, but giving orders. Francis bit his tongue and simply nodded.

Little brother Lalu Ganesh devising plans for everybody. Controlling the lives of everyone in the family from a long distance, like he held a remote control for people. "You come to America first, then we arrange everything," was how Lalu had started it.

After landing in Chicago Francis found out he was expected to apply for a Green Card at the earliest chance. Instead, Francis wanted nothing to do with America. Just go back to India.

"Well, in that case you better start making money for the plane fare then." Lalu actually said that. Francis fumed. Is this why Francis had obeyed his old mother? To work like a slave, and make wages for his own return ticket?

True, for a whole year, Lalu had exhorted. "As soon as you come here, we'll start papers for green card." Francis saw little reason to leave India other than see his daughter. Lalu used money, goodwill, and lawyers to bring him, Francis, to the US. If only on a temporary visa. "First you get here, then we get green card," became Lalu's mantra.

"Green card, yellow card. Humph.. just go see your daughter at least once," mother Ganesh said to her Christian son.

"You and America might agree with each other," said his bedridden father. "After all, they are a Christian country and you are a Christian now." The senior Ganesh was ever the positive-minded person.

"Your little brother works so hard for all of us," had been a refrain for as long as Francis could remember. Then came the pleas 'go see your daughter.' And lately, the entire clan added a new slogan,"Why aren't you in America too?" Even the street urchins in the village broke into a sing-song whenever he passed, *"Francis Phani unkkle - Going to Amme-Rikkaa."* It was set to the tune of a different Bollywood movie melody each time the urchins sang. W*ho told the cursed ugly snots?*

Phani Ganesh, aka Fakhruddin, aka Francis Ganesh, eventually spoke just two words, "Yes, okay." Let Lalu arrange for papers and plane ticket.

So now, this place called *Khana-Khazana* in Chicago.

****

Food, food, food - twenty-four hours a day - food was for sale. Customers of all sorts - Indians, Pakistanis, Nepalis, Bangladeshis, vegetarians. Even Africans came to eat! And white people too. All sorts of foods to all sorts of people.

Food, food, food, all the time. Except during *Ramzan*, when festive crowds thronged mainly after sunset, including curious Americans. Khana Khazana did not just serve food, but it also sold the groceries needed to make the foods at home. Endless arrays of shelves loaded with Pan-Asian food stuffs. Even crazier, diners ordered so much food they took home containers filled with their own leftovers.

Francis found it amazing that all the activity took place in just one building. It was unreal, magical, like the cave of Ali Baba or a film studio. Maybe it's a foolish dream. During work hours, though, it sure felt like a nightmare which he prayed would end. Maybe just as soon as he reached the goal of five thousand dollars. A goal his little brother set for him.

***

Not being located on the main strip of Devon Avenue turned out to be an advantage, Khana Khazana grew rapidly and became a hangout for night people. Cabbies, teenagers, those who slept by day, and students from a nearby college campus - all loved it. Being a couple blocks away from the main drag freed it from thick traffic. It made Khana Khazana unique in Little India - you could park near it. One of the things Francis discovered soon after coming to America was that Indians won't go any place that didn't offer free parking.

Francis Ganesh learned too, that Khana Khazana not only raked in a lot of money, it also paid out a lot in salaries. Workers came and went at all odd hours. One word from his brother Lalu Ganesh was all it took. "You can start working right now," Ali Bhai, the owner of Khazana said at once, at their first meeting. Francis was shocked. His younger brother really could make the universe run in Chicago!

Another thing that Francis found was that Ali Bhai liked to pay some workers in cash directly. No worries about taxes, tips, or pay stubs. Other eateries did that too, but Khazana remunerated better. His own acrobatics as a cleaner of dining tables, were matched by his growing appetite for work hours and dollars. But fact remained, that in America *you worked like a donkey to get rich like Ali Baba.*

Gita's father realized something else. It's a lot better to be a cash-paid donkey in America than be a beaten-to-death real life donkey back in India. A real donkey back home would be carrying a washerman's load to the Laundry Ghats on the banks of the river *Musi.* Maybe eat a bit of straw. Back home, donkeys didn't make dollars. Oh well, some dogs eat better than others, men working like donkeys ate best. They even get to fly in an airplane.

Francis Ganesh suddenly found himself standing by the kitchen sink, nodding his head, his lips moving, and his jaw twitching. He stopped himself short and looked around. The Mexican boy was nowhere to be found. But, the wizard of the chopping knife, Castillo the Filipino cook, was looking at him curiously, and then he began to grin.

Francis felt his face burning, ears ringing. He fled to the dining floor at once. The sight of a large table full of dirty dishes and cutlery settled him. He began to 'bus the table' with bare hands and felt a feeling of calmness come over him.

Francis and Castillo

Francis lowered his sinewy frame slowly into a folding chair at a shabby table in a corner of the storage area. He knew that the business of Khana Khazana would keep going, with late night patrons, but his own shift ended. He wiped his face with some paper towels pulled off a roll that sat upright on the table, and leaned back against the paneled back wall, took some deep breaths, his cheeks puffing, and blew air out. The last westbound city bus would arrive in half an hour. Francis wanted to be on it. To go home to his daughter's apartment for a good long sleep.

He took a folded piece of paper from his pants pocket, laid it on the table, and smoothed it out. He was looking for the pencil he alway carried when Castillo, the junior cook, approached the table wiping hands on a towel slung over shoulder. Castillo dragged a metal chair over to the table, its legs scraping over the rough cement floor, sat down and slowly cracked his neck.

Francis wished to be alone, but couldn't really object. Everybody who worked at Khazana used that table at some point, often to rest their feet in the middle of a long shift. That corner of the storage area was almost like a break room. He took in Castillo's smooth round face, scrubbed and wiped clean, with little hair, no beard to speak of. Just wispy short sideburns. *This fellow grins like a baby angel, but the way he wields a knife!* Francis felt a thump in his chest as the image flashed across his mind, of veggies being handled by Castillo, the knife a mere blur.

"So you finally sit down, huh, circus man. Watchu writing?" Castillo asked, leaning over the table. Francis saw spittle parked at the corners of Castillo's mouth as he spoke and recalled how Castillo's jaw rarely moved sideways when chewing food. *Strange fellow.* The cook craned his neck to look closely at the paper that lay on the table between them.

“Writing down my work hours,” Francis said without looking up.

“You write them down on your own paper? You don’t write them in the book kept on Ali Bhai’s desk?” Castillo asked.

“I write both places.” Though he was quite tired, Francis tried not to show his annoyance at the unwelcome intrusion. He knew the Filipino cook to be a talkative and noisy fellow, mouth clattering khut khut khut, sounding just like a knife on a chopping board. Francis had never gotten over his early unease with Castillo. Now, with the fellow sitting so close, he felt unnerved, and his nose itched.

“Let me see that,” Castillo reached out.

Francis remained calm, and let the cook pick up the paper and look at it. The Filipino gasped and his eyes widened, “You worked all these hours, circus man? Where do you find the time?”

“I find time.”

“Never seen anything like this, Francis,” Castillo said after a while. He shook his head. “Your numbers look so neatly written. So perfect, man. How you manage to write like that?”

Francis gave a tiny smile but said nothing. He knew his written numbers looked pretty, but he let the other fellow say it out loud. “Man, these numbers look like they were printed by a typing machine, not handwritten,” Castillo spoke slowly. Francis remained silent.

“Hey, Chico check this out,” Castillo called the Mexican

dishwasher over. "Ever seen such writing?" Young Chico came over to look, gave a low whistle, and shook his head a couple of times. He smiled at Francis and walked away without saying anything.

Francis knew from experience that Castillo was just the latest person to be impressed by his hand-entry of numbers. He has always had a steady hand, and taken lessons in pencil-drawing in Middle School. His teachers praised him, and said he could become a painter, maybe earn money creating colorful cinema posters and billboards. But, god planned differently. Now, Francis Ganesh, the busboy-donkey, sat in the dingy storage area, amidst stacks of bags of rice, flour, pulses, and pungent spices. His handiwork reflected in Castillo's round eyeglasses, the cook still mesmerized.

Impressive columns of numbers. Date, time in, time out, hours worked. The columns of numbers didn't zig-zag at all. The numbers of each entry were placed precisely beneath the ones above. The lines of entries went straight across, without going up and down like waves. The columns were so regular, even the spaces separating hours and minutes fell in line. *They could drop a plumb line on my decimal points!* The paper was not lined or ruled. Yet, Francis's entries looked like columns of soldiers on a parade ground. Solid figures in a neat order with no break in the ranks.

Francis smiled, eventually. He was pleased, both because of how much Castillo was impressed by his penmanship, as well as by the buggy-eyed shock on the Filipino's face at the number of hours worked. He waited for Castillo to say something, ask questions, perhaps. Francis could tell him stories. But not tonight. Tonight Francis was tired and wished to go home and sleep.

Castillo handed the paper back to Francis, saying "You're

something else bro. You should work in an office. Maybe a bookkeeper or something like that."

Francis found his discomfort with the chopping man easing. *Not a bad fellow.* "How many kids you having Castillo?" he asked the cook.

"No children. Maybe next year, or two years. My wife says we buy a house first, then have the baby." Castillo added with a chuckle, "Can't have a baby living in a studio apartment." Francis nodded.

"What about you Mr. Francis, you making all this money to buy yourself a nice house?"

Francis remained quiet. What was he going to say? There was nothing to say. *Does a donkey care why it's carrying the loads?* And then there was this. In less than half-an-hour this Castillo fellow went suddenly from calling him circus man to brother, and then from just Francis to Mr. Francis. Maybe, he is a good boy after all. Anybody younger than him was a boy or child to Francis. *So few Americans really knew how to respect old people.* His bus wouldn't arrive for a while. A short chat with this boy is good, to pass the time before going out into the cold.

"No Castillo, I am not going to buy a house," said Francis. "I am going to New York next month." That was all Francis wished to say. But even that little answer seems to set the fellow off and launch a praise of New York City. How it glittered at night, how colorful life there was, the hustle and bustle, pulsing with activities at all times of the day. "You know, Mr. Francis, they call it the city that never sleeps."

Francis listened attentively, nodding occasionally, his own face showing no emotion or interest. He was also careful to not reveal his newly found sense of ease and comfort with the junior cook. In spite of it all, his nose itched again as images flashed in his mind, briefly, of vegetables under Castillo's bent fingers.

"So, Mrs. Castillo hails from New York?" Francis asked. The cook replied, "Upstate." Whatever that meant, Francis didn't care. He only wished to hear about traveling within the city. He asked Castillo about it. "Oh, yeah. Kimi has a big family and some of her cousins live in the city. We stay with them," said Castillo. Followed by another monologue about the trains and how one got around using the subway, the buses, etc.

By the time they left Khana Khazana, and Costello walked him to the bus stop, it was too late. Francis missed the bus. The Filipino insisted on giving him a ride home. "It's all my fault, sir," said the boy. "I kept admiring your penmanship and made you late. No problem for me..."

Francis was pleased by Castillo's politeness. Even more so when Castillo told him, "You did a double shift, Francis, so just relax and rest. I'll wake you when we get to your daughter's place." But, relax, is not what Francis wanted. He just found a fellow who was knowledgeable about things of value. New York city's airports, how people changed flights, went from domestic to international terminals, and vice versa. And many such questions that Francis wanted answered. Castillo will know all the details, and Francis would stay awake and listen. The many questions that Francis couldn't ask his brother Lalu, or that young policeman Warangal. And definitely not that noisy Kumar fellow.

Castillo was the answer to all of his questions.

Gita cooks a meal

Francis opened and closed cupboards at random. Now the door under the sink, now the one holding coffee cups and saucers, now the one that held the spice jars. So many *shelphs*, so much space. For one little girl who was not even married. Back in his own parents house, there was a single rickety light-wood *shelph,* from which the condiment containers threatened to tumble down. Francis shook his head for the hundredth time at the depravity of it all. People craved to come to this country just to own space.

He watched his daughter flit about the kitchen. She moved quite gracefully, he thought. Reaching methodically for the bottles and jars, she placed different-sized piles of seasoning material on a wooden board the size of a banana leaf. Oil heated up and began to fume in a large pan on a rear burner of the stove. Gita was preparing the mixture of spices for a *turnover.*

The way the free end of the sari went around one arm twice, and held at an angle. The way the end of her braid was folded back up her neck held with one silvery hair clip, and the way she glided across the kitchen, like one in total command. Francis smiled. It was like looking at own mother, as he remembered his younger years when he used to be home a lot.

Francis shook his head to loosen the grip of memories, went over to the hallway closet and pushed the door open. The bi-fold slid open on its track., Francis looked all around the inside of it, more space, when all those clothes could be put into one nice bundle. He began another round of inspection of the kitchen cupboards. In no particular order.

"Oh, please, ayya. Kindly, sit and rest. This is a big meal I am making." Her voice was sweet, as always. Francis liked that part of his daughter. But, his little girl, who learned to read and write under his tutelage, now acted like a know-all, just because she lived in America. The little girl, who they said wouldn't stop crying whenever her father was not home, now ruled the roost, like she was in-charge of life itself. It was all due to that little brother of his. Francis heard, rather than felt, the sound of his own teeth grinding, but it was her voice that jolted him back to the present.

Gita was saying. "We will have at least four more people. I don't know how many will come with Lalu uncle. I have a lot of things to do. Here, have some chai." Again, Gita was so calm. Francis was impressed and irritated at the same time.

"Are you making okra and cauliflower, daughter?" he asked.

"No, ayya. it will be brinjals today. Americans call it eggplant. Funny name, isn't it. Instead of the long and slender type, I bought the fat bulbous type. I am stuffing them with a mixture of lentil powder and curry paste," she turned to smile at him. "I put onion and crushed sesame, just as you like it, ayya."

Snort. "Daughter, you know that I really like potatoes and peas mixed with coriander. Eggplant, you are making for someone else." He put a little extra something into his voice on *someone else*.

Gita didn't respond. She had just 'turned over' the heated spice mixture into the cooked cauliflower, and the burst of steamy, spice-vapor might have been what caused her face to turn away and tear. He coughed too, more vigorously than he needed to, but Gita didn't turn to look.

He saw her move things along. She dropped fragments of saffron into the boiling basmati rice, stirred once, sniffed the aroma, and covered it with a heavy lid. After turning down the heat under the rice, she moved to the other burner and dumped a vegetable mix into a boiling pot of crushed-lentils-in-tamarind water. Stirred the mixture, set it on medium, and covered it.

Francis thought about what his daughter said earlier, about the number of people coming to dine. It will be crowded, where will they sit? He had already noticed something silly about Indian families in America. They owned giant-sized dining tables, but used it only to park the food they cooked. People themselves didn't sit at the table, but instead spread themselves around, and sat everywhere. Some people ate with the dinner plate in their laps. He shook his head again.

Gita was busy with the eggplants, slicing them deeply from the fat end, until they were held just by the meaty part near the stalk. The brinjals splayed and looked like four-legged stools. She stuffed them with a mixture of roasted, sweetened lentil powder, spices and onions. Tied up with string to hold it all together, the plumped up brinjals looked like strange pregnant beings laid out in the wide pan of a hospital ward. Gita filled the space between the beds with curry leaves, crushed peas and chopped onions. The ladle-full of mustard oil began to heat up, and Gita turned the eggplants over every few minutes.

Francis, watching it all, said, "Daughter, you set them up to look like the long rows of seats on an airplane." She smiled distractedly. Francis kept looking at the eggplants as they were rolled over, heated, and browned.

Taking a last sip of chai, Francis set the mug in the sink, and went back to his chair to brood. It was Kumar who irked him most. Always chatting, abruptly switching to meaningless bursts of smart talk, and absurd cackles. The Kumar fellow was insolent. Francis could deal with that. But, what he could not grasp at all, was the quietness of the young policeman they called Wrangler. As if his real name Warangal was not good enough. The word was good enough for a great city and a great Indian kingdom. But this boy comes to America and immediately the word Warangal is twisted into Wrangler. Silly, isn't it, and so irritating. Something else about the young man bothered Francis. An indifference toward Francis, avoiding talking to Francis, the older brother of Lalu. It was bad arrogance. No respect for the elders. *Police or not, that Warangal boy has no manners.* Francis felt quiet anger welling in him.

When the guests finally arrived, Francis noticed that there was no end to Shetty gushing over the food. The lanky right hand man was just like a headmaster or inspector. He peeked under every lid, and poked every dish with a ladle. Some he stirred, others he inhaled the aroma. He turned the chunky sambar with the ladle a few times. Shetty praised everything. *All too familiar in my daughter's house.* "Gita, Gita. This is fantastic. Super." Will he clap his hands like a child?

Francis was still thinking of saying something when Shetty took charge, and began carrying the food dishes to the dining table. He also laid out the condiments, napkins, spoons etc., and put ice in a big jug of water. *Like he probably done before.* Gita acted as if all that were quite natural. When Shetty turned the exhaust fan over the range to the ON position, it was Gita's turn to gush. "Thank you, thank you. I totally forgot, big-brother." She smiled, *Like she got a birthday present or something.* Francis frowned, why would his brother employ anyone named Shetty?

They loaded up their dinner plates with Gita's food and took seats, to partake of it. His brother sat at a small wooden side table. Shetty and Warangal were seated on the long couch, with their dinner plates on tray stands his daughter placed in front of them. Francis seated himself on a wobbly three-legged stool in a corner. Holding the plate in his wide left palm, he mixed the food with his right and ate. He was careful to not spill a single grain of rice. His daughter took her plate to the far end of the kitchen counter, bent over it, and ate with a spoon, adding seasoning to each item as she went.

What really got Francis most was Kumar. He ensconced himself in the only comfortable piece of furniture, an over-sized, over-stuffed, fake-leather, single sofa. Its footrest was out and Kumar looked very comfortable, with a large plate of food in his lap, a fork in one hand and a beer in the other. He didn't move at all, and let Gita ply him with seconds.

Lalu said little, except to Gita. He was giving her tips on cooking. It's a good idea to toast sesame seeds lightly before grinding them. Use mustard oil when you can. She should try stuffing green bell peppers just like she did the eggplants, but go around with the thread a couple of times. Otherwise the peppers give way. Be generous with the channa atta. Make the gravy thicker. Use tomato juice, just squeeze the whole tomato with your fist. Gita looked attentive and nodded at everything her uncle said. And, when Lalu sat back down at his little table, Gita brought only to him, a saucer laden with sweets. Others got up and served themselves. *What, she couldn't bring one for her own father?* Francis forced himself to say nothing.

Decision

Francis Ganesh watched his younger brother reach into his satchel and pull out a folder. "Your return ticket, Francis. Decide on the date you want to leave, I will call the airline and confirm your seat." He placed it on the kitchen counter and gave it a push toward Francis. Like, that was that.

Oh, that travel agent talk again. Yes, return ticket all paid and ready. Yes, just fix the date....ugh. It was the third time in two weeks that his little brother, born some seven years after himself, and master of everything America, dispensed travel advice.

He picked up the folder and studied the flight timings, how long it would take, and if it was any different than the time it took to come to America. Francis knew his time in America ended when he refused to file papers for a green card. He knew when he left the village that his US stay will be a short one. He *had to* experience America, to see with his own eyes how his people lived, see how his daughter lived away from him. Sure enough, they all looked rich, but lived with empty spaces everywhere: cupboards, closets, hallways. But the space was not empty, they filled it with junk. American junk for the working class Indians, and made-in-India junk for rich Indians who could afford expensive imports.

Whatever. The one thing Francis knew for sure was, Indians worked hard in America. Like donkeys that carried loads of washing. Or, dirty dishes. Some donkeys carried loads of curries, or cooked curries for others to eat. Francis had seen enough, Indians lived like beasts of burden. That Kumar fellow, he was a donkey too. Except, he carried no load, he only brayed.

"Coffee is ready." It was his daughter's voice.

****

"I should get on the plane in Chicago only?" Francis asked, directed at no specific person in the group - his daughter's group. He was still looking over the folder. Getting no response from anybody, he said, "I want to go to New York City first, and from there take a plane to India."

Lalu shook his head, "Why Francis? You already have a ticket from Chicago, why change it?"

His daughter chimed in, "Ayya, I wish you to stay. But, if you must go, leave from here. I will have so many gifts for you to take. Load your luggage right here, without worrying about transferring it."

Lalu was still shaking his head slowly, when Warangal piped up. "Francis uncle, just because the map shows New York is nearer to India than Chicago, doesn't mean it will cost less. You actually will pay more money. For the second flight between Chicago and New York."

Francis offered no immediate response. His daughter said through sniffles, "Ayya, keep the direct flight, don't change it. Actually change it all, cancel all of it. Just stay in America with me." Francis made like a nod, but said nothing.

Shetty spoke up, "Phani, sorry, Francis, my brother. That is almost twenty thousand rupees," Shetty spread both up-held palms, open and closed twice. "All that unnecessary spending. Think of things you can buy for our old uncle and auntie," referring to the elder Ganeshs. Francis noticed the waiter fellow's slip up with his own name, but forgave it, since it was corrected quickly. *Phani is now Francis. Phani is not Fakhri either, keep it in your head, you donkey cook.*

He took in Shetty's figure, neck askew with that habitual head tilt of his, leaning against a wall next to a window. A bony man, a pretend-cook, standing next to a radiator which pretended to heat the room. Pathetic. Pathetic heating device, pathetic waiter, pathetic donkeys all.

The silly lean man was still talking, “Think brother, twenty thousand rupees. You worked very hard for it. Why throw it into a drain?”

But, Francis was not okay with cheap advice from people who know nothing. Nothing at all about Francis. That’s right. It’s my money and I will do what I want with it. Yes, down the drain even, if I wish it.

Not unexpectedly, Kumar the wise, spoke up, much to Francis’s annoyance. Said Kumar, “Francis sir, you made a lot of money at Khana Khazana. Hold on to it and enjoy the convenience of a direct flight...” To which, the others didn’t show any outer sign of agreement. Even though they only looked impassive, Phani knew they all thought the same as Kumar.

Shetty spoke lowly, “New York is a confusing place, brother. You have to go from one airport to another. You have to take buses, maybe a train if the buses fail. You could even miss your flight to India. Lots of problems.” Shetty sat back like there was nothing more to say.

Warangal looked to Francis like he was resisting saying something. But, when Francis stared hard at him, the younger man relented. “New York buses and trains can be dangerous, Phani uncle.” Pause, and a slow resumption, “That’s what people say. But, maybe not for you, hehehe. You’re a tough guy.” It was not amusing to Francis.

His own idea was good and no one rejected it outright. Francis continued to say that he wanted to take a connecting flight through New York. Connecting Flight - something he learned about recently, and unlike other travel terms like standby or confirmed booking, he spoke the words connecting flight with authority.

Francis looked around, but didn't focus on anybody in particular. He gazed at one person and then another. He felt his mind drifting too. He knew vaguely that others were looking at him. He worked to bare his teeth and twist his lips into a smile. *There, I showed them how happy the idea of New York makes me...*

"I want to tell people that I was in New York City." He now grinned fully. "I came all the way to America, I should see New York."

The ensuing long silence was pierced by only one thing. His brother Lalu laughed, chortled, and almost choked on his coffee. Once recovered, Lalu wouldn't stop laughing.

Francis departs

Lalu said to me, "Hey Kumar, let's go drop off Francis. You received him at the airport about two months ago, now join us in sending him off." Well, what was I going to say? Deny my friend some relief from the stress he has been under? Naw. I couldn't do that. So, I went. It so happened that Warangal went too.

In his infinite wisdom, Lalu chose a remote parking lot. It was already decided that Francis wouldn't be dropped off at the curb and left to his own devices, but that we would all go with him into the terminal. Get him checked in, assist in the preflight formalities, and enjoy an extended farewell. So, it made sense to park for cheap. But, did it have to be this far away? O'Hare Airport provided several parking lots, from which folks could ride a small train to any of the airline terminals. But it turned out Lalu chose a lot even farther away, and it didn't have direct access to the tram. As if he read my mind, Lalu said, "Closer parking is a lot of money, Kumar. Twenty-five dollars for just one hour." He was right, of course. By the time it was all done and over with, we could be looking at a pair of Benjamins. The remote lot we entered probably cost a small fraction of that. Still, I couldn't resist a bit of ribbing.

"Are you sure we are at the airport, Lalu? I don't see any planes." He didn't respond, and quietly drove through the wide aisles looking for an open slot.

"I can hear the planes, sound is everywhere," said Francis. It provoked a chuckle from Lalu, "See, Kumar, just proves there is an airport nearby. Aha, here is a spot, our lucky moment." Lalu backed the car into a well-lighted empty spot, and we all got out. I helped get the bags out of the trunk. I carried the smaller duffel while a quiet Warangal handled the heavier pull along suitcase.

"From here we take a shuttle bus to the train," Lalu said to no one in particular, and led us to a nearby bus shelter. In no time, the free bus came along to take us on a little winding route, picking up more travelers along the way. Gita and Francis sat together on the bus, and Lalu gestured for the rest of us to sit a few seats away. The extended farewell began in earnest.

Gita was quiet throughout the day, in a way that was not like her. Since her father announced his intention to return to India, they spoke very little. His decision was a big disappointment to her. I spent a lot of time with the Ganesh family the few days prior to Francis's departure, and in all that time I did not once see Gita smile. She carried on with talk of cooking and recipes in a lively fashion. But today, all day long, she spoke only perfunctorily, short phrases like, "lunch is ready," or "who wants coffee?" Not directing anything at any specific person, and never addressing her father at all.

Lalu and I sat a few rows back and watched Gita and Francis whispering, Francis shaking his head, Gita sniffling. Her head rested on his shoulder. Warangal sat apart from us and stared out the window quietly, as if he took a vow of silence. I wondered a few times during the previous week if the young policeman found Francis intimidating. And, if he did, could it be due to the difference in their ages. But, Francis was a peasant and Warangal a metro policeman. No, something else subdued Warangal in the presence of Francis. I couldn't imagine what that could be. I should have spent more time worrying about it, but I didn't. Looking back, that was the most foolish lack of curiosity I suffered during the entire affair.

Our parking lot mini-bus pulled up at the terminus where we would board the people mover system. I rose and walked to the exit. Gita was wiping her face and straightening her hair. Francis's hands were lifted up slightly, raised in his lap, and palms open, like he were holding an imaginary book.

We made our way to the tram and boarded the lead car. “This train is completely automatic, isn’t it,” said Warangal, the first words he spoke all afternoon. “Nobody driving it.”

Lalu grinned at him, “Yes, yes. Just like you officer, it’s run by auto-pilot.”

Gita turned to her father and said, “I rode on this before, ayya. This train is like magic. Opens and closes doors like it is on a clock, but nobody driving it.” She perked up, pointing to the runways, car lots, and planes taxiing. Her efforts were impressive. Fighting sadness, seeking moments of lightness, finding cheery things to say. She was composed enough now to call her father ayya again. But her father, he was not there at all.

A family of four boarded the tram at the same time as we did, and two screaming kids were looking out the front window as the vehicle rolled. The little boy made choo-choo sounds, and made believe he was driving it; his little sister grinned, clapped, or picked her nose. I noticed Francis nod and smile at the kids.

A mellow voice from the overhead speaker announced Terminal Number Two and the names of airlines that had gates there. Our group filed out, with me bringing up the rear. “Bye, bye” trilled the two children behind us. Gita turned and waved with a smile. Her eyes were reddening already. We accompanied Francis to the check-in area, where I stood a short distance away, and watched the crawling line carry Francis forward through a maze of stanchions.

Warangal seems to have found his voice again, “Mr. Kumar, this whole thing is crazy, him changing planes in New York.

He will get lost over there." I shrugged, there has been enough talk about that already, I let it pass. But Warangal's show of concern was interesting. I tried to recall if he had voiced a strong opinion during dinner the previous weekend at Gita's apartment, when the rest of us tried to get Francis to fly to India direct from Chicago. My recollection was that Warangal was silent much of that evening too. He and Gita were exchanging looks during dinner. I thought both were resisting the urge to roll eyes whenever Francis opined goofy ideas, such as the need to reduce 'time in the seat.' Or, wanting to see New York City's lighted skyline, if only from the sky. Warangal's concern now seemed genuine. Maybe, he found some courage with Francis's departure close on hand. Francis received a boarding pass, and the Ganeshs huddled together. Lalu talked animatedly, Francis nodded slowly, and Gita looked from one to the other, dabbing her eyes. Warangal and I stood apart and talked quietly about the weather, and then shook hands with Gita's father wishing him a safe trip. As he went past the checkpoint and looked back to wave, I thought back to my younger years.

Going to the airport or train station was a big event back then, almost like a festival. We not only dressed up to celebrate the event, we remembered it for days to come. There was a sense of romance to places of transportation, and we drank of it fully. We observed all that went on around us, and long after departure time, we lingered, or rather malingered. That habit found its pluses in my later life due to Chicago's capricious weather. Flights got canceled abruptly, or returned to the gate after the so-called departure. Just because Francis disappeared into the crowd past the magnetometer, we couldn't assume his plane took off. A storm of some sort was moving in from the north.

So we did malinger, and watched the flight notation go off the information board. That's when I said, "Okay let's go home."

Lalu offered to drop me off and I accepted. Gita remained tearful, Warangal remained grim-faced, and I struggled to keep the conversation alive. It was an emotional situation for all of us. In that sea of turbulence, a little bit of my imagination died, but I didn't know it. It would be months before I realized what that entailed.

Francis in New York

His wheeled suitcase trailed behind him. Pulled by the short strap of a leash, it wobbled like a reluctant, overloaded donkey. He saw that there was only one solitary agent behind the ticket counter at the Air India check-in. A North Indian woman in a Punjabi outfit.

Francis thrust his ticket folder at her. The lady looked questioningly at first, but took it after a few moments. Francis had an idea about what she'd say, but wasn't exactly sure what she'd *do.*

The lady looked at her wrist watch, studied her computer, and then peered down the concourse toward the security inspection area. She shook her head. Francis met her gaze straight on, as she gave a short rapid speech. He didn't follow her, except for the words sorry, late, door, sir. But, he needed to engage this lady somehow. He continued staring at her. She spoke slowly now. Francis put on a confused face, and said: home, Hyderabad.

She tried again, even more slowly. A halting explanation, with her head tilted, palms open, and speaking one word at a time. Francis repeated the words he recognized; late, gate, doors. He was not surprised that there were no other Indian ticket agents since he arrived quite late. He knew he was going to miss the flight. But right now, he should get her to make some arrangements for him. Costello said it could be done. Francis must make her pity him, somehow. But, his English was not good enough to tell her what he precisely wanted. *I need this woman to give me another ticket.*

The lady adjusted her kameez, pulled the sleeve back, Francis knew she could not figure out exactly which Indian dialect he spoke. She switched to gestures and signs. She pointed to her own wrist watch while shaking her head and then moved her palms like parting and coming together of curtains. She tapped her index finger next to the departure time, and handed the folder back to him.

Francis stood looking confused, staring alternately between the unattended ticket counters and the north Indian lady's soft round face. He pushed the ticket folder toward her again, like she should do something with it. But there was only frustration: sighing, tapping her pen on the counter, fiddling with papers. *But, she didn't walk away... wants to help me..* He hoped he cut a sorry figure, standing alone in the vast terminal area, while other passengers were already at security and passport control. Crews began taking down the maze of stanchions around him.

The airline lady tried another round of words and gestures, and Francis responded with a gesture of his own, using hand movements he learned in Old Hyderabad. He shook his right hand, only thumb and pinkie extended, the middle three fingers slightly bent over the palm. To an American it might look like Francis was sliding his hand on an air guitar. But she, an Indian, would know that classic Indian gesture of a question - what, why, where, when? One gesture, many questions: *She must know that!*

The ticket lady made some calls. She looked from Francis to her own watch, to the computer. In between, she glanced at the ticket Francis held out. When done, she set the phone down and shook her head with a finality. Francis stood there and kept staring at his ticket folder. He spotted an Indian fellow, one of many who were at the airport to bid farewell to family members, and beckoned him. The ticket lady and the stranger exchanged some rapid fire dialog in English. When it ended, the stranger turned to Francis and spoke, like a father to a child.

Francis found himself at the receiving end of a mixture of several Indian languages: Hindi, Urdu, Tamil. Gujarati, Oriya, and god knows what else. But the man spouted a lot more words familiar to Francis than the lady. Francis understood some of the words and repeated them. Departure, push back, gate, takeoff. The man looked pleased.

Francis let hopefulness show on his own face, not ready to smile yet. The other Indian man repeated the explanation, now using some of the same hand gestures as the ticket agent. Francis couldn't get on the plane. Plane's doors close soon. Even if a boarding pass is issued now, the fellow seemed to say, Francis wouldn't make it through security in time.

Just as I thought...

But, there was one other thing which he needed to get done. He stared unblinkingly at the ticket agent, pawing his luggage and chewing his lip. The ticket agent stopped tapping her pen on the counter, looked at Francis, and declared, "I am re-booking you for a flight to Hyderabad. Um, just a sec." Finally, she said it. *Re-booking,* the one word Francis understood quite well, thanks to Costello.

The ticket woman picked up the phone again and spoke in a more sedate voice, in a mixture of English, Urdu and Punjabi. With a lot of laughter and rolling of the eyes. Francis showed gladness on his face as the woman and her keyboard each made noises of their own. Finally, she said, "Okay, we got it. But, your flight is not until the day after tomorrow, confirmed seat. You can come tomorrow and try, you'll be standby." The lady gave a big sigh. Francis had an idea what it all meant, but let the other Indian man explain. The man looked very pleased, *like he himself had issued the ticket...*

Francis took the paperwork handed by the lady and said "Thank you" with a slight bow. That seemed to please the Punjabi lady. She said gently, "Sorry for the problems you are having, but you'll be heading home soon." And then she added quickly, "Oh, here, this might help, 50% off a hotel room near the airport. You pay only half," she handed him a large green flier. It had giant-sized numerals five-zero on one side, and a list of names on the other. "You'll be home soon Sir," a quick plastic smile flashed on her face, and then she disappeared behind a door panel.

Francis felt his heart beat fast, but he was pleased and felt in control. He gripped his ticket folder firmly and left the area immediately, practically dragging the groaning donkey behind him. He went quickly down to the ground transportation area, feeling a lightness in his step and a warmth in his palms. The hotel coupon got crumpled and absently stuffed into a pant pocket. In the New York chill outside the terminal building, Francis located the bus he heeded and boarded it.

Not bad for a fellow doing all this for the first time. Going from one New York airport to another turned out to be easy. That Kumar fellow made it sound like a complicated process. But, it was Castillo who really knew how airports worked. *Everything worked just like Castillo had explained a few days earlier.*

The shuttle bus sped toward Laguardia Airport. Francis felt an occasional thud in his chest. His skin began to heat up and his whole body shook all of a sudden. He rested his water bottle between his thighs, closed his eyes, ran imaginary prayer beads through his fingers, and mumbled a series of incantations to force his mind to slow down.

****

Two Days Later.

Francis, aka Fakir-ud-din, aka Phani Ganesh, exited flight 2017 from Chicago, and joined the river of humanity flowing through the concourses of New York's Laguardia Airport. He carried a small worn suitcase by its handle, and wended his way to the level of ground transportation. That area was also crowded with travelers, greeters and airport workers. Francis's ears hurt from the plane ride, now compounded by the noise of announcements, rumbling luggage trolleys, and loud voices of people moving in every which direction, seemingly randomly. The area smelled of sweat, oil and food odors. He walked past a set of baggage belts, car rental desks and an information kiosk. He found the food court, and proceeded to the only familiar eatery - one with the ever bright yellow letter M.

He bought french fries, a cup of yogurt, and a large coffee. He also requested four creamer cups and three sugar packets. He sat in a corner and consumed the food quickly. All around him, people milled about, shouting greetings amidst a lot of hugging.

The atmosphere was oppressive, but he tried to spend some time regaining calmness. He felt an ancient urge to buy cigarettes but fought it off. America as a whole seems to have given up on smoking, even frowned upon it. He remembered the days when Indians traveling abroad was a new thing, and everybody wrote home about how cheap cigarettes and newspapers were in 'The States'. But, he now saw with his own two eyes that things were different. Nobody in America smoked or read. But they ate. Yes, Americans ate food all the time, everywhere. At home, in restaurants, in movie theaters, in parks, in their backyards. Not only that, they spent huge amounts of money at grocery stores. And on top of it all,

Americans ordered food in restaurants to bring home and eat, or even had it delivered to the house. All that eating made them fat, ugly and misshapen.

With his belly full, a warm feeling come over him, he leaned back and closed his eyes and breathed drowsily. He ran his hands over his face and sat up abruptly. How did he look? Dirty, ratty, disheveled? He sniffed under his shirt, it was not too stinky. There won't be a way for him to take a real shower, not without spending precious dollars on a hotel room. These American airports were not like railway platforms back home, which often had a public water faucet, and a person could actually bathe village style, crouching under the spigot.

Francis dumped his empty food containers in a trash can in the washroom. He gave himself a sort of a wash, using liquid hand soap, and using up the paper towels in two dispensers. He took his shirt off, rinsed it out with some hand soap in a wash basin, and let it flutter for a few minutes under the hot-air hand dryer. He put the shirt back on while still wet. It was only two-thirty in the afternoon and there could be time later on for a more thorough cleanup before the final leg of his journey.

Going from one airport to the other in New York City was easier the second time around. He took a window seat on the shuttle bus with confidence. But, as soon as he sat, he felt different. His stomach tightened. Castillo has been right about everything so far. Things worked just as the Filipino cook had explained. The flights, the transfer between airports, getting a new ticket issued for two days later than the original date and so many other things.

Lalu wasn't the only smart man. That Filipino brother-man knew just as much, if not more about how things worked in America. But, in this strange country, things could still go wrong.

Francis wanted to be at the Air India counter quite early this time around. Make sure the re-booked ticket worked without any problem. He shivered at the thought of being stuck at JFK, not being able to board the plane.

****

End of Book of Phani

****

MAY, 2005

"Rough winds do shake the darling buds of May,
And summer's lease hath all too short a date:"

William Shakespeare, Sonnet 18., 1609

May box of mementos

The month of May did not start any better than April. In some ways it was worse. Instead of focusing on whatever was happening 'on the ground' to move the case along, I got caught in the swirls of the past. May turned out to be a month for *memmories.*

Since the day I set foot on American soil, there was this fascination with all things USA. Some stuck to me, many others peeled off. Country music was one that stuck like glue. There was a country lyric to suit every sad moment (just as there was, I found out, a rock lyric for every angry sentiment). There were nifty lines of country songs that could be seized on any given day, and over the years I suffered them all - songs that is, not sad moments.

The would-be writer in me, loved the emotive colors of country lyrics, their easy storytelling, and best of all how every singer pronounced the word memories with an extra drawl. *Memmories* became my touchstone to lingering pathos.

On that last day of April, I found myself in a state of contemplative idleness, as the small portable radio on the window sill played music station WCM, FM 93.7 - 'Chicago's exclusive country.' That station became a favorite source of music for me during daylight hours. (At night, I turned to the baleful, improvisational, wordless melodies of north Indian singers of *khyaal* music on my aging tape deck.)

Between sets of country songs the program host read some news items, and said "Finally Spring has sprung and there is warmth in the air." My little radio remained cool to touch and carried on with songs about the past. Randy Travis, an early favorite, came on, crooning laments.

"I am "diggin' up bones, I am diggin up bones;
Exhuming things that's better left alone."

How did Randy know what I was doing right then? There was this sense of love and loyalty to Gita. And then, my kitchen-challenged bachelor's gratitude for the hundreds of curry dishes cooked by her uncle. Dishes he made for the world, but I enjoyed more. The curry lingered and stirred memories in me. So, beyond curry, what was I digging for?

Gita Ganesh was not coming back into our lives. She went on to be re-born elsewhere, in a form unknowable to us. Unless, of course, she attained Nirvana. In her own lifetime she couldn't tell us what happened. And in her new life, she probably has no idea about Gita of Illinois.

The cycle of life demanded that memories, even those that country singers pronounced *memmories*, be compiled just one lifetime at a time. Hey there, you Soul, discard memory upon entering the next life. The wheel of life, death and rebirth rolled on as long as it didn't get a flat tire. Lalu and I should have known this business of karma instinctively, and moved on. But we couldn't. I certainly couldn't. Memmories clung to us.

We lived in America now. That meant that we must know everything. And, know everything as one long elaborate sequence, and in excruciating detail. The more there were things that we couldn't do anything about, the more we craved to know. After all, in America we *could* know everything. So, while cops focused on the present, I went the way of Randy Travis, diggin' up bones.

***

Cops had advised Lalu that Gita's apartment in Des Plaines,

Illinois, be kept available, unused, for future reference. It wasn't the scene of crime, nor a place to be staked out. It was a just-in-case type of suggestion, nothing official. That polite suggestion was enough for Lalu to not enter it in the weeks following news of her death. I understood his own personal reluctance.

So when, on that last day of April, Lalu called me up and said it was urgent that we go to Gita's apartment, I was more than willing. It was located in a suburb that adjoined Chicago, just a few miles west of Little India. Lalu wanted to pick some things to send to his parents in India. Truth be told, I was excited. To see her inner sanctum post-mortem. How will the space feel without her?

The building's super looked suspiciously at us. I explained why we were there. His demeanor changed instantly, "Oh, that poor thing. So sorry about that." He became solicitous, "Picking up some memorabilia, huh. Sure," he held the door for us.

For his part, Lalu said, "There are things her family should have. I know my niece purchased some special things to send them. Gifts from America." The super nodded, polite but incurious. I carried a sturdy corrugated cardboard box, the kind that food stores accumulate by the dozen. We went in.

The air was stale and oppressive, but I was beginning to feel pumped. Water and light connections were still on, as was gas. Lalu chose to not disconnect them when Gita's death first came to light. It was his way to stay connected to Gita. While her death remained unsolved, keeping the lights on was his slender link to someone gone, but not yet entirely let go.

The cardboard box filled up quickly. There was clothing - nice woolen suit material for Gita's favorite teacher back home;

three Japanese-made saris for an aunt; dresses for her niece Wasitha, a little girl still learning to play jump rope.

Lalu then pulled something from a glass-doored kitchen cupboard that caught my attention. It was a plastic replica of the Statue of Liberty about the size of my forearm. Its looks were modified. The sculpted folds of clothing on the statuette were painted to look like a sari. A bright vermilion dot was painted on Lady Liberty's forehead. And, a braid of hair was also painted on, and styled to curve over the left shoulder of the statue and come to rest on her chest, ending with a tiny pearl-like bead.

Miss Liberty looked like a sassy college girl in a typical Indian college town.

"Gita's handiwork," said Lalu flatly, as he wrapped the statuette in a pale blue silk scarf bearing a view of Chicago's skyline.

He Lalu placed more items in the box. Picture postcards of Grand Canyon, Lake Michigan and St. Louis Arch; tee shirts with pictures of Sears Tower, American flag, and Chicago sports teams.

I couldn't help but smile when I saw the last items he put in the box: a shiny round tin of Fancy airline-style smoky almonds, a bag of candy corn, a larger bag of chocolate kisses. All-American treats for villagers just peeking over the rim of their wretched no-longer third world.

We left the apartment after stopping by the super. "Please, keep an eye on the place, we'll be back some other time," Lalu told him. The man nodded okay, "Hope they catch the killer soon."

While Lalu seemed satisfied with our task, and the super

waved goodbye, I felt a desire to hang back. I began to feel the beginning of an itch to search through the entire apartment. Yes, I wanted to go diggin' up bones and exhume, what if anything, her death had buried.

***

We stopped at the post office to ship the box. Ever the organized person, Lalu had brought a satchel of supplies with him. Box sealing tape, thick tipped pen, white paper to serve as a label. He even thought to bring clear, wide sticky tape to protect the label!

Before the final sealing, Lalu pulled something out of the satchel. "Want to see?" he offered. A dozen prints of photos he had personally taken. Photos of Gita at work and play.

Gita blowing out multi-colored candles set into a yellow-frosted birthday cake.

Gita, sweaty and smiling, holding an enormous ladle, stirring some sort of bubbling liquid in a giant wide mouthed vessel.

Gita beaming into the camera, standing, seemingly at the edge of a precipice of some sort.

Gita dressed in the uniform of high class wait staff - black pants, white tails and a bow-tie - at some party, and bearing a platter of *hors d'oeuvres.*

Gita giggling, a hand partially covering her face, and showing only one eye through slitted fingers.

And then, the stunner of them all…

Gita in devotion. On her knees, bowing down, touching

forehead to the floor in front of a deity at the Hindu temple in suburban Illinois. She was dressed in full native Hindu garb, true right down to the flowers in hair, bangles shimmering. Her bare feet showing off the bright color of henna, and slender silver anklets. To my mind, at that moment, that photo of Gita carried echoes of the rapturous posture of a would-be bride seeking divine blessings.

It was a stack of happy memories. I should have smiled, but couldn't. My hands shook and my stomach tightened. I felt Lalu's hand patting my shoulder, and I let the pile of photos slip into the box. He sealed it, handed it over, and paid the clerk.

As we left the facility, I was struck by the oddity of the situation. Suddenly, it was Lalu doing the consoling. He looked lighter and more square in the shoulder. His face changed once the postal clerk took over the cardboard box. On the other hand, it was I that seemed to have grown heavy. In the glass pane of the window of the postal facility, my face looked dark, distorted, and unrecognizable. And I kept having the nagging sensation that a part of me stayed behind in Gita's apartment.

My friend came to me

"My friend came to me with sadness in his eyes."

That was the first line of a song written by George Harrison about sitarist Ravi Shankar, and sung by the Beatles at Concert for Bangladesh. I was in high school back then, and grew up watching the song become the anthem for a generation. That line rang in my ears the instant Warangal entered. I let his sadness be.

What could I do though? There he was, seated at my desk, at my place of business, and using my bandwidth of a T-1 connection. A massive change from his previous visit to my place. Yet, he avoided looking at me, looking me in the eye.

He sat unmoving, silent, barely tapping his fingers on the old wooden door set on saw horses which made for a table top. Just laid his palm flat on its recent coat of varnish, odor still lingering in air, while the desktop computer hummed its warmth.

Warangal, aka Wrangler, was evidently not yet a true cowboy, not yet a fearless American. Showing that special vulnerability that only a villager from rural south India living in a milieu of strangers could. All his sense of ease, and being at 'home in America' gone away. He began to sob, not looking up, not looking at me. As if, he suddenly remembered that he was the alien here.

The tall lean frame of a good policeman, his body was not quite deflated but nearly... What's that word? I couldn't quite think of it, but groping for the word yielded the image of a kid's toy, a thumb-push-figure made of beads and coils. One press of the bottom and the whole figure collapsed, and snapped back upright when let go. Warangal was like that push-up figure.

Somehow the bottom of the toy was pushed, and the wrangler fell off his horse, lost the lasso, and became a plain collapsed pile of pieces.

He eventually turned, even as knobby brown knuckles gripped the computer mouse tightly. I saw the cursor go wild, matching his own jerky movements.

"Am I on the right web page bro..ther?" he asked. I nodded.

His thin black lips that usually stayed curled in a permanent smile, now flattened out into a sliver of a crack on a granite face.

I remembered the fact that a luck in timing made Warangal a favored cadet at the training Academy. The Chicago Police Department had already committed itself to diversity. And, Warangal garnered plenty of goodwill. The rookie cop was greeted at the precinct with a barrage of questions about his schooling, ethnicity (not that it mattered, they all said,) and his name. Just like that, his new buddies decided that Warangal should be re-christened Wrangler. And that was that. The nickname even made it to the chalkboard roster behind the desk sergeant. He ceased to be Warangal.

"You the new guy, just come from Academy? Wrangler, right? Nice to meet you. I am..." So it went. Pretty soon even the Indian oldies who lived off Devon Avenue gave up their very familiar and comfortable words, Krishna and Warangal, and took to calling him *Opheesr Wrangulaar.* I used to sneer at things like that. But lately though, I've been more indulgent of my paisano's linguistic foibles in America.

"What are we going to do Mr. Kumar?" opheesr wrangular wailed from his perch near my deck. "All destroyed. All destroyed Mr. Kumar," he let go of the mouse and grabbed his head with both hands. And with his elbows on his knees, the convulsions spoke volumes.

I poured us some tea from the kettle, sipped mine some, and stared at him. Surprising, how much the death of Gita Ganesh moved him. And why? What was I getting myself into here? Maybe, I didn't know people as well as I thought?

Miss Agnes, my favorite tabby, and the unofficial mascot of *Wings of Desire*, jumped on to the computer table, advanced, stretched slowly across the keyboard, walked over Warangal's fingers. Her whiskers tested the static emanating off the boxy computer monitor. Then leaped onto the stony shoulders of the immobile man, mewled as if to say grow up guy, and hopped off. She moved with an elegance and true indifference that I envied right then.

I regarded the twenty-something Gita to be family. She was considered ready for marriage, and also to succeed her uncle, or fully go independent in catering. Unlike her fellow Indian sisters and brothers who were born and raised in the land of wealth, and lived in big mansions in the suburbs of Chicago, Gita kept a low profile. "You know Kumar uncle, I never heard this word suburb before, what is this burble burble?" Yes, that Gita, dead far from where she lived, and even farther from where home was. And somehow, *that death got Krishna Warangal all shook up.*

The Wrangler now straightened out some and stood up. But he was still agitated, like the inflatable tube man at a car dealership or some such cheesy consumer venues. Compressed air alternately filled and paused, with each shift of the valve. And the dancing puppet, its arms flailing, faltering and flailing again, beckoned passers by to come check out the used cars. Krishna Warangal's figure and gestures would have been comical were it not for the grief that rendered his face dark.

Lips pursed into a line as flat as his voice, and alarming in its fierce dejection. What was this tube puppet drawing attention to?

There was a tightness to my throat and neck. I was sympathetic to his pain, but then again, the weight on my neck may well have been the orange tabby. She jumped onto *my* shoulders and began to get comfortable. Seeming to whisper something her snout tickled my ear. That peculiar feline odor brought me back to reality. It got me to ponder the wickedness I was to delve into. Gita Ganesh, the beloved niece of my beloved curry maker, what was she doing in the middle of a field, in the middle of a god forsaken stretch of a highway? Why was the young policeman so vexed?

"What about your contacts in the Department, they not helping?" I asked.

"The Lieutenant is helping, trying. Even called the state highway cops officially."

"And.."

"State Police is cooperating, but.." A return to convulsions, much to Miss Agnes's amusement apparently. She jumped off, raised tail and went over to curl up in her favorite spot, made up of my old tee shirts. I envied her even more now.

So, this is what it came to. One scared and forlorn, sick young man; one aging broken-hearted kitchen boss; one very dead sweetheart. And then me, an over the hill frustrated intellectual. A self-proclaimed writer - unpublished, unsung, and unkempt. Ever holding a pen that perpetually threatened to dry out from disuse.

Forget history, forget sad songs. The world immediately

around me has gone crazy. I was surrounded by folks whose hearts were wounded, whose bodies were morphing, and whose minds seemed rent. Folks worse off than me. What was I to do with the lot? Was I the only one here with no loss of my own?

I too lost something, didn't I? But then, I was a writer, wasn't I? In that case I had better be in good order to set the order of others right. I better do something before I lost *my* wits.

The second week of May

What began as a bad May, got worse in one week. The Question, was asked.

What about the body?

The subject came out of the blue and ignited dread in me. If Lalu had ever thought about it, he didn't indicate it. Shetty and Warangal were all sealed up in their own brooding. As for me, I had been overloaded with playing detective, period.

It's understandable that Lalu's old parents longed for 'one last look' of their granddaughter. But still, nobody was ready for that question.

What stunned me though, was who actually raised the issue of Gita's body: her father Phani. In a telegram no less.

SEND BACK MY DAUGHTER'S BODY STOP PROPER FUNERAL MOST IMPORTANT STOP DEMAND POLICE SURRENDER GITA. STOP

Telegram! That big daddy of all messaging methods would freak out most people. 'Oh, a telegram, wow." Not Indians though. Indians love telegrams as much as they like travel by train, dips in holy rivers, and English language acronyms.

My daughter, said the man who finally broke his silence. I was at a loss for words. But Ganesh, he exploded:

"*Bewakhoof* wants her body?" Lalu gritted his teeth, "Let him come and get it."

"The man just wants a final look at his daughter before the pyre is lit," I said.

"Oh, he is going to light it?" Lalu pivoted from his hips and spat out his disgust, "How he shows his face, huh. How? On the cremation grounds, how? The man has no shame?"

"It is *his* obligation. The poor girl had no man of her own. Neither a husband nor a son. And no brother. Who else to put the light to her, than Phani?" I said.

"How can she have a male of her own. Phani neglect his duty. Never look for a husband for her. Never ask me to look. I am uncle. You are uncle. What is Phani to her?"

"He fathered her! He is expected to do the cremation, Lalu," I said.

"I don't care. Let a furnace do it, right here in America." His right index jabbed downward.

The slow and stoic Lalu was gone, replaced by fitful cattle rampaging through a field of dried cow chips. Or, like that American TV commercial, a bull in a china shop.

"Go easy Lalu," I said to him. "It is bad enough that a father has to cremate his child, when the natural order says children should be conducting funerals of parents. You are going to deny even that to your brother?"

"Kumar, don't you see, he doesn't care. Phani care only about himself. Maybe not even...." The trail off in his voice felt to me like a hesitation. Lalu cooling off. I was wrong.

"Phani stayed away from everyone for years. His own daughter. Now she is dead. And he wants her back now?" Pacing and hard breathing resumed.

I didn't have any answers. There *were* no answers. Cops hadn't said a word to us in nearly two weeks. I just let Lalu rant away.

"She write him many letters, Kumar. Every year. I myself mailed some, so I know. Gita write him letters for Diwali, Sankranti, Ugadi, Holi, every festival. She ask about his health, what job he doing. Phani never reply. He not even send a card for Gita's birthday."

"He surely is an oddball alright," I said.

I had used the oddball a few times already. I didn't think I could be any harsher toward a brother of my friend. I couldn't condemn Phani, or could I? In any case, unlike before, Lalu did not grin when I said oddball.

"Tell me, Kumar, how a person don't care about Gita when Gita alive. But now cares about her funeral? Phani had chance to live in America, be with his daughter. He said no then. Now he likes her dead body?"

Lalu Ganesh, who has been coping with his niece's death somewhat admirably, finally looked crushed by karma. Worked hard all his life and planned good things for others. But the gods, they willed the outcomes differently.

He stopped abruptly in the middle of the floor facing me, arms spread wide and eyes dewy, "Phani the only person cares that much about Gita?" He wheeled and strode into the kitchen. The door swung wildly and squeaked.

What's there in the kitchen to soothe Lalu now? His family album, which he said inspired him for over a decade, would probably not do the trick now. Nor was he likely to get solace from the smudgy smoky teakwood statue of his namesake deity, Lord Ganesha. Or, the sandalwood scented incense burning in front of it. The odors of curry and cooking oil will be his only consolation.

"Kumar sir, one doubt in my mind, sir," said Shetty in a low voice.

"Yes Shetty..." I said.

"Yes sir, Lalu need a lot of money, sending Gita sister home, yes?"

"I expect so, Shetty. I'll have to look into the costs. There'll be a lot of paperwork."

"Very good, Kumar sir, I..." Shetty paused.

"We have to get the body back first. I'll look into that too," I said.

"Soon?" Shetty asked.

"Could be. But sometimes we have to ask a judge to tell the government to release the body," I sighed. "Many steps are involved, Shetty, before our Gita is back home."

"I am thinking, Kumar sir, we all help Lalu. So much cost it is, to send Gita home. We all put the chips in," he said.

I nodded slowly while my brain caught up with Shetty-speak.

"Oh, you mean we all chip-in, to help Lalu with the costs?"

"Yes yes sir, we all put chips in. I have not too much money, but I can help. Other workers will help. Gita is our sister. Lalu give us our jobs in America."

“It’s a wonderful idea, Shetty. Bravo, my friend.” Shetty beamed.

“I will research the costs. By the way, the word is chip-in, not put the chips.”

Shetty nodded with a look of satisfaction. He deserved it, I suppose.

****

Detective Mullins offered an effusive greeting over the phone. “Hello Kumar, nice to hear from you, how you been?”

Despite my delight with his good mood, it was the guarded version of me that came out. “I am quite well, Mike. Glad you made time for me. That in itself is a good thing. You also have some news for me, I hope.”

“Ah, yes about the case. Your niece, I mean Gita Ganesh. How is Lalu saab doing, by the way?”

“Truth be told, he is feeling agitated. Waiting for news everyday. But he is a tough guy. He is dealing with it,” I said.

“That’s good. It must be hard running the restaurant under these stressful conditions. Minding the kitchen, suppliers, etc....”

“Any new developments, Mike?” I asked.

“The case is progressing nicely.”

“So, that means… what?”

“You know something Kumar, I haven’t been your way, up north, in quite a while. I think I will rectify that soon.”

He is stalling.

"Mike, you will be welcomed with open arms on Devon Avenue. You will be cheered by all of Little India, sir," I said.

He chuckled, "Don't have to tell me. I always feel the warmth and hospitality when I go out to eat samosa."

Why is he doing this? I've got to bust this stalling tactic,

"Mike, I want to talk about Gita's last rites. When can we expect to receive her body?"

A pause. Sound of papers being shuffled, but I really didn't think he was going through any notes or case files.

"Yes, the body. Fact is, it is not up to me. The medical examiner's office decides it. Once all procedures are completed, they will contact whomever is on the paperwork as the next of kin of the decedent."

I tried to control my breathing. Mike's answer was exactly the type of police-speak that Lalu wasn't cut out for. The reason Lalu was happy to have me around. People in big jobs speak different, Kumar, as he said.

Once I felt my breath and voice to be level, I said "Detective, we have been patient about this. So many days have passed. The girl needs to be on her final journey. At this point it's not just about culture or religion. It's psychological too. About closure."

"Of course, Kumar, of course. I am with you, totally," he said.

"So then, what's the delay? No one has contacted Lalu yet."

"Probably still running tests."

"When can we expect the body, Mike. Where is it anyway? We can go there and ask, instead of bothering you," I said.

"Oh, No. It's not a bother at all. Right now, I don't know where Gita's body is. The medical examiner has control, I just don't know which one. The city morgue, or downstate. I can find out for you, Kumar."

More stalling. Could he genuinely have gotten side-tracked?

"Any idea how long the tests will take? Don't they usually take all the samples they need, and be done with the body in just a day or two?"

"Hey, that's pretty good, you know your stuff. Yes, that's how things usually work. The ME wants to make sure they have all the right samples. After the preliminary results, they must have decided to probe further. That could be the holdup."

"What additional tests?"

Pause on his end, palpitations on mine.

"I am not sure that I really know the answer precisely, Rama. I'll find out. You know what, I will make that overdue visit soon."

More sound of papers being shuffled. It made me wonder if that's why people keep stacks of papers on their desks: the rustle of papers was the language of dodging.

Carrot & Stick

I spent some time later that day with Mr. Guinness. The topic of conversation, between me and Triple Stout, was not so much why my detective friend was being cagey, but rather why he wasn't hiding it.

Mullins will sometimes offer an entire set of facts, or illuminate an event, or a scenario. At other times he just hinted. Offered a scent, so to speak. Sometimes the hard details he gave were mostly junk, such as the scene where Gita was found. The things he withheld were critical, such as the exact cause and manner of death. The cause, he wouldn't say. The manner, we sort of knew. Homicide, evidently.

Was he putting the bait out, knowing that a meddler like me can't stay quiet for very long? Mike's pattern of keeping us informed was just to tantalize. His purpose was, what? To tease us? Naw. To frustrate us? Not intentionally. Was he trying to draw us out, and see if the Indians were hiding something. After all, a cop didn't have to tell us nothing. But, he *was* telling me stuff, why?

Halfway through the six-pack, Mr. Guinness agreed with me: Mike was stringing me along. He dropped crumbs, daring me to pick up the trail. Do I dare? The answer was a definite yes. Mullins was dangling the carrot. I was to provide my own stick.

Breaking & Entering

The light drizzle didn't bother me, but the temperature was quite a different matter. It was not cold enough to bundle up, and neither was it warm enough to peel off a layer of clothing. In the end, I wore jeans and a flannel shirt under my trench coat, sans umbrella. An umbrella would have been awkward and conspicuous.

I had been out all day, running from one business to another on Devon Avenue, chatting up storekeepers and waiters. Pumping people for their views on Gita's death. It turned out to be a foolhardy venture. After all, I was dealing with *my* people, whose concern with other people's problems could be as fleeting as a butterfly, or more rarely, as tenacious as gum under a shoe. Time to be on my own.

I turned up the collar of my thick red flannel shirt as I entered the block in which Gita's apartment was located. The drizzle thickened into a steady light rain by the time I walked an additional block past her building, turned left, and doubled back through the alley. I crossed the intervening street, and after a few more yards found myself next to somebody's garage.

Facing me was a fence made of what they call chicken wire. The trash cans inside the yard bore numbers indicating that I was at the back of the correct building. I turned my baseball cap around, made the bill overhang the nape of my neck, and keep rainwater off my wet shirt.

The famously fickle weather of Chicago was having a grand old time messing with me. The wind picked up, temperature dropped, and rain intensified. I silently cussed out the barometer, the thermometer, the wind-meter, and the whatever-meter. So much for the idiom spring has sprung, which Chicagoans so loved to say.

I turned up the collar of my trench coat against the growing chill before jumping over the fence. Truth be told, I actually scrambled over it, thankful that it was just an amenable apartment building, and not some sort of a medieval castle or cloister. I double checked the numbers on the trash cans to ensure that I was at the correct building. I was. The rain now hit me with its slanted bullet-like drops.

It was a duplex kind of a structure, a pair of three-apartment stacks joined all the way along a single mud wall, as some say. Plus, there was a garden apartment in each twin-half. Out of that total of eight units, five had lights on somewhere, four glowed like lightning bugs indicating televisions. Only one was utterly dark and was directly above my head. That would be my target.

I ascended a typical Chicago back porch made of wood. A short set of steps, turn at a small landing, and another short set of steps leading to a full width landing that was the backside of an apartment. Repeat the alternate short and full landings. Damn! Too many wooden slats, too much potential fot creaking and groaning wood. At once, I took back all the cuss words I tossed at the weather instruments. The pelting rain and the whistling wind were my noise-drowning allies now.

I imagined a creak with every step, but there really wasn't any. Just one corner plank groaned under my weight, and a lightweight that I was, the sound flattered me more than it startled. The weather conditions triggered an enormous itch in me, in my lungs, in my mind. It would be a perfect moment to light up a pipe, to have the bouquet of Reverend Raspberry tobacco on my breath. And for the added whimsy of a Sherlock Holmes fantasy.

Once on the landing that was the back of Gita's apartment, I pulled out my 'kit'. The stout butter knife got pushed in the space between the window sash and the frame. I wiggled it about, ran it from side to side to loosen the dirt and jiggled the lower glass pane gently. No dice. I repeated the process wedging the tip deeper and dragging it farther than before and along the sides. Still nothing.

I swore silently and took out the other tool in the kit, a short mag-lite. Shielding the beam like I was supposed to (that's how the pros always did it in the movies), I shined the light where the upper and lower sashes met. Was there a securing device? Was a locking mechanism tying the two?

There wasn't, and relief flooded my being. I took a breather, filled and lit an imaginary pipe and took a few puffs. Then I resumed. It took some adroit physical contortion. Push up against the lower frame's edge with my shoulder, my left palm fully spread out against the glass for purchase, insert the short blunt knife at an angle to increase leverage. Plop! With sound barely audible, the slight adhesion caused by three weeks of being kept shut gave way. I raised the sash and stepped in her kitchen.

I was determined to solve every mystery of Gita right then and there. Know everything that needed to be known. Let there be no mystery at all. *Talk to me Gita.*

The mini light came out again. I played it around the kitchen, looking in each cupboard and base cabinet. Not much of anything interesting. I looked in the proverbial coffee can, candy jar and the unlabeled ceramic containers. Not much besides crunchy Indian snacks.

I entered the bedroom and stopped short. This was a lady's

chamber of refuge. A private place of the female heart. *Should I really be doing this?* Doubt and hesitation gripped me out of nowhere. I was about to do something vile and violative. I stood brooding, chewing my lip, sweating. Moisture dripped in random drops from my trench coat. I had shaken it while ascending the porch steps. It no longer shielded me but I had kept it on.

Her inner sanctum kept beckoning, and would not let me step back into the hallway, or depart the apartment altogether. I went to the kitchen for some paper towels to mop up the rain drops on the floor, and take a breather from my chaotic thought process. How could I justify my breach of a dead woman's privacy. Where could I find the reason? Well, as it turned out, I found it exactly where I stood dripping. Something I hadn't noticed before.

The louvered, bi-fold door of the closet in the passageway wasn't fully closed. The fold lay at an angle of hundred and sixty degrees. That left a gap of some six inches through which I could see into the closet without even trying. Inside that closet, close to the baseboard, was an electrical outlet with a dying night light plugged in. It felt like something was moving on the floor, I gasped and nearly lost my balance.

Good thing I didn't slip or collapse, the closet's edge was a handy straw to clutch at and regain myself. The night light was on its last leg and was flickering, giving an illusion of movement. The light flickering combined with my own wound up state gave me almost a head-spin.

After wiping up the polished wooden floor and gathering my wits, I inspected the closet thoroughly. Scattered on the floor were an assortment of items, which a cursory glance showed they were gift items for Francis to take to India. Many were still in original packing. Some I remembered being bought by Gita or Lalu on Devon Avenue. Trinkets, toys, children's dresses, souvenirs, tourist crap.

It was evident that just before leaving Gita's apartment, on his last day in Chicago, Francis must have gone into a frenzy and dumped all those items. He wanted no part of America, apparently. Not to live in, not to carry back with him. Daughter or no daughter, he put America behind him, shoving his daughter's America into a hallway closet.

It explained the strained behavior of father and daughter during their final week together. Especially, that last day when Lalu drove us all to the airport, and we rode the people mover system to the airline terminal. Was there something more? What else happened between father and daughter? Something that I didn't know, Lalu couldn't know. Perhaps, that something shed light on why she died so far afield, in a godforsaken farm. Well, to the bedroom, since it has to be.

Goose pimples erupted all over me, in part from the chilly air in the room, but mostly from the chill I felt from within. Lalu would be enraged, Francis would kill me (or, maybe not care at all, that thought occurred to me too). I shouldn't even be in her apartment, let alone her bedroom.

The first thing I found was a pair of brand new shirts from Sears laying on her made bed. The size tags hinted that Gita bought them for her father. The shirts were carelessly unwrapped and unpinned, as if someone might have held one in front of them and didn't bother any further.

On the night table were a writing pad and pen, but nothing was written on it. In the waste bin by the bed was a crumpled, green colored half-page sheet with big black numerals, seven and zero on one side, and a list of some sort on the other. I flattened it out into a rumpled square, and proceeded to look through the dresser drawers. Nothing in them that would be out of place in a young lady's room. I decided to leave.

It was some sort of an instinct rather than a calculated thought that made me look again in the bottom drawer. I pulled it out all the way and looked at the contents in the glare of the mini-mag. A soft packet the size of a book stood out. Something was wrapped in a cloth with images of green cardamom pods on a blue background.

I laid it on the bed and unfolded a large square scarf. Nestled in there was a stack of letters. Lavender in my nostrils. Instinct said they were love letters. But from who? I re-wrapped them and stuck the pack in the inside pocket of my trench coat. I had to jiggle the drawer between the rails to slide it back, and noticed the clothing items shift a bit. And underneath her intimates: a round plastic pill holder, with dial markings for each separate day. *Wow, Gita was using birth control.*

Less than an hour after I broke into her apartment, I baled out the same way I came. Hopped the fence back out and scurried. The rain had stopped, the wind had slowed, and the cool breeze dried my skin in no time. *I obtained clues*. I was on cloud nine. It felt for a while that I could solve any problem in the world.

It was obvious the apartment did not contain any weed or weapon. Naturally so, since the poor girl didn't even smoke or drink. On the other hand, a different issue reared its ugly head. Gita was a girl with secrets. And, a secret lover.

Detention

I rushed over to the Blue Mountain the next day. I didn't take the packet of love letters with me. There would be time for that later. A passing glance at them was enough to give me an idea on how to quiz my friend Lalu about many things, including his innocent niece Gita. Today would be a day of storytelling, of the sort even the green photo album might not match.

The temps normalized during the overnight hours and a light breeze put everyone in a good mood. Even the bus driver smiled, and said "Nice to see you brother, you gonna have a day, or what?"

"For sure Daryl," I said. "The tips I gave you last time helped?"

"Totally, totally. Gracias, my friend." he replied. "You know something? My son don't roll his eyes at me as much. I don't sound so foolish, I guess." Daryl laughed heartily. I gave him an American smile and an Indian nod. He beamed and said, "Next time," and closed the bus door after I alighted.

It went with my pigment. People assumed I either owned a donut shop, or I was a nerd. If the word computer came up, I was expected to be an expert of sorts. Daryl, who didn't know of my Internet Cafe business till today, somehow just *knew* to ask me computer questions. I gladly gave him my card, but didn't foresee what good would come to me because of it. As the saying goes, if you got nothing going for you, at least be lucky. And, as *I* say sometimes, make some luck of your own, even if you didn't know you were doing it. Serendipity, anybody?

I timed my arrival at Lalu's restaurant to coincide with the end of lunch hour. Sure enough, the last of the lunch customers were leaving and the wait staff began taking down the buffet set up. I was about to flip the sign to Closed, when one last customer came out of the darkness. Before I could raise a greeting, Mullins whispered, "Kumar, let's have a quick chat," and ushered me out the door.

*****

It should have been pretty hard to do, but I did it: I dozed off in a police lock up. Yes, I did. Hard to believe. Once I got over the shock of Mullins's decision to take me into custody, exhaustion overtook me. His stubborn silence didn't help either. I let the tension of the previous forty-eight hours ease me into a snooze.

Vaguely familiar voices down the hall from my cell woke me. I blinked to wipe tiredness off, just in time to see Lalu Ganesh and detective Mike Mullins approaching the holding cell. With them was the 'night captain' of the precinct station. Bringing up the rear was a person in a rumpled suit, dimly familiar.

"As you can see Mr. Ganesh, your brother is quite comfortable," the Captain was saying.

No response from either Mullins or Lalu. A slight cough from the fourth guy whom I still couldn't place. A cell phone shaped like a candy bar appeared in his hand, and he was struggling to use his stubby fingers on it.

"And, how are we doing this morning, Mr. Kumar?" asked the Captain, as if he were some nice and elderly family doctor making a post-fever follow-up.

I offered no response. The fourth guy coughed again. The other three looked at him. That's when recognition hit me. He was the fellow who usually drove State Senator Mr. Josh Howard around Devon Avenue and the Rogers Park neighborhood. The Senator's driver - that's what I erroneously thought when I first seen him in Indian restaurants and parades - turned out later that he was the senator's office manager, Mr. Stern.

He spoke up now. "Really, Captain Jim, why keep him here at all? Surely, you aren't going to recommend charges?"

I craned my neck to catch something of the dialog, but the fellows moved around the corner, but not before I caught Mullins's voice: "... his own good.. Cool down.....will be fine.." Followed by some overlapping comments and assenting grunts from others. I imagined Lalu nodding vaguely, if only gravely. Wow, how many bigwigs of Devon Avenue did it take to make this visit possible! Rudiments of a new joke about screwing in a light bulb were forming in my mind.

I sat back down on the long wooden bench bolted to one of the walls. The cell's other inmate - was that the right word - looked at me archly, and asked, "What was that all about? You is somebody?" I just shook my head.

The voices in the hallway faded, and I was left to my own thoughts. In the situation that I was in, being in detention could be a sort of a badge of honor. But, only if it gave me some street-cred on Devon Avenue, and, if it prompted people to reveal stuff I didn't know. On the other hand, I could be branded a loser and be mocked. Worse yet, if things went too far officially the wrong way, it could affect my business license. I didn't know...

"Hey," said a voice, and my eyes flew open. Lalu was standing outside the cell, with Mullins a few feet away. Lalu looked like he was carrying two loaded sacs of rice. Mullins didn't even look in our direction.

Lalu whispered to me, “The police say you must stay now. You will come out later.” Ganesh and his odd habit of speaking in broken sentences and strange short-cuts of expression. By police, he meant Mullins. By come out, he implied I will get out with no charges. It all made sense. My friend the detective was pissed off at me, punishing me. Well, so be it.

I patted his hand, “Thank you, it will be alright.” Lalu nodded and left. I sat back down on the bench, and my ‘cell-mate’ resumed.

“What you do for a living bro?” he asked.

“I am, like, um, a writer”

"What do you write, political stuff?”

“Good heavens, no.” I replied.

“I figured you pissed somebody off with your writing. You wrote comedy stuff?” my bench-mate ventured.

I shook my head.

“Let me guess, porn. Right? Lots of money in porn.”

“Naw man, I just write a blog, community news, you know, about my people. Devon Avenue.” That should sate his curiosity, I thought.

“Devon Avenue, huh. Yea, lots of Pakistanis and Hindus, right? You worship Allah, man?”

I looked at him with something of a smile and a non-committal nod. But he was still curious.

"I like Allah, man. Don't know much about him though. Hey, I hear some politician came here to check up on you."

"No, it wasn't the politician, it was his driver who came."

"Ha Ha ha. I knew you was a comedian."

I became somewhat concerned when, about an hour later, a group of three disparate individuals were brought into the cell. I watched and wondered what would happen.

It seemed to be some sort of a protocol of the holding cell, for occupants to ignore each other at first, then scowl some, and eventually chit-chat about random topics, if they so choose. Behavior that reminded me, again, of a waiting room at the doctor's, except there were no out of date magazines. I got nosy as usual, and inquired after each one as to why he was brought in. But, they just scowled and said little.

The pretend journalist in me was having a good time when the same two officers who brought me in, cuffed me and escorted me out. Around the corner through a different hallway, to a smaller cell. This one didn't stink of sweat or bad breath, and had two shorter benches. It looked like I was to be the only occupant. Well, I would miss conversing with the criminal elements, but I was grateful to be in 'solitary,' so to speak.

The afternoon wore on and shift change occurred. I nearly dozed off again. Scraping sound and sharp odor woke me up gradually. A giant of a human being, an African-American gentleman with a shaggy gray beard and a shiny head with just a curly fringe, was mopping the floor of the hallway, and making a serious effort to not notice me.

He came close and whispered, "You the computer guy?" Gee whiz, am I being profiled again? I nodded slowly. The mopping continued as he mumbled, "I am Moses. Larry's uncle."

Larry, Larry - I nodded very slowly, and amid goosebumps and all, the light bulb went off in my brain. "Number Eleven Lincoln Bus," was all I muttered. The mop guy stuck a piece of folded paper in my hand through the bars and continued running the mop. In the manner of those who act like everything is okie-dokie, he hummed a tune to himself, as he retreated away from my cell bars. Excited as I was, I still managed to doze off again.

*****

It was mid-day by the time Lalu drove us back to Blue Mountain, where a double dose of hospitality awaited me, thanks to Shetty. Two plates of samosa instead of one, a plate of chicken biryani, extra-strong spicy tea, and two steel bowls of different desserts: mellow, spongy gulab jamun, and delicious stringy burfee topped with crushed nuts. I wolfed them down while the kitchen staff watched with some amusement. Lalu waited patiently. Eat something first, right?

"So, Kumar..." he said. No statement or questions. The bags under eyes spoke for him. If there were the tiniest curl of a lip hinting satisfaction on his face, I chalked it up to that universal joy all great cooks feel when people eat. The staff didn't leave our area, they in fact made themselves ready for a campfire tale. I stayed silent. Not even a belch.

Finally, Lalu asked, "Tell me. What is wrong with you?"

"Nothing." I replied. My mind was on numerous things at once. First of all, gratitude to be out of hell's ante-chamber. The tribe rallied for me. And then, there was the other stuff, the more important ones. Gita's pills, Warangal's love letters, Larry's messenger. On top of it all was my own muddle: Mullins dropping hints and Kumar chasing clues.

How do I explain all that to Lalu? Especially, when it's Lalu that needs to explain so many things to me. About Gita, her life and her loves. Right then, it felt to me that Lalu owed me more explanations than I owed him. That he might know more than he realizes. Not a good spot for a good friend to be in. Not a good time for my expose of Gita's heart. So I surmised.

Gita drove downstate?

In another first - less than a week after I was detained and released without charges - Detective Mullins asked me to 'come downtown.' That too in a tone he never used before. Come ASAP, no so small talk, no humorous comment, no use of the casual Rama.

"Kumar, we should meet, at once," he said as soon as I had answered the phone. Nothing regular about that summons. It was a good thing that I had some coffee in me. "Good Morning to you too, Mr. Mullins."

"Yes, good morning. We should meet immediately. There is something we need to address."

"Sure, how about we eat some samosa?" still trying to keep things regular and light. 'Twas no use.

"Please come downtown, You know where it is."

Who is this new Mullins guy? Way too solemn. He wasn't asking me to a seminar or a social gathering. This was a ten-four situation. "Oh, sure, Mike," I said.

In spite of myself, I put a positive spin on the invite: he called on his own, and that means that he has news. But, there was a negative too: the way he plunged into the topic.

****

"I don't know what to believe," he said, with unwavering eyes. "Do I believe the persons I consider to be friends, or, do I believe the computers, the hard facts?" He opened his palms out. "The receipts and records." I waited, resting easily in an armchair across the desk from him.

Mike resumed, his elbows on the desk, hands extended and palms out. No edge in his voice. "Everybody assured me what a sweet innocent thing, the little girl was," he said. "Kumar, you all led me to believe that Gita was this washed pearl, babe in the woods type of person. I see different now."

Ah, a sudden concern about Gita. "What gives, Mr. Mullins?"

"How long have you known her personally?" He asked.

"I don't recall when she came over. But I do know that her uncle sponsored her," I said.

"Did she always have her own apartment?"

"No. She lived with him the first few years. She didn't move into her current place until three or four years ago."

"And, she never had a car of her own?" Mike, focused on banalities.

I shook my head. "I do remember she had access to a car owned by her friend, Kamini. Gita was allowed use of the small car, a blue Nissan I think. Gita did a lot of jobs for Kamini's mustard jar business."

"Ah, yes. Anything else?" Mullins asked.

"Lalu let her use his own car for the catering jobs. I understand those events rarely went too long, and she brought back the car for him each night."

Mike is stalling, something amiss here. Patience, patience. And then, Mullins changed direction.

"Did Gita have a boyfriend, Kumar? I mean, is it common for Indian girls to be dating, do you know?"

"She is Indian, Mr. Mike," as if that explained it all. Did Mike bite it?

"Was Ganesh saab looking for a match for her, then? Isn't that what the elders do in your community?"

"I don't think Lalu made any attempt in that direction Mike."

"You are killing me, man. So many non-answer answers. I know you mean well, you are fond of Lalu's little girl and she treated you as nicely as she treated her own uncle. But, you got to help us out here." Mike didn't look exasperated, only sounded like it.

"We should get Lalu into this conversation, and Shetty," I said.

"Shetty. Is he that lanky gent with the awkward smile?"

"Yup. He and Gita did a lot of catering jobs. You know, Mike, come to think of it, they traveled together in the suburbs quite a bit. He still doesn't drive. It was Gita who drove them to the catering events: parties, birthdays, Name Ceremonies, and such. Yes, I am sure she did most of the driving."

The detective pushed three photocopies toward me. My eyes grew wide. It hurt when I perused them. "I don't know Mike. I don't know what to say. I just don't know what to think." My voice faltered and my words failed. Those documents made me feel pathetic.

Mullins leaned back in his swivel chair and tilted back a bit, "Try, Rama. Try to explain." His arms spread out in a disarming invitation to a dialog. But, his face remained immobile. His use of my old first name, which at other times conveyed informality, now sounded flat. Like a habit, not a genuine feeling. At least, he has not gone fully hostile on me yet.

I placed my hands on his desk, palms down, leaned into it, and summoned up a force of conviction to my voice, that wasn't in my heart. I tried not to feel like a supplicant, "Believe me Mike, this comes as a complete shock to me. I never had reason to think of Gita as driving around. I always thought she was taken by force or under duress." I stared at the documents he laid in front of me.

"Why do you think she needed *to rent a car*, when her uncle had a nice comfy one?" Mike asked, speaking slowly, tapping the photocopies, stressing the word rent.

"Don't know. Sure would like to know, though."

"Why did she go downstate, who do you think she went to meet?" Again, he emphasized by tapping the date of the rental car.

"I don't know, Mike. Can't guess why."

"Do you think Lalu Ganesh knows?" Mike asked.

"I, honestly, don't know, Mike."

"You don't know anything, do you, Rama?" There was an edge to his voice now that was concerning. But, at least, he continued using Rama, which meant we were still being informal. Interrogatory, yes. But cordial too. I tried to relax, breathe easy, and think. Think!

Had I ever a reason to discuss Gita's driving habits at all? It was always Lalu who drove me around. It was he who picked up workers, or urgent supplies for the eatery. When catering a large gala, Lalu rented a van to load up. I made a mental note to quiz Shetty and some of the Patels on Devon. Mullins continued his probing gaze. The eyes grew steely, but not daggers yet.

Mike's chair settled back to level. "Why did Gita rent a car two days before her death? he asked. "Come, come, Kumar, you must have a theory, some shred of an idea. After all, you know her like family?"

Know her? At the moment, hardly.

Kumar grilled

Just when I started to feel like I didn't know Gita at all, Mullins switched tracks, he asked about Shetty.

"Nice guy. A polite fellow," I replied. "A real 'curry of the earth' type person, you know."

Mullins chuckled, and the mood across in the beg desk lightened. "Even for a writer like you, that's too much. The Bible refers to 'salt of the earth' people. Is this other thing a Hindu Bible sort of thing?" His tone indicated indulgence and renewed cheer.

"Salt or curry, same difference," I said. "His people have been feeding Indians for decades, as cooks, servers, restaurateurs, hotel owners," I said.

"His people, his people?" You going racist on me Rama?" Mike's chuckle grew into a smile, the tone remained the same, non-accusatory.

I ploughed on. "A whole tradition of cooking exists along the Western Ghats of India, among people named Shetty. In some cities, the name is synonymous with food service."

The detective managed to turn his look of amusement into one of interest.

"It's true, Mike. Thousands and thousands of eateries flourish in some states due to folks named Shetty."

"And that makes him innocent?" Mike asked.

"What I am saying is that he is ambitious and works hard. He is working toward his own golden piece of America. I trust him, he wouldn't betray the curry either, hehe."

"There you go again, blogger-man," said Mike. "Explain."

"What you said earlier about the Bible and salt. They say people were paid in sacks of salt in olden days. Don't know if that's true. But, it is a fact that Asians hold fealty to be a virtue. When a person receives hospitality, he is honor-bound to not *betray the salt.* A disloyal person is a salt-thief, someone who betrays the salt he ate. *Namak haram.* Quite a colorful phrase, huh?"

"So, you're saying Shetty will never betray his curry master, Lalu." Mike said.

"Precisely."

"Hmm, you sure love them words, don't ya?"

I smiled, nodded. But, Mullins loved his questions more.

"Couldn't Shetty have been lusting after Gita? After all, she is.. er was an attractive young lady. He spent a lot of time with her, driving around, out of the sight of Lalu Ganesh…"

I didn't care for that kind of talk, and cut Mike off. "Oh, they were always focused on their jobs. No hanky-panky," I said.

"How could you know, you weren't there?"

"I wasn't there, but I observe people, Mike," I said.

"They could have sneaked around. People do that, don't they?" Mike asked.

"I doubt it, Mike. Things don't work like that among *my* people," I said. "Unless the police know different."

Well, he was the police, wasn't he. Mike never admitted if the case was transferred to Chicago. Was he really in charge of it?

"Hey, What do I know about how Indians live? I am just a cop. That's why I have you explain things to me." Mike said. Yup, he said that, and with a straight face too. It earned him a disbelieving stare from me. But, I needed him to keep playing ball, so I stayed silent, and after a while he obliged.

"Was her uncle looking for a suitable match for her? Isn't that how it's done among South Asians?" Mike asked.

"True that, but Lalu had no such plans. I think he would have told me." I replied.

"Why not?"

"I should think that Lalu expected Gita's own father to take initiative on that front."

"Do you know if her father did?"

"None that I know, Mike. That entire episode of his visit became a giant fiasco. The man was crazy and left abruptly."

"Yes, Lalu told me all about his sudden departure."

"Mike, Shetty should be above reproach, as far as Gita is concerned. You realize he is so much older than her," I said.

The detective leaned back in his chair, drummed fingers on his chest, and took a sip of water. After a minute or so, he sat up straight again, looked me hard in the eye, and said, "Alright, I'll buy that for now,"

That was the easier part of the grilling.

***

I had no answer to Mike's other question, "Why did Gita rent a car just days before she was killed?" It came out of the blue, and felt like an attack. Even worse was the shock I had felt from the fact of it, from seeing the photocopies of the rental contract she signed. I knew Gita used Lalu's car for catering jobs. She was saving money for her own vehicle. I knew nothing about a rental car. *Was Mullins trying to trip me up?*

"I have no idea, Detective," I said. Mike tilted his head this way and that, but the eyes were fixed on my face, scanning my expressions. What was there to scan for, other than puzzlement on my part?

A bunch of questions were already forming in the back of my mind. When did she rent, from where, how long was the rental period, what was the mileage when returned, did she list any other drivers? *But most of all, Mister Mike, how do you know any of this stuff, who sold you the tale, sir?*

"This comes as a shock, Mike. Frankly, I am puzzled. How on earth did you guys even stumble upon this?" I meant it as praise of police work, but I don't think it came across that way to him.

"Well, Mr. Blogger-man, the police have their ways. The real question is, why you don't have any answers?" He rolled his chair close to his desk, drummed his fingers on it, and said, "I would think Kumar, that a smart, eager sleuth like you would know your subject more fully." His smugness was cheeky, but that jab of his wasn't quite as tongue-in-cheek as I might have wished.

"Honest, Mike. It is confusing. In all my conversations with Lalu, this possibility never come up. I am sure Lalu would have said something," I said.

"He would, huh?" the fingers still tapping the desk in front of him.

"I bet my life on it." I said.

Hoping to wish away a puzzle that l couldn't explain, I asked, "Are the police a hundred percent sure about this rental business?"

"Absolutely, but you can go look into it for yourself. In your own way." said Mike. *What the heck did that mean, look for myself?*

"And the returned car? Where was it found?" I asked.

He hesitated, examined the backs of his hands, probed my face once more, and said, "Technically, it was not returned. It was abandoned."

"Oh my goodness, abandoned where?" I asked.

"In a remote parking lot at O'Hare Airport," Mike replied.

"So, it just sat there gathering dust?" I ventured.

"Yes, dust, and parking tickets. Quite a few citations." Mike said.

Understanding dawned on me slowly. Parking lot employees wrote down the plate number of every car, every day. Tag numbers, make & model data, and parked location of the vehicle were recorded. Some travelers forgot where in the vast parking area they left the car, but one simple phone call brought out a customer service car. They advised the driver where the car was parked. If needed, they gave a ride to the location. Even changed tires, jumped dead batteries, etcetera. Cops had access to the data, and ran plate numbers through their own computers to find unpaid traffic tickets, expired licenses, and stolen cars. It was a *system*, alright.

As Mike took his time studying my face - and seeing the wheels spin - I got the feeling he didn't regard me as an equal partner or confidante. At the same time, I didn't feel under scrutiny either. It was one of his characteristic gazes. Gray eyes under bushy brows didn't flutter or pierce, just probed in a liquid gaze. This one sought information without giving out any of his own. But, a slight tightening of his mouth said he gave me too much already. Oh well, I needed more, a whole lot more. So, I pushed, "And the car was originally checked out from..."

"Same place, O'Hare Airport. But not at an automated kiosk at the terminal, or via a reservation." Mike said.

Again, an understanding dawned on me slowly. I blew a low whistle.

"That's interesting," once again the answer formed in my mind even as I spoke. "The rental was an impromptu decision. She probably took the shuttle bus from the terminal building to the Rental Complex. If car rental happened beforehand, they would ask for flight information, name of the airlines etc., show the arrival ticket or something." I noticed Mullins's nods urge me on at first, but slow down to a long pause.

"How did the car get back to the airport, and how did you find out about it?" I asked.

"We are the police, Kumar. We have our methods." he said.

Apparently, hard information wasn't going to be forthcoming. Mike laid his palms flat out on the table and curled his lip. Eyes unblinking. *Well, the blogger- man is on his own now.*

But then again, it was quite like Mike. Withhold hard facts, hit me with soft revelations. The detective has been doing that all throughout our acquaintance. He was an adroit questioner, regardless of whether he and I were adversarial, or cooperative.

Over the years, he had been slow to trust me, quick to respect Lalu, and unwary of the others. Trust did build between him and me over time, but his esteem for Lalu Ganesh grew even faster. Either way, officer Mullins was a good friend to the Indian community, and I respected that. What I really needed was hard police facts on Gita. Sadly, the detective turned that faucet off.

I too leaned back in due course. All I could muster was, "I have got a lot of thinking to do, Mike." It was time to stay cool and cordial. Especially, since he veered off in a new direction.

"As long as we're talking stuff, what about Officer Warangal, might he be involved?" Mullins asked.

I gasped, probably paled too. Again, it came out of the left field. Why would Mike cast doubts on one of his own professional tribe? Did he regard Warangal to be Indian first, and only then a cop?

At a loss for words, I let a blank expression take over my face. Mike tilted his head this way and that, studying my face. He checked his pockets, an obvious empty gesture. At the same time. he leaned in a bit and cast a demanding look at me. An old, forgotten, and uncomfortable feeling came over me. Mike the cop had made me feel that way some years before.

Throwing questions at me, probing, seemingly distrustful. Fixing me like a moth, pinned under glass in wax.

I took a couple of deep breaths and loosened my grip on the armrests. It took some time, before I could refocus on the heart of the matter. The subject Mullins brought up was Warangal, not Kumar. I didn't expect Mullins to link Krishna Warangal to Gita Ganesh. It left me feeling like I was missing something.

Mullins eased back into his chair and rolled back. He swung his legs sideways to sit side-saddle in the plush chair. I didn't take that posture as meaning that he blinked first. But rather more like he fired his torpedoes and dived.

Rental car

I sidled up to the crawling yellow vehicle with a revolving light atop. Its driver was a young Latino man. An equally young Latina with long nails was seated next to him, using a keyboard. The mapping crew, recording license numbers of cars parked at O'Hare.

The driver rolled his window down, "Did you misplace your car, sir? I got all the locations right here."

"Thanks but, No. Nice of you to offer, though. I'm just wondering, how's your shift going."

"It's going," he stroked his chin. "Same as any other day. At least, the sun is out. Right Maria?" Maria didn't respond.

"If you got car problems I can call for a service truck. Get you a jump or something." He offered again.

"Thanks again, I am really curious about this whole thing you guys do. It's a terrific thing for customers, but it must get on your nerves, the tedium. No?"

The young man looked at his coworker and asked, "Done?"

She had a tablet-like device in her lap and she pressed a dainty finger upon it, one key at a time. Her other fingers were lifted in air, and nails with glitter gel caught sunlight. "Okay, move," she said, eyes still on the gadget.

The vehicle inched forward, I along with it, till it was put in Park again.

"Must get boring doing this eight hours a day," I said again.

"Naw, not boring. We got our tunes, our snacks. She does the actual writing down," he tilted his head toward his coworker. "She is the smart one."

Glitter gel nails giggled. She turned her head toward me.

"Julio is jealous because I get to use the *compewter* and he is just my chauffeur," she lifted up her hand-held device. She giggled again. Everything sparkled, the screen of her tablet, her nails, nose ring, and one steel capped canine on her upper left. The young man didn't blush, he beamed.

I asked the on-the-job lovebirds if they remembered a recent event, a worst-parked vehicle. "It was parked a long while, it seems. At least, that's one stall you didn't have to go to every day, right?"

They did what lovebirds everywhere did. They looked at each other before answering. "Oh, you mean the rental car?"

I nodded. "Sorry to bug you like this, but it involves family. Someone died..." I paused. They both said, awww, almost at the same time, before I resumed.

"Cops know that I am doing these questions. What do you remember about that car?"

They looked at each other again. Glitter gel put her tablet on the dashboard, pushed her hair behind her ear, and leaned forward to address me through the driver side window. Her body shifted familiarly over Julio, the left arm comfortable on his shoulder.

"It was a compact car, parked wrong. They didn't use a stall. Just pulled up over a yellow-stripe area," her thumb pointed to the right.

"Yes, my detective friend told me about it. Left abandoned, ticketed and towed. Maybe you can add more?"

"It was towed, but not by cops. The rental company came and took it. Right over there," she pointed to a building one infield distance away. "Go check with 'em."

"It was parked real close to the tram station. Like they just stopped the car and ran to catch the tram," said Julio.

Maria added, "Yeah, our boss said the car's tags were current so the city might not be in a hurry to tow it. He just notified the rental company."

"Did your manager look to see who left the vehicle, the security cameras?

"There is cameras in the tram station, the cashiers, and some fence line. You know, catch car thieves," Julio winked. "I don't think they care about a car coming in to park. They care about cars leaving without paying." *Funny.*

"Cops never came?" I asked.

"I heard somebody say that one officer came, don't know what he did."

"I can see why the city would leave it here," I grinned. "A new ticket everyday, easy revenue. Those rental companies have loads of money." We all laughed about that. I headed in the direction they pointed.

****

A grizzled old man, slovenly and gooby looking, leaned against the side wall. His face looked caved in on the left side, and his mouth pulled to a side as he lazily picked his teeth. I asked him who was in charge, and he twanged "Jojo inside." He pointed to large double doors at the far end.

I entered a space crammed with service counters, baggage clusters, sulking kids and anxious adults. I parked myself in a corner of the room, and looked for a woman who most likely would be in a spiffy business attire, scarf and a company pin on her lapel.

A wiry young fellow wearing mousse gel hair passed me by at a brisk pace which hinted at a bright future in junior management. Jo Jo, said his tag. Aha, it's Jo Jo, not Jojo. He kept darting in and out of different offices behind the counters. A classic clipboard, a small tool kit on his belt, and a multi-colored ball point pen in his shirt pocket. With a slide rule added to the shirt, he would be a perfect throwback of a NASA engineer.

I stopped him during his third pass with my question and he cut me off. "You not renting a car? Okay. But hey, can you come back in half-an-hour, I will be on my break then?"

Jo Jo passed by several times. At one time, I chuckled at something he said to a customer, and said *Touche.* On subsequent passes we exchanged snappy banter about Chicago's weather and sports teams. By then I was part of the scene. I cornered him during his sixth pass. "Listen Jo, this is important. I really must talk to you. Only you can help me."

"Kay, I'll take my break now," he said, and we went outside.

"My name is Jorge Jowicki," he volunteered. Pointing to his tag, "I really don't like people calling me *Horhay*."

"Kumar," I extended my hand and grinned. "You shouldda seen my name before I got off the boat. Yea, I understand." A part of me mused about when everybody smoked cigarettes publicly. I always carried a packet, and wonderful conversations would ensue when two smokers met and broke ice.

Jo Jo sipped his gluten-free fruit drink. "What's this about a rental car? You didn't rent it?"

I took a photo of Gita out of my shirt pocket and held it in my hand.

"No Jo Jo, I didn't rent the car, a young woman did. She *was* my niece. Thing is, the car was left abandoned in the Economy lot and you guys had to tow it back to your side of the fence. Recall that?"

Jo Jo took a big swig, wiped his mouth with the back of his hand. "Oh yeah," he said. Belched once, and continued, "We all laughed about it, because it was so dirty. Sitting there, end of an aisle. Splattered with slush and puddle waters. And bird poop. Wash Me scrawled a bunch of times."

"Abandoned. Not properly returned." That's what my cop friends said.

"What's your interest, what happened to your niece?"

"She is no more. I am digging for facts. This rental is a lead."

Jo Jo nodded, drained his drink, belched again. Squinted into my face and said, "Okaayy, what do you want?" His eyes were drawn to the photo in my hand.

"Oh, just a few little pieces of info. Where the car is, what you found in it, what you guys did with it, etc."

"Humph, is that all?" Jo Jo said. His tone was flat. I couldn't tell if it was sarcasm or a real question.

"Ideally, I would like to know how many miles were driven, any damage to it, etc. But cops would have looked into it, and I can always ask my buddy about it."

"Why don't you?"

"Sadly enough, this case is not sexy enough or high profile, you see," I shrugged. "Just a little brown girl. I gotta make sure things don't fall through the cracks. My niece, after all."

The fruit drink seemed to have calmed his nerves, he laid it out for me.

The manager became worried when cops contacted him. Their car was rented by a woman who later died. He asked if the cops will impound the car, but they said no. A lone technician came, examined it for whatever, took some photos. That was it. Jo Jo was told to take the vehicle out of rotation, and park it for the time being.

"I gotta go. You still got questions, talk to that guy. He is the only car washer on duty today." Jo Jo vanished.

Well, well, well, the car wash guy turned out to be Mr. Gooby himself.

"Yes, sir, remember that one. I done washed it. The machine was broke that afternoon, and I used manual spray wand and elbow grease. The vehicle is settin' over there," he pointed to a fenced off area.

“Glad you remembered, sir. You cleaned the inside too?”

“Naw, the boss man said it ain’t gonna be rented out for a while, why bother... Funny thing is, I was also on duty when that car went out too.”

“Yeah?”

“Yasser, I just done run it through the washer and took it out front. Where they sign rental papers. Nice Hindu lady.”

My heart fluttered, stopped, willed itself to restart. I sweated. My mouth went dry. Is this where it all comes together? But, but, but there could be so many Hindu ladies. So many harried travelers that leave cars at rental places with keys under the mat.

“You sure about the customer?”

“Same complexion as you. I don’t discriminate, you mind. She your girl? You looking for her?”

“My girl alright, but just to be sure.” I extended my arm toward him. I had Gita in my palm.

“Oh, yeah, that’s her alright. Pretty, if I say so myself. I kinda like the ladies with a bit more meat on them, though.”

“I need to locate her, talk to her.”

“How did you come to lose her, bud? ”

“Men and women have arguments, don’t they?”

"You telling me...” He smiled.

"Is the car unlocked, can I look inside?"

"Sure," said Mr. Car Wash guy. "Listen buddy, don't lose sleep over that little thang. There is lots of fish in the ocean, and some are bitin'." A nudge, a wink.

"Yes, can I see the inside of the car?"

"I guess it don't hurt none. You look harmless," a chuckle.

It was dank and smelly inside. As if some youthful employees had used it for recreational-smoke breaks. Some fast-food wrappers were about. A plastic supermarket shopping bag, a partial roll of paper towels, a travel size packet of tissue. Under the passenger seat, an old fashioned paper map, accordion-folded, to show Northern Illinois. I put it in my jacket.

I opened the glove box. No bloody knife or confession letter, haha. Just a couple of receipts. I pocketed them. Tried to memorize the mileage but luckily remembered the trip odometer. It read 427. Kilometers, I noticed, not miles.

When I got out, the car wash man looked different. He looked pleased with himself. He didn't look quite as old, or slovenly, as at first. He done did his good deed for the day. He helped me, yes sir, he did help.

I thanked him profusely, and turned to walk away. There was a hand on my shoulder. I heard his voice, "Don't worry mister, she ain't for you. Looked to me like she liked the other guy a whole lot more."

The Other guy

I couldn't think or breathe. It was all I could to turn around and face the car wash guy squarely. There was recognition on his face. His statement stunned me, and I could see that he felt bad about it. His face sagged and softened, went tired, and he looked old again.

"That guy surely ain't no better looking than you," he said. "You can be assured of that." A forced laugh. "And that's no BS."

I couldn't decide whether to bale out of there and spare myself further hurts, or probe deeper and torture myself with what might be sordid details. Analysis paralysis. Mr. Gooby sir decided for me with his own brand of talkativeness. "They seemed close, you know. Didn't take eyes of each other. Whispering, sniffling. Like I said, he ain't got nothing on you, mister. You'll be jes fine. Take care." He turned around to leave.

I laid a shaky hand on his arm and engaged his rheumy eyes directly, "I am wondering if this other person with the lady..." I didn't get to finish the query, ('was he a white person, a dark person or what').

Words slithered out of his mouth along with spittle. "I knowed what you is thinkin." He shook his head. "No, she ain't run away with no young buck or a Hollywood stud."

"She was with a man of my complexion? A Hindu man, was he?"

"Guess he was. Same skin tone as you, same age too."

More shock, more paralysis. *Older Indian man?* Something clicked and I blurted, "did they have a lot of luggage?"

"I am not a cabbie, mister. Not my job to load or unload bags. Jes wash cars is all." He walked away.

***

During the ride back home, my mind was as noisy as the train. The steel-on-steel rattle of the wheels, the din of the underpasses. and the garbled announcements. One huge melee, but no match for the buzz in my mixed-up mind.

Gita didn't run off on a whim with some white college guy. At least, that was something. And, she didn't elope with some obscure Bollywood wannabe. That was even better. Or, was it? Who on earth could have lured her away from a happy secure life on Devon Avenue? What older Indian dude could do *that*?

I had entertained some suspicions as a matter of course, about Warangal, Shetty, Ghose, and assorted single men of Devon Avenue. But, I had nothing on them, yet. And, if Gita tried to run away with an older Indian, why was young Warangal acting so secretive and distraught lately? Why didn't Lalu have any clue?

At Logan Square station, I transferred to a city bus that took me homeward. A new sort of confusion took over my mind. When the day started, all I sought to find out was where Gita drove the rental car to. Instead of answering that I wound up with a zillion other questions.

What started it all was, how did the rental car come back to the airport? The rental agreement was in Gita's name. Her body was in a farm a hundred miles away, yet the car returned to the airport? What sort of magic was that? The rental car was no Lassie to return home unerringly. Not even *Narada* who could travel freely through all known levels of Creation could do that!

No, it wasn't magic. It was some evil person who drove the rental car back. Is it possible that Gita brought the rental car back herself, was then forced to abandon it, and got taken away? Naw, that's too many branches off the Fault Tree, said my analytical mind. The dumber part of me just wanted to know what evil did Gita encounter?

I inventoried the known unknowns. It made for a bad enough list. Where else did the car go besides, apparently, the farm where Gita was found? What did the mileage I wrote down on the rental car signify? What route did the car take? Did it get any traffic tickets, if so where and for what violations? Did it stop for gas?

There was an old Hollywood film-noir movie I once saw, in which a body is found slumped in a taxi left in front of a police station. The detectives note the amount of money on the meter and drive the taxi in a dozen different directions to see where it matched the exact fare. I couldn't recall the ending of the movie, or if the cops succeeded in estimating the distance the cab was driven. But, I did stop to purchase a large detailed map of Northern Illinois. And a planimeter.

Walking home from the bus stop, I got restless from the echoes of Mr. Gooby's words.

'They looked like they were intense...They was cozy, not lovey-dovey like. Her eyes were on him all the time. Just saw them for a few minutes, mind.'

It was the last thing I expected to discover today. But, who was the person with her? She must know him, right?

Did she go willingly, or was it under duress?

Who drove the car back to the airport?

***

Back in my apartment, I retrieved some leftover KungPao from the fridge, and began to pick at it without warming it first. I tried to get comfortable in my single sofa with its pretend Lazy-Boy styling and an equally pretend leather cover.

The gooey cold food was my symbol of a cosmopolitan existence, where I could pretend to exist beyond the bounds of curry and pickled mango. Something kept flashing in my mind between chopstick pickings. What was it?

Man, I am getting old.

I went back to the fridge to get some teriyaki sauce packets and returned to the living room. My plan was to spread the map out, and run the planimeter to see where the mileage I wrote down from the rental car took me to.

It hit me when I stirred the sauce into the noodles. A similar fridge door being closed with care, like I wanted to ensure nobody could tell that I opened it at all. Where was it?

Naw, it wasn't the door closing or door hinge. No, it did have something to do with a fridge door. What was it? Got to be something else about the fridge door, not the action of opening or closing it.

I put KungPao aside and took a deep breath, relaxed, and closed my eyes and opened my ears. Some slow and steady breathing took me past the cloying smells of Asiatic foods.

Get lost cold teriyaki. Hello odors of stale air freshener and faded curries.

A business card, a paper with some directions written on it. Or was it a hand drawn map with miles written on it?

There was a fridge door that I opened multiple times. But which one?

I am opening and closing doors. I keep it closed a long time. My eyes sweep the door, yes there are some magnets, an Indian flag magnet, a doctor's office number, phone numbers of some Indian stores, a scrap of paper with a handwritten number 'Doctor Dental Reddy'. Something else, what is it.

I gave up the auto-hypnosis after a few tries, emptied more sauce packets into the KungPao and ate the leftovers. The TV news showed flights being delayed at all Chicago airports due to sudden micro-bursts and thowers--

I jumped up and rushed to my own fridge and closed my eyes. I saw it clearly then... In Gita's kitchen. A passing glance at the fridge door. What was it that I had seen?

A ticket stub, LGA-ORD-LGA, payment method CASH in block letters. Flight# 327 Dep 16:11 Mar/30

I returned to the couch and slumped in it with a sigh. It didn't make no sense. Why would Gita have a ticket stub from a flight? What did LGA mean anyway.

Thanks to a million shows filmed in the Big Apple and Hollywood, most everyone in the world knew that LAX was Los Angeles and JFK was New York airport. Being a Chicagoan, I knew the initials ORD referred to O'Hare Airport, (technically ORD stood for Orchard, its original location at an apple orchard in Bensenville, Illinois).

But what on earth was LGA and what was it doing on the door of a refrigerator. Just the stub and not the ticket itself. It must have had a name of the passenger on the stub part too. What was it? What was it doing on a refrigerator door and held by a Chicago flag magnet.

What else on that fridge door?

A business card. Of Dr. Bharathi, 'voted Illinois's best well baby doctor'. The back of the card showing an upcoming ultrasound appointment.

Ms. Honeycutt

I found Ms. Honeycutt in the sub-basement of the building that housed the morgue, located at the corner of 22nd & Ogden. The pleasant looking lady was the mistress in charge of the dead bodies resting in chilly freezers. I got there somewhat early and watched her from the back of the 'cutting' room. She was dealing with a bunch of people in lab coats and smocks holding some sort of forms, and formed a cluster in front of her.

Ms. Honeycutt inspected the forms one by one. I saw her finger run down each sheet, methodically tapping at four or five spots. After satisfying herself, apparently, she would mark a corner with a highlighter. Her caramel colored fleece hoodie was pushed back, revealing light brown hair with blonde highlights. From time to time, a big grin appeared on her face suddenly, and disappeared just as suddenly.

I kept rehearsing in my mind how I was going to approach this lady, who seemed casual at first blush, but turned out to be meticulous and quite procedural. Would she be amenable to my shtick, I wondered. The smell of the air around hit me out of nowhere, and the sharpness of it, the sterile nature of it jolted me out of a reverie. Along with the thought that sincerity might be the best way to reach this earthy lady.

Her eyes crinkled at something occasionally. The fawn color lipsticked mouth parted a bit and a comment would slide out.

Like, "This one, signed who? Professor Skulnik or Sklotowsky, can't tell, yeah okay,"

Or, "You didn't put down the grant number in this box, it should have eight digits in it. Oh, I see that you squeezed it down over at the bottom but you put only 7 digits. See darling, if you had put it in where you shouldda, it's gonna have enough space." Big grin on, then off.

And, to a grizzled old fellow in an open collar shirt and a worn out green smock, "You come for more glial cells doc? Still chasing meth crystals in the brain?" Again, grin on, grin off, but only more softly for the doc guy.

So went the proceedings while I waited. She lifted her head up a couple of times to give me the once over before she returned to her supplicants. The group eventually left. At last, it was me and Ms. Honeycutt, face to face. I was nervous.

"You the Kumar guy who kept calling me all week?" she asked.

"Yes," I said.

"What tissue you looking for?"

"I am not in research. But you're right, I have done histochemical studies. But that was way back in my past. Thanks, by the way, for agreeing to meet me, Ms. Honeycutt, hope it wouldn't make you miss your train."

"Don't worry about it. I asked you to come at this time cause all I gotta to do is file paperwork. You can talk while I do that."

"It looked busy there for a while," I said.

"We get a lot of research people at the end of the day. The cadavers are all ready and prepped. I set up requests for the night shift autopsies. Grad students, PhD candidates, people on government grants, all sorts of tissue hungry people come here. Swoop down like vultures, hehehe."

"I noticed how you handled them, you were part bartender

remembering ‘the usual’, and part flight attendant, keeping passengers in line,” I laughed.

“So, you are *not* here to pick over the stiff for your little bits of tissue. Is that what you’re saying?”

I chuckled as I nodded my agreement.

“No grant money, huh” she said.

“Mercifully, I am not one of those who lives for science. My reason is different,” I said with a slow and deliberately awkward grin.

She responded with a grin of her own style. “And what is that?”

“Well, it’s a bit delicate,” I mumbled. “Mind you nothing wrong, nothing official...”

“Just delicate, huh...”

“I know your brother Larry. He usually drives the Lincoln Avenue bus Number Eleven? I often ride it to Devon Avenue. My friend owns a restaurant over there.”

“My brother? Oh, you mean Larry? Larry Joyner!” Ms. Honeycutt’s face became full of teeth. A wholesome joyful face. “Larry, he my cousin, we grew up together, same house, same grands. Yea, that’s okay. We are almost like real brother and sister.” She loosened her fleece jacket, sat down on a round steel stool, and signaled for me to sit too.

“Larry gave me your information and said you might be able to help me.”

Ms. Honeycutt kept eye contact for quite a while, sizing me up.

A slight grin continued and the happy face didn't fade out at all. Her eyes softened too, and I began to regret that I was going to put such a nice person into a bind.

"I have been hoping that Larry would've told you about me," I said.

"Now I remember, he sure did. You are the computer guy Larry likes. He always asking people computer questions. You give him your card once? He goes on the internet and looks everything up. He sharp. Says you two talk about food and police work a lot."

"Yes, we do that. I answer a lot of his questions, but I didn't know he was in total online immersion."

"Larry is like that. But me, I don't touch that stuff. I go home, relax and watch soap operas," she giggled.

"I am glad Larry mentioned me. It just makes it easier for me."

"You shouldda tole me over the phone that you're friends with my brother. Instead of something about a body to collect and you didn't have a Release Number..."

Ms. Honeycutt now gave her classic big grin, except it was expansive like in a cartoon where it was all mouth and no face.

"So, what's you and Larry up to now, Mr. Kumar?"

I was feeling relaxed enough that I wanted to show her the picture of Gita, which I did.

"This is Gita, my niece. Actually my friend's nice, the one who owns a restaurant on Devon Avenue. Him and I are real close, like brothers..."

She put a hand on my arm, "Brothers, huh. Just like me and Larry. You know, Larry tried to get all my family to go out there and eat your food. But we never did though. Larry love butter chicken, biryani type of rice and all that Indian and Pakistani food."

I just nodded and let her go on.

"Thanks to you, Larry connected all his things, you know, modem, cables and stuff. Used to be all he did was watch sports on cable TV. Now, he talks about interesting things. What happened to this sweet pea? Such a pretty girl," she handed Gita back to me.

I took a deep breath, "She is in here, in one of the drawers." I turned to face the back rooms of the facility. Tried not to choke up. Ms. Honeycutt, on the other hand, let out an unhesitating gasp, a hand to her mouth, eyes wide and totally still. I put Gita's photo back in my pocket.

"I feel you baby, I am sorry," she touched my arm again. "I don't see how I can help. You need to see Dr. Bansal, he'll be here in a couple hours. Go get coffee or something." She pronounced Ban Sal. But I'd recognize the name of a north Indian cousin anywhere. Also, I had seen his name on the staff listings earlier, when I first entered the building. Doctor Bansal, I am sure was a nice guy, but he was the last person I needed to see.

"I think I'll do that," I said. "But you can help me before that. I need to see what the coroner's report said. Why he recommended a full autopsy, why they sent the body over here from downstate where it was found."

Honeycutt's eyes darkened and hardened slowly. "What's going on here? You playing at being a cop, or what?"

"Believe me, nothing nefarious is going on here. Cops are being super tight lipped about Gita's case. We just want to know where it is going. I need to see the report."

She sat back down, and so did I. We stared at each other for some time during which I examined my fingers, nails and the backs of my hands. She put her fleece jacket back on, buttoned it, picked up her purse and placed it in her lap.

"Please," I said. "We know it was not a natural death. Quite possibly a murder. I hate to let the case fall through the cracks."

"Sorry babe," she whispered. "The records aren't here. Even if they did, I could lose my job, I shouldn't even be talking to you." She stood up, but I didn't. I swiveled around on the hard seat of the stool. And eventually engaged her eyes.

"Things happen around us, Ms. Honeycutt, for reasons not always known to us. When Larry sent word to me to contact him, when I was in police lockup, I didn't know what would come of it. All's I knew then was that an elderly African man mopping the floor, handed me a slip of paper with your brother's number on it. On a different occasion, a blue-haired dog I had never seen before, came over to stand next to me and comforted me in a cornfield. Things happen…"

"A mop and pail? Did his overall say Moses? Yeah? That's my uncle Mo! Old as Moses hisself. Won't retire ever. Keeps working, keeps his head down. Good Lord! He sneaked Larry's number to you, huh," Ms. Honeycutt grinned again.

"Let me see that picture again." Took it from my hand. This time she caressed Gita's face, felt the stiff paper between her fingers, and whispered, "So this is the little girl you went to jail for, huh. Lucky she had good uncles."

"Just an overnight detention," I mumbled. "Got out with no charges. Your uncle Moses saw me that afternoon. I didn't never really think anything would come of it," I sighed.

Ms. Honeycutt disappeared while I was in my soliloquy, I realized.

She came waddling back, hand bag tucked under her arm, scarf around her neck, and heavy in gait. She sighed, laid a hand on my shoulder, and steered me up off the stool, and out of the darkening oppressive closed space.

During our walk out together, Ms. Honeycutt gave me what she could, and what I dreaded to hear.

"Okay babe, this is what's going on. The ME here is asked to do a full autopsy including the special protocols the legislature passed recently for young women of child bearing age, the whole works. They already know the girl to be pregnant. They trying to see if it's connected to whoever killed her. A lot of DNA testing."

Now they all know

I couldn't wait to share my new knowledge, so I showed up the next day at the Blue Mountain much earlier than usual. My report wouldn't answer everything, but it was a step forward, and Lalu should know about it.

It was well before the start of lunch, most of the food preparation was done except for the tempering of food. The kitchen's door to the rear alley was open and a big fan was going. Lalu and Shetty each worked with a ladle the size of a hubcap. Hooray, they were roasting spices in oil. As I looked on, they turned over the hot mixtures of *masala* into the latest cooked curries: mixed vegetables, potatoes and peas, okra, and sambar. Loud sizzles and clouds of warm smoke erupted instantly, and got chased into the alley by the blowing fan.

The two cooks placed tight fitting lids over the tempering, wiped their faces and smiled at each other in triumph. Another battle won against bland food. *Viva La Curry,* I suppose. The air in the kitchen crackled and my whole body tingled. Invisible molecules of masala overwhelmed my senses for a minute or two. And then it all settled down. Gone away were the dull stale odors of the previous day. In with the fresh, tingly, sharp odors of a new-born curry.

I inhaled deeply and returned to the dining area where Lalu joined me. Ghose was left in the kitchen to stir up the curry dishes and load them into large trays for the self-service buffet.

"Lalu, I have some new..." I began, but he cut me off. "Eat something first," rushed out of his mouth.

A tray of snacks appeared, courtesy of Shetty, along with water and chai. My compatriots watched me take the first few bites. Even after all the years, I was still regarded as a guest. With that ritual behind us, they could all join in some well deserved snacking before the lunch rush.

The other staff, consisting of two Mexican young men, were on the floor setting up tables for the buffet spread, and put place settings, water glasses etc., on dining tables.

Ghose joined us, but jumped up when the front door dinged and in walked Krishna. "Opheesr Warangal," Ghose exclaimed. He rushed to hold the door open. Krishna strode in, and without taking his jacket off, settled into the chair pulled out by Ghose. Lalu continued to wipe his face with a thin towel that reeked of the kitchen. Shetty sat side saddle to display his full lanky frame. Warangal slid his chair back a bit, much farther than needed for comfort or legroom. *What was that distancing all about?*

"I managed to visit the mortuary where Gita's body is being kept," I said. "They found out many things about her death." Lalu leaned in a bit and shifted in his chair, kept wiping his face. Shetty and Ghose gasped, and breathed through their mouths. Warangal pursed his lips, stared off into the distance in stony silence, and leaned noticeably farther back in his chair. More distancing. Hmm.

I hesitated momentarily, but went with my instinct. I put off any mention of Ms. Honeycutt, her bus-driver-brother Larry, or the nittty-gritty of how I came by any of the stuff I learnt.

"Our Gita died of foul play. They think she was choked to death. It is a case of murder. They say there are many clues on her body indicating that Gita was killed by someone very strong. Someone she probably knew and trusted. Police are not ready to give us the body." Warangal nodded very slowly, still not looking at anybody. The rest of them stared.

The bubble of silence didn't last, the two young Mexican workers approached Lalu inquiringly, who nodded. The fellows went about with the finishing touches to the buffet, they lit warming candles under the curry trays and poured ice around bowls of yogurt dressing, leafy salads and desserts. Fresh deep fried papadam, and pakora took their place in the lineup.

I looked at each of the four fellow Indians around me in turn, "The medical examiner says that more tests need to be done..."

Lalu erupted, "Still doing tests? What tests, why tests?" He slapped the table. "Gita is dead, they need a test for *that?*" His face darkened and trembled even as the words shot out of his mouth.

"What tests, Kumar sir?" said Shetty." Life has gone out of her. No medicine can make Gita live again. Why more tests." His hands spread out like a book opening in the middle.

Young Ghose, his mouth agape, rapidly looked from me to Lalu and back. Still breathing hard, he tried to slither out of there. A wave of his boss's hand made him sit back down. Lalu tried to get hold of himself. He looked at me long, and not so hard. He spoke slowly and tapped the table with his full palm after each sentence.

"Kumar, go to your friend, the detective." Tap.

"You two help each other before." Tap, tap.

"Mullins must explain to you now."

Tap, tap, tap. Three in a row.

"What tests, why tests, why delay. We need Gita's body.

Cremation, most important." Many taps, soft and tapering off. Lalu was done, and went back to a stoic face,

The Indian in me knew that Lalu Ganesh wasn't talking to me like a child. His was a cultivated patience of the finely honed kind. But then again, the same Indian in me also realized that Lalu right then was also a person at his wit's end. The next stop could well be a full blown conniption. *Tread carefully. Reveal gradually. For sanity's sake.*

"Oh, definitely, the cops have to explain," I said. You can rest assured that I will make sure they do. Gita's body is being kept in cold storage. There won't be a violation of flesh, er ... she will be suitable for cremation. If we want to do it here."

"We are not sending her to India?" Shetty asked.

"That can be done too. There are special ways of shipping the casket. We can send the body home packed in special ice. Once there, the family can place her on firewood just like any other body and do the cremation ceremony."

"Gita sister needs a ticket?" Ghose asked.

"Yes, Ghose. She needs a ticket, so to speak. An expensive ticket. For the box, ice, permits, doctor's letters, permission slips."

"Same plane as people?"

Shetty chuckled, "Why do you ask Ghose, you want to go with her?"

Warangal finally spoke up. "Remember Ghose, you can't put her on the seat next to you. She will travel inside a cold box in the belly of the airplane."

"Like a suitcase?" Ghose's face showed pain, and gave himself a Siva-slap at such a bad thought.

I explained the options, that it depended on what we could afford. Passenger planes charged more, and our people back home would have to go collect the box. Cargo planes were cheaper, but took longer to schedule, arrange for inspection, but they make a door delivery.

"So many problems, Kumar sir. When it is my time, I wish to just die in my own village," said Shetty. "What about you, Ghose?"

"God decides death."

"Your wish, Ghose. *Your wish*. Don't you wish to be near the river Ganga when you die?" Shetty asked.

"Ganga River, Chicago River. Not different," Ghose said.

"But you are a Hindu, Ghose. Ganga is our mother," Shetty persisted.

"God wants I die near Ganga? He buy my plane ticket."

Mild titters all around, except from Lalu. He remained thoughtful and only pretended to follow the banter. But, at least, he was breathing steadily again.

"What about you Kumar, you want to die here or India?" asked Warangal.

"Let me see what American heaven looks like first. I will decide then."

"Haha, good joke, Kumar saab," said Shetty.

Krishna spoke up. "You have to light up a joint first to get a preview of heaven, Kumar. But, do it away from my sergeant. He is not flexible like me, hehe."

Titters again, but this time not on the face of Ghose who looked confused, but spoke up anyway. "Opheessir Krishna, where you die?"

Krishna tuned on an air of thoughtful silence. His face clouded over and looked way more grim than the silly turn in our morbid chat warranted. His mind was elsewhere. Surely, it couldn't be on his own death? Naw, it's gotta be something about Gita's death. Shetty looked at me, and I returned my own look of concern.

Warangal went into the kitchen and returned with a fresh cup of chai. "You people are bad in the head," he said. "One of our friends is dead, you just talk about what's a good place to die, and how to ship the body. Bad, just bad." He just stood there with one hand holding a mug of chai, and the other on his hip. Blowing softly on the hot tea, sipping noisily.

I got the impression that the young Indian policeman was trying to be part of the group, and yet couldn't bring himself to share fully, or tell us what he was thinking. After all, he must know by now, that I had more than an inkling about him and Gita being in love.

"There is something else," I said. Four pairs of eyes upon me.

A group of Americans came in, smiled at us, and proceeded to pick through the buffet offerings. We smiled back at them, watched them settle into their own banter and munching.

I faced my group again. "The doctors say that Gita was going to be a mother. She would have had a baby in a few months. By *Diwali* or *Dusserah.*" Don't know about the others, but it sure was a relief to me to get that off my chest. I didn't relish giving the news. It just had to be done.

Lalu spoke, his voice week, hollow, tired. "So this is what you are hiding, telling us slowly. First you tell us she was in love, like an American girl. Then you tell us how violently she died. Now, you work your way back in here, and this time she is a mother before marriage." Lalu looked defeated. Life seemed to drain out of him leaving him slumped and shrunk, looking like a saggy sac of flour.

There was moisture in Shetty's eyes. Ghose's mouth hung open.

"I am sorry Lalu, but that's the truth. Doctors confirmed it."

Lalu's head hung down and he didn't raise it for a long time. And, when Ghose rose to slip away into the kitchen Lalu didn't stop him. I thought I heard Shetty sniffle, and just waited for Lalu to face me.

Eventually, Ganesh did raise his head and asked, "So, who has Gita been spending time with?"

I looked around the room before answering. Officer Warangal was nowhere to be seen.

"That is where the new test come in. Some people who knew Gita will have to take blood tests. Us too," I wove a circle around us three. "Excuse me, but I need to freshen up my chai." I went into the kitchen and asked Ghose about Officer Warangal. He pointed at the door to the alley and said, "Gone."

When I returned to the dining room Lalu was standing, seemingly preparing to go somewhere. “Don’t worry Kumar. You don’t have to tell me the name of Gita’s secret lover. I don’t care.” He looked at Shetty who was still dabbing his eyes. “My friend Shetty, get ready. I won’t enjoy doing this food business anymore.” He patted Shetty on the shoulders.

And just before entering the kitchen, Lalu paused, stared at me and said, “You continue as a detective. Keep digging. Remember, you are not planting a fruit tree, you are digging dirt, just like a grave digger. You enjoy digging?” Lalu shrugged and answered his own question, “You are good detective. Bad friend.” Lalu shrugged again and slid into the kitchen.

I couldn’t say that I was shocked by his reaction. Such things happen between friends - bad news bears and all. But, what concerned me was that Lalu’s words were delivered softly, not due to other people being in the room, but it was his own sense of near defeat. Specially, when he said these last words: “Don’t worry Kumar. I am not angry with you or anybody.”

*****

My Dear Sashanki,

I find myself in a great big new turmoil. The facts are rather murky, but Gita's death is a full-fledged police case now.

I could use your insight and maternal wisdom. Could you stand to deal with learning about another deceased young lady, without being stirred up about your own Durga? To my thinking, Gita actually couldn't be that much different from Durga, age-wise. If you feel that you could handle some additional details, kindly let me know.

Here in America I feel somehow lost about the matter of this young girl's death. I need to hear from you - both as an Indian mother, and as someone I respect. Have you heard of Skype?

Your friend and Well-Wisher,
Anand Kumar, Chicago.

****

My Dear Mr. Kumar,

Thank you for your most recent.

Yes, feel free to write about Gita Ganesh. It speaks to your kind heart and sensitivity that you are sickened by her tragedy. I am quite anxious to know the details of her death, and your plans to help Mr. Lalu.

My memories of meeting with her uncle are a bit dim, but I do remember that she helped me make that special dinner at your doctor friends' home. I recall her as being pretty, energetic and full of plans for becoming a caterer.

My first thoughts are that it takes an exceptional kind of

courage for an Indian girl to live abroad away from her parents. You further say she has her own apartment separate from her uncle's bungalow. That's even more audacious for a Hindu girl. Loneliness presses upon young women who are left to their own devices, far more so than it does on young men. Only the most gregarious and piquant of single Indian women can fend for themselves emotionally. Our girls are particularly sheltered emotionally. And cherished by their families. Being cut off from the extended family, loneliness could become a source of anxiety and self-doubt. Lalu is a good man and he loved his niece very much. She had that. But is that enough for a marriageable girl?

What actually happened? Email me the facts as you know. I am all ears.

Sincerely Yours,
Sashanki.

PS: You enjoy writing letters, and that's good. But, you know, it's also okay to talk on the phone now and then. I would enjoy listening to you.

PPS: I don't have to tell you, a computer guy, that when in a rush, you could email me.

****

My placid morning

The trill of the telephone interrupted my placid morning of classical music, a colorful three-egg omelet of cheese, tomato and bell peppers, and the two-inch thick Sunday Chicago Tribune. That unwelcome sound upset me, to say the least. It's not often that I had all the ingredients to make breakfast, at least not all at the same time. And the Sunday paper was, of course, a ritual all of its own. I set the fork down and headed over to the phone leaving the coffee mug steaming.

Had I been paying attention I would have realized that the call from my friend, Lalu Ganesh, should be more puzzling than vexing. But, the mood I was in at that moment, I only felt annoyance. I wasn't mentally prepared for what was to come. The Caller ID showed he was calling from home and not his restaurant, the Blue Mountain. That made it curious already. Second, the tone and the brevity of his words made it even more curious.

"Kumar come immediately, the police also coming." Click.

The cryptic request and the abrupt hangup were not surprising given what's been going on. Gita's death and its investigation have been proceeding in fits and starts. But, there was something else, a quiver, in Lalu's voice that I had never heard before. It puzzled me, and my shoes went on at once. I remembered to put my thinking cap on too.

There was also the word police, too generic and vague. I really had to stroke my chin about that one. Fortunately, it was a long train ride to Lalu's house on the far Northwest side of Chicago and I had time to ponder the matter, between sections of the Sunday paper.

My first reaction was that Lalu was contrite about his reaction to my revelations about Gita. Partial revelations, of course. I didn't unload the more grievous details about Warangal's letters and such. But, that didn't involve police coming to Lalu's bungalow. It had to be something else Something that couldn't wait a visit to the Blue Mountain. Did someone visiting the restaurant tell Lalu some new fact about the case. If that were the case, why didn't the call come from Blue Mountain? The train was racing and reverberating through the subway tunnel, and so was my mind.

A new message or query from India perhaps? Something so ... so what? Accusatory? Abusive? Did a friend of the Ganesh clan who just got news of Gita's death, pickup phone and assail Lalu across the oceans? Lalu had been through so much incoming invective, he would have became a past-master at it. The poor guy's shoulders became too soft and slumped, to even make like a shrug.

As the train emerged from the tunnel and settled into a steady rumble, so did my thoughts. It occurred to me that this particular phone call by Lalu had a cryptic quality all of its own. The quiver in his voice indicated distress. I felt immense pity for the poor fellow, all over again.

A sense of *deja-vu* arose in me. The unease I felt as the train swayed along, on elevated tracks under blue skies, echoed my ride on #11-Lincoln bus to Blue Mountain in early April. It seemed like ages since I first learned of Gita's death. But, unlike that April afternoon, when I bolted out of bed and rushed to learn of Gita's passing, this time I was in my element. I had just taken a leisurely bath, clipped toenails, cologned up, and worn clothes fresh out of a dryer in the basement of my apartment building. I intended it to be my sort of a comfy, newspaper & omelet type of Sunday morning.

This time though, I didn't feel any hint of Ms. Agnes, the tabby, on my clothing. There were no reminders of her odor, her paws or her shed hair. I usually sensed the cat about me. But, on this train ride to Lalu's house I was without a reminder of Ms. Agnes. The clatter of wheels only added to further the disorientation.

Lalu's house was located in one of those parts of Chicago that journalists and people involved in real estate loved to describe as a 'bungalow belt'. A succinct description of a neighborhood where houses had little variation, streets were regular, children left toys on lawns, and every home sprouted a television dish. Bungalow Belt said it all. Solid citizens lived here. Folks here were respectable.

I walked the five short blocks from the train station toward the bungalow belt with my collar turned up against the light breeze, but with the zipper of my down vest undone. It was that sort of uncertain weather with which Windy City often teased its residents. I expected Lalu's street to be a beehive of activity with lots of police. Instead, it was more like all quiet on the western front.

Only two vehicles could be recognized as out of place. One was an official marked car parked in the front, but with no lights flashing. The second was an unmarked car with a blue stuck-on light on the dashboard, pulled onto Lalu's driveway. I recognized it as the big gray Chevy sedan of our good friend the detective, Mike Mullins.

The street was quiet, the homes were quiet. Just a typical Chicago Sunday morning, people still waking up, not too much astir. Lalu's house was a cream colored, recently-roofed, solid, brick octagonal, with a four-step cement walk-up leading to a squarish landing. I went up the short flight of steps, past a wrought iron bench and flower pots on a ledge, and through an unlocked front door.

The inside of the house was equally subdued.

What's the scene here, man?

"You Kumar?" I heard before I saw the uniformed officer, a youngish fellow who had his cap under one arm, and the proverbial flip notebook in the other. And taking my answer for granted, he motioned me toward the hallway leading to the kitchen, "They're in the back. Garage."

A beat cop who seemed to know it all. The images I conjured up during the train ride, chalk outlines, yellow tape, flashing lights - they all vanished instantly. But that only mystified me further.

I walked down the kitchen and picked up voices coming from beyond and went through the back door of the kitchen into a screened porch area. It's the sort of bright enclosed space that home sellers like to call a Florida Room. Through the screens surrounding the Florida Room, I saw Lalu and Mullins standing on the apron in front of the garage.

The door of the garage was mostly down to just a few feet off the ground. The blue paint of the garage floor vividly contrasted with the dirty-gray, chipped asphalt of the driveway. Why on earth was the door open only partially? More mystery...

Lalu nodded me over. The detective made like a gesture of a hello with one hand, while his other still lay on my friend's shoulder. Mike seemed to be patting Lalu. Comforting him?

"Gentlemen, what's going on? Lalu, you sounded so upset on the phone, so abrupt. What happened. It's all so quiet out here."

The two gents looked at me and each other.

The detective said, "It got taken care of for the most part, Kumar. I think it is best if you explain, Lalu saab," Mike paused.

"Thank god, Kumar, you came. You missed most of the madness. Thank you for coming right away," Lalu gushed, and abruptly grabbed me, hugged and smothered me. Moisture on my shirt sleeve said a lot. When he finally let go of me, and wiped his tears off, Mullins raised the garage door all the way up and beckoned me.

With the sun not yet at zenith, Lalu's Honda gleamed with a quiet dignity and shimmered nicely. It sat to a side of the large space, with plenty of room left over. Mullins stood in that space and shined his light up. He waved me over.

Hanging down from the highest beam of the garage was a white rope, half inch thick, tied tight at the top. The end dangled above our heads, and had a clean tip like it was recently severed. A short three legged wooden stool lay on its side nearby.

Lalu remained on the apron and let Mike show me it all.

"You missed most of the action, my friend," the detective said finally. "I got here just as the ambulance was leaving. Lalu saab called me right after he called 911."

The radio on his hip crackled. He put it to his ear and cocked his head. I only heard gibberish and static. But the detective apparently heard English and made out what was transmitted. He looked pleased and nodded at us.

"They have him on a ventilator, needing assistance with breathing. I think he'll be alright."

I looked at Lalu who was still misty eyed and nodded.

The detective spoke again, addressing Lalu directly: "You are in no condition to drive. The officer will take you to St. Anthony's and bring you back home after you talk to the doctors. I will follow along." Mike headed to his own Chevy sedan.

I turned to Lalu. He uttered a single word, "Warangal."

Riding in police car

As the police car sped along North Elston Avenue, I tried to lean back and gather my thoughts. I couldn't. My mind, and my body, the two seemed to run away from each other. I was literally in the edge of the seat. Lalu had no such problem. He looked composed, closed his eyes, and breathed easily.

I should have been worrying about Warangal, which I kinda did, but couldn't get past my initial reaction to entering the back seat of the police car. My first thought was that it was a unique, but disturbing, way to be driven anywhere. Especially for a non-criminal. The ride we were being given was, after all, an act of kindness. Courtesy of our detective friend. I should be grateful for that, I told myself. But, I was in a zone, a zone of conflict, odd in its own way.

It did not feel like any ride I ever got. My whole body felt most peculiar: I didn't sweat, palpitate, or get nauseous. Why would I? However, I just couldn't relax. An old and unforgettable sensation I couldn't name vibrated in my body. My back, forearms and chest felt warm and heavy. Though I tried to focus on the suicide attempt by Warangal, and the reasons for it, my mind did its own thing and obsessed over my immediate environs.

Sitting in the back of a police car and having a police officer drive us was no limousine ride. Sure, the officer was polite, even kind, but I *knew* that he was no chauffeur. *And*, it didn't feel like a taxi cab ride either. The officer driving us was too clean-cut for that. The vehicle didn't have flashing lights or siren turned on, but there was no mistaking its feel of a police car. The smell of sweat left behind by criminals, the constricted space of a wire-screen cage, lack of door handles, they all screamed police car. Events of the day already had me discombobulated, the ride in a police car worsened the feeling.

The abrupt phone call (which was becoming a habit with Lalu), my abandoned breakfast, his latest misery, and the sight of a rope hanging in the garage - they were disturbing enough. But, the thought of the noose tightening around young Warangal's neck, and how he must have suffered, compounded it all to an unbearable limit.

Questions kept popping in my head, as to how Lalu discovered Warangal in the garage, who cut him down, etc. Now isn't the time for all that curiosity, I told myself. I was too distraught to probe Lalu. But getting a nice ride to the hospital, courtesy of our thoughtful detective friend - I should have been pleased, but wasn't. I was stirred up in an ancient sort of a way. I felt like a criminal, and not a criminal, both at the same time. There was also a sensation that I done wrong. An uneasy feeling that I was entering some place unknown, even though I *knew* we were going to see Warangal. And, maybe, get some unasked questions answered. *I should try and get outside my mind. Maybe, actually, get back into the right form of it?*

The dispatch radio in the cruiser was turned down, but somehow the young cop seemed to hear it quite well. He picked up the mouthpiece a few times and whispered into it. Like it was a matter of course. It wasn't a matter of course to me, and it didn't do anything to ground me in the present. The ride to the hospital was more disturbing than the ride to the bungalow belt.

We pulled into a circular driveway in front of the emergency entrance. I wanted to say or do something to comfort Lalu, but found myself shaking. Sweat began to bead on my forehead. Lalu laid a hand on my forearm and patted softly. For the second time in as many weeks, it was the grieving uncle doing the comforting. And it was I, Kumar, the brash valiant private seeker of truth that needed it.

***

We entered the hospital building through an underground entrance and took a short elevator ride to the general reception area. The clean hospital air immediately cleared the fog in my mind, its antiseptic sharpness a welcome reprieve from the police car.

Calls must have been placed ahead of our arrival. Seeing us approach, the lady at the desk rose, ready with a clipboard. She looked us up and down silently, and decided we were the right people. She peeled off two hand-written name tags and proffered them to us, one in each hand. As if to say, you guys figure out who gets which.

"Go straight down, turn left at the second, elevator to third floor. The nurse's station will guide you." She gestured with two fingers, then three fingers, followed by a chopping motion. Like a football umpire calling downs and signaling to the camera. I stuck my badge over my shirt pocket, gave the lady my thanks, and hurried after Lalu. He was already walking with his badge held between his fingers.

We missed our turn in the long hallway. Lalu showed his hospital tag to a nurse coming out of a supply closet. She read the patient's name and the unit, said "Oh, yes," and escorted us to the correct elevator.

I never felt so physically ill at ease as when I stepped off the elevator. The floor, walls and everything else about the Emergency Unit was pristine and clean beyond pale. The extreme nature of it heightened my sense of anxiety. It didn't feel like I was going to see a person who just had a close brush with death. Rather, it felt more like I was in a time and place that was more after-death like.

“It’s okay,” I heard Lalu whisper. The lady at the nurses’ station looked at her own, fancier, clipboard, and nodded, and led us through a smaller maze.

“Be very quiet, he is awake but resting. Fifteen minutes.” Unlike the receptionist downstairs, she produced no hand gestures, just sternness. Lalu and I nodded our heads, both together. Finally, we were in sync, ready to look at our young friend.

Emergency Situation

He looked about as wretched as I expected. After all, the Emergency Room wasn't a place people went to by choice. It was where folks found out they were in worse condition than they thought. Is it possible that all those medical machines in the room made it look worse? Lalu Ganesh, standing next to me, remained silent, stoic, and seemingly opinion-less.

Liquids flowed through a variety of tubes connected to Warangal's body. Like, there were more tubes outside his body than inside. Glass, plastic, rubber and chrome fittings everywhere. An array of gadgets with digital displays emitted colors, and lights blinked. They surrounded the headboard of his hospital bed like an electronic halo for the suffering. The whole thing looked like a science lab, minus the blue flame of a Bunsen burner and gurgling liquids emitting foul smelling gases. The object of all that medico-technical adoration, Warangal, just lay there looking deflated.

"Hello, young man." His eyes opened upon hearing my voice. There was fear in them. However, I forced myself to pretend I didn't notice it, and motioned for Lalu to approach him.

"How you feeling, son?" Lalu asked.

Warangal raised a cord-connected hand, made like a nod and mouthed okay. Lalu moved closer to the bed, sandwiched Warangal's hand between his own two palms, and murmured: "Don't worry about anything. Get your strength first. Important." A single tear rolled down Warangal's cheek at the contact. He looked at me, his lips moved, but I couldn't read anything. Maybe, they merely trembled. During the remainder of our visit, his tear-flow was intermittent, his eyes would close. Whenever he opened them I saw an inner terror. Whatever was going on, it got me worrying.

"I spoke to the doctor," said Lalu. "You are completely out of danger. Happy news,"

I nodded agreement, Warangal blinked.

There was a Minerva collar cradling his neck. I was surprised by that, since I often associated it with a broken neck, and here was Warangal alive and conscious. I made a mental note to ask the staff about it. Just then, a nurse came in, completely ignored everybody in the room, played with some devices, and left just as indifferently. "Excuse me, ma'am," she already brushed past me, and out the door.

Lalu kept patting Warangal's hand gently, "You will be okay, we will all be okay. Get a lot of rest." He set the patient's hand down softly. I nearly expected Lalu to lean in and ruffle the hair on Warangal's head in that avuncular way, but he didn't. Instead, he turned to one of the displays and became absorbed in its study, hiding his face from us. I guess that meant, cue Kumar.

I moved close to Warangal's bed, adjusted the sheet covering him, and did my own Hindu-uncle thing. "So, they are taking good care of you, are they?" I asked. Made a show of perusing the electronic halo around his head.

"Yes, thank you, " he could barely get the words out.

"Looks like the nurses come by regularly to check on you," I said. "That's very good. A good place to get strong fast."

Warangal mumbled something inaudible. When he saw that I had no reaction, he signaled with his eyes and by raising his other hand, with a beckoning curl of fingers. I leaned in close.

"Any arrests?" Warangal whispered.

I shook my head.

"Come back soon, sir," the words struggled to expel themselves out of Warangal's mouth.

Lalu turned around. "We will both come to see you, my boy," he said. "We will come two or three times a day." I nodded my agreement with Lalu's sentiment. Warangal closed his eyes.

No other words were spoken by any one of us for quite a while. We listened to the electronic buzz, the intermittent beeps, and an air flow hissing somewhere, the only markers of time. Warangal appeared to have fallen into a peaceful sleep.

Lalu and I looked at each other almost simultaneously, nodded to one another, and we quietly slipped out. I turned in the doorway to take a look at him. Quite peaceful though his face was, I hoped that whatever the source of Warangal's terror, it will have drained out of him while he slept.

Warangal whispers

The building looked different the second time around. In the pristine sunshine of an unseasonably hot spring day, St. Anthony's Hospital and Cancer Center on North Elston Road, did not look as forbidding. It looked pleasant, actually. An older construction with some Gothic styling to it that made it almost cheery, like a fairytale. Fresh spring shoots on every tree made the premises look happy, and smell nice too.

I felt optimistic. Some ideas were taking root in my mind. I had come to the hospital alone. I know, I know, Lalu Ganesh promised to visit Warangal daily. But the man has a restaurant to run, which took all his time, and he has little to spare. Let Ganesh immerse himself in cooking and serving food. He needn't be bothered, right? Right. My optimism was further enhanced when I learned that Warangal has been moved to a regular room just that morning.

The patient was up and awake. The tubes and wires were still connected, the science lab still active. If I looked at his face hard enough, I could have imagined some color returning to it. Yesterday's pallor flooded over by various fluids.

"Looking good, you are, young officer," I said, in a chipper tone, which I myself resented when doctors used it with me. But, which I now hoped would compel Warangal to respond.

"Thanks for coming again," he croaked.

"I see that you still have that thing," I said, pointing to his neck brace with one hand, and circling my own neck with the other. He stared for about one second and quickly averted his face. I felt instantly contrite. It wasn't meant to embarrass the poor bugger. My gesture of neck-grabbing just happened. God knows, the young fellow didn't need reminders of anything, least of all a rope around his neck. But, at the same time, I wondered if my thoughtless gesture might just jog him into a chit-chat.

"Is there something I can do today for you, Anything?" I asked.

He faced me again and spoke feebly, "Where is Ganesh?"

I hesitated, "Er, he is so busy with cooking etc. Why bother him? Plus, what can he do for you that I can't?" I hoped that that was conspiratorial enough, just between the two of us.

"He is good man," said Warangal.

"But a busy man," I replied. "Someone who leaves matters for me to deal with."

He spoke haltingly, "I should," gasp, "tell you something," gasp gasp, "Important."

Uh oh, here it comes, I thought, and leaned in close.

"I didn't kill Gita."

"Wrangler, nobody said you did!"

"Mullins knows I didn't do it."

"What, you guys talked about it? When did he question you?"

"When we first got news."

"But why? What basis did he have to question *you* at all?" I had to ask.

"He knows Gita and I went on dates."

Wow, finally things were falling into place. Maybe this rabbit hole has a bottom, after all. Mullins, Warangal and Gita. But wait, so Mullins knows Gita, and has seen her or met her while she was alive? I had always assumed that since Gita rarely showed up at Blue Mountain during daytime, Mullins might have never personally met her, even if he knew of her. Things looked different all of a sudden. It's good that the young man admitted to the affair. But, there seemed to be more things I didn't know; and didn't know that I didn't know.

"How does Mullins know about you and Gita going out together?"

The Wrangler took a long deep breath, gathered himself and whispered, like it were still a secret. "She came to the precinct one time." I felt bad about his struggle, the gasps. But had to plow on.

"And you never told Lalu any of this?"

Fear and darkness came over his face. His lips trembled and a sob tried to emerge. His frame shrank back into the softness of the hospital bed.

"Glad Lalu is not here," Warangal said.

"Cheer up Warangal," I said. "We all just want you to get strong first. Things will fall into place slowly."

"I respect Lalu, Sir," Warangal said.

"How many times did you and Gita go on dates?"

"Several."

"How many is several?"

"Ten, maybe twenty."

I snorted, no value to badgering him about the gulf between ten and twenty. Let Warangal tell his story, his way.

"Did you double date with another cop, or someone else?"

"No."

"So, nobody else knows about your dates, I mean, no Indians, Lalu's friends?"

"No."

"You two must've been in love?"

Warangal sighed. His eyes stayed closed for quite some time. Was it due to exhaustion or some sort of ruefulness at having his secret busted? He was letting things spill out, little by little. Will it mean that the look of terror will leave his eyes finally?

"We don't know how long you'll be laid up here. You will need some change of clothing, fresh underwear, toiletries, etc. You want me to get them?"

"Thanks a lot," he gestured toward his pants hanging on a hook behind a medical machine. "Keys in the pocket."

I left the room with a pat on his arm, a cheery smile, and a kiddi' joke. "Hey, Warangal, why was number six sad?" Why? "Because seven ate nine." Most Indians wouldn't have got it rightaway. But, the American hidden inside Warangal got it. His smile matched mine. But, as soon as the smiles faded, that look of fear returned to his eyes.

I snoop, again

For the second time in a month, I went noseying. This time in the bachelor pad of the other member of the duo of secret lovers. Even as I turned the key to Warangal's place, I suffered the odd necessity to justify myself. Walking in hesitatingly, I told myself that what I wished to do was not snooping, but a look-see. Shake the tree to see what fell. Rough winds of May and all that. Unlike Gita's apartment, which I broke into, entering Krishna's was by invitation. I had the keys, so no way should I be feeling guilty. But, I did.

Mu trepidation mounted even as I did the easier part of my mission. I went to the bathroom and gathered some toiletries, his electric shaver, etcetera. I stopped by the kitchen to see if the fridge had a stock of a favorite soda. Yes, it did - two six-packs of a popular root beer, but in the weird European, diet size of eight ounces, instead of the usual American twelve ounces. *Hmm, not a thirsty fellow*, I picked them up and returned to the living room to lay down the supplies. I smacked my forehead as they did in a commercial for a juice drink: 'wow, I could have had a v8.' In my singular focus on exploring his apartment, I left the hospital without checking with the medics about Warangal's feeding: could he swallow, drink juice? *Oh, well. He is alive, and Gita is not*. I should stay with the plan.

It was all India and Chicago in Warangal's front space. Chicago more prominent than India. On the wall above a long couch was a pretty large Municipal flag. Golden sunlight filtered by large windows fell on its nice horizontal blue stripes, and the middle white bar bearing four red stars, (a popular joke had it that the stars denoted the four men of the Daley clan who held sway over the city). One of the other walls had a collage of photographs of Warangal: graduation from the police Academy, swearing oath, in full uniform, scenes from life as a police cadet. The collage was flanked on one side by an elongated, framed poster of the skyline at night. And, on the other by a photo of sunrise over lake Michigan - the great Eastern sky looming over shimmering waters, boulder-strewn breakwaters, and a distant water intake crib. His self-pride capped off by a pair of flags above his collage, India and USA, with the American to the viewer's left, of course. I should have been moved, and was, somewhat. I also remembered the reason I was there at all: the total mental collapse I saw at the tip of a dangling rope in Lalu's garage. I sighed, and went into his bedroom to gather some clothing items.

I was stunned.

Once again, a bedroom turned out to be the key, just as it did in the case of Gita. In Warangal's place, it was the bed itself. Lying wide open on the well-made bed was a suitcase sloppily loaded with clothing items. Three pairs of pants, some handkerchiefs, an air pillow, four shirts, and one tie. At least one shirt still had pins in it, sans wrapper, like it was just bought. It was also very different from all his other shirts. More Hawaii, less Chicago. *Where was he going?*

That question became moot right away, being overshadowed by one other object, that I had expected to see anyway. But, somehow, the act of actually seeing it turned our world upside down.

An inter-office type manila envelope peeked out from under the tropical shirt. Its flap was undone and the contents peeked out. I could make out orange tinted papers imprinted with Gita's name. A nice gentle bouquet of lavender on them.

BOOK OF GITA

Book of Gita Ganesh, Lalu's niece

(Flashback - October, 2004 Thru March, 2005)

Liebfraumilch

Gita stood in front of the dresser mirror studying her reflection. She turned her face this way and that, tilted her head, and grew tall in the neck. In the flickering light of a lavender scented candle, she pulled her braided hair over the right and then the left shoulder. The regular lights were turned off in the motel room, except for the bedside lamp which she had draped with her bandanna, a large pale blue square of chiffon, printed with images of green cardamom pods.

Which view did she look best in? When she pulled her hair back to the right and turned, the single-pearl stud made her ear look pretty. When she did similarly on the opposite side, the silvery bell on a slender chain sparkled, rolled, and caressed the fine hair there, now matted. That was good too.

She took another slow lazy look at her two side views and gently removed the jewelry. Into her purse they went. She brought the hair braid over her right shoulder and pulled it across her face like a veil and breathed in the bouquet of *sambrani.* Her grandmother had sent the crystals a year earlier. Gita used just a pinch at a time to burn and let the smoke scent her hair on special days. Its gossamer fragrance in her hair recalled happy times growing up, and a grandmother who fulfilled so much for her.

A quick finger-rake down through the braid, and a shake of the head, her hair spread across her back. She leaned close into the mirror to check the skin around her bindi, and caught a glimpse of him on the bed.

Krishna Warangal lay on his back, sleeping, snoring softly. With each of his breaths, there was a waft of lavender and gentle flutter of the scarf. His face had a bluish tinge from the filtered light. "Looks blue, just like a god. All the great gods are blue in color," Gita murmured. The name Krishna suited him so perfectly. He looks good, and he protects. She wanted to return to his side, to feel his skin against hers, but decided not to stir him awake. Instead, she sat in a comfy cushion chair by the foot of the bed, tucked her feet under her, and leaned back with eyes closed, sighed in happiness.

They had been lucky so far. A getaway trip they craved finally came to reality. Lalu uncle didn't even ask what her plans for the day were, and there were no catering jobs scheduled. The small town of Frankfort, Illinois was far enough away from Chicago. It was so off the beaten path for most *desi* people of Devon Avenue, nobody would miss her.

Everybody in the little town was friendly, the young ladies all decked out in interesting Germanic attire for the tourists, clothing Gita had never seen before. Waiters and waitresses fussed over guests and offered explanations of menu items with patience. Their waitress was indulgent, laughed and didn't seem to mind the faces Gita made when some meat ingredients were mentioned. "I know exactly what you will enjoy, honey," she said. And returned with a steaming plate of what she called 'Bavarian Vegetables'. Gita didn't know what that meant but it was delicious, a blend of broccoli, cauliflower, carrots, beans, asparagus, Lima beans, All steam cooked and smothered with butter sauce and mayonnaise. Krishna indulged in some kind of *wurst something*. A policeman needs to eat that sort of food, to be strong and protective, she told herself.

They strolled through the streets of the little town admiring the architecture and historical features mentioned in the brochures. At one point they reached out hesitantly and held hands. It was the first time they dared to do that outdoors, and then, only because they were so far from Little India.

She felt free and comfortable in her blue jeans and kurti with its embroidered sleeves and frilly collar. And kept thinking how smart he looked even when not in uniform. So trim, and carried himself well.

He abruptly dragged her into a pub against all her protestations. They sat in a quiet corner, and he ran down the list of names of different beverages. "Do you know a lot about beers?" she asked.

"Oh, not really, just picked up some tips at the precinct house," he said. "Actually, all my knowledge comes from box labels and commercials," he added with a chuckle.

"You are being too modest, Krishna," she said. "Someday you will rise so high in rank, Lalu uncle will be so proud. Even Kumar uncle will be bowing his head to your accomplishments." He beamed as she squeezed his hand.

"Here is one that I heard about," said Warangal. Grasping her wrist, he used her index finger to point at a name on the list, "Liebfraumilch, see, this word means 'milk of the beloved woman'. Now here, St. Pauli's Girl, that one refers to an old walled quarter of monks. Some say that the name refers to a ..." lowered his voice and whispered into her ear. And enjoyed her blushing.

During their short time in the pub, Gita listened to him intently, not really absorbing anything. What she would remember most about that visit was the moment she had her first taste of beer. Her first taste of alcohol, in fact. It just happened. He insisted and she relented. She didn't like it or hate it. She made faces. Warangal wiped the foam off her lips.

A few yards from the pub, a clothing store was putting out items for display on the sidewalk. Racks of hangers and bins of accessories. Krishna stopped, bought a bright blue fleece vest for her, “you’ve been hugging yourself. You must feel chilled.” Gita was pleased, “This is perfect, the light jacket I put on this morning, that was too optimistic.” He drew her close. “Behave Krishna, we are in public,” she said, but got close anyway.

They left the town of Frankfort just after sunset.

“I loved this day, Krishna. Feels like I visited a whole different country. Thank you for taking me away from everything.”

“I enjoyed it too,” he replied. “It is nice to change our routines a bit, ain’t it.” She smiled. He had started doing that lately, saying short expressions like “ain’t” like Americans. She wondered about her first taste of beer, whether she would try it again if a situation ever came up.

“Really Krishna, I think I spent a day in Europe.” To which he could only offer a mock smirk, “Europe is not a country, it’s a continent.”

“Oh, you silly policeman,” she rolled her eyes. Leaned into him and rested her head on his shoulder. “But, you are my silly policeman,” a squeeze of his thigh, and dozed off in the car. And didn’t stir until he patted her awake a block from her apartment.

She wondered if Krishna expected a parting gesture of some sort. A caress, a hug, maybe an American kiss. She knew Americans kissed at the drop of a samosa, whereas Indians didn’t even do it in bed without blushing. She took the bandanna out and wrapped it around her head with a knot under her chin. She brushed the tails of the scented scarf on his face, murmured a throaty ‘love you’ and exited the car. She tucked the scarf against the gathering chill of the evening. In her unit, she turned the light on, lifted the shade and waved.

The beams of the car flashed to say 'okay good'.

Her heart pounded. Watching his car pull out, she didn't feel a sense of separation. She and Warangal belonged together, and that wouldn't change. She did take a big step forward today which could affect all those around her. No matter what, she thought as she fell into sleep, all happiness was hers.

Casablanca

Part-way through the movie, Warangal sensed Gita yawn, even though she tried not to be obvious about it. She stifled it by tightening her hold on his arm. How could she be bored by *this* movie, he wondered. He was enjoying the World War II drama playing on the large screen. The black and white images invoking a past long since gone. The different nationalities, military uniforms, and the intrigue about something called transit visa. On top of it all there was what his fellow older cops talked about - a famous piano song by a black man. Warangal found the movie absorbing, and couldn't believe that Gita was falling asleep during *Casablanca*. All the same, he shifted to snuggle close.

A week earlier, he had asked the guys around the precinct house to recommend an old romantic movie. Several names were thrown out, but the older cops said Krishna should watch the movie with 'great drama scenes' and starred Humphrey Bogart and Ingrid Bergman.

"Now, that one is a classic. *Casablanca*, you should see it," said a younger female officer who happened to be getting soda from a vending machine at that time.

That had settled it for Warangal, and he looked through listings of theaters that showed old films. The Arts section of the Sunday Tribune showed that Doc Films Society of the University of Chicago was in the midst of a retrospective of Ingrid Bergman movies, and perchance, Casablanca was due to be screened that very Thursday. It sounded like a plan, but would they drive all the way down to the South Side to watch it?

"Nobody will know us there, Krishna," Gita said. "We'll be safe there."

"I thought your feeling safe was due to being with me?" Warangal teased.

"Ha ha, my funny policeman, you always make me feel safe." Gita poked his arm, "But, you know what I mean. There won't be anyone there to recognize us and carry word back to Lalu uncle, or worse tell my father."

"It's a university campus, with highly educated people. There will definitely be some Indians. Though, I hope not many of them attend an old Hollywood movie."

"You are right," Gita caressed his arm. "College campuses are loaded with Indians. Professors, engineers, science students..."

"Don't forget spelling bees," Warangal smirked.

Gita let out a tinkly laugh.

The spelling bee contests became a thing with Warangal lately. They fascinated and annoyed him at the same time. At first, he was curious about them, being a poor speller himself. But, somehow Indian children seem to have taken over the whole scene, and Warangal thought that peculiar.

"The language belongs to Americans, but our kids are the experts?" Warangal said that there was something phony about the whole spelling contest thing. "It doesn't make any sense."

"Don't worry Krishna," Gita laughed, "I am sure there won't be any spelling bee kids in this movie theater."

"There better not be," replied Krishna. "If I hear anyone saying 'use Casablanca in a sentence' we are leaving." They laughed heartily at that.

Both of them looked forward to the darkness of the theater, the closeness. Watch the movie on a big screen, maybe hold hands. It would be an exciting evening, like being on a date, just like Americans.

When the scene came, in which the famous song 'a kiss is just a kiss' was playing, Warangal felt Gita's breath on his neck. Her eyes were closed, mouth agape and snoring lightly. He nudged her awake and asked, "Should we leave?"

"No, no, no," she replied and straightened herself in her seat. She took a sip of her soda, and turned her attention to the screen.

"What's been happening, did they get married yet?" She took his hand into her own.

Warangal whispered, "I don't think this is the kind of a movie in which they get married," and turned back to the screen.

"That's too bad," she said. "I like movies to end in marriage scenes."

They finished watching the movie without any further chat. During the drive home, they continued their silence but sat close together. She let him drive with one hand on the wheel and the other wrapped around her waist. Just like Americans did in so many movies she had seen.

Equinox Ugadi

Even before her father came to America it was difficult for Gita to go on 'dates' with Krishna. But now, with her father around, it was nearly impossible to sneak out.

Francis made demands on her every hour that she was home. From coffee time in the morning, through lunch and dinner hours, to night hours when she was asked to explain something or another about a TV show. Her time was his. Gita had little breathing room. Whenever Warangal and Lalu came visiting, Gita had to act reserved. Warangal too put on an act of distance from Gita. She could clearly see frustration on Warangal's face.

Within days, Gita too began to feel the suffocation and was ready to take a chance. Luckily, her prayers were answered, unwittingly, by her uncle. Lalu decided to take Francis on a trip to Indiana, "We will look at some business opportunities. Farms, real estate, horses, many things." The brothers would be gone all day. "If necessary, we will spend the night with the Sardar," said Lalu, referring to an old Sikh friend who owned businesses in La Porte county. That sounded even better.

"All day to ourselves, Krishna. Wonderful, no?" Gita said to Warangal in a phone call to the precinct house.

He agreed, but they both knew full well that there was danger lurking. For one thing, they will have to deflect any questions from her father and uncle. Were Francis to ask what Gita did all day, she will have to lie. Could Gita look her father in the eye and tell a convincing lie? She had no clear answer.

The day the two Ganesh brothers drove to Indiana coincided with *Ugadi* in India. It was the start of the Hindu New Year on the lunar calendar, celebrated on the first new moon that came on the heels of the Vernal Equinox. Gita suggested a trip to the Lake County, Illinois beaches. They could drive up Lake Shore Drive, north on the winding Sheridan Road, and on towards the Wisconsin border.

She had a picnic basket packed and ready, along with a sturdy blanket and a pair of thick woolen shawls. She also filled a large round steel box with the special item: the supreme symbol of the first day of the Hindu new year - *Ugadi Pachadi.*

The pachadi was a snack treat: pieces of green mango mixed with jaggery, salt, neem blossoms (sent by her grandmother), and tamarind juice. Gita was up early and made everything from scratch. Peeled and cut the mango, soaked the raw tamarind pods in hot water, melted down the jaggery cubes into a watery syrup, and mixed the items of the Ugadi chutney. Its many flavors evoked the variety of life's events in the year to come. Eating that chutney on the morning of Ugadi, was a centuries-old way of ushering in the New Year. Millions of Indians regarded it as a foretaste of life.

"We will stop at the Baha'i Temple and feast on our multi-taste chutney," Gita said, as soon as the drive began.

"It's a temple, not picnic grounds," Warangal said. "We agreed to have our spread near the lighthouse."

"Yes, yes, for lunch. But this is Ugadi chutney, we have to eat it in the morning, at the start of *our* new year." She shook her head. "We shouldn't wait till later."

"Why couldn't we go straight to the lighthouse garden, roll out our blanket and..."

Gita didn't let him continue. "Oh, Krishna, are you being deliberately difficult? We should eat our *Pachadi* in a special place. A temple is a good place to start the day. Any temple is okay." She played with her braid. Laid a hand on his shoulder and said, "We really can't go to the Hindu temple, you know. Too many people will recognize us there."

She looked at him as he drove silently. She knew he was seeing her point when he flashed her a quick smile. After some miles went by, and the sun began to gather height and heat, she lowered the window glass and let the breeze coming off the lake ruffle her hair.

"Really Krishna, this is so nice. We start a new chapter in our life, on *our* Ugadi day." She returned her hand to his shoulder and ran a finger around his ear.

He said with a straight face, "I didn't know we were writing a book. What did you name this chapter?"

"Ha ha, my dear officer, you tell me," she reached for his sides, intending to give it a poke, but ended up grabbing an inch of his belly fat. Instead of recoiling, she grabbed him firmly, "Ooh, somebody here is quite healthy." And, laughing, let go of him.

"It's all your fault," he said, with a pout. "You and your wonderful cooking. I enjoyed your uncle's cooking without putting on weight." He patted his tummy, "But now you feed me exactly what I enjoy. See what happened."

Gita laid a palm on his belly and ran it around in a gentle caress. Almost like an American rubbing a Buddha for luck (she saw that on TV recently). "It is a nice belly," she said.

She saw that he was not displeased by her comment, but still, he said, "Can't you see, I am out of shape? I should hit the gym and melt this."

“No no. No need to do that,” she said. “I like my man bulky in the middle. It’s a sign of prosperity. And, people will know you are being cared for by a woman.”

Gita was pleased with herself as she said that, but saw him roll his eyes.

“It’s true, Krishna. All Indian women think this way,” she said. He laughed heartily at that and said, “If there is going to be a belly on someone, it is better that I look prosperous. A belly showing on you could be troublesome.” He turned to her and wiggled his eyebrows.

She met his gaze for a few moments and turned her head to the passing scene. Waves lapping gently against the boulders at water’s edge, the sky and the lake merging into a single formless blueness in the distance, and the solitary tower of a water inlet crib stuck in the vastness of Lake Michigan. A small flock of birds hugged the shoreline, moving together, changing directions, dipping and rising, swiftly. In ways that seemed to defy all rules of physics.

Gita flipped her braid forward, smelled the sambrani on it, and turned toward him again. “You know Krishna,” she murmured, “I wouldn’t mind it. The belly, I mean..”

He looked straight ahead and negotiated the several turns of the twisty Sheridan Road. It was a mile before the road straightened out. They drove in silence until they reached the Baha’i Temple.

They walked around, admiring the airiness and the filigree work of the marble edifice. Gita chose a discrete spot where they fed each other a spoonful of the Ugadi chutney. Simple ceremonial dollops of it. Roll it around on the tongue, recognize the flavors, and gaze into each other’s eyes. They held their arms out like a couple about to commence dancing, or like figurines atop a wedding cake.

Strolling through the gardens of the temple complex, holding his hand, Gita felt satisfied that a ritual has been performed. She had unbound herself from restraints and old values lately, but honoring the new year in this way, in such a location, was somehow comforting. Partaking of the traditional mixture restored a bit of herself. She had really not strayed that far afield, and even her father, as confused as he might be about the different beliefs that tugged at him, even he couldn't stay angry forever, and would have to approve of her decisions.

She was ready to enjoy the rest of their picnic date.

LOVE LETTERS

Love Letters

The missives from Krishna were not always quite in proper letter form. They were just randomly jotted short notes, apparently, using whatever blank paper was at hand, with whatever writing instrument he could grab. His notes were somewhat moody, often petulant, and always naughty in some part. His words and expressions were jocular, even teasing. His state of desire in them was plain.

On the other hand, Gita's letters to Warangal were written on thin sheets of pale orange paper that came from a custom writing pad. The initials GG were embossed across the top in an old English script. Curlicues, daisies and bumble bees ran across the bottom. The space in between was not lined. It didn't need to be. Gita wrote perfectly straight. It was a penmanship so practiced, it suggested good schooling. Indians called it Convent Education, meaning that her classes were taught by Christian Brothers and Sisters. People of different faiths in India admired such schools for the 'discipline' the nuns imposed, and many sent their children to such schools. And yes, the nuns made the students practice penmanship for hours everyday.

**

Warangal's letters to Gita, were clumsy, varied, and looked disheveled. Quite unlike the trim looks he personally sported. They were wrapped into a bundle, and hidden under her intimates. The stack was imbued with a bouquet of lavender - a scent at once delicate, feminine and quite un-Indian. Gita cherished Warangal's notes in that timeless, private way women valued their memories.

Most of Gita's letters were written in English, with a generous sprinkling of words in her native tongue of Telugu. Like most

Indians, she loved English language acronyms for all things Indian, such as NRI (non-resident Indian), OCI (oversees citizen of India), or LBW (Leg Before Wicket - a type of fault in cricket play). She used a fountain pen of bright burgundy colored ink. She wrote in the style of the British English of an earlier generation of Indians. What some Americans called the King's English.

Gita's penmanship *deserved* to not have pre-drawn lines on the paper. Her sentences hung in mid-air as it were, with compact dashes, curvy loops and flourishes. Letters slanted to the right a bit, the words looked like someone resting on a couch and stretched out in languor. It was an elegant curvy script strung together like a garland of polished gemstones. It invited the reader to reach out and caress the letters.

**

Warangal seems to have composed his messages at different times from his workplace. And, he wasn't picky about what he used to write with: a blue-ink ballpoint pen, a fine tipped red felt pen, a number two pencil, even a magic marker. He seldom signed his full name, using a single letter K, or xoxoxo, and always dated them at the bottom. Gita treasured them all with that same lavender treatment.

Gita wrote all her letters at night. She put the time and day of the week at the top of the note, but not the date. Sometimes she put the time at the bottom, as part of closing thoughts. She used post-scripts. His letters weren't meaty enough to have any.

**

All of Gita's letters were mailed in plain white Monarch style envelopes of the kind sold by the bundle in Dollar stores.

They were not sealed with kisses, but affixed with special stamps issued periodically by the post office. Jack-o-lantern, snowflakes, Christmas tree, red hearts, the US flag...

A stack of Gita's letters to Warangal were found in a manila envelope, the kind used in offices. That inter-office envelope itself was in a suitcase flipped open on Warangal's bed. Along with a couple of shirts and pants thrown in.

**

Real answers would come eventually, once Warangal came out of the hospital, once he gathered enough strength and courage. But for now, the love letters would tell a tale all of their own. On any other day, in any other universe, I should have died of shame to read those letters. But, the knowledge that I would share them with people who I thought were more normal than I, helped overcome some of my shame.

******

<u>From Gita to Warangal.</u>

I like Warangal. Oh, I don't mean just the word, or the name, or you yourself the person. All those things, in fact. What I like most is the sound Warangal. All those 'A's just roll off my tongue. I also like the sound of your speech, when you talk like a policeman.

Do you like history, Mr. Policeman? If you do, you probably know that Warangal is a modern word derived from an ancient Telugu word Orugallu, the name of a city. That name gradually became Orugul, Orungul, and finally Warangal. You probably know all that. Lalu uncle said once, that he heard you were a good student in school. What do you think, Mister Officer Wrangler?

(This, presumably an early or first letter of Gita, had no salutation or signature, just a smiley face scrawled at bottom. It was written on a plain piece of paper.)

*

From Warangal to Gita .

(Written on a sheet of commercial writing pad promoting some law enforcement products. Off-white paper, written in a black ballpoint pen ink.)

To my second most favorite Indian cook in Chicago, you can guess who the top one is, right? You write so beautifully.

I would love to know more about the place I came from. You seem to know a lot more. I am happy about it.

Guess who? You better get this right!

(No name or signature, just a yellow smiley sticker).

*

From Gita to Warangal.

(She now started using her signature custom writing-pad.)

I already told you I love Warangal, I know all about Warangal, and more.

My grandparents often took the family on picnics at the site of the old historical fort at Warangal. We would pack enough food for the day and drive our bullock-cart there. Sometimes several families would gather together and ride a bus over.

I had forgotten how much I enjoyed those days until I met a real person named Warangal. In America! When I hear your name spoken by my uncle, or see you in some shop on Devon Avenue, I am reminded of those picnic trips. My mind brings up the great fort, the fabulous sculptures, the carved single stone pillars, and the great gate built by Kakatiya rulers. You know, the stony arched gateway. Its picture is in all our school books.

So many sweet memories come to me from your name, Mr. Warangal.

Delicious onion pakoras and strong pepper *bajjis* cooked by my grandma. Small unripe mangoes my little brothers used to fell from roadside trees. Hot and spicy mixtures of lentils and puffed rice we used to buy from wandering snack vendors. The chili pepper in the mixture burned our mouths sometimes so bad, we would run to the public tap to rinse our mouths out.

You must have picnicked there too. After all, you were named after it.

Wishing you a good night full of dreams of your own special memories, this is Gita, admirer of things Warangal, closing out the First Tuesday of the first month of Chicago's Autumn.

G

*

<u>From Warangal to Gita.</u>

Greetings to the one who likes Warangal.

I enjoyed stories of your picnic memories. They reminded me about Warangal Fort, Queen Rudrama, and other chapters in

History classes I skipped attending. Luckily, during exams I could crane my neck and copy answers off Vivek, whose desk was in front of mine. Sorry.

I am thinking how lucky you were as a little girl to have a grandmother to cook so many snacks for your excursions. Why wasn't I your relative or a permanent guest in your house? I would have become your grandmother's favorite eater.

As someone who loves many things about Warangal, you should know that there are no other likable things about me except the name. But, I hope you will go on liking Warangal, at least the town!

Other than that, you see, I am just a dumb American cop who eats donuts all the time, hahaha.

Officer, not Gentleman.
K.

*

From Gita to Warangal.

(Written, like the earlier one, on her personal stationery pad.)

Hello, my policeman!

Wasn't that a nice Diwali Gala set up by the P & P Mall. Lalu uncle says in all the years he had known Mr. Patel and Mr. Patwardhan, this was the super best party they gave. They always invite Lalu uncle. Such a nice turnout, no?

The fellow playing music was crazy and made silly remarks. But, he had good taste and played some great old songs. Rafi, Lata, Mukesh - I love all those singers, don't you?

Krishna, you looked quite handsome at the party. So nicely dressed in a traditional kurta and a waistcoat, like a Moghul nawab or prince. May be I should call you the Prince of Warangal from now on.

Looked to me like you didn't eat much at the banquet. I was watching you. Everyone at our table made a good job of feasting, but you fidgeted and nibbled. Why? Where was your mind during dinner? Kumar uncle, on the other hand, ate enough for a cow. Sorry. But, that poor man doesn't get a chance to eat gourmet food often, it seems. Why he won't find a suitable lady and settle down, I will never know. You should ask him, Krishna.

Sorry, I am starting to yawn. So, I will sign off this one, the night of the first Monday of November. Gita

PS: Holidays will be here soon. Are there office parties you have to go to? Do you celebrate Christmas?

PPS: Do you get any days off, how many?

*

<u>From Warangal to Gita</u>

(Written on a sheet imprinted with the letterhead Great Lakes LEOS Association.)

My dear Gita, you worry too much about my wellbeing. I am honored that you do, though. I *was* feeling a bit nervous at the Diwali banquet. You see, before we all sat down, I nearly spilled the beans, as Americans say. Yes, I am embarrassed to admit. I almost told Kumar that you and I went to see that movie Casablanca. You know how Kumar is, always going on about old American films. He mentioned Casablanca while scooping some biryani on to his plate, and I blurted out that I saw it two nights before. Luckily, I recovered quickly and said it was on cable, and avoided mentioning us being together. Whew, I never know what Kumar will bring up, I have to be careful in future. KW.

*

From Gita to Warangal.

Dear Mister Policeman, How you go on with your poses and views. I am not fooled that easily. We both know you love living in America. Why tell me how much you miss the village life of your schooldays. By the way, you looked so smart the other day when you came with some fellow officers while I was loading up a catering job. If only your mother could have seen you that day, in your crisp blues and shiny brass, *(heart symbol). GG*

PS: I like signing with the new name you gave me.

*

From Gita to Warangal.

(Written on her custom writing pad.)

Krishna, I have a suggestion. How about you and I go away someplace for a day or two? So many well-to-do Indians go away to India in December because of Christmas holidays. I helped in the catering of several weddings already this season. I even did two entire events that Lalu uncle booked but could not do himself. I am ready for a break. Think of some place you can drive us to. Not too far. Overnight trip will be nice. But even just a day trip, I will love that. Your *GG.*

*

Warangal to Gita.

(Written on a plain bond paper, crisp and white, with a ballpoint pen in royal blue ink).

Dear Gigi,

Are you trying to take me away to some remote place and put me in your spell? Is that why you want an entire night by ourselves? Very naughty of you, but a very good idea. It is hard to plan at a time like this, so we will have to play it by the ear, as my desk sergeant says. I will call you as soon as I know the time is available, and if it is right for you also, we can getaway impromptu? Agreed? Krishna.

*

From Gita to Warangal.

(Written on her custom writing pad. Though the pad is made of thick enough paper, she doesn't write on both sides. Instead she uses a second sheet.)

My Dear Krishna, what an extraordinary outfit you came up with for the New Year's Day party. Like the Nawab of Golconda or Maharajah of Mysore. So very handsome you looked. No Bollywood thespian could match you. But Krishna, did you really have to wear that stupid sports cap reading I love New York, just because the whole banquet hall was watching the dropping of the ball in Times Square? Sorry, I apologize. I should only say positive things on this happy day. We just finished one hundred days of our friend-ship. We are lucky that Lalu uncle hasn't caught us. I hope he doesn't ever. Or, at least, until my father comes to the US. Then we can jointly tell them all.

I overheard Lalu uncle talking about it with Mr. Khan of the India Bank. It looks like uncle is gathering sponsorship papers for *ayya*. When are you coming over? Tell me in advance so I can make something special for you. Sankranti will be here soon.

Have to close this now, I hope you will be thinking of me. I will always be thinking of you, including on this Eleventh Day of the Moon, and a sacred Tuesday night, wishing happy Vaikuntha Ekadasi, yours ever, *Gigi.*

*

From Warangal to Gita.

Gigi, is that a good short form for your full name, does it sound okay to you. I am loving saying it, short and sweet. It was a great party. Except for that Indian stiff acting. Americans go wild at midnight and start kissing each other like crazy. We should have our own separate celebration of January first at some other time. Yes?

So, in that Bollywood movie in your mind what were we doing? Were we doing a rain-soaked dance, or leading groups of dozens of men and women in a colorful field under blue skies?

The kind of jobs kids these days want to get into couldn't be imagined. Policeman, FBI agent, one kid even wanted to be a fireman. Ever thought Indian kids think like that? Every kid had at least one parent who was a doctor. Wow. Meet soon?
Krishna

*

From Gita to Warangal.

Dear Mr. Officer, I am going to make a *pukkah* South Indian meal on January 26, Republic Day. So, actually we will be dining after midnight of the 25. We will watch the parade in New Delhi live. A catering customer lady showed me how to do it with a small thumb drive she gave me. Won't it be fun? Please mark your American policeman's calendar. GG

*

From Warangal to Gita.

I might be scarce for a few weeks. Can you forgive me, dearest? Heard that your father is coming next week. It wouldn't look good for me to be around a lot. You should have a chance to get used to him. He should get used to Chicago. Lalu Ganesh said that you and him will go to the airport to receive your father Phani. Let's give him a few days to to get used to the weather and foods here before I visit him. It might be a good idea if I actually met him at Blue Mountain first. Hey, here is an idea. How about if you cook a real Indian meal all by yourself and invite 'friends' of your uncle Lalu. Your dad will be impressed by what a chef you have become. Kris

*

From Gita to Warangal.

O, my policeman Krishna, you can arrest this GG *gopika* on the Fourteenth of this month. She won't resist, I promise. You are given almost two weeks of advance notice. Bring your flute, O my Lord Krishna, and this cattle girl will rejoice. GG.

PS: It may not be funny to you, but for some reason, I always burst out giggling when I write the new name you gave me, GiGi - Giggle, giggle.

Happiness

“We should tell ayya about us, Krishna.”

“No, not yet.”

“Why wait?”

“We just wait.”

“He will be pleased. You are a police officer in America, and I will have my own business soon.”

"And, that will make him happy, you think?”

“What father wouldn’t be?”

“Hmm, your father is not like any other father.”

“Why dig up the past? He is here now. *With me*. I just know, he will be pleased with you.”

“You are a good daughter, Gita. Still speaking on his behalf, after all these years. He doesn’t value our lives, or America.”

“Don’t say that! He lived so long without me around. It’s all too new for him. He *will* come around.”

“Hah, not likely. Unless what you really mean is that you feel you abandoned him so long, you miss him, and feel guilty too. Did you forget *he neglected you* for years?”

She sniffles, and the sniffles turn into sobs. He draws her close. They stay silent for a while.

“What you say is true Krishna, but I have hope.”

"You hope what?"

"He will not deny me my happiness, or my love for you."

Warangal snorts, and that says it all.

Their vehicle gathers speed as it leaves rural counties behind, and heads Chicago-ward.

"We should tell him before we register our marriage…"

"No, we tell him after we do what we always wanted. Don't give him room to argue. We make it *fait accompli.*"

"What's that?"

"It means something has already happened…"

"Aha, like shoot first and ask questions later?"

"Haha, what a thing for a girl like you to say."

"I have to keep up with my cowboy lingo, right?"

The car leaves highways and negotiates the boulevards of the big city. Gita opens her eyes and says, "You're right about that fatecompli, whatever, idea. Sometimes, it is better to ask for forgiveness than to ask for permission." He pats her arm and murmurs about being on the same page.

Now on the home stretch, on the Kennedy Expressway, Gita straightens out, adjusts her seatbelt, and turns to face him fully.

"We will do it, Krishna," she says, uses her fingers to brush her hair back. “I will place an order for marriage rings, I know exactly how I want them. You will love it.” She settles back and closes her eyes. She correctly imagines a smile dancing on his lips. She sighs contentedly. A little later, she feels a nudge, and hears his voice: “Home, madam.”

*****

End of Book of Gita

*****

The Emails

Sent via Email: (May, 18,2005; 04:12:25 UTC)

Sashanki, my friend:

The worst has happened, and I am completely at a loss. You see, it seems Gita was in love, got pregnant, and that may have led to her death, somehow. I know the person involved with her, but I am extremely uncomfortable with that, in that they both kept the affair a secret from ALL of us. None of us suspected a thing all these days. How is this possible, why was this done in this way? Why didn't they just come out and say just once that they were 'going out' or something like that? Do you understand what I am saying? Sasha, I am completely confused and angry at what I have found out. What am I going to do now? Anand K.

*****

Sent via Email: (May 18, 2005; 11:2:16 UTC)

Dear Anand,

I sense your intense anxiety and the rude shock that caused the said anxiety. In your shoes I would take a step back and examine the scene, if I may. You indicate how you all were shocked at the news. You virtually shouted it out all in caps. It was as if you had a right to that information. You don't. What has happened was between two young people, it's their problem, not yours. You may have a commission to dig up the facts for her uncle, but that's it. You may not feel offended by what you found out. Plus, the youngsters may have their own reason to keep it to themselves - didn't you say her father visited her? May be they told him, did you think of that? Oh, my friend, Anand, I know you mean well, that's why you get so worked up. That's part of your charm. Please take a broader view. Give everybody's point-of-view a chance. You will see.... Sasha.

*****

<u>Sent via Email:</u> (May 20, 2005; 19:49:55 UTC)

My Dear Sasha,

I am deeply grateful to your words of wisdom. They speak well of your acumen, as well as they do of my impulsive affinity toward my friends. I should carry on with the task assigned to me by the forces of Fate that brought me to this point. But going forward, your words will ring loudest in my ears. Thanks, yours, Kumar.

*****

MAY-HEM

Lalu shouting

"Why did he do it in my house, Kumar?" Lalu wailed, pounding the air with his fist. "Why, Kumar, tell me why? So many trees in the park, he could have hanged himself from anyone of them. Why my house?"

Each why got its own pounding. His thumb stuck out so his fist looked like a claw hammer. I recognized that Indian gesture. The more the thumb stood out, the more demanding the question.

"It's a cry for help," my tepid response.

"But, why did he have to try it in my house?"

"A bit mysterious why he chose to end his life in your garage," I said.

"Mystery? What mystery? So many methods to die, Kumar. Why hang himself in my garage?" Lalu seemed to be trying to keep his voice and breathing level. He failed on both counts. And the air kept getting hammered.

"It's hard to read Warangal's mind," I said. "In the hospital, he looked scared and tearful. Thank god he is stable. Given time, truth will come out."

"Why didn't he find a big tree or a light pole? My house, my garage. Why?"

I could see Lalu was fighting tears. Grief and anger made for a bad combination. My intuition told me that he was not done venting, and would continue to drive the invisible nails. I wished he would stop pacing and sit, so his breathing could slow down.

"Self-harm is a strange thing, Lalu. I read somewhere that many suicide attempts are half-hearted."

"Half-hearted, whole-hearted, or a half-a-kilogram, I don't care! Why he want to finish off? His life is so good. He is well-settled. His parents proud of him. They even looking for a suitable match for him."

"Did he know that?" I asked.

"He should. His parents say, 'Lalu find a girl in America.' I search here, they searching back home for a nice girl."

"Well, maybe that's not what he wants. Maybe he wants to be free of their plans for him. Social workers say a person may try a suicide, but on the inside they really want to live. It means the person is troubled for some reason."

"Kumar, what you say is not correct. You make excuses for fools. I help people, and then they do this. Run away from everything. What's wrong?"

"Of course, you help people. You sponsored Warangal for visa and supported him. You helped others. This attempt by Warangal is his personal issue. Nothing to do with you."

Lalu ran his hands over each other, scratched his elbows, drilled an ear with his pinky, rolled his head and massaged his neck. And wrapped arms around his own shoulders, like he was giving himself a hug. The whole thing made it seem like he found parts of his body he didn't know he had. His breathing eased somewhat, though. After a while, he said, "Why Warangal has problems, I don't understand. He is having a good life."

"He must have suffered a sudden blow. Extreme pressure, Feeling lonely and hopeless."

Lalu looked at me like I was from a different planet, speaking a strange language. He found more body parts to massage, rub or shake loose. He made faces, but not of agreement. He was all snorts, no nods.

"I ask, what is the meaning of using my house. Can you tell me that?"

"Um.. Probably couldn't think of any other way. Somehow connected to you. We'll know soon enough."

Lalu's breathing eased some and he sat down. The fists eased a little bit on the claw-hammer look. Kitchen workers ventured out onto the floor bearing trays of snacks, drinks and chai. Lalu gestured to Shetty to sit with us. Others lurked behind the giant double doors.

"If he lives..." Lalu closed his eyes and bowed his head for a second, "I pray to *Lord Balaji* that Krishna survives. When he is released from the hospital, I will give give him a beating, he will wish he actually died." Lalu gritted his teeth, but his fingers unfurled. The figurine of elephant-god Ganesha which dangled from a gold chain around his neck twinkled once and disappeared under his shirt.

The irony of Lalu's words made me chuckle. Did that unconscious humor mean that he was relaxed enough to receive the news I had? Or was it the opposite, and I should desist any more chat, so as not rile him up all over again?

"There is something that you should know," I said. "And, it might explain some things, but not everything,"

Lalu sipped his chai.

"It's about Gita, and Warangal," I added.

Still no response. There was an odd silence, as if Lalu wasn't listening.

"Gita was in love with Warangal."

"Silly, like a school kid. Yes, Krishna has personality like a Bollywood hero," Lalu almost grinned. But he caught the look on my face and stopped short.

"It's not a girlish crush, Lalu. Real love. Warangal has been having a love affair with your niece for months. I saw love letters."

Lalu jumped up and stood trembling. A mug full of chai spilled out. His lips parted but no sound came. Shetty too jumped up at once and pulled Lalu's chair back, ready to steady his boss.

"I am sorry, Lalu. It shocked me too. But it is a fact," I said. "We can't doubt or deny it."

Lalu pounded the table. Real fist, real table. The silver and the snacks trembled into disarray. When the air settled, Shetty broke in, "What you say Kumar sir? You say our Gita sister and our Krishna brother..." His voice failed him even as he bade Lalu to be seated. I ignored the familial words imputed in Shetty's confused heart. He was only too shocked. I got up to take a break.

"Sit. Tell me everything you are hiding," barked Lalu.

I sighed. We all sat down. A kitchen worker came over, his head down, and sorted out the table. A new jug of chai and a new tray of snacks came. I took a deep breath, took a sip of the fresh hot chai, and looked hard at Lalu.

"I am not hiding anything, Lalu. You are getting it as I learn it. It was good of you to come visit me when the police had me locked up. I appreciated that you brought that man from the State Senator's office. Mullins could have been tough with me if he chose. And, you never pressed me about the break in. All that was good. Here is the fact. I found love letters written by Warangal to Gita," I paused to let Lalu absorb it.

Lalu's jaw tightened, the eyes remained wide. "You never told, er you, er, anyone? About the letters you found?" he asked.

"I haven't told anyone till now. Even Mullins doesn't know."

Lalu slumped in his chair. "I don't believe anything. You speak nonsense," he said.

"There are letters, Lalu. Not email or chat. Written in his own hand, some even used police stationery."

"You had *no* right to be inside Gita's place, you shouldn't have broken in." Lalu didn't have the strength to shout, but the darkness on his face articulated what his mind couldn't.

"Remember, Lalu, we've been after facts for weeks. We wanted to know what happened to our Gita."

"She is *my* niece, not yours," he said, finding some of his voice again.

"There are other things I found, stuff cops would not be thinking have value."

"Stop it, Kumar. You are ruining Gita's name." Lalu raised his voice a bit.

"Far from it, Lalu. I am only trying to show you what she was going through."

"Okay, okay," Lalu shouted. Sat up straight in his chair and waved his hands about. "What, what, what things?"

"Something we didn't notice when we went to pack up that box of gifts. You remember that day, right?" I didn't wait for his answer. "We saw nothing odd on that day. But when I was in there, I noticed a mess in her closet. Smashed gifts, figurines Gita bought, souvenirs she wanted her father to take back to India with him. Looked to me like somebody had an angry outburst about something."

"Is that all, that's your evidence?" His voice really rose. "We know my brother is er od, oddball, you said so yourself…"

I sighed. "Lalu, it was not Warangal only who wrote love letters. Gita wrote to him many times. He has a box full of them."

"How you know?"

"I saw them, I have them. On my second visit to St. Anthony's, I asked for his keys to pick up some clothes and toiletries for him. The letters Gita wrote him were right out in the open. I don't think Mullins knows about that either. Gita and Warangal were going out on dates. For several months, I think."

Lalu was agonizingly slow to rise out of his chair. Even more deliberate in looking at all the corners of the dining space, the floor, the ceiling. He finally settled his eyes on me and let loose.

"You rotten man! I asked you to find out what happened to my brother's daughter. You tell me she is bad girl. I think you and police are friends, so you can find out things. Now you tell me you know things police don't know. You hiding things from police? I think you mix good with Americans, and you speak English good. But, you tell this nonsense about troubles and crazy suicide points."

The pause in his diatribe was not voluntary. He was running out of breath. He came back to the table we were sitting at, and pounded it with force. Spoons and forks flew in air again. Chai in cups splattered. Except mine, which I held and continued to sip from.

Hands on hips, he bellowed, "I said Kumar will help, he is good with Americans. But no, just like white people, you think we are bad people."

It is the way he said 'we' that stood out. Not just his voice, or the finger that jabbed at his own chest. Something else, his eyes, said that that 'we' excluded Kumar.

"Get out, get out," Lalu shouted. "Don't come back to Blue, blue... Nilgiris, it's not for you anymore. *Jao, chale Jao*."

All that shouting, the breathless anger - I felt sad and got up to leave. I neared the door when Lalu croaked, "Wait wait."

I pushed the door open just in time to hear Lalu blurt out, "Shetty, quick quick, fresh chai for all us." As if that chai for '*all* of us' now included Kumar too.

Who knows what might have transpired had that tea order come just seconds earlier? As it happened, I was out the door already.

Out on the street, on my Devon Avenue, I didn't see any suspects. The mania with which I searched for a murderer in every face, melted away. There were no killers lurking in doorways. I saw pretty goods in store windows. Mean-looking aunties smiled.

Sidewalks of Devon

Insistent odors wafted out of the eateries. I paused for a moment at the corner of Devon & Rockwell and inhaled deeply. The heavy North Indian strains of thick masala simmered in hot oil, and the sharply explosive intensity of South Indian spices, mingled and delighted me.

So, Lalu wanted no part of my truths, or the name I coined for his restaurant. 'Blue Mountain' was my idea, due to how the American Smokies reminded me of the Nilgiri Mountains of south India. Lalu and I loved both those two mountain ranges and their blue aura. Since every other eatery on Devon Avenue was named India this or India that, it felt more authentic to call the new restaurant Blue Mountain. Lalu loved the concept. Yet, in a moment of rage, he stumbled over the name of his own business: he mangled the English words, couldn't say Blue Mountain, and struggled to say the Sanskrit word, *Nilgiri*. Both mind and tongue failed him.

I felt neither remorse nor turmoil. Just weary, empty, and different. Or, maybe it's the street that was different, due to the way light cast on the storefronts by the *karma-sakshi* in the sky - the hour of the day. Whatever, the goods in store windows and the weekend Indians who gawked at them made for a myriad of images. An emptiness within me was getting filled. But, there was also a desire to be alone in the crowd, to be like an alien sauntering on the unassuming dirty sidewalks of Little India.

"Hey Kumar, how you sir? Hello hello, Kumar sir." The gravelly voice from behind me was Keshubhai, just stepped out of his own Indian fast food joint named *Sangam of Taste.* It was a popular eatery that served snacks of a North Indian persuasion. His fingers wiggled in a beckoning gesture, but his head leaned over the curb as his mouth spat out a stream of betel leaf juice into the gutter.

“Aha, Namasthe, Keshubhai. All is well?” I asked.

He straightened up, wiped his reddened lips with the back of a hand and growled, “Oh, Yes. All good, all good. What about our friend Ganesh, he good?”

“About as good as can be expected, you know. I’ll tell him that you inquired.”

“Do that.” Keshubhai’s voice dropped. “Any news about Gita ben?”

“The authorities are working very hard. Still figuring out why it happened and who did it.”

“Good good good,” he nodded, looked over his bifocals and asked, “Lalu thinking about selling his restaurant, yes or no?”

“I don’t know, Keshubhai. Hope your business is good?”

“With your good wishes and God’s blessings.” His stained fingers pointed up. “Business is good. Come in, Kumar, let’s have some chai.”

“*Maaf keejiye* but, I have to be somewhere else. Next time, perhaps,” I touched his elbow and turned to go.

I heard him rasp behind me, “Call me when police tell you something.”

Everybody wants to know. But not me, not anymore.

The street had changed so much from its ghost-town looks during my PhD days. Thousands of Indians came to work and study in Chicago. Businesses sprang up along affordable Devon Avenue. The presence of stores brought more Indians to the area, and so on. The cycle kept turning until the turkey of a sleepy street morphed into a dancing peacock of real estate.

I found myself in the doorway of India Book House. It didn't sell many books, but survived by selling video discs, music CDs, Hindu idols, and books on yoga (mostly to young white college students).

Right by the entrance, inside, I encountered a rack loaded with weeks-old magazines and newspapers from different parts of India: Gujarat, Punjab, Telugu, Marathi, and Tamil regions, as well as the Hindi Belt. And, tons of newspapers in the Urdu language.

"You came after a long gap, Kumar," said a female voice. It came from behind the glass display case which reached high like an old-fashioned pharmacy counter. Alpa Mehta, the owner rose up slowly behind it and smiled, her round face accented by a brilliant saffron colored forehead mark. "Still looking for Vedic calendars, Kumar saab?" she asked.

I shook my head. "Downloaded one last week and printed it out," I said. "But, it is very kind of you to remember. How is Mr. Mehta, and where are the kids?"

"The kids went roaming." She pointed to the street. I nodded and smiled.

Alpa sighed, and said, "This internet will be the end of bookstores. Everybody downloading everything. Nobody buying anything. Things are just too easy." The *kajal* on her eyelids looked dull and dry in the fluorescent lights making her appear tired, even though her lips continued to smile.

"Got to flow with the times, Mrs. Mehta," I said, as I moved through the aisle, past shelves of books and dictionaries. And, shelves loaded with trinkets, incense sticks, costume jewelry and figurines for every religious tradition of India. It kept my mind occupied, but I was still stung by Lalu's words. At the same time, I worried more about his mental state than mine. As agitated as Lalu was by the news of Gita and Warangal, would he be able to handle what might yet come?

I heard Alpa behind me. She stepped down from her perch and followed me in the aisles. "By the way, Kumar, it is very sad what happened to that girl. Your friend Lalu is her *mamuji,* isn't he?" She paused and then, "I hope they catch whoever did it. Such a sweet girl." *She is sweet. Everybody says so.*

It seemed to me that just because Lalu threw me out, there was no way I could sever all ties with the situation of Gita. We were all in it, that's for real. The whole of Devon Avenue was becoming invested in it. The tiff between Lalu and me couldn't really go on too long.

I crossed the street in the middle of the block without waiting for a break in traffic, just like other Indians, and came to face a beauty salon. *Beautiful Dulhan* said the gaudy overhead sign composed of photos, slogans, and price lists.

Images of arms and faces decorated with exquisite designs and elegant scrolls in the vivid red color of *mehendi*, what silly Americans called henna tattoos. The signboard also promised *Eyebrow Threading Special.* A shy face peeked from behind a bridal veil *Be the Best Bride.* I took in the sign before entering the store, and was struck by the fact that the happy shy bride depicted on the signboard was unmistakably a white lady, not Indian.

It was perfumy inside. "Kumar sir, welcome, welcome. You visit us finally, vah-re-vah," the middle aged lady owner greeted me. Her head tilted forward, and she touched it with her right palm held upright, touching chin and forehead.

"Mrs. Mumtaz, thank you for your greeting," I returned her salute, a classic Muslim-inspired gesture. "I can imagine that you are surprised."

She bade me to be seated, snapped her fingers at a young lady lurking in the back, and ordered tea for two.

"Mr. Kumar, I only see you at festivals and meetings. This is your first visit to my poor shop. Please accept my humble hospitality." She bowed and fell silent.

A sweaty young man carried in a full-service tea tray and namkeen. Only after I mixed the tea and took a first sip did the lady speak again, "You want to ask me about mamuji's little girl Gita, yes?"

Yes. And, everybody knows what's on my mind…

"Bravo, Mrs. Mumtaz. With a sharp mind like that, how can this not prosper?" I waved my hand to cover the salon chairs and make-over stations. She touched her face again with her palm. A blush on her face, reflected from the henna on her palm.

I drained my cup of chai and reestablished eye contact with Mrs. Mumtaz. She voiced the tale without any further prompting by me.

"Mr. Kumar sir, you already know that Gita beti and Ganesh saab are well-liked. You have been in Chicago a long time. Long before many of us settled here. Gita was a good client. She didn't visit often, or make too many demands. Maybe, she bought a small round tin of kajal, a tube of mehendi, or a packet of bindi stickers. Everybody here loved her visits, we all talked about cooking techniques, banquets, spices, etc."

"I am not surprised, Mrs. Mumtaz. You pretty much are the unrivaled beauty authority for all Indian women who visit Little India." Her palm touched her face again. I nodded and continued. "Mrs. Mumtaz, you are often hired by the parents of young women, aren't you? You specialize in bridal parties?"

She remained silent for some time. Eventually, she sighed and chose her words carefully.

"Mr. Kumar sir, I have heard rumors. You probably did also. Gita *beti* lived by herself. Some shop girls say that Gita found a way out of loneliness. It is not for me to say that she has a boyfriend or anything like that. She would have made a very attractive match for anyone. The women who work for me are all married. They go back home to their husbands after work, and when they are here they gossip. I got the impression that Gita ben anticipated getting married later this year. That's all I can say with confidence." She ended abruptly.

"Any idea who the groom would have been?"

"Not at all Sir. We could tell her interest in makeup and beauty items was increasing since last summer. I believe she has also been asking questions about bridal jewelry. But she was tight-lipped about any details."

"As long as we are talking about this, did she have any appointments coming up, or did she miss any recently?"

Quit it man, stop chasing ghosts...

Mrs. Mumtaz thought about it for a while. "Gita always talked to me only. I set her timings and assigned who should do the work, whether it is eyebrow threading, or learning to do a makeover, or anything. So, I can say no, she didn't miss a date. Does that help?" She looked at me directly. No more formalities or excessive courtesy masking the real topic. Part of me wanted to disregard it all and just walkaway. But, the worse part of me won out.

"Mumtaz *begum,* you helped me a lot, *bahut shukriyaa.*" I stood up, ready to leave. But one last question popped in my head. "Anybody show particular interest in Gita, do you know?"

"There was a white police detective who wanted to know everything about Gita. I told all facts. He never came back." She paused, "Oh, you mean," paused again, and said, "you mean, anybody else interested in Gita personally?"

Yup, begum. I am getting mired again...

"See Mr. Kumar sir, like I said women here gossip. What else can they do, talk lipstick all day? Clothes, Bollywood movies, and jewelry. Cooking and men, that's all there is to talk about. When Gita visited, we talked about all those subjects and more." Mrs. Mumtaz chuckled and I nodded.

"To answer you directly, Mr. Kumar, an unmarried woman is a favorite topic for everyone. Rumor is that the paunchy fool who manages the gold shop two blocks away is looking for a wife. I hear that his gaze is upon Gita. Another man I have heard about is the owner of the Currency Exchange at the end of this block. He asks about Gita all the time. We don't know why. But, he does have a son who is Gita's age." She shrugged.

"All this helps, Mrs. Mumtaz, thanks."

"Do you think the white policeman is working hard on the

case? What should I do if he comes back?"

"Tell the truth, Mrs. Mumtaz. Always." I stood up.

"I hope you will re-visit my poor house, Kumar sir." Formality returned. She too rose from her seat. "When everything is settled down, please bring everyone in your family." She bowed again.

I returned the gesture, "*Qudaa Hafeez,*" and left the store.

In my peripheral vision, I caught her pleasant face in the glass wall, and a goodbye wave of the hand.

Rhinestone Cowboy

I tapped on the glass door of Lakshmi Jewelers a few times, loud enough to rise above the din of the street. A pot-bellied fellow with a slow swing of arms padded over to the cash register and pressed a button under the counter. The front door clicked open. He ensured that the door re-locked after I entered, and walked up to meet me.

He was sharply-dressed in a dark suit, wore a gold watch, and a pendant made of gold-tipped double-tiger claw. His face bore a twist of lips that naturally bordered on a leer. He was the man mentioned by Mrs. Mumtaz. He went by one name only, Ranajee, and his greeting was stiff.

"You bless us with your visit." He extended a hand, and a waft of patchouli followed. I nodded as we shook hands.

Ranajee didn't offer me a seat. Nor did he ask what I wanted to examine: rings, necklaces, bangles, or what. He diagnosed correctly that mine was *not* a gold-buying visit. After all, I wasn't accompanied by women or family.

"Thank you for letting me visit, Ranajee sab. I know you prefer to give appointments." I swung my hand around, "You keep the place secure."

"Oh, yes, yes. Everybody on our street knows you. You are a respected member of the community." I bowed, as much in acknowledgment, as at the pictures of gods and goddesses on the wall behind him. One has to show respect to the gods who made gold, as well as to the person who dealt with gold daily. Ranajee didn't order tea either.

"I was wandering about on the street today, and remembered something," I started. "You have hired my friend Lalu Ganesh for catering jobs. Were they all good?"

"Oh, yes yes, Mr. Lalu is a great cook. The best. I give menu, they bring food. The best, yes." And then added what I considered a non-sequitur, "Are you a complete vegetarian yourself?"

"Did Gita do most of the food service for you, sir?" I asked.

"Yes, a lovely lady she is," he adjusted the gold chains around his neck. Another gust of patchouli. I knew that he meant to use the word *was* with reference to Gita, but like most Indians, he didn't bother with that distinction. I let it pass.

"We still don't know what actually happened Mr. Ranajee. Nothing new from the police," I hoped that I cut a sorry face, if only to get him talking. But then again, I did really feel sorry for myself at that moment. *I seem unable to free myself from this mission.*

"My heart breaks, sir. You and Mr. Ganesh, friends for a long time."

"I ate hundreds of meals cooked by Lalu," I said.

"Yes, yes. Naturally, we feel grateful to all those who feed us. We honor our food-givers."

"So true, Ranajee," I said. "That's why I do the best I can, to help my friend."

"Yes, yes. I am guessing that you are feeling very badly for Lalu Ganesh, and even more about Gita ben," he said. His lip curled when he said Lalu's name, the eyes shone when he said Gita.

"Time will reveal everything, Ranajee. Can you tell me about Gita shopping here. Anything you know?" I asked.

“Very polite, good cook. She bossed the workers nicely”.

“What else?”

“Every one knows, a very pretty girl.”

“She ever buy jewelry here?”

Very slowly, “I don’t think so....”

“Please try to remember, Ranajee.” I said. “She might have come with a man? Maybe a white person.”

“Oh, if she came in with a white fellow, I would have remembered...”

I persisted, “It’s possible she shopped for an inexpensive item, like a simple necklace or bangles made of rolled gold.”

“I don’t think so. But, I will ask Mrs. Verma. She is not here today.”

“So, you never spoke to Gita in the store. She might have wanted to buy something for her father when he visited America?”

Ranajee chewed his lips, “I am now thinking that maybe we did talk once or twice.”

“It would be very helpful if you can tell me the details. I promise I won’t tell the police or anyone else.’ I said.

“No, no, no. I don’t really mind if you tell the police. I would have told myself.”

“What are you saying. Ranajee?”

“There was a white policeman who came asking about Gita. Questions just like you are asking. He said he was a detective. I answered everything truthfully. But that fool was asking all the wrong questions. What actually...”

Insistent banging on the front door. A noisy family at the door. Women, children and an old man stood outside. Ranajee looked at his watch and then at me. I shrugged, and let the poor fellow personally go open the door and eyeball each potential dollar as it streamed in.

For the benefit of the family that just entered, Ranajee proclaimed loudly, “Kumar saab, your order will be ready by two-thirty, you can pick it up then.” The family looked back at me, and behind them Ranajee gave a shrug and a baleful look. I nodded my thanks as I left.

****

I wanted no more human interaction right then. I wasn’t sure any progress was being made in the case. I wasn’t getting any real help from Detective Mullins, certainly not by my fellow Indians, who only fed me bits and pieces. What I did discover and conveyed to Lalu only resulted in outbursts of angst. Was I chasing ghosts, or my own tail?

The sidewalks of Devon Avenue got a beating that afternoon. Words, broken thoughts, and incomplete phrases bubbled to the surface and burst into nothingness. It's always the same thing that happens, when my mind is abuzz and I felt mixed-up or lost. Bits and pieces of old remembered poetry, Bollywood songs and American Country songs, all mingled into a bad mishmash.

Walking on the dirty sidewalks of Broadway....
Singing the same old song....of Gita Ganesh
Like a little Indian cowboy ...
seeing the same little tree again, ...
Where I knew every storefront and doorway ...
Like an old Asian cowboy....

Yes, it did feel like I was actually wearing rhinestones and a stetson hat. Was I in the wrong place at the wrong time? Should I even be bothering about Gita at all? I pounded out my paces until I came upon the intersection with Kedzie Avenue. One entire mile! I crossed the street and turned around to walk back on the other side.

Not to worry, I told myself. I am not losing my mind. Everything will be clear after I talk to the paunchy gold merchant. Somehow he will steer me in the right direction. I felt angry at the interruption by the noisy Mathur family, just as the jeweler was about to spill something. It was like chewing a morsel of rice only to catch a grain of sand between teeth. Yet, I found myself in a zone of patience. Why was I being so patient? Was it an innate Hindu steadfastness, or was it an American optimism? Whatever the reason maybe, the uneasy Kumar who left the Blue Mountain a few hours earlier gradually melted away. I headed back to the jewelry store with a clear head and a steady gait.

On Devon Avenue, everyone knew everything. Especially jewelry merchants. They knew everything that went on on the street, and who was who. To know gold was to know people.

Gold Merchants Know

My 'walkabout' continued without my running into people that recognized me. Something the jewelry store owner said kept rattling around in my brain. Something about a foolish white cop who 'asked all the wrong questions.' It has to be Mullins who went around and interviewed storekeepers. Now, any astute detective, let alone Mullins, would know what questions to ask, wouldn't he? Yet, Ranajee wasn't impressed by the policeman's questions. Why was that?

It took all the patience I could muster to prowl the area at leisure, and not rush back. My hope was that in the meantime Mr. Ranajee would have made a nice sale to the Mathur family. A good sale put a jewelry man in a happy talkative mood. I needed Ranajee to talk. It turned out he did make good sale.

He called it a story. "Let me tell you the whole story, Kumar sir," he started. And what a story it was...

A white detective came in and asked a lot of questions about Gita. He didn't look like the usual tough guy cops seen on TV, more like a Columbo-type detective, but better dressed, and not looking like a scarecrow. On the other hand he wasn't dressed in three piece suits like in some of those New York cop shows. Never in uniform, though. Twice he came in and showed his shield both times. "Funny eh, Kumar, like I would forget a white face asking about gold here on Devon." *For god's sake man, get on with the tale...*

The detective wanted to know all about Gita. He had her picture and Ranajee identified her readily. Who on Devon Avenue couldn't, right? Right. The cop asked about what sort of items Gita bought, their general price levels. How high was the most expensive thing she bought, how she paid for them. *That figures, what else?*

Like, the policeman wanted to know the total number of times Gita might have made purchases of jewelry. Ranajee smirked when he said this. She came in often, Kumar sir, she was like a frequent flier. Small items, but a loyal customer. *Yeah, a regular big shot buyer, eh..*

Ranajee must have read my mind. Smirked again and said, "You see Mr. Kumar, it is not what you thinking. That white detective also was disappointed when I told him that all of Gita ben's buying amounted to peanuts, really. Necklace for a child, rolled gold of course; gold laced thread for a baby's name ceremony; small silver chalice for First Food ceremony. One time it was a silver plate for writing the child's first alphabet in sacred rice, you know, that type of things. See, all those wealthy doctors were having Gita and her uncle cater food to their grand events. Gita ben found the perfect way to make the families happy with small ceremonial gifts. Great marketing, if you ask me. The white officer didn't like it at all when I explained these details. He was off in his own world of detectiving. It's a different world alright, *this whole 'detectiving' thing...*

"What the officer wanted to know most was about the men who accompanied her, whether I knew who they were, and if she ever came in with the same man more than once."

"And...?"

"Of course, I knew all the answers. But the detective didn't look like he liked my answers. Kumar, I am not a gossip, but I answered the questions. I knew everybody who came in with Gita ben. Shetty came in a lot. The vendor of sweets came in once or twice. Ghose came in once. Men escorted her to the store when darkness fell, or when the crowds thinned out. You know, it's just the Indian sort of thing, be a bodyguard for the lady. Many of them didn't even come inside. Just stood outside smoking. You know, we all know each other on the street. But the white detective didn't like my answers at all."

It wasn't the dryness of the scalp that had me scratching my head at this point. Something was wrong. Very wrong. In fact, everything and everybody sounded wrong. I am missing something here. More head scratching. I looked long and hard at Ranajee, nodding slowly, reluctantly, and wishing he would go on. Once again, the gold merchant relented.

"She was a clever person, Mr. Kumar," said Ranajee with a smile. "Gita ben bought very low cost but tasteful gifts for the families she did catering to. I don't think she ever made a big fuss about it. People spent hundreds of dollars on these catered affairs. Gita would gift the matriarchs with a pair of bangles, a set of toe rings, a small silver box, things like that. It made the older women honored properly, and they recommended Gita to others."

"Amazing," I agreed.

"I told her to tell Lalu Ganesh to buy a whole bunch to keep in stock ready."

"Did Lalu ever make such a bulk purchase?"

"No, no. I don't think she even told Lalu about it. It was her own clever little habit. Charming, if you ask me."

Finally, I asked Ranajee about his original comment "all the wrong questions." It fired him up and set off great excitement in his voice and face. It was as if he discovered a new continent or a brand new temple ruins.

"Like I said, the cop asked about people who were with Gita.

Who came inside, who didn't, and who sat close to her. He wanted to know if anybody acted friendly and sat too close to her. He tried to get me to gossip about her. Funny, the white detective asked a lot of questions about a lot of things, but he never asked me about people Gita *talked* about."

"Yes, Ranajee. Astute of you...."

The man leaned into my face as only Indian men do sometimes to reveal their own genius, "Gita was planning on getting married. She bought a set of wedding rings. American style bands."

I nearly fainted, but was saved only by the way I had leaned over the counter. Ranajee right then moved to a back shelf, and didn't see me sway. I just held on to the counter, and by the time he returned the moment passed. I was clear headed enough by then to focus on what Ranajee carried. "These are the bands," he held up two open cases. "His and hers. She had the words Ginger and Cowboy engraved on the inside, and a heart symbol." He set them down on the glass top of the display case.

"What no diamonds?" I said only half-jokingly, to keep the man in good humor and stay communicative. I picked up each small case in turn, admired the sheen of the satin cushion, the gleam of the metal and the small letters on the inside. They felt good in my palm. I warmed all over, as if Gita herself were standing in the room with us, approving, smiling. Ranajee spoke, and the moment passed.

"Here is the thing, Mr. Kumar sir. I have no idea what those words signified. She never explained them to me."

"And they never got picked up?"

"I am coming to it. She said a police officer will come and pick them up. But the only cop who came was that white detective with his stupid questions."

"And the white officer never asked you about the wedding rings?"

"I am also puzzled like you, why he did not. Mr. Kumar, the officer only wanted to know about the men who came in with Gita ben. He got their descriptions and took off. I am glad that you are now asking all these things. You will tell Ganesh?"

"Of course, sir. When did Gita order the rings?"

The man scratched different parts of his head in succession: scalp, chin, forehead, behind ear, and made faces like actors in a French movie. He finally said, "Got it. She came on St. Patrick's Day to order them. I remember now the green scarf she wore. Said they will be picked up before *Gudi Padawa*. Something about a New Year's Day in her native district, or something like that. Should I get a calendar?"

"No, no Ranajee, I know the exact dates."

"Of course, of course. A writer like you is already knowing such things. All this helps? Poor girl."

"Definitely Ranajee. You serve our community well, even more than with just your business. Very nice. Thanks a lot."

I asked to see the bands one more time before I left. He obliged, but seemed unable to take his eyes off me.

Ginger and Cowboy.

They truly belonged together. The sight of the wedding bands filled me with a mysterious joy, my heart palpitated as I imagined them on the young lovers' fingers. Ranajee's eyes never wavered as he observed me keenly. He was, after all, a gold merchant.

Bad Day at Blue Mountain

I returned to the Blue Mountain. I couldn't have stayed away anyway. Shetty and Ghose were overjoyed to see me. Lalu and I kept going as if stuff never happened between us. That he did not throw me out of the restaurant, and that I didn't leave in a huff. I told myself that sometimes it is better to focus on the bridge and not on the water that passed under it. Moreover, I now had the added testimony of the gold merchant to bolster my case, if bolstering is what was needed at this point.

Warangal was still the matter on hand. His near death affected Lalu as much as Gita's actual death. "What bad did I do, god is punishing me?" He said, over and over. Having no real answers, I resorted to letting my hand and head movements do the talking.

Lalu aged more in the few days after we visited Warangal in the ICU than he did in the months since we learned about Gita. Grief is like that sometimes - it grows like compound interest.

I compared notes with Shetty that afternoon and we agreed that just in the past one week, Lalu became less talkative, lost his arm swing, slowed down over all. When he made the curries, his hands didn't move as gracefully as before, but rather doddered like those of a recovering stroke victim.

"I am worried, Mr. Kumar sir," Shetty said. "The food isn't the same. He is messing up the masala."

"You think he knows?" I asked.

"That is why I worry, Kumar sir. Lalu doesn't know he is off. He thinks all is okay."

"Is the business down, you think?"

"I *know it is, sir.* Not much but quite a bit...definitely down a bit."

"Catering jobs down too, huh?" I asked.

"After Gita sister, not right away. But now, he is not taking that many orders. Some yes, some no. What reason? He doesn't explain." Shetty chewed his lip.

I patted his arm, "It will get better soon, Shetty. Things will fall into place, I am sure." A brave smile on my part, and he perked up some. "Sergeant Mike says he has some new information coming next week. He will share it with us, definitely," I said.

"Something that will really tell us what happened to Gita sister, sir?" he asked.

"I am hoping. So you just keep an eye on Lalu."

There was moisture in his eyes as I left. Only to be called back by a noisy rapping on the window from inside. A bag of snacks in Shetty's hand, and a semblance of a smile on his face.

****

Even as Chicago's weather got warmer, the case stayed cold. Blue Mountain was taking a beating. I didn't want to add my own anxiety to the mix. Shetty will be fine, Lalu will be fine. We will all be fine. Just hold on to that thought, I told myself, as I walked along the strip darting in and out of stores.

I took in the the sights and sounds of Little India. Screams in many languages, pulsating Bollywood tunes and people just crossing the street at random, disregarding traffic. Devon Avenue put me in a world all of its own. I wallowed in its energy, its power, and like good poetry, its ability to transport me to worlds away.

****

In the grandly named Mall of India, I saw a familiar face trying to cut through the throng of Indo-Pak shoppers coming towards me. He was waving, attempting to catch my eye. It was Ghose, the short and skinny kitchen helper from Lalu's restaurant. "Saab, saab, Kumar saab," he said, "Shetty sent me to look for you. Come, come. Some police are at the buffet table." In his own mixture of Hindi, Urdu and English, Ghose said Lalu wasn't there yet, Shetty was nervous, cops were there. It was a crisis.

I never claimed to be clairvoyant, but this was too much of a coincidence. Me making a lame assertion, to assuage Shetty's feelings, that Mullins will have news, and now cops showing up at Blue Mountain? Police have news already? What gives, Mr. Blogger-Man? We headed back to the restaurant.

Friends smarter than me have often told me that good authentic food brought in critics, and critics brought in customers, but only taste buds brought in repeat diners. At the Blue Mountain, above all, great popularity came from pricing and the vast array of dishes Lalu provided at his daily all-you-can-eat buffet. The higher priced weekend buffet was pretty awesome too. Crowds were sometimes so big, diners waited at the bar, where oddly enough the prices of beers varied too. Par for the course. After all, white people seldom noticed or complained about such things as prices in ethnic eateries. No harm, no foul. But, police running around couldn't be that good for image.

I needn't have worried, it was not on-duty cops, but Mullins and some of his friends. The detective must have brought them over to eat some samosa. Lalu wasn't anywhere. He has been getting pelted from every direction. The latest attack from the rumor mill said that Lalu himself got Gita killed because she was growing too strong as his direct competition. Would have been funny if it weren't so stupid.

Shetty was relieved to see me back.

I shook hands with Mike. He seemed genuinely pleased to see me, and made the introductions, referring to me as a writer.

Six policemen come to eat Indian food as Mullins's guests..

That thought wouldn't have mattered much were it not for one fact. The food at Blue Mountain sucked that day. I sampled the buffet while it was being set up. No Lalu to supervise and taste test. The mixes of masala were already messed up. *Where was Lalu?*

The six people from the police department sat at a large table, birthday table Shetty called it. Four men, and two women. Two of the six were African-American, evidently a couple. He was muscular like a patrolman or a detective. She was a looker, elegant with nails and hair, both introduced to me as officers. None of Mullins' guests were in police uniform or openly armed. One guy was in a technician's garb, smock and all, and looked vaguely familiar.

One of the two women, the wife in the black couple, kept referring to the buffet as Pakistani food, Her husband kept gently correcting her that they were at an Indian restaurant. "Oh well, whatever, they are all brothers," she shrugged, but wouldn't give up the word Pakistani food. I watched her eat later and noticed how much she relished the food. *That* was a glad sight to see.

The white girl still wore a job ID on a lanyard. It said SUSAN, indicated she was a lab tech. Susan smiled and said, “I actually don’t care who cooked the food. I just love curry. I fell in love with it in London during my gap year travels. Curry is my passion.”

Mullins chuckled, “Your real passion, my dear, is that red-headed lad, Rourke, you met while dancing.” The others just smiled. Mullins added, “You never tasted curry before him, and have not eaten it much since.”

“Thanks for ratting me out, uncle Mike,” she let out with a hearty laugh.

Mullins admitted to me later that he once dated Susan’s mother, an old-time nine-one-one dispatcher, and that he would never let it be known at work, that it was he who got Susan a job at the police lab. All I thought at the time was how there were so many uncles around.

Mike said two of the guys in the group were from different beats, they worked with Mike at different times and still called him Sarge. One was a Puerto Rican, the other had a distinct drawl that I couldn’t place.. The group made for a regular Jesse Jackson rainbow coalition.

I worried. *Why did Mullins bring cops with so many disparate jobs? Was this just a cultural outing, or was this his brain-trust, a second set of eyes? And, where the hell was Lalu?*

From the phone on the back wall of the kitchen I kept dialing him every few minutes. Sooner or later he has to pick it up. And he did. ”What do you want? Told you not to bother me,” came the bark.

"Hello Lalu, I am so glad to get in touch with you," I said.

There was instant calm on the line. That was unusual for Lalu lately. Even more unusual, I told Lalu for the first time ever, how his food sucked. His breathing eased, "So, what is going on there?" he asked.

"You have six VIP guests from the Chicago Police department wanting to enjoy your cooking. Shetty can't baste chicken like you can. And he is nervous that you are not here."

There was silence on the line and a pause to his breathing. Just to drive home my point, I added, "Lalu, we need your Chicken Tandoori, now."

"Okay okay okay, you tell them your stories. I'm coming. Don't say nothing."

When a man says okay three times, I believe him. When he says it rapidly like Lalu did, I trust it. So, I returned to my new favorite people, lovers of Pakistani food and London gap-year curry, to tell tales of my own world travel, global cuisine, and personal misadventures in cooking. The guys loved and laughed at my stories more than the gals. Mike just sat and smiled. But amidst all that clatter, I could feel the gears mashing in his head with the same thoughts as mine, *What is going on, where the hell is Lalu Ganesh, why is this food not like anything I tasted before?*

Shetty meanwhile, outdid himself in terms of hospitality. He hovered about, refilling water, setting up masala chai, providing finger bowls for each guest, replacing cloth napkins stained by curry.

There was a booming sound. And a continuous sizzle.

Out of the kitchen strode Ghose, blowing a conch. It was an enormous pink shell with six elegant spikes and a wide mouth. A saffron colored ribbon hung from its front tip. Ghose was blowing the conch shell like he were some kind of a medieval warrior. In his left hand, he held a pair of finger cymbals he clapped. Behind Ghose came, at a majestic pace, Lalu Ganesh, carrying a giant platter. It held hot, hot sizzling cast iron servers on which sat muted red tones of a dozen chicken pieces, surrounded by fried onions, lemon wedges, cilantro and steam.

"To our special guests," he proclaimed to the room. There was applause as he placed it on the serving stand between the two ladies. "Very hot, plate very hot. Careful," he said. The ladies vied with one another for the privilege to serve. The lover of Pakistani food won out and seized the tongs. Other diners looked on in awe, some smiled.

They dined in joviality. The ladies had questions about the recipe. The guys had questions about what they called the ceremony. I made up stories for them. The group took turns playing with the conch, hefting it, and blowing into it. Mike said very little, just looked at me and nodded.

When the lunch hour ended and the front doors were closed, Shetty broke into smiles and tears. Lalu slumped into a corner booth, and Ghose insisted on blowing the conch once more.

"Mr. Kumar, Mr. Kumar, you are a great man, sir," Shetty gushed. "Oh, Kumar sir, you have pulled a *tamasha* out of a disaster," he said. Yes, I did. But then, even the most unschooled and wretched of Indians will offer the easy wisdom: life itself is one big spectacle, tamasha or make believe. Gita and Warangal were all too real.

Memorial Day Weekend

I tried several times over the next few days to seek a meeting with Mullins. He didn't answer the phone or return my calls. I left a voice mail saying I need to talk about Gita's rental car, urgently. No dice. His silence was a bit annoying. Lalu was worsening, the case was dragging, and my mind was overheating. I needed things to move along.

The whole rental car thing was one of my major known unknowns. Mike was good enough to tip me off to it. I really wanted to tell him what I learned at the airport. Plus, there was the matter of the love letters which I unearthed. But, when it came to the unknown unknowns, I was at the end of my rope. It was time for Mike's unlimited resources to further my quest, and for him to let me in on what was going on.

Finally, this morning, "Hello Kumar, don't you have any other case you are working on, hehehe. Gita is the only case you got, hehehe."

"Very funny, Mike. See, I am known as the one-case sleuth, sure you saw my show on TV, haha. Yes, I do have a one track mind."

His response of, "Aha" was tepid, not cheery at all.

"So, what's on that one-track of your mind, pal?" Mullins asked. The word pal was a new one. It could mean either he was being too chummy, or too standoffish. I couldn't tell which. Did it bode anything?

"I know a few things about the rental car, Mike. And, a few things about her daddy who could have become a granddaddy. I just can't seem to fill in the blanks."

A certain length of silence... I couldn't time it or give meaning to it. Just waited with my own silence.

“Come out and say it, Kumar. What blanks do you think need filling?”

“Can I come downtown, Mike? Just catch each other up on where things are. Just lay my cards down, so to speak.”

“How interesting, my friend. A mind reader you are…”

Now I am a friend? I held my breath. With blood pumping in my ears, I was at a loss to scan the situation. He did it for me.

“My friend Kumar, this is a coincidence. You want to come downtown and lay your cards. And I want to go uptown and lay my cards down. Interesting, yes? Let’s meet at Lalu’s place.”

Another pause, during which I imagined Mike checking his watch, his desk calendar and jacket pocket for car keys. I held my breath. “Kumar, meet me at Blue Mountain around three o’clock. The lunch crowd should be gone by then. Bye.” Click.

****

City bus 11- Lincoln reached the end of McCormick Blvd and turned east onto Devon Avenue. Two blocks in, I already counted more than a dozen out-of-state license plates on cars driven by my fellow brown Americans. Or, as Mullins would say, ‘Kumar’s cousins.’

“Memorial Day crowds already, huh,” I said to Larry, the driver.

“Never fails,” he shook his head. “Even regular weekends, same thing.”

Long weekends brought out the inner bulk-shopper in my cousin. Huge bags of rice, wheat flour and *atta,* giant square tins of cooking oil, saris by the dozen. Indians in America hell bent on a pilgrimage of a different sort. The longer the weekend, the more packed were the SUVs; the warmer the clime, the farther the cousins came from. Today's farthest license plate? Nebraska, most likely Omaha.

Larry heard me muttering the names of states as I read out the tags. "You got relatives in all those places?" a half grin on his face.

"Probably, more than you got cousins in Serengeti," I said. Not quite knee-slapping humor, but lately a fixture of our banter.

"No doubt, no doubt," Larry chimed. The grin bloomed into a full hearty laughter, and he said, "And they are all coming to see *you,* hahaha."

"Yup, they love me. But they love shopping even more."

"No doubt, no doubt," Larry giggled.

The sluggish traffic inevitably annoyed local white people who transited the street. Larry got paid by the hour, and laughed heartily whenever we heard someone shout 'go back to your country'. Lately though, I noticed that it was Indians who shouted that epithet at others, like the Caribbean people, especially on days the West Indies cricket team thrashed the India-XI.

"Hear that partner," Larry said after one particularly loud outburst.

"Larry, sometimes you just can't go home again," pleased with my own wit.

"Ain't that the truth," he replied. "I heard you went to see my sister at the morgue. She help ya?"

"Oh yes, she was helpful," was all I said. He looked at me hard and long, nodded, and kept the bus inching forward. He didn't push for details.

The show on the road went on around us. People darted in front of cars to cross the street, drivers leaned on the horn, slammed brakes or both. *Welcome to Little India, pal.*

When the bus reached the bridge at the old donkey-baseball park, I said my thanks to Larry, "I'll walk from here. It'll be just as fast." He tilted his head. I blended into the throng on the old crumbling narrow sidewalk, and drifted eastwards toward the heart of Little India. The avenue was a sluggish artery clogged with Muslim beards, Hindu saris, North Indian turbans, dollar-faithfuls, and faithless seekers. Memorial Day weekend in America - not always good for making nice new memories.

****

Stepping into the Blue Mountain was like entering a tomb. Most lights were off. It was quiet, and smelled of stale curries scraped off cold serving trays. The dining room was cold and drab. The only sounds were the colorless strains of instrumental versions of film songs. A sort of Bollywood's own elevator Muzak. The yield of the recently installed padded carpet under my feet, was the only sign of life, or movement. Then I saw him.

Mullins sat at a side table with his back to the wall and facing the entrance, the usual hospitality of chai and samosa in front of him. He didn't look any different either. A manila folder next to his cup of chai and a half nibbled samosa. I sat down and smiled.

"Hello Kumar, it seems your friend just went down the street. That young man Ghose seemed a bit unnerved when he saw me, but..." he waved his hand at the tray in front of him, "...but perfect Indian hospitality. First Class courtesy as always."

While heaping that praise, Mullins didn't smile, simply held my gaze. Shetty came from the kitchen mumbling "Sorry sorry," switched on more lights, and returned to the kitchen. No further activity could be heard back there. Evidently, we were to wait for Lalu's return.

"So, Mike, what is going on with the case?" I asked.

"How do you mean? You should know. You've been going all over the place!"

"Hah. I am running from pillar to post, as they say."

Mike had no response. I took a different shot. "I've been running like a chicken with its head cut off!"

A slight chuckle now.

"I hope you begin to fill us in once Lalu gets here. Oh, by the way, were you waiting long? I was stuck in traffic. It's crowded out there."

He just nodded. I got the feeling that Mullins wasn't going to be talkative till Lalu got back. I looked about the dining area, but realized that the detective's gaze was fixed on me.

Some sign of activity in the kitchen. Sounds of voices and washings. Lalu came in through the big double doors.

"Hello, hello. Sorry to keep you waiting," Lalu shook hands with Mullins, "Oh Kumar, good you came."

“Anybody know when Warangal is getting out?” I asked.

“I took him home yesterday. Forgot to tell you, Kumar,” Lalu’s voice. I was looking at the detective’s face while he watched mine. Lalu’s words sounded distant, from beyond a wall or words carried by a wind that changed its mind.

I nodded slowly. Mullins seemed to approve something in his own head. Lalu unexpectedly spoke my thoughts out loud. “You brought something for us, Captain Mike,” pointing to the folder.

“Yes, but I do have another request too. Request to you Lalu saab. I need an address in India for your brother, Phani Ganesh.” He pronounced it *Fanhee.* “I believe it’s a small town near the City of Hyderabad.”

Shetty, Ghose and a Mexican young man, all came out onto the dining floor now. They flitted about, turned more lights on, and kept up a buzz of activity. Trying to transition the dining space from a lunch buffet setting to a dinner hour decor. Flowers in vases, candles in decorative glass containers, cloth napkins in rings, upgraded salt and pepper shakers. Dressing up a city pigeon to look like a Himalayan lake swan.

“Why do you need Phani’s details?” asked Lalu.

“He is Gita’s father, after all.” Mullins said.

“Yes, but you never ask before, officer,” Lalu persisted.

“Well, we have to be thorough and look into everything,” Mullins said.

Lalu’s face was consternation itself.

"Sir, he has gone away. I mean to say, Phani went back a long time ago. It was a week before Gita..." Lalu didn't finish. He couldn't finish. His voice cracked. Shetty, who brought in a tray of snack reinforcements slipped away. I stared at the tiffin laden tray and the giant teapot. *What's going on here, what is Mullins up to*?

Mullins was saying, "See Mr. Lalu, I know that your brother has gone away. He flew from Chicago O'Hare on the ___ day of March. He took an American plane from here. For completeness of my paperwork, I have to have a questionnaire answered by him."

"Complete paperwork?" Lalu looked at Mullins. From Mullins to me and back to Mullins. Confused and a neck pulse visible like a twisting snake crawling up. "You closing the case detective saab? Not tell us who killed Gita?"

Even as I waited to see what tack Mullins would take, I caught sight of Shetty who returned to the floor and hovered.

"Oh no, Ganesh. The case not closed at all. But the leads are getting narrowed. Almost any day now. It's a routine questionnaire for the file. We need the answers. There is a small American visa office in Hyderabad. Fanhee can go there to give answers."

"But, but, our father reads and writes English good. Phani too. They fill their own forms in English, you know."

Suddenly Mullins face softened. Not a lot, just a shade less grave.

"You misunderstand me Lalu saab. It's not about the language or translation. You see, the visa office in Hyderabad has staff authorized to be notary public. Authorized to witness signatures on documents acceptable in US courts. What we want *Fanhee* to submit is an affidavit. We need that formality."

I must admit to squirming in my chair a bit. Lalu, on the other hand, appeared comfortable. And just sat there comfortably. All activity ceased around us. Lalu's lips trembled and twisted into a stupid grin, like, *can you believe this, an affeeda-Wit?*

During the next few minutes Mullins spoke rapidly, explaining that he was seeking to add to the file. He already had a statement from Warangal, he had a statement from the workers and owners of some of the stores strung along the Avenue, some prominent doctors who hired Gita as a caterer, even the alderman's secretary who knew Lalu well.

"There is quite a bit of a file on the young lady, Lalu saab. The case is reaching the final stages."

Mullins should have left it at that, right? But no, he had to wrap it up in the usual copper's jargon bullshit. "We expect to apprehend the suspect imminently. Your help in these last stages will be greatly appreciated."

Lalu was amazingly placid by the end of that little spiel. He seemed oddly unmoved except for that grin-like fix of a twisted mouth.

"What did Warangal say to you, officer?" I asked. Lalu's head jerked as if he wanted to know the same.

Didn't Lalu have a chat with Warangal after they left the hospital?

"That he and Gita were good friends. And that you all took Fanhee to the airport and saw him off. Date and time confirmed to me under oath. Not only by officer Warangal but also by Mr. Shetty here."

"What else do you already know about Phani?" I asked.

"Just what officer Warangal said, something about how his girlfriend's dad was a tough nut to crack. Didn't explain why he thought so. I'll say this though, the young Wrangler wasn't sad about Fanhee leaving."

Lalu's face gradually relaxed as it lost the risus-like twist of the mouth. He stood up, and along with him rose an edge in his voice. "Many many interesting things you told us, Captain. Thanks a lot. You know everything. If not, you can find out anything you want. Go to the Indian Consulate downtown. They keep records. Get Phani's address from them."

It would be incorrect to say that Lalu was angry. But the way he shot up to a standing posture said a lot.

Detective Mullins, however, remained seated and calmly pressed on. "That may be so. I would rather you give me the information."

"No," Lalu exploded. "You can call the Immigration office. They give Phani visa, they have his address." He seemed ready to stomp out of there, but the detective's quiet sigh
caught him short.

"I still have this to talk to you about, gentlemen," Mullins tapped the folder in front of him.

Court orders

The index finger of Detective Sergeant Mike 'Moonshine' Mullins went tap, tap, tap on the blue folder in front of him. It reminded me of movie scenes in which the judge uses a gavel. Bang, bang, bang, "I will clear this courtroom." Just like in the movies, silence fell upon the dining room at Blue Mountain.

"My captain wants this done today," Mike said, more calmly than the movie judge. Continued silence from us Indians.

He looked at each one of us in turn and continued. "Captain Jones thought it important enough that I was told to bring these forms personally, instead of mailing them." He opened the folder and slid the contents out. The forms looked official and very very legal. There were the Great Seal of the State, blanks along the edge to write people's names in the fashion typical of bureaucratic paperwork.

I felt chilled even though I saw this coming, I wasn't quite prepared for the bluntness in Mike's voice. For one thing, he wasn't ruffled by Lalu's rudeness. And for another, I saw a total failure of what Indians often thought of as 'power of the place'. We were seated in Lalu's place, where Lalu ruled the roost. But it was Detective Mike who held the edge of authority. Lalu's power of ownership couldn't discount Mike's presence. Sure, the sergeant continued with his famous befuddled look, but his words hit us like pelted stones. We Indians remained quiet, and just looked at each other.

Into that sense of helplessness, Ghose brought a fresh tray of chai and snacks. Batter-fried chili peppers this time: slender, long green things coated with curried lentil paste and deep fried. They bore an oily look and a hint of recent sizzle. *Mirchi*, Hmm. I prayed for hot chili seeds to escape his bite. And luckily, Mike continued in his 'eat samosa' vein, and no errant pepper seed got bit into. Unwittingly, Ghose's appearance did some good. His chai exuded an extra waft of ginger. Between that and the chili peppers, I found something else to focus on, besides the blue folder.

A Chicago journalist once famously described Mullins as a *Detective of Manners,* implying that the sergeant was least likely to commit a cultural *faux pas.* Crime reporters on television spouted similar copycat punditry: Homicide Mike was an 'ethnic specialist'. In the numerous legendary ethnic enclaves of Chicago, Mullins got along with everyone. Little Warsaw, Little India, Pilsen, Caribbean Town, Vietnam Village. You got minorities? We got Mullins for you!

Lalu bolted upright. And sat back down just as abruptly.
"What nonsense in these papers?" he asked.

"What I have here are court orders," Mike said flatly. "Signed by the Honorable Sklendowski, the judge in charge of the Second Family Division of the Municipal Court. He approved the Chicago Police Department warrant application for a Paternity Test in the homicide Case # —— . Gentlemen, we need to know who the father of Gita Ganesh's unborn child is."

It was a recitation bereft of all warmth, and it didn't stop him from resuming to munch on the *mirchi* and sip his chai. A part of me marveled at Mike. He tilted his tea cup, pouring the chai on the saucer, and blew on the hot beverage before sipping it Indian style. He might have been a rickshaw puller in small town India.

Silence continued on the floor. Even the helper staff smelled that something was afoot and retreated to the kitchen. I could make out some heads in the square glass panels of the double swing doors of the kitchen. The doors were still, but not the faces behind the glass as workers took turns to peek through.

I dared to break the silence. "What's the point, detective? What do we care about the father? We want to know who killed Gita, right?"

Nods from the Indians, naturally.

"The police think that identifying the father may help solve Gita's murder."

I had to object. "That doesn't make sense, Mike," I objected. "Why would whoever got her pregnant want to kill the mother of his child.? It makes even less sense to assume that one of us is involved somehow. What would being a father prove? You know all of us were right here in Chicago when Gita supposedly died?"

Nods all the way around again, among the Indians.

I pressed on. "Is it just us here, or are there others you are seeking blood tests from? What about Warangal, Gita's customers, others on Devon?"

I sensed a jerky movement from Shetty, who gave me a sharp look, like he worried that Lalu might throw me out again.

Mullins tried to shift the mood with a ready-made boilerplate response. "My advice to you gents is not to worry about others, but think about excluding yourselves."

I should have been ready for Mike's spiel. I had questions that couldn't be framed properly due to the storm in my brain. And, I couldn't speak due to the parchment that lined my mouth. The sweet toothy face of the morgue lady Ms. Honeycutt flashed in my mind, and I thought of her foreshadowing of this moment. The love letters between Gita and Warangal flashed too. Is Mike just casting about, or does he have a master plan? My spine tingled.

Ghose whispered something to Shetty, and it turned into an exchange of mumbles.

"What, what? Speak it loudly," said Lalu.

Shetty spoke up, "Ghose asks if we are going to be arrested. I told him no."

Mullins and I said at the same time, "No, no."

"We just have to take a blood test, Ghose." I rolled up my sleeve as I would at a testing lab, and gesticulated. "It will help the case of Gita sister." Ghose picked up the enameled kettle and topped off our cups. Steam coming off the hot liquid exuded a touch of ginger. Mike seemed particularly delighted by it. Looking at Ghose, he let crack a smile, raised his cup and saucer, and said, "Delicious chai."

"I don't understand," the first words spoken by Lalu Ganesh in quite a while. This one not directed at anyone. But I was all ears as I knew that it could fall to me to answer. "What happened to Gita, okay she was killed. Who killed her? Nobody knows. She got pregnant before she died? Okay for that too. The father killed her?" Here Lalu's face went through more contortions than possible, I thought. He was a one-man debate show. Both asking and answering questions, like a sage sitting under a tree querying pupils.

"So, Gita died fighting? Or, she died accidentally?" Lalu now pointed a finger at Mullins. "And, now you want our blood tests. You know, why. Yes you know," Lalu stabbed the air in front of the policeman. "You know none of us have anything to do with it. So, why our blood tests? This new DNA stuff... I don't know it… It is all twisted evidence."

"Mr. Lalu, everything you say has a grain of truth in it. I will admit that I don't have any idea who killed your Gita. That's why I am asking for help."

Wow, Mike was smooth.

"How the tests help?" Lalu wasn't mollified.

"It is important that we know who was with your niece when she died," was all Mike said.

"Okay, you find we all were there. We were with her a day before, two days, three days before Gita passed away. Means what? Nothing." Lalu insisted.

"I am referring to the day, the hour, and the moment the young lady passed," Mike was still, as Indians say, flying kites to see which way the wind was blowing. Only, it wasn't a direction that anyone at the table liked.

"Trust me people, the tests will help. The department believes that knowing who was with Gita will help. Knowing who fathered her baby will help."

I imagined Lalu's internal dialog going in circles, frustration mounting, and looking for a way out of a dizzy vortex.

"What would be the next step, Mike?" I asked Mullins, "After the blood tests, and you know who the father is."

Mullins was ready for that too. "Well, we'll cross that bridge when we come to it. For now, we have to follow Judge Sklendowski's orders," tapped the forms again. He must have thought he made the sale. He now moved in to close the deal.

“My job is to find out all about Gita’s last hour on earth. Who was with her? Asking for blood tests doesn’t mean that I think something suspicious is going on. Unfortunately, we don’t have any photos or videos of those last hours. Science has to help us. The father could be the key....”

A tingling sensation began in my spine and rose, like the *kundalini* serpent. I was triggered by the word father being bandied about, and the ambiguity of who the father was - whether it referred to Gita’s baby daddy, or Gita’s own daddy. The vagueness ensnared my imagination.

Mullins’s closing pitch worked. Lalu grabbed his form first, and then we all signed the papers. Mike gave us pamphlets on testing centers and left politely saying, “Na-ma-stay”

Ever the ethnic specialist, the Detective of Manners.

Kumar's next move

Go away and don't come back, Lalu said, a week ago. Man, why did I return after that fight? I should have stayed angry. Maybe even gone on a road trip.

Wait, you don't own a car, have to rent one....

I was never thrown out of any place. Not a bar, not a restaurant, not even a grocery store. By girlfriends, yes. But never by a business.

It was an old English teacher, Mr. Narayan, from High School, he used to get excited about old sayings. He had a theatrical manner of speaking English proverbs, like they were not part of what he was saying but dialog quoted.

Funny how Mr. Narayan didn't use the word proverb, and called everything an adage - "Boys, we enjoy some adages for what they simply say, like 'Make hay while the sun shines.' Others we enjoy because of how they say it." He'd pause, strike a pose and exclaim: "Faithful are the wounds of a friend." Spittle sprayed out when he said lines like that. "Boys, that sort of adage lasts for ever, beautifully constructed." Faithful are the wounds of a friend - that adage lived, in my brain.

Yuk, this tea is cold. It's the worst... sweetened spicy chai that's gone cold.

My crusty old teacher didn't make much sense back in the school days, but that adage as he called it, did stick with me, and played in my head like a broken record. People do say they are lucky to have me as a friend, don't they? Yes, but did it mean I should suffer it all?

Lalu knows curry, but has no clue about people. My own damn fault for being so curious and caring. What the hell are you trying to prove, Kumar? Suffering such slings and arrows?

I do it for Gita, Sir. A daughter without a daddy. Hey, I like that, and hope I can remember to use it somewhere. A daughter without a daddy. Not an orphan, of course, but without a real caring close-by daddy. Lalu tries. We all have to worry about a little girl like that.

Damn, this chai.

No good will come out of these blood tests. Anybody with half a brain can see that. Gita and Warangal were an item. So, why fuss with the forms? Mike is playing some sort of a long game....

"Hey, hey, mister writer," a shake of my shoulder, and the clatter of cups and saucers. "You don't have to be thinking like a detective. Remember, Mr. Mike is finally doing his job." Lalu's voice was almost normal and level, but there was no gladness in it. His face was still drawn, with tired sunken eyes, and no smile. He dragged a chair with exaggerated noise, and signaled Ghose to bring us some food.

I approved of what Ghose laid in front of us. A plate for each, with one leg of chicken, one nan, a ladle-full of biryani, and some dal. And after a nod from me, Ghose brought me a steel bowl bearing two small balls of gulab jamun that gave off a delicate rose aroma without half trying.

Lalu ain't ready for nothing. Not for post-mortem results, not for DNA tests. What can be done now? I looked around the room before addressing my favorite Indian food items.

The place began to fill up with groups of customers near the buffet. Oohs and ahs from Americans, and the usual muted grumbling from Indians. Practically every item on the buffet spread had some flaw for the fussy Indians. Sambar too thin, okra pieces cut too thick, not enough coriander in the potatoes, curry leaves too fragmented, dal dish not thick enough or oily enough. I could pick up the soft complaints in at least three languages, four including head shaking. *This is not how we make it.* No dish on the buffet came up to the standard of *their* family - typical Indian dissatisfaction with food not cooked by mother. But, that did not stop them from gorging on the 'all you can eat' buffet.

Lalu, ever the faultless host, let me take a few bites of my food first. Then studied my face and said, "Your policeman friend is ready to solve the case?"

I gave a slow nod. "He seems to be putting all the pieces together."

"I am thinking, you got your own answers, correct?" Lalu asked.

"Only Mike has all the hard data. But I do have an idea. More than one actually."

"But, your idea not same as police, correct?"

"We know that Gita was killed in an act of a violent outburst. I think she might know her killer from way back, or a part of her life that we don't know. Honestly, even I am not sure about my own ideas."

"Hmm, what you say is confusing," Lalu said.

"Gita's recent life was not fully known to us. I started looking for one thing, but I found something else. I go in one direction, only to find I am on a blind side street. Easy to get lost, like when we used to go to roam in the old parts of town as kids. Narrow curved lanes that went this way and that, never straight. Trust me, Lalu, science will show us exactly what happened to Gita."

"All I know, Gita is a good cook of Indian food. She learn everything I teach… She never disobey me."

'Never disobey me,' whatever that meant. Family love and blind spots, they go together, don't they?

Lalu asked a different question, "Gita died because of her love affair?"

"Love breeds optimism, not despair. People in love don't seek to die." What else could a writer say?

Lalu continued his 'thought boxing' by hurling ideas at me. "Kumar, it was you who said Warangal was in love with Gita. Look at all these love letters, you argued. Gifts were exchanged, you said. They went on dates, you said. Tell me then, why…why a boy like him, he is in love… why he try suicide. When we see him in the hospital, I put no pressure for answer. You answer now, why try suicide? He not serious about his love?"

I only had seeds of an answer. A variety of phrases, images, and bits of thought were buzzing in my head. They were calling out to be organized. They were also strongly calling for Mr. Guinness.

"I am going over to *Khazana* and talk to that Muslim friend of yours who owns it."

"Why, you looking for crazy Muslim dishes, like brain, liver and goat meat?" Lalu wasn't being funny. Just a question without curiosity.

“There is a couple guys there I want to talk to. Fellows that work in their kitchen,” I said.

“Why you want to talk to....” Lalu trailed off into silence for a few seconds. Let the words tumble out slowly, “That’s where Francis worked. I made him work, so he go back to India with some cash.” He fell silent and became thoughtful. Well, that ‘some cash’ was actually cash under the table, but that wasn’t my point.

“I just want to see if Francis got close to anybody during those weeks.”

"What you are saying?” Lalu started.

“Nothing, I just want to see who knows what. If any of the kitchen helpers at *Khana Khazana* got to know your brother well. That’s all.” I might have been a bit breathless.

Lalu’s lips were drawn back to form a lifeless slit, “I thought you are not detective anymore. Well, well, well. I won’t tell Mullins that you are still on the case,” he gave a mirthless chuckle.

JUNE, 2005

Khazana & Clues

I left my fellow Indians stewing in their curry. Devon Avenue hit me with a sense of *deja vu*. I had done a similar walkabout a few days before. But, this time it wasn't so random. I was going to connect the dots. Seeds of some crazy ideas were tickling my brain cells, struggling to germinate, needing to be watered.

The mile-long stretch was all clues and no compass. I knew where to start now. And then connect up each dot with Gita. Don't forget about people who knew Gita; they are dots too, I told myself. Yeah, people are dots too, slogan with a silly ring.

Who was the most proximate person to Gita during her last week on earth? Her father, right? Okay, but *that* doesn't compute. Her father wasn't on the scene when she died. Or, was he?

*****

"Nijam-ud-din saab is working today?" I asked the man behind the counter.

He was a lean man in a white, knit skull cap. He stretched to his full height now. Stroked his long thin beard, peered over his round bifocals, and tossed his head in a sudden recognition. "Ah, Mister Kumar sir, yes yes, Nijam saab is in the back, coming soon. Sit, sit please. Will you kindly be having chai?" I nodded. I had to. Accepting hospitality was an obligatio almost. It greased the small talk, and there was no time like the present to ingratiate myself to a gracious compatriot, right? Right.

Tea and Nijam arrived at the same time. The big round man with the enormous belly unrolled his sleeves as he sauntered out of the kitchen. A faded shade of red henna tint still clung to his tapered beard. The owner of the famous local eatery, Khana Khazana, looked every bit the 'storehouse of food' himself, just like the name of his business.

"These are difficult times, Kumar," he said, as he sat down and pushed tea toward me. "That little girl getting killed like that..." He clucked his tongue.

I nodded. "Thanks for your time Nijam saab, just some simple questions if I may."

"Sure, sure. This getting killed is not good. Anything new? Police news? What you are wanting to know? You are having some important questions. Am I right?"

It wasn't a rain of questions. Nijam was being solicitous in that special Indian way, where just saying *what can I do* wouldn't cut it. Courtly manners required asking the same question in different ways, specially with offers to help. I recognized that gesture of effusiveness, and jumped at the chance.

"*Bahut shukriyaa*, Mr. Nijam. You did a kind thing by employing Gita's father for a few weeks. So the poor fellow could return home with some dollars. Nice of you."

Nijam nodded, "That's not a problem at all, Kumar saab. There is work to do, I see a person who want money. So...." he waved a hand. As if, hiring people who didn't have a work permit, and paying them cash under the table, was the most natural thing to do. Which, of course, it was in many of Chicago's ethnic neighborhoods. I nodded.

"What I want to know, Mr. Nijam, was there anybody Gita's father talked to a lot. Or, maybe spent time with?"

"I know that the cook gave him orders a lot. You want to talk to the cook? You know, Lalu bhai's brother was the silent type. A couple of kitchen workers talked to him regularly. Most of the others ignored him."

"Do you personally know the fellows who chatted most with Francis?"

"Mr. Fakhri, or Francis, or whatever he called himself, was a loner. During breaks he sat by himself, he ate rice by himself, even talked to himself sometimes..."

"And..." I prompted Nijam. His eyes wandered as he surveyed the place, made sure things were running smoothly. Then turned back to me again and said, "I should say he worked non-stop. Even a donkey wouldn't work so hard. Sorry, Kumar, don't take this wrong, I hope."

I smiled, "Of course, nothing implied there, Mr. Nijam. We all knew about that side of Gita's father. Once he put his mind to something... You didn't say anything offensive. The man did work like a donkey, period."

Nijam looked relieved. "There was one particular man, a Filipino guy, who bounced around different places on Devon Avenue. I gave him a job in the kitchen and he loved it. He spend a lot of time with your girl's father. Those two worked many shifts and same odd hours together. I will give you his number."

Nijam accompanied me to the door. He lowered his voice and said in a jovial manner, "This Filipino fellow, I stole him from the Patels' shopping mall. He was most unhappy working there." The large man gave a sudden burst of laughter.

I patted him on the shoulder, "Well done, Nijam saab, well done." I knew what my next stop should be.

*****

The six pack of Guinness proved to be quite companionable. Mister Triple Stout flowed with a thick floral odor, went down smoothly, and even more importantly it tickled some neurons way back in my limbic system. Best of all, Mr. Beer listened well.

So, who cares who fathered Gita's baby, and what's that got to do with who killed her or why? Why the DNA tests, and what's Mullins's game?

Mr. Guinness didn't answer.

At least five people on earth probably have a solid idea about the truth of paternity, regardless of what Mullins's bullshit court forms aimed to show. Two of the five knew for sure, the other three had a strong idea.

Gita knew who her baby's daddy was, unless she went the route of the anonymous sperm bank thing. One could say that such a thing might be far-fetched. But hey, Gita had been surprising us lately quite a bit. Hokay, what next?

The father himself. Or, 'the daddy man hisself' as the lady who sold me the Irish six-pack might say. Assuming that a daddy man really existed, and did the deed in flesh and not in a test-tube sort of way, my vote went to Warangal being that guy. In fact, so should everybody's vote. The jewelry shop man nailed it for me with those wedding rings. It was sly, how Gita dropped a hint by telling him to expect a policeman to pick up the rings. Mullins going around asking questions only confused the gold merchant. At least, he kept his mouth shut until I pried the secret loose.

Three other people knew about the paternity well before anyone else. One, Mullins knew it for quite some time. His performance in the restaurant was just window-dressing.

Second person: I suspected it, and needed no proof after reading those love letters. That, of course, didn't stop me from obliging Mullins with the test. After all, how else was I going to figure out what the Detective of Manners was scheming?

The third and last person to suspect Gita was a mom-to-be would be Gita's father. Did he know who the actual baby-daddy was, and how would he know that anyway?

*****

Patel & Patwardhan Mall bustled. I managed to locate and corner Shankar, a smelly old acquaintance of mine going back some years. He seemed glad to see me, and after the by-now-mandatory exchange about Gita, I asked about the Filipino man.

"Oh, Oscar. Yes yes yes," he said. "Nice fellow, always smiling. Good worker. Always talking about home. Why Kumar, why talk about him now?"

"Just curious. It seems Gita's father knew him while he was working at...." I left the rest unsaid. Everybody knew everything on Devon Avenue.

"Yes, yes. Too bad Gita's father don't like America. He could have made so much money. Worked like a donkey, that man. Very very hard, he worked. That Filipino man, what you are wanting to know?"

"Was he nice and normal, or what? Was he also a bit, er difficult like Gita's father?"

"Oscar is okay. He liked all our foods, he liked working here. But, he always talk about wife, kids, home."

"He missed his own country that much? Like Francis? Is that why the two got along?"

"No, no. What country? It's New York. The Filipino man talked about New York all the time. His family is there. For some reason he lives here alone. He might be converting to Islam or something. He and Francis talk all the time about New York City. Oscar told me sometime ago... Listen, I have to go, come back later. We'll have tea and talk."

*****

I opened the cardboard box into which I had been throwing things I thought were worthy of stroking my chin about. Little slips of thought, short questions, fortune cookie like sayings, and assorted clues. Items that I thought were clues to Gita's killing.

- A crumpled piece of a half-sheet. Unfurled and smoothed out, it read 70% in huge letters that took up most of the space, tiny letters said 'off the first night'. The other side of the half-sheet had a map.

- A flier, with another map, this one hand-scrawled on the back side.

- Receipt from a gas station, curled paper, folded twice and creased... placed into a shirt pocket? Or put in a purse like a woman might? Most guys I knew left them hanging out of the slot on the pump, looking like a tongue sticking out.

- An actual map of Illinois, printed, official. Rand-McNally type. A style of map not prevalent any more thanks to countless gizmos telling people where to go and when to turn the car.

- Note to self about broken dolls on the floor of Gita's closet.

- Note to self about a business card from an OB-GYN on Gita's fridge.

- Note to self about a roll of mints found in the glove box of the rental car.

Didn't Gita's father say something about Life Savers and rubber tires? Mr. Guinness didn't answer. But Mr. Filipino might. Or, would he be tight lipped too?

*****

The Filipino man was smiling. That's the way I found him when I dropped by Khana Khazana. Mid-morning customer flow was slow and mellow. Cab drivers and Loyola students indulging in a leisurely late breakfast. Lunch hour loomed, and Oscar was chopping vegetables with a vengeance. His smile was captivating.

"Kumar, yeah I know of you. You are buddies with that crazy guy's brother. Good buffet tables they are having over there, Blue Mountain restaurant." His speech was staccato and spit riddled. Explosive guttural vocalization was punctuated with sounds made by the chopping knife against the butcher block.

I tore my eyes off the samurai action in front of me and looked around for a few moments before finding my voice. "Glad to catch up with you, Mr. Oscar. I thought that maybe I talk to you about Francis. Heard that you two spent a lot of time together."

"Francis? Oh, you mean Fakhri? Yeah, quite a guy, that Fakhri dude. A bit crazy, I'd say. But man, could he carry dirty dishes. He could go non-stop like an Energizer Bunny." He set the knife down and did a quick impression of a TV commercial for the battery, taking a few quick steps in the cramped space. I laughed. The Filipino thought of Francis as a rabbit while the Indians thought of him as a donkey. The knife-man laughed too and asked, "What you want to know?"

"What did you and Francis talk about most?"

"Can't think of anything specific. We talked about whatever, everything. He wasn't that talkative at first. You know, we'd all be busy doing our jobs and Francis, or Fakhri, would suddenly come up to me and ask a random question, like how many countries I visited. Or, what was New York City like."

"He was obvious about his dislike of America, was he?"

"Funny though, he said he enjoyed life here. He just didn't want to stay in this country a long time. It was weird like that."

"What's the deal with New York City?"

"I told him I am from there. My family still lives in Queens. Francis was totally curious about the airports. He wanted to know how to get from one to the other. How things worked at JFK."

"What for?"

"I don't know. Guess he wanted to change planes in New York. How to take the train or bus from LaGuardia to Kennedy. Where to stay if he had to."

"*Stay* in New York?"

The Filipino shrugged.

"Anything else he asked about?" I wanted to know.

"I don't remember anything particular. Why you asking all these questions?"

"Oh no special reason," I said quickly. And then more slowly, "He really didn't call us when he got back to India. We just wondered if he got lost or wandered off for a few days. He gets lost easily, you know."

"But he left months ago, you asking now?" The Filipino looked skeptical. He stopped chopping, ran the knife through a sharpener, and looked up suddenly. "Yea, I can see him wandering off just to piss people off. An angry fella. You know, he asked me a lot of questions about what happens if he missed his flight. What if he couldn't transfer, the bus broke down, or he wanted to go sight-seeing in New York. I explained to him how to rebook a flight, what standby meant and what confirmed seat meant."

"You must have thought it was all a silly talk, right?"

Oscar didn't hesitate, "You know something, that Francis dude was a real hillbilly. He didn't even know what a boarding pass was, or a seat assignment. Everything to him was just 'ticket'."

"What was Francis worried about?"

"Like he didn't want to transfer to his next flight right away, on the same day. I explained it's called a layover and how it works."

"*Wwhat,* Francis wanted a layover in New York?"

"He wanted me to explain how it works. You know, could he postpone boarding his plane to India for a couple of days later than originally booked?"

Kumar's Long dark night

Since I began tilting against windmills on that dismal April Fools Day, eons ago, I discovered so much about Gita that nothing should have fazed me by now. Yet, my stomach knotted whenever I thought about the tree under which Gita's body lay. Why was she so far away? Did someone plan it, or was it happenstance? Who could be so dark and diabolical as to snuff out two lives? The worst of it was: could the perp be someone in my circle? The windmills didn't answer, leaving me with dark thoughts, and a sincere beer thirst.

*****

"You partying hard tonight, huh. All by yusself," said the nice lady at the corner liquor store.

I grinned. "Yup. It's been a fabulous partee, so far."

"Wish I could join," she said, all dimples and flying beaded braids. "But I gotta do the shift." A long sigh. "And go take care of my babies." A soft smile.

"I too wish you could join," I said. "You'd be a sounding board."

"Naw, naw, I won't be bored, er excuse me…" she turned to a customer seeking attention.

Well, I wasn't going to be bored either, what with my heart threatening to burst, my mind buzzing with dire thoughts, and the air around me with a chill unusual for the month of June. I hunched my shoulders in an attempt to shield my chest while the case of beer shifted from one hand to another. All the while, the backbencher neurons in my brain did their thing.

When I was a kid flying kites in Old Hyderabad, whenever the thread got un-spooled and all tangled up, most friends just abandoned it and bought a fresh reel. I, on the other hand, used to sit under a street lamp or a shop window, and slowly unravel all two or three hundred feet of it. Slowly teasing one loop at a time. I alone never lacked for kite thread.

*****

The roll of mints kept drawing my attention. It wasn't exactly the kind I enjoyed. I preferred spearmint discs with a solid core in the middle which burst its flavor into my mouth. But, this particular mint that I thought might be a clue, was a ring. Some Indians called all breath mints life savers, but only some brands of mints looked like circles. The back of my brain has been gnawing at this roll since I first found it in the rental car, and now it hit me. There were more wrappers in the glove box. The mints didn't necessarily belong to Gita. Her father loved them. During his hours of playing cards and Parchese, late nights at Blue Mountain, Francis used to mash on peppermints. Francis found many American words funny, including Life Savers. In his brief, bedazzled American exposure, he conflated words, images and ideas utterly alien to most foreigners. All motor vehicles were cars, all round things were wheels. He ranted about how rubber tires on the sides of boats did not save lives, and how his own elder father hated the old Indian one-paisa coins with a hole cut out of them to save copper. Holding up a mint, Francis would say, "Where is the rest of this *pipperment*?" and point to the hole, and laughed at his own wit. Funny stuff maybe, but did that mean Francis was in the rental car with Gita? Naw, not likely.

Two other things from the rental car were more telling, though. A map of Illinois, the kind sold at gas stations even in these days of the internet. The second, also a map, was hand-drawn, or rather more like driving directions, to a medical clinic. Handwriting can be figured out pretty easily by a lab, but that wasn't an issue. What it all said to me was that the two maps went together as a clue. Gita drove the rental car to visit Dr. Bharathi, no doubt. A business card I lifted off Gita's fridge during my break-in supported the idea. As to the purpose of the visit, I couldn't tell yet. Fact was, however, the doctor specialized in womens' health, spoke same dialect as Gita, and we all hailed from the same general region in India.

When Detective Mullins called me downtown to question *me* about Gita's lifestyle, he showed me a copy of the car rental agreement. The difference in the mileage on the rental contract and the mileage I wrote down in the return lot closely matched the route someone marked on the large state road map. Between Chicago and Lincoln in downstate Logan County. I hadn't noticed it before, but I could see clearly that the marker pen simply did not connect two points on the map. Its tip was dragged one way, from downstate to Chicago. The marker ink showed sections of trailing smears ending in plump 'head' halts. All head marks pointing to northward. It was a line made by a series of short strokes. Someone traced the route to Chicago!

Whoever drove the car back to Chicago wanted to ensure they didn't stray. An American would not do that. Only someone completely unfamiliar and bewildered by the Interstate Highway system would go to that extent to reassure themselves. That map was found beneath the driver's seat of the rental car.

Within the many folds of the map was a gas station receipt: one wedge of cheese pizza, soda pop, three rolls of life savers, and one bag of potato chips. Should I then believe that Gita stopped at a rural gas station late at night, and bought junk food?

Could someone besides Gita have driven the car back? Possibly.

As she lay dead under a tree? A shiver shook my spine. Whoever drove the car, they must have been in a frenzy. Which explained it being parked sloppily near the People Mover station at the airport. Who was that person, where did they go?

Note to self: Check with Mullins about cameras on the highways around O'Hare, the toll plazas and the gas stations. *If he didn't do it already that'd be a shame.*

Mullins theorized that Gita was most likely killed by a person she knew and not by a rando, (as the expression went these days). The FBI says that a quarter to a third of murder cases never get solved. While spree killers get the most press, murder remained the most intimate of crimes ever. Who was so intimate and vengeful in the case of Gita?

There was a revealing moment a few weeks earlier, after my visit to the morgue and Ms. Honeycutt. I forced Lalu to sit down and listen to me: "This makes total sense, Lalu. Warangal and Gita were truly in love and wanted to get married." Ganesh's initial shock was followed by a weird sense of relief that her baby's father would be someone we knew. Warangal, one of our own tribe, was a far more acceptable paramour than a stranger we didn't know. "He is one of us," I recalled Shetty muttering, and Ghose nodding. Yup, that's us, Indians in America, of different mores than the cousins we left behind in the old country.

Gita dared to be different, independent. But not too much. It was all fine as long as she kept it in the tribe. But her father, how might he have reacted if he knew Gita had a secret lover? I remembered Lalu's answer, "It will kill Phani." Lalu gave a dry laugh and muttered, "But he will kill her first." Lalu's breathing halted for a few seconds, and with dread on his face said, "Phani will kill young Warangal too." At the time I thought it was all crazy talk. I couldn't believe that even nutty Francis could actually kill. Whatever, I must now face the fact that *Lalu believed* his brother's rage could be murderous. But then, would Francis have *known* that his daughter was expecting?

I dashed over to my desk drawer and dug up the digital camera. After some clever rigging I managed to get the photos to show up on my television set. Bunches of photos of the day of Phani's depature, and at the airport. Different combinations of father and daughter with other people. Lalu and Gita. Francis, Shetty and Lalu. A photo of Francis and Warangal taken by Lalu. Gita moved away at the last moment and was seen in a side view. Her belly prominent. She wasn't wearing a sari or jeans and shirt like she often did. A little baby bump was evident under baggy Punjabi attire. Why didn't anyone notice that before?

As the night wore on, my fourth beer turned out to be a dud. It just slid down my gullet without helping me any. It didn't provoke even a single new thought. But the fifth one, it tickled something and an event flashed unexpectedly.

Shetty heard father and daughter quarreling, about a week before Phani's departure, "No ayya, I like it in America. I don't want to go back with you. Uncle Lalu is a good protector for me." Francis raised his voice according to Shetty. "You and Lalu don't even live under the same roof. What protection will he give?" Gita cried but wouldn't change her mind.

"You are getting old. I will find you a good boy in our village. It's my duty as your father. My brother doesn't know such things."

"Ayya, please understand. Lalu uncle got you a visa, bought you a plane ticket, and now he is trying to get you a green card. I want you here. *You* can look after me *here.* We don't have to go back. You don't have to go back. Please, stay in America."

There was more shouting. Shetty fled to the kitchen. He did, however, hear the sound of a hard slap. When he peeked, Gita was seen running out with her father after her. The two of them stood on the sidewalk for quite a while. Her head bowed, her father shaking his fist like an air-hammer.

During a catering job the next day, Gita acted like nothing happened. But Shetty had been worried enough to relate the event. *Underline the name Francis with a red ink.*

I crushed the beer can and tossed it to score, into the trash basket. It rattled around with a dull sound. I saw the proverbial monkey wrench in my thought process. For all his craziness, rage and lunacy, fact remained that Gita's father couldn't have been in America when Gita got killed. As they say on cop shows on television, 'I liked Francis for Gita's killing' but I would be hard pressed to prove it. He was already in India. Unless, he wasn't.

Hey riddle riddle, put me in a muddle.
The cat and the fiddle ....

A couple of swigs of the sixth beer washed the rhyme out of my mouth. In place of rhyme, I needed Reason. A reason for somebody to kill Gita. And, if it's not Francis, who? And if Francis, how?

In one thousand and one movies, it's the same old drill. Push pins on a cork board, sticky notes, colored thread connecting clues or photos. Firm jawed cops staring at collages for hours. For me though, it was a bedspread with two large pillows, and two armless chairs for extra space. And, pieces of paper laid out and rearranged every few minutes, in shifting sequences of argument. Somewhere in there was an answer I dreaded.

You made the bed, pal. Go lie in it.

Night without end

Tired though I was, it just didn't seem feasible to lie down and rest, what with all the material spread across my bed. Should I hit the couch, or just plan to re-set the puzzle pieces on the bed in the morning? But, something else was going on at the back of my brain, something tingly, something vague rather than a clear thought. As if, the clues abruptly switched to a dialect I could grasp.

I dashed over to the bathroom sink and gave my face a thorough scrubbing, washed the drowsiness out. Set up Mr. Coffee for a fresh pot, and broke open some new pads of sticky notes of different colors.

A classmate back from college days, who migrated to the USA to become a professor of pathology in Chicago, reconnected with me recently. Dr. Bhaskar Rao and I hung out during community events in Little India and some of those occasions grew into satisfying sessions of college style, 'shoot the breeze.' Bhaskar would offer pithy nuggets, such as 'there are no diseases, only sick people', or 'same disease, many faces,' and so on. *Minds mot*, I'd compliment him, grinning at my own wit (playing off *bons mot*). For diagnosis, he'd say, one has to firmly exclude the many unlikely candidates, and then look for solid evidence to nail the last remaining one. What's my diagnosis going to be in this knotty case?

The knot I needed to undo was Francis being in two places at once. Show that he was not where we all thought he was, but with Gita at the fateful hour.

The man we took to the airport *was* in our environs. Somehow.

I grabbed the wall calendar from the kitchen and began to go through all the entries on it, printed and handwritten, attempting to reconstruct events of the recent past. It was a good thing that unlike 'the kids these days' I hadn't fully given up my analog ways.

Pick a specific date, ask myself if I spent the entire day at home, at my internet cafe, or did I go to Devon Avenue? Was I solidly sure of that? Place a star on an eventful date such as meeting Warangal, encountering Francis. April 15th, the day I always filed taxes. I celebrated that achievement the next day with a Blue Mountain buffet lunch. Think, who said what during that event? March 17th, for example, was St. Patrick's Day. Did I talk about it with anybody, who did I see that day that wore green? What did Shetty or Ghose say two days afterwards, for example. What day was it that Lalu took Francis to Indiana to look at some franchise opportunities. Did I go to Blue Mountain on that day, see anybody? Probably not, didn't even go to Devon Avenue since I knew Lalu wouldn't be there. The days dragged on, the calendar got scribbled, and I wouldn't be denied.

I told myself that tedium held its own reward. Fact was, it helped to have piping hot fresh coffee, flavored with peppermint syrup. *Pipper-Ment* as Francis might have said it. The upside of tedium was the mixed bag of things other people said and did, which I recalled and noted. A twist of the cliche: what did Kumar know and when did he know it. The calendar whispered to me like a dead body to a forensic examiner.

The very day Francis arrived in the USA, Groundhog Day, Lalu begged me to not use his brother's real name Phani, but only use Francis. Eight days later, staring open mouthed at the beast of an SUV I had rented for our road trip, Francis asked a zillion questions about how to handle it. Looking back on it, he may have sounded clownish, but I now think he was serious, "I like to watch how people drive." I smiled as Francis went on, "So easy to drive a car in *Ummericaa*. No gearbox, no clutch, no other car hitting you." My eyebrows rose at that, and an equally simple response came out of him: "India driving horrible. Here just follow white lines..." I remembered my eyebrows not lowering.

One week prior to his departure from O'Hare, Francis made a big stink in front of everybody about changing his ticket. He wanted the direct-route flight changed to one with a change of flights in New York City. He said with a grin, "I want to tell people that I visited the Big Apple." He seemed unaware of how silly he sounded. Or, maybe, he actually was?

In the days before he quit the busboy job at Khana Khazana, Francis had extensive discussions with the Filipino man about airports in New York, layovers, missed flights, re-booking etc. "That man didn't even know what a boarding pass was," I recalled the smiley, knife-happy, chop-chop guy telling me.

When Gita rented the car she was accompanied by a man. "Same complexion as you..." in the words of the carwash guy. I passed it off as mere coincidence. And, I was too agitated to ask for a detailed description. But now I was certain, it was Francis. Somehow he got Gita to come rent a car. Somehow he was in Chicago. Back to the bed spread and clues. Something in there was trying to tell me something. But what?

My mind had been going in different directions since the day I broke into Gita's place. Love letters, birth control pills, doctors' names, broken toys, abandoned gifts, stuff on the fridge door... Each item pulled me one way and then another. Okay, ignore all that stuff. Focus on Francis's movements.

Stuff on the fridge door? Yes, of course! There was a ticket stub held under some sort of a magnet. An airline ticket stub, LGA-ORD-LGA it read. It was the sort of paper ticket still issued sometimes, even in these days of e-ticket and ticket-less travel.

I didn't know at first what that stub meant. Now I was sure, LaGuardia. What I fleetingly caught sight of, on the fridge door, was a part of a ticket. For a round trip flight someone took between New York and Chicago. Francis, it has to be. The crumpled piece of paper I picked up off the floor in Gita's closet, from amongst the smashed toys and gifts, was a coupon that airports gave out during bad weather. A coupon for steeply discounted hotel rooms near the airport, and given to travelers whose flights were canceled or missed. The stub and the discount coupon from LaGuardia put Francis in Gita's place. I didn't have the dates or names for sure, but if my theory was right, it spoke of a very cunning man. And a diabolical one at that.

Do I dare go on with my bewildering hypothesis? As the geeks say, do my random thoughts compute? Chicago police could resolve the matter easily with a few simple phone calls. Would Mullins even entertain the thought, or respect my hunches? Can I make him see the dots I am trying to connect?

That sip of coffee was awful, yuk... muddy cold. I went to the sink to rinse out the mug. The sun had risen and shone through the kitchen window. The whole place was bathed in redness. Everything, the walls, the air and even the dust in the beam of light looked red. It was not the easy tint of an innocent morning sun, but a disconcerting bloody redness.

Too wound up to sleep and too tired to stay awake, I settled in the lone single sofa to jot down my talking points. The reasons why Francis would be a strong suspect, how it could at least be shown that he returned to Chicago. Once again, my mind meandered. My heart kept going. Why did all this fall to me? Why didn't Mullins already figure this out, he was the professional, wasn't he?

Yes, detective, get on with those phone calls. Check the flight manifests. Francis could have paid cash for his ticket, but he would show some identification. Make your checks, you'll see how foolish it was to collect DNA from cooks and kitchen workers.

It was hard to believe that Mullins was so unimaginative. Did he even trust me at all? That made me get up and pace, thinking. The sun must have been up fully. My entire place was bathed in light.

Mullins has always been cordial. The so-called Detective of Manners became a friend to me and my people. No doubt about that. Yet, in the case of Gita, he was stingy with information, sparing in offering guidance, and showed just enough courtesy to keep us looking up to him. On the one hand, he humored me enough to keep me going. He offered tips for sure, but they often came after an interrogation-like chat. He must know a lot more than he let on. Mullins was practically Warangal's boss. Wouldn't the young man confide in his departmental elder, more than his tribal elders? That must be why we never heard of Warangal taking the blood test. Mullins was steering me like a ten year old does a paper kite. Is it possible Mullins was exploiting us for police purposes?

An older black janitor in the police lockup gave me a number to call. Ms. Honeycutt of the coroner's office said he was her uncle ("as old as Moses hisself"). Uncle Mo, placing a piece of paper in my hand, had whispered, "You some sort of informant?" We parted hurriedly, but that highly unorthodox comment mystified me. I now remembered that an hour earlier, I woke up from sleep on a small bench in the cell. Voices in the hallway: a political operative, Lalu, Mullins, the Night Captain, all talking. "He does things for me in the community," Mullins was saying, and "Aha, okay," the captain responded. A few hours later, they released me to Lalu's care.

Either the breeze failed or my blood was boiling. My mind

remained in overdrive as I contemplated Mullins and me in this cosplay, with him bordering on perfidy. Yet, sleep took over.

When I awoke, the room appeared to be bathed in a light similar to when I fell asleep. My calendar said that Summer Solstice was around the corner. So, I figured it had been a long sleep that lasted some ten to twelve hours. But unlike in the earlier light, I now felt alert and optimistic. I had reached conclusions. About Francis, about Warangal, and about Mullins. I cleaned up and headed to the Blue Mountain.

The abyss

The gloom was palpable and hit me the instant I walked in. Lalu was seated in a corner sectional and didn't sing out a hello. Instead of basking in a curry-induced euphoria, my friend looked crumpled and defeated. It was as if the banquet and the curry were long gone, only stale odors lingered. I slid into the chair across from him and that's when I noticed. In his hands were clutched, some rolled up official looking papers, and in his eyes a waterfall on pause.

It was alarming to say the least. There I was, ready to give Lalu my final briefing on Gita, along with my grim take about her father. And, share my dark theories with him first, before confronting Mullins. Instead, I find my old pal in a new crisis. True, he has been deteriorating lately, right in front of my eyes. Each week a little worse in the face, leading now to this look of a cornered animal.

I looked from the papers in his hands to his eyes, and back. And, tried to find the proper words to form questions, even as my face showed those same questions. Lalu didn't say a word, just got up abruptly and went into the kitchen. The double doors swung back and forth restlessly before settling. The crumpled wand of rolled up paper was left on the table. I unfurled and smoothed it.

Aha, results of the blood test. I made the paper as flat as I could and studied it. Name, address, date, blah blah. Signatures of an assortment of persons, notices of privacy, disclaimers, and other gibberish. A goodly amount of explanatory notes on the back of the page, with some really tiny numbers referencing entries made electronically on the front. Other imprinted stuff, issuing office name, the official government form number, blah blah. Nothing dramatic, so far.

On the second sheet was a table which took up most of the space and was also filled in by computer. Running my finger across the columns, DNA Locus, Alleles Called, Donor 1, Donor 2, Combined Paternity Index,. Running down the left side was another list. A series of the so-callled 13 locus regions officially named by the FBI as standard parameters for US law enforcement, and admissible in courts. More boxes below that table, some conclusions and more caveats on the third page. Finally, at the bottom of the third page was what I was looking for: Not Excluded. Two words that stirred Lalu to tears. I scanned the pages over and over to see if this was comparing Lalu's DNA against Gita's or her baby's. Neither. Did Lalu misunderstand the report or did I miss something?

Daughter without a daddy

[Flashback to late March, 2005]

Phani grinned at his daughter. The door was stood wide open. Gita stared at her father in shock. He did not move to enter but continued his grin. She didn't stand aside or gesture for him to enter. The grin turned into a cackle as he took in her looks. A sleepy disheveled face, wide staring eyes, and utter bewilderment. Her breath came haltingly. There was a glow on his face now. He looked pleased, he stunned his little girl, yes he did. Still out in the hallway, Phani looked past her into the apartment, at the kitchen passageway, toward the bedroom. Could somebody be coming out of there? There were no movements. Just two hard-breathing people.

Gita capitulated first. She fell to her knees, touched her fathers's feet and said, "Come, come ayya, come inside. Tell me everything." She retreated back into her apartment, still shooting questions at him. "Did you miss your plane? Miss the connection? Did you forget something here? You have passport, right?" And a dozen others. His sudden appearance at the door, the grin and now his silent stare.

Phani stepped across the threshold and sat in a chair close to the door as a casual visitor might. He sat lightly, almost tentatively. Like he might bolt up and leave any minute.

Gita dashed to the kitchen and returned hurriedly with a tumbler of water. He drained it in one big chug, didn't hand the glass back, just stared at his daughter, like a teacher or a king might. Like it was his sheer presence that said it all, and like it was up to Gita to talk and explain. Gita remained mute, put her head down, and shrank back into the couch across from her father.

Francis grinned again, he looked more relaxed now, though his own underarm odor wafted up, and his grimy collar brushed against the bristly hair on the nape of his neck. His powerful lungs pulsed with controlled intensity. The single light fixture from the Casablanca fan cast a faint yellow light which made both father and daughter look sickly and pallid. Stale odors lingering from an earlier dinner, enveloped the pair and added up to a feeling of being trapped. Phani bore down on his daughter. She hadn't looked him in the eye again since first opening the door.

"You thought you will never see me again, right?"

A slight sob from her.

"Didn't expect to see me, right?"

A sniffle and a wail this time.

He stood up, hands crossed behind him, and standing squarely in front of her said, "You thought I went away, gone out of your life, right?"

A whimper and a nod from Gita, and he exploded, "Wrong!"

The force of his shout seemed to have stirred and roused her. She stood tall and erect, but soft. Her eyes wet and wide, she uttered one word. "Why?"

The look in his eyes felled her. She crumpled to the floor and didn't hear his clear words.

"Teach you a lesson."

In the beginning

[Flashback to late March, 2005]

Her eyes went wide. Mouth snapped open too, but no scream came out. After the first shocked expulsion of an out-breath, her lungs began their own struggle along with the rest of her body. Air moved neither in nor out. Pressure from the hands around her neck was too much. Pain from the squeeze on her throat grew severe and unrelenting.

Why is this happening? Rama! Krishna! All you gods, why, why.. Stop this, stop this. Uncles! Uncles! Somebody make this stop!

Gita Ganesh felt like she was about to pass out. Blood pounded in her ears, as if all the waters of all the oceans flowed through this giant seashell by her ear. Except, there was no such conch, only large soft hands that completely enveloped her neck. The braid of her hair came wriggling and hissing over her struggling face. She sensed the bouquet of the *sambrani* crystals she burnt that morning to perfume her hair: light, evanescent, ethereal. Smell of sambrani in her hair, hands around her throat. *Get away from me, get away...* She struggled, the hands tightened.

O baby, O my little boy-Krishna. The image of a smiling *Balakrishna,* the infant god, flashed. Darkness took over.

Detective of Diplomacy

(Current Time / Day before Solstice)

I probably should admit that I was on the verge of a boil when I entered District Eleven building. Though glad that Mullins agreed to my frantic request to meet, I was nonetheless pissed off at him, big time. I didn't wait on formalities or good manners this time. Not even with the Detective of Manners.

"Detective, this is the worst thing you did. The way you harangued us - all of us - into taking the blood test."

"What's your point?"

"You put Lalu through hell."

"My dear Kumar, don't you know that your friend was already in hell. And, it was due to his brother."

"You should have explained to him. You laid a trap for him."

"What trap?"

"You knew who the real father was."

"They all knew who the real father was, Kumar."

My face must have been a question mark at that state ment. How could they know?

Mullins continued. "You told them, didn't you? You broke into Gita's apartment, you found the love letters, the pills. You showed everybody that Warangal and Gita were having an affair."

Of course, I did. Somewhat triumphant about playing detective, I told everyone at Blue Mountain. Even got throwed out of there by an angry Lalu, who wouldn't hear a bad thing about his beloved niece. I even snooped around Warangal's place under the pretext of bringing fresh clothes to him in the ER.

You mean to say, Mr. Mullins, you knew all along...

"Detective, did Warangal confide in you directly about the affair and pregnancy?"

"We are both sworn officers, Rama. You remember that, right?" Besides a softening of his tone, there was that familiar soft touch of my first name.

"Then why did you ask us to take a blood test?"

"You forget, Kumar, this is a murder investigation, not a game of who's your daddy"

"So...what are you saying?"

"What I am saying is that I needed a DNA sample for forensic evaluation."

"To discover what?"

"To match the scrapings from under the fingernails of Gita."

"You did say she was strangled..."

"And, boy did she resist. I have to love the way she must have fought. The little lady scratched the hell out of ...." Mullins's voice trailed off.

“Why didn’t you just come right out and tell us about it.”

“After the bird has flown the coop?”

“Why didn’t you ever mention Francis as a suspect?”

“I expected you, Kumar, to do it.” A mild chuckle. “Seems like you loved the task thoroughly.”

“You were handling me —“

“You handled yourself. And pretty well, I must admit.”

We were still standing. I sat in the folding chair and chose my words.

“Okay you’ve been devious. Clever. Maybe even justified. But why harp on the DNA of all *my* people.” I even managed to sound unsurprised that I said my people.

“Come come, Kumar, you know how science and databases work. There aren’t that many Indian criminals on file around here with blood samples.”

“You are building a DNA database of all the Indians you could badger and browbeat? How is that right?”

“Probable cause, my friend. The judge agreed that in the case of the homicide of one Gita Ganesh by strangulation, in the county of Cook, with the likely suspect in absentia, all relatives, coworkers and close associates can be asked for DNA samples to exclude them.” He intoned. And then less flatly, “The case is aggravated by pregnancy. We are talking about two lives, not one.”

“But couldn’t you just wait to get a sample from Francis, to be collected by the FBI field office in India?"

"Sure I could. I could also be dealing with a missing Francis for years. Francis wandering off to the Himalayas, leaving Gita's murder unsolved. Why not check out the DNA profile of the brother living right here?"

"But Lalu thought you were accusing him of, er... of violating his niece. What a horrible thought you had."

"Technically, I didn't know that he hadn't. Though I did think he didn't. I just wanted the DNA to exclude him."

"He was so dejected by the report which said he was not excluded."

"Sadly it happens sometimes. Especially where two brothers are involved. There would be enough similarities between their DNA that Lalu couldn't be excluded totally. Not without a good sample from his brother. Gita's fingernails yielded DNA too contaminated to offer enough alleles at separate loci to be dissimilar enough to exclude Lalu."

"You sure can obfuscate, detective. Even I don't use that many negatives and double negatives in one go."

"Well you know what I mean, Rama. Her nails contributed enough to confirm a connection to Lalu's DNA, but distinct enough to show it had to be Francis. But good news though. We were notified this morning that Francis gave a sample. That should match up nicely with Gita's donation."

"When will that test be done, when is the sample arriving?"

"Oh, there are some excellent labs in your own hometown. We'll let the Cell Biology Lab in Taranaka do it. You know, the spirit of cooperation and all."

I smirked, the detective of manners is now a detective of diplomacy?

Mullins shrugged, with a reluctant smile.

"No doubt you are still expecting a sample for your own records and for retesting here." I said slowly.

He nodded. "For purposes of admissibility etc.." No shrug or smile this time, of course.

"I couldn't have done this without you. You did all the work. You're a hero, Kumar."

MEGHA DUTAM (KALIDASA)

आषाढस्य प्रथम दिवसे मेघमाश्लिष्टसानुं,
वप्रक्रीडापरिणतगजप्रेक्षणीयं ददर्श ।

आषाढस्य प्रथम दिवसे मेघमाश्लिष्ट सानुं
वप्रक्रीडा परिणत गज प्रेक्षणीयं ददर्श ।

Ashadhasya prathama divase
Megham Ashlishta Sanum,
Vapra-kreedaa parinatha
Gaja prekshaneeya duhduhrsa

Megha Dutam
By Mahakavi Kalidasa,
India (circa 500 AD)

On the first day of Ashada he saw
A mountain-top-embracing cloud,
to all appearance,
like a butting elephant preparing
to thrust against a wall ..

Cloud Messenger
Translated from Sanskrit into English prose,
by H. A. Ouvry, CB, London, 1868.

In the preceding, the order of stanzas is as follows:

Original Sanskrit,
Original Hindi,
English Transliteration,
Oldest known English translation.

Closures

Close unttil further noties, read the makeshift sign, a flap of a cardboard box taped to the inside of the glass window.

I watched some hungry fellows stop, read the sign, and move on to forage at the pasture land of buffet spreads down the block. True devotees of Blue Mountain, however, paused long enough to scratch their heads, peer inside, and wear a look of dismay. Then gaze longingly up and down the avenue, as if to ask, where are you good curry?

Closure of the eatery did not surprise me, its suddenness did. I watched inexorable changes in Lalu over the weeks and months. He became sluggish and rotund in the weeks after Gita's death. He grew silent and sullen when word of Gita's romance came out. All those around him noticed how dark his mood became after Warangal's attempted suicide.

It was ironic that my efforts to boost Lalu's spirits failed, due to my own success at playing detective. The more news I dug up, the more Lalu despaired and ditched shifts in the kitchen. The blood tests must have broken the man in the end. Life, like gravity, finds its own measure. But, Lalu wasn't the only one that went through changes.

Gita's father was nabbed and faced imprisonment, either in India or here in the US, depending on how the battle of Red Corner Notices got settled at the Interpol.

Gita's secret boyfriend, Warangal, got his police job back, thanks to his union. But, he wasn't going to be making Sergeant any time soon.

Gita's catering business would pass to the devoted Shetty, as would, in time Blue Mountain. The eatery reopened but Lalu stayed closed up, buried in a quiet, private hell.

Mike 'moonshine' Mullins, the favorite policeman of Little India, made Lieutenant that month. He trimmed his mustache and gave up the avuncular look, but continued to say 'love the samosa' whenever he came up to Devon Avenue.

That still left me, hanging...

The Gita-Warangal-Lalu-Francis episode amounted to a sad story of ordinary mortals. Had the story concerned great personages, it would have been called a Greek Tragedy by pundits. But, the Indian part of my mind hankered for something different, a happy end card. As every moviegoer in India knows, no matter how many reels have rolled by, it is the last hundred feet of film that really charmed. Lilting songs, jiggly dance numbers, and shabby fight sequences - the audience can take 'em, or leave 'em. But the ending, the ending must satisfy the Indian way.

That's why *Subham!* mattered. The word meant a state of universal wellness, and it was the last word in cinema. Indian movies end with a happy event. It could be a wedding, a childbirth, gods triumphing over demons, or John Wayne's Hindu cousin riding off into a sunset. *Subham.* With or without an exclamation mark, the word *Subham* was literally the last thing the audience saw on the screen, the end card. Indian movie honchos, even those who don't chomp on fat cigars, but only spit betel juice out of the corner of the mouth, they too fret about the end card.

If recent events of my life made for an Indian movie, what end card would I project?

The impending summer also brought on a number of realizations. One of them was how cheap and widespread

Broadband had become. Internet Cafes were going to fade away like real estate offices and travel agencies. Wings of Ether was doomed. What will take its place in my life?

I had often thought that all well-imagined lives should be like a wall shelf with matching book ends. Even the shabbiest life could wind up safe somewhere in celebration...somehow. Maybe in a work of fiction even. My real life - *my American life* - needed a tidy and real end card.

New Delhi has been calling my name. My mustard friend Sarada Sashanki was the only true and sane thing in my life during that turbulent spring. She gave me useful tips to understand young single Indian women living in the US. Sarada telephoned me regularly. I reciprocated, and the phone lines were getting hot.

I made my move one morning that June. I pressed into service a favorite English troubadour's famous poem. Modern pubs and singles bars had no line to match the greatest pickup line in all of poetry. Christopher Marlowe would have made a great wingman.

Come live with me and be my Love,
And we will all the pleasures prove
That valleys, groves, hills, and fields,
Woods, or steepy mountain yields.

That was just the first stanza. Would Sashanki care for Marlowe's sentiments? Will she notice how much thought I put into my thoughts?

So, on the longest day of the year, a day of seemingly never ending sunshine and endless possibilities, I set out on a journey that was a longtime coming. I sent Christopher Marlowe's madrigal to Sarada from *Wings of Ether*. Later, I read it to her over the telephone.

My heart was grinning. My mind was running a marathon. I was aware of the corniness of the lines, and the cadence of the stanza.

On the other hand, the silence at the other end of the phone line made for a heart-stopping roar in my ears, and electronic pulses between our two phones seemed to play hide and seek.

Into that stillness of heart and thought, slowly crept my mustard lady's soft voice.

> *Ashadhasya prathama divase*
> *Megham-ashlista saanum*
> *Vapra-kreeda parinatha*
> *Gaja prekshaneeya duhdursa*

Great lines of Sanskrit poetry written by Kalidasa, picturing the onset of monsoon. The ancient poet singing about the welcome clouds that looked like elephants head-butting mountains, to yield life-giving rain. Vertical sheets of moisture plunging into the furrows of land that had lain fallow. First rains upon the parched earth on the first day of *Ashadha*, the Indian Month of Rainfall.

Sashanki just read to me the most famous Sanskrit couplet known to millions of Indians by heart. Did she merely quote a poem about the current weather? I didn't think so. I was convinced Sarada wished for more than good things for herself.

That invocation of rain falling over cropland was a wish for a state of Universal Well-being, a note of subham. It's not for nothing that Kalidasa's poem was titled *Meghdoot,* or Cloud Messenger. It carried a message of optimism, the eternal heartbeat of great poetry.

Listening to her over the phone my own heartbeat quickened, gathered speed, and thudded like clouds gearing up to deliver a thunderstorm of Ashadha.

GLOSSARY

Ashadha - Name of a month in the Hindu calendar. In the Luni-Solar calendar, it corresponds to June-July period. The first days of Ashadha usually coincide with the onset of southwest monsoon rains in India. Spelled variously: Asadha, Ashada.

Attar - perfume, scent or cologne.

Auntie - In contemporary urban India the word auntie is often used to describe a middle aged lady to whom one is not necessarily related. Used almost synonymously with Madam or Ma'am. And, of course, also a true aunt.

Ayyappa or Ayyappan - A Hindu deity popular in Kerala and the south of India generally. Venerated for his discipline and celibacy.

Bajji - A lentil fritter composed of deep- vegetable: potato; cauliflower; long chili; or even carrots.

Balakrishna - Little boy-Krishna. Krishna is the only god worshpped by Hindus in his little-boy form.

Beti - daughter

betray the salt - Salt in this context is hospitality received. To betray the salt is to be an ingrate. In the extended sense, it is disloyalty or outright betrayal. A classic example of English verbiage applied to Old World senssibility. See also *Namak Haram* below.

*Bewakhoo*f - An Urdu word, means 'without common sense.'

Bindi - Mark on the forehead, made of vermilion

paste, powder or sticker. Shaped round, oval or flame-like. Worn by Hindu women of childbearing potential. Absence of a bindi often marks a Hindu woman as a widow.

Bonda - A spherical form of a fritter.

Brinjal - a vegetable, purple in color and comes in different shapes. From the French Aubergine. Known as eggplant in North America.

Bustee - neighborhood.

Chee-Chee - An explosive expression of derision, or dismissal.

Chudidar - A tight fitting Indo-Pak pants.

Deeksha - A period of intense religious observance, usually includes fasting, abstinence, avoidance of intoxicants, prayer and specific attire, for periods ranging from a few days to several weeks.

Desi - A person from Des, or Desh, A compatriot. An Indian paisano.

Dhaba - Diner, a Punjabi style cafe and fast food eatery, often roadside and open late hours. Popular all over India, with many imitations in the USA.

Dulhan - Bride, newlywed woman. (Hindi)

Dusserah, or Dasara, also known as Vijaya Dasami - A Hindu festival that is celebrated over a ten day period to recall triumph of Good over Evil, manifested by Rama defeating Ravana. *Ramlila* and *Durga Puja* are major events of this post-monsoon festival.

Ekadasi - The eleventh day in the waxing phase of Hindu lunar month, three days prior to Full Moon. While every Ekadasi is honored with prayer and fasting, the one right after Dark Solstice is considered most sacred. Millions of Hindus believe gates of heaven stay open on that day.

Gadha - Donkey, Jackass

Ganesh or Ganesha - Also known in Sanskrit as Ganapthi, Vinayaka, Vighneswara. Most popularly translated as the Elephant God. Ganesh Festival in India is celebrated on par with Diwali.

Ghadiya - A short, practical time span in Hindu timekeeping, generally regarded as equal to 24 minutes.

Gudi Padawa - Hindu New Year's Day, celebrated along the Western Ghat regions of India.

Houla - Fool

ji or gee The suffix -ji or -gee denotes respect. Similar to -San in some East Asian languages like the Japanese.

Kajal - traditional Indian black mascara, usually applied to the edges of the eyelids rather then on the skin of the eyelids. Also called Kohl, katuka.

Kalakand - An All-India favourite sweet, made with reduced milk, flavoured with cardamom and saffron, and topped with nuts. Hundreds of recipe variants have been created by US Indians.

Kalidasa - Sanskrit poet of supreme note. Revered by Indians. Exact date unknown, circa 500 AD. Always referred to as *Mahakavi* or great poet.

Karma Sakshi - Literally, Action Witness, a moniker of the Sun, used by Hindu poets to denote that he sees it all.

Kathori - A small, shallow bowl, usually steel. Used to serve a single serving of curry, rice or dessert. A typical dinner plate has several kathoris on it to keep the various flavors apart.

Khayal or Khayaal - Classical North Indian style of singing, full of free floating imagination and improvisation, at different speeds. From Persian - to imagine.

Kurta - Typically collarless, it is a long flowing tunic worn by men and women. In modern times, stylistic differences have become quite vast, including the length, collar, and buttons.

Kutha - Dog

Maff Keejiye - Excuse Me.

Mamuji - Uncle

Meghdoot or Meghadut - Also, Meghadootam or Meghadutam. A poetic work of the mighty Sanskrit writer Kalidasa. Widely translated as Cloud Messenger.

Namkeen - Salt biscuit, usually served with chai.

Namak Haram - Literally, Salt Thief. To betray the salt. An Urdu expression. It means to be disloyal to one's employer, master or benefactor.

Narada - A mythical wandering troubadour who goes through all the worlds. A great character of Hinduism.

Neem - A bitter, astringent leaf of a tree widely found

in India. The twigs of neem tree are used as a toothbrush. The tender shoots and dried flowers are used when astringency is indicated. Not to be confused with *nimbu* (lemon).

Pachadi - a Telugu word for chutney. Generally, any uncooked mash of veggies and spices. A special recipes is used only on Ugadi comprising every taste sensation known to the palate.

Pallu (palloo) - Free flowing end of the Indian sari. Drawn from the waist in front, over chest, and draped over shoulder. Often elaborately decorative. Sometimes drawn over the head to look like a hoodie, could even be drawn over face like a veil.

Payasam - Milk pudding made with either vermicelli or rice, rarely pearl sago. Often garnished with roasted nuts, raisins. Always makes for 'a good occasion'.

Pukkah - Proper, true.

Ramzan - Indian spelling for the more familiar Ramadan

Saab or Sab - shortened from Sahib. Sir

Sambar, or Sambhar - Liquid curry of vegetables, notably pumpkins, okra, and moringa (drumstick)

Sambrani - Benzoin crystals, used by Indian women. Sprinkled over hot coals, produces fragrant smoke that is used to perfume hair.

Sayam Sandhya The hour of sunset, when light changes rapidly.

Shiv Ling - An ellepsoidal or elongated polished stone, used as a representation of god Shiva. Most famously popularized by Steven Spielberg as the Shakara Stone.

Siva Slap - The phrase Siva Slap was coined by Mr. Griz, an American aficionado of life on Devon Avenue. It perfectly described the classic Hindu gesture of a gentle double self-slap, using palms to touch the opposite cheeks at the same time. Comparable to Christians crossing themselves, the practice of Siva Slap is a Hindu expression of contrition, after a bad thought or slip of tongue.

Subham! - Universal Well-being, also a common on-screen title card, end card of movies.

Subzi - Vegetable dish, vegetarian curry dish. Also spelled subji, subzee.

Tamasha - Spectacle, show.

Tongue-toucher - Indian dining habit of dipping a finger very lightly into a potent chutney and then touching one's own tongue. This momentarily heightens the spiciness of a morsel of food. Several Indian languages have words that refer to the practice. The English phrase tongue-toucher was coined by the inimitable writer Santha Rama Rao, and popularized by the books on Indian cookery by the great Madhur Jaffrey.

Tuglak - Mohammad bin Tuglak, (Tuglaq or Tuglakh), one of the last emperors of the Mogul dynasty in India. He was infamous for erratic acts and irrational decisions. History books refer to him as 'crazy Tuglak'. It's a popular put-down to call someone a Tuglak.

Qudaa Hafiz, also Khuda Hafeez - Go With God, a parting salute widely used in India, of Persian and Arabic origins, via the Urdu language.

Ugadi - Hindu word for New Year's Day. On the lunar calendar it is observed either on the first new moon, or the first full moon, after the spring equinox.

** * *

ACKNOWLEDGEMENTS:

Cover Art By: Rc Marie

for details email to: **raya.chisesi@gmail.com**

Several readers of Phoneix and Chicago areas - novelists and would be writers - have offered valuable insights at different times in the making of this book. I am grateful to all of them, but it must be understood that any faux pas are exclusively my own. A successful book can have many good mothers, but only one *baad* father. In that spirit, I thank all the participants of Schaumburg Writers Group, Red Sands Novel Workshop, East Mesa Writing Group, Hangout and Write @ Starbucks, Poetry Open Mic, and other compatriots in ink. Down with the blank page!

ABOUT THE AUTHOR

Sp Venkata

He left his heart in Chicago. But she keeps tugging at him. The deserts of the American Southwest beckon to him with the sharp lure of a cactus. What's he to do, but take out the longest thorn needle and dip it into the deepest inkwell of life, losses, and insights? He lives like an American and thinks like a cowboy, but is one hundred percent Indian...

PRAISE FOR AUTHOR

This is so good!

- IEN NIVENS (POET, NOVELIST, AND FRIEND)

From the nicknames and witty thoughts on America to the customs and mouthwatering food descriptions, I was intrigued by every page. I especially enjoyed following along with Kumar as a detective... I cannot recommend it enough if you like a good mystery intertwined with cultural insight into life on Devon Avenue in Chicago

- RAYA CHISESI

It is a well-paced book.

- ROBIN (FRIEND, POET, AND POLYGLOT)

Love the descriptions of Indian food!

- GEORGE MONTGOMERY (NOVELIST AND INDOPHILE)

A Touch of Ginger kept me wondering until the very end. Great mystery seen through the eyes of a man driven to find answers.

- FRAN LYONS

LITTLE INDIA TRILOGY

Anand Kumar, a sometimes-employed writer, blogger, and internet cafe owner, finds himself involved in probing into murders that happen amongst his people in Chicago's Little India. A frustrated intellectual, he feels the urge to insinuate himself into the police process. But will his sheer charm and wit carry him through, or will his efforts backfire? The official American detective in the cases, Mike Mullins, is patient, kind, and crafty. Kumar's fellow Indians are eager and hopeful. We see Kumar go through changes as life throws one crisis after another at him. Will he be destroyed in the end, or will he somehow eke out a triumph of sorts? Let Kumar tell the story...

A Touch Of Ginger

Kumar is at his best, tilting against windmills, when the lovely niece of his best friend is killed a hundred miles away from Chicago. There is no shortage of suspects, only of evidence. Could Kumar do it? Could he unravel the mystery?

A Murder In Mustard

A murder at a Spice Show in Chicago. Three prinicipals, Indians all. Kumar is called upon by the gentle Detective Mullins to assist in untying this sub-cultural knot. Could Kumar do it, without entangling himself up in the process? Especially when the two women he has to befriend and investigate turn out to be polar oppossites? And, he is drawn to both of them?

A Concubine In Cardamom

What can you say about a girl who is all sweet and spice. Spice as in Cardamom? She shows up as an Anamika - nameless, identity-less - in an alley of Chicago's Little India, dead and beautiful. Kumar is intrigued, then ensnared, and finally wounded - all while trying to give her a name and an identity. He wishes he hadn't, but he was fated to do so. The mystery girl turns out to be not so mysterious, after all.

BOOKS BY THIS AUTHOR

A Touch Of Ginger

Little India Trilogy - Part 3

A Muder In Mustard

Little India Trilogy _ Part 2

A Concubine In Cardamom

Little India Trilogy - Part 1

Sugar Parrots - A Decameron Of South India

Poems Across A Continental Divide